ATTACK AT THE BUTTE

The attack came on the morning of the third day. The Sioux came in such numbers, even with Remingtons in their hands and a sheer stone wall at their backs, Story's riders were awed.

All the wagons were already drawn in close to the butte. The teamsters and many of the riders lay behind wagon wheels or steadied their rifles across a wagon box. The Sioux seemed bound for a head-on clash, but before they were within range of the rifles, they split their forces. Half rode north of the butte, while the rest circled to the south.

"They aim to ride in from both flanks," Story cried. "Those of you who are handiest to the left, concentrate your fire. If you're nearest the bunch attacking from the right, go after them. We can't come out of this with whole hides if we're all shooting at the same fifty Sioux."

The outfit followed Story's lead, and when he judged the galloping warriors were close enough, Story fired. And twenty-nine rifles roared . . .

THE VIRGINIA CITY TRAIL

Ralph Compton

St. Martin's Paperbacks

This is a work of fiction, based on actual trail drives of the Old West. Many of the characters appearing in the Trail Drive Series were very real, and some of the trail drives actually took place. But the reader should be aware that, in the developing of characters and events, some fictional literary license has been employed. While some of the characters and events herein are purely the creation of the author, every effort has been made to portray them with accuracy. However, the inherent dangers of the trail are real, sufficient unto themselves, and seldom has it been necessary to enhance their reality.

THE VIRGINIA CITY TRAIL

Copyright © 1994 by Ralph Compton.

Cover photograph by Comstock Images.

Map on p. v by David Lindroth, based upon material supplied by the author.

All rights reserved.

For information address St. Martin's Press, 175 Fifth Avenue, New York, NY 10010.

EAN: 978-0-312-95306-5

Printed in the United States of America

St. Martin's Paperbacks edition / September 1994

15 14 13 12 11 10 9 8 7

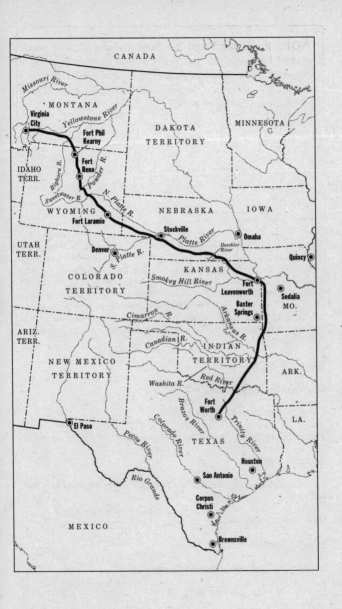

AUTHOR'S FOREWORD

Not a man in Texas trail-driving history had more determination and cool indifference to the dangers of the frontier than Nelson Story. Born on a farm in Meigs County, Ohio, in 1838, Story was orphaned when he was fourteen. After two years of working his way through Ohio University, he was qualified as a teacher, but Story's dream reached far beyond a little country schoolhouse. In 1854 he boarded a steamboat that took him to St. Louis. There he traveled up the Missouri to Fort Leavenworth, Kansas, arriving with thirty-six dollars and a determination to move west.

Despite Story's youth—he was only sixteen—he was hired by an outfit that freighted west from Fort Leavenworth. The young man from Ohio silenced those who thought him too young and inexperienced. Story became a bull whacker, took his turn at night guard, and sought the advice of the old-timers who knew the mountains and the prairies. He became a dead shot with rifle and pistol, a dreaded adversary with his fists, and led the charge against Indians who had come to regard wagon trains as a source of horses, weapons, and scalps. By the time Nelson Story was eighteen, he owned his own wagon and oxen.

When gold was discovered near Pike's Peak in 1858, towns sprang up quickly. Gold-seekers were willing to pay almost any price for supplies and equipment, so twenty-year-old Nelson Story bought another wagon, six more oxen, and moved his freighting business to Denver. Following the great gold strike at Alder Gulch, Montana Territory, in 1863, Story went there, built a store, and began hauling goods from Utah. But he found the life of a merchant too tame, and had been around the camps long enough to know something about mining. Story got gold fever and bought a claim he felt hadn't been worked out. By spring of 1866 he had forty thousand dollars, but Story was a marked man. It was a time when infamous outlaw sheriff Henry Plummer and his band of road agents were murdering men for their gold. Nelson Story, cool, quick, and deadly with a gun, had become captain of an Alder Gulch vigilance committee. From December 21, 1863, to January 11, 1864, Story and his men captured and hanged twenty-four of the road agents, including Henry Plummer himself.

Nelson Story's next venture led him to Fort Worth, Texas, where he bought three thousand Texas longhorns and hired a crew of Texas cowboys. Texans were already trailing herds north, and Story planned to avoid the glut at Sedalia and Kansas City by taking his herd to Quincy, Illinois. But approaching Sedalia from Baxter Springs, Kansas, Story quickly found there was no possible way he could reach Quincy, for there was no graze. Moreover, there were toll collectors, some of them demanding as much as two dollars a head. Texans who had gone ahead of Story's herd were selling for what they could get. Story backed off, trailing along the Kansas border. He would take his herd west, to Montana Territory.

Story would begin the western leg of his trail drive in Fort Leavenworth, the town where he'd begun his life on the plains as a bull whacker. He had friends there he could trust, and he bought work oxen and wagons. He loaded the wagons with equipment and provisions and hired a crew of experienced bull whackers. Since he was heading for the bloody Bozeman Trail, he would make the drive as profitable as he could. He took the old Oregon Trail west until he reached southern Wyoming, driving north to reach the Bozeman at Fort Laramie. Army officers at Fort Laramie tried to talk Story out of going farther, but Story had an edge. His twenty-five Texas cowboys were armed with Remington breech-loading rifles.

Their first fight with the Sioux came south of Fort Reno. One cowboy was killed and two were wounded. At Fort Phil Kearny, Commander Henry B. Carrington forbade Story to continue, but Story moved out in the darkness. On October 29, five hundred Oglala Sioux, led by Crazy Horse, attacked Story and his men. After heavy losses, Crazy Horse withdrew, and on December 9, 1866, Nelson Story's drive reached Virginia City, Montana Territory.

PROLOGUE

Virginia City, Montana, December 21, 1863.

"*I* am innocent," George Ives said confidently. It was
the password of the infamous Plummer gang to
which Ives belonged. He stood on a wooden box, a thir-
teen-knot hangman's noose about his neck. The other
end of the rope had been looped over a beam in a newly
constructed building, pulled taut and tied to a spike
driven into the floor. Four men with drawn guns stood
between Ives and those who had come to see him hang.
One of the four men was Ken Tanner, himself secretly a
member of the Plummer gang, and it was Tanner who
spoke.

"Back off. Sheriff Plummer's been sent for, and we're
waitin' for him."

"Like hell we are," a miner shouted. "The Dutchman
was killed an' robbed, an' when this Ives was caught, the
varmint had the Dutchman's mule. Now this miner's
court says he's guilty, an' Plummer ain't gonna change
that. Hang the bastard."

"I say we're waitin' for the sheriff," said Tanner, "and
I'll shoot the first man makin' a wrong move."

Even some of the vigilantes who had captured Ives
seemed intimidated, and Ives grinned. But the grin
changed to a frown as a tall man with sandy hair, a
three-day beard, and a cocked pistol in each hand el-
bowed his way through the vigilantes.

"I'm Nelson Story," he said, "captain of this vigilance
committee. George Ives has been tried and found guilty

by a miner's court, and he's going to hang. I'll kill the first man who interferes."

His cold blue eyes were on those four men with drawn guns, and one by one they backed down, Tanner being the last. Story kicked hard, sent the wooden box tumbling, and George Ives was left dangling at the end of a rope. The lawyers hired to defend him turned away, unable to bear the grisly sight. Ives revolved slowly, his face contorted, kicking his life away. The four men Story had backed down glared sullenly at him, and Story glared back. He made no move until he was sure George Ives was dead. Then he backed away, into the ranks of the vigilantes with whom he rode.

"His friends can cut him down," said Story. "Let's get the rest of them."

In knee-high boots and sombrero, Nelson Story was six and a half feet tall. Belted around his middle was a pair of 1851 Colt .38 caliber revolvers, and he could draw and fire as swiftly and as accurately with one hand as with the other. After the hanging of George Ives, the weather changed dramatically, and Story moved to take advantage of it. He gathered his vigilantes in the bitter, bone-chilling cold, before first light.

"There's three feet of snow on the plains," Story said, "and fifteen to twenty feet in the mountain passes and draws. Plummer and his bunch will try to quit the territory, but they can't get out until the weather breaks. We have them trapped, and we're going to finish them once and for all."

Bannack, Montana Territory. January 10, 1864.

"Let's hang the others first," said a miner, "an' save Plummer fer last. I want the low-down, murderin' son to watch his pards die, knowin' he's gonna foller 'em to Hell."

There were shouts of agreement, and four of Plummer's gang went to their deaths without complaint. But Henry Plummer, whose bloody reign had resulted in the deaths of more than a hundred men, begged for his life. His hands bound behind him, the infamous outlaw sheriff fell to his knees.

"Please," he wept, "I don't want to die. I'm not prepared to die. Cut off my fingers, a hand, a foot, but let me live. Have mercy."

Some of the vigilantes turned away in disgust, but Nelson Story faced this man who deserved no quarter and would be given none.

"You murdered men for their pokes," Story said, "every one a better man than you. You deserve no mercy. You're going to pay with your life."

The gallows had been built by Plummer himself. He was dragged to it, and his crying and begging didn't cease until the rope cut off his wind. In all, Plummer and twenty-three of his outlaw companions were hanged by Nelson Story's vigilance committee. But several Plummer lieutenants escaped. One of them was Ken Tanner, and he vowed to kill Nelson Story.

Nelson Story was only twenty-six, but having been a captain in the band of vigilantes that had destroyed the Plummer gang, Story had become prominent and respected. He moved to Denver and began his own freighting business, accepting a contract to haul for the government from Fort Leavenworth west to Wyoming. As Story rode the high plains with their abundant grass, an idea began to take shape. Miners wanted beef, and at Fort Leavenworth, Story had heard that Texas cattle were selling for two dollars a head. Why not go to Texas, buy a herd, and cover the high plains with longhorn cattle? While Story lacked the money for such a venture, he wasn't lacking in ingenuity. Having spent considerable time in Virginia City, Story knew something about gold mining. With a final load of trade goods—two loaded wagons and sixteen loaded mules—Story headed for Virginia City. He bought a gold claim that hadn't been properly worked, and by late fall of 1865 had accumulated thirty thousand dollars in gold. Money had been depreciated because of the war, and for his gold, Story received forty thousand dollars in greenbacks. Knowing the risk he was about to take, he sewed ten thousand dollars into the lining of his coat.

Preparing to leave Virginia City for Texas, Story encountered Tom Allen and Bill Petty, two young bull whackers he'd known in Denver.

"I reckon I've had enough bull whacking," said Petty. "I'd like to hire on for the drive from Texas."

"Welcome," Story said.

"I'd like to go too," said Tom Allen. "One day these mines are gonna play out and there won't be enough work here to keep a man in plug, but I'd gamble there's enough grass on these plains and in the mountain draws to last forever. I wouldn't mind havin' me some seed cattle. I got near two thousand dollars. You got any objection to me buyin' as many cows as I can, and then trailin' 'em north with your herd?"

"None," Story said, "long as you don't mind riskin' your scalp."

"Nels," said Allen, "I purely admire your sense of humor. Ever' time I climb up to the wagon box and take that trail west out of Leavenworth, I'm offerin' my scalp to outlaws, Injuns, and anybody else wantin' it. By God, if I got to fight, then I'm ready to fight for somethin' that belongs to me. Bill, you ain't rich, but you're as well off as I am. Why don't you buy some cows and trail 'em with us?"

"Can't," Petty said. "I just hired on with Nels, for wages."

"Consider yourself fired," said Story with a grin. "Now you can buy cows of your own, and I'll have you helpin' fight Indians for nothing."

"That'll be some ride, just gettin' to Texas," Tom Allen said. "Any idea how far?"

"I figure it at fifteen hundred miles," said Story. "We'll ride south across the divide to Fort Hall, cross the Rockies again into Wyoming, and go south to Denver. From there we'll cross Indian Territory into Texas and ride on to Fort Worth."

Fort Laramie, Wyoming Territory. December 1865.

Story and his two companions spent the night at Fort Laramie, and it was in Bordeaux's Trading House that they met an old mountain man known only as Coon Tails.

"Yep," said Coon Tails, "I been through the territory a time er two. I got friends amongst the Cheyennes an' Arapahoes. I oncet had me a Cheyenne squaw fer a while."

"I can use a scout who knows the territory," Story said. "We'll be going to Fort Worth from here, buying a herd of Texas longhorns and driving them across eastern Indian Territory to Quincy, Illinois. Interested?"

"Mebbe," Coon Tails said. "Depends on if'n I git paid in gold coin. I ain't wantin' no Yankee paper."

"Gold it is," said Story. "A hundred dollars for the drive."

"Two hunnert," Coon Tails countered.

"Hundred and fifty," said Story.

"Deal," Coon Tails said, lighting his pipe.

"We ride at first light," said Story.

1

~~~~~~

Fort Worth, Texas. February 1, 1866.

*N*elson Story and his three companions arrived in Fort Worth in the early afternoon.

"Wal," Coon Tails said, "I dunno what else this place has got goin' fer it, but they's a blessed plenty of blue bellies."

"Texas and all the South is under reconstruction," said Story. "We'll have to report to the officer in charge and identify ourselves. Since the war's end, there are renegades from both sides looting and killing. Us being strangers in town, we'd best find the soldiers before they come looking for us."

Before they reached the end of the block, a pair of Union soldiers confronted them. One of them was Negro, and neither seemed more than a year or two out of their teens. They stood in the muddy street, their muzzle loaders at port arms. Story and his companions reined up.

"We're from Montana," Story said, "here to buy cattle. Take us to your officer in charge for whatever clearance we may need."

"Ride on the way you're headed," said the white soldier, "and take a left at the next corner. From there you can see the unfinished courthouse, and the post commander's tent in front of it. Ask for Captain Clark."*

Story and his men rode on, and when they turned the corner as directed, Story could see the pair of soldiers following on foot. Having stated his intentions, he found it irritating that he and his men were not trusted to ride to the officer's tent without an armed escort. Reaching the tent, they were eyed suspiciously by a corporal who stood near the closed flap of the tent. He faced them, his rifle at port arms, a question in his eyes.

"We're from Montana," Story repeated, "here to buy Texas cattle. I want to speak to Captain Clark, the post commander."

Before the soldier could respond, the tent flap was swept aside, and the officer who emerged could only have been the officer. He was smartly dressed, and from the epaulets of his blue tunic, captain's bars flashed in the afternoon sun.

"I'm Captain Clark," said the officer.

"I reckon you heard what I said," Story replied. "I'm Nelson Story, and these men are part of my outfit. I only want you to be aware of our purpose here. Is there any reason why we can't ride from ranch to ranch, buying the cattle we want?"

"None that I know of," said Clark. "However, I must remind you that Texas is under federal jurisdiction. If you hire Texas cowboys, they'll need permission to leave the state."

Story and his men were still mounted, and Story sidestepped his horse nearer, so that he looked the captain squarely in the eyes when he spoke.

"Obviously I don't have enough men for a cattle

* Fort Worth had won the county seat election over Birdville in 1860, but the courthouse was never finished, because of the war. It was destroyed by fire in 1873.

drive, Captain, so I will be hiring riders. Is that going to be a problem, getting permission for them to leave Texas?"

"Only if they have taken up arms against the United States," said Captain Clark. "In that case, it will be left to my discretion. Those who fought for the Confederacy will be required to sign papers, swearing never again to take up arms against the Union."

"Thank you, Captain," Story said. He rode back the way he had come, with Coon Tails, Allen, and Petty following.

"Them federals is a hard-nosed bunch," said Petty when they were well away from the officer's tent. "The war's done, and they whupped the Rebs. What's to be gained by keepin' 'em penned up like a bunch of mavericks?"

"Reconstruction is a cruel punishment conceived by a few vindictive men in Washington," Story said, "but as long as we're in Texas, the law's what they say it is."

Story and his men rode past saloons, cafes, pool parlors, and several hotels. Story seemed to know what he was seeking. They rode south, the town thinning out, until they reached what was obviously a large livery barn. On one side of it was a six-pole-high corral where four horses picked at some hay. On the other side of the barn was a long, low building built of logs and chinked with mud. Above the door, across the front of it, was a sign that read: YORK AND DRAPER. *Drover's Supplies, Livestock, Wagons.*

"We need information," said Story. "We'll start here."

They dismounted, Story leading the way into the dim interior of the building. A long counter ran from wall to wall, with a swinging door at each end. On a stool behind the counter sat a bald man wearing an eyeshade, working over a ledger by the light of a lamp. He looked up as they entered, and Story spoke.

"I'm Nelson Story. We're from Montana, here to buy cattle. I'll be needin' riders as well as cows."

It was an unasked question, put in a manner that invited a response, rather than demanding one.

"I'm York," said the man at the counter, "and I can't be of much help to you in findin' cows. Just about everybody that can raise a herd and afford an outfit ain't sellin' locally. Had a dozen drives go up the trail last fall, and there must be fifty more plannin' to move out in a month or so. I ain't sayin' you can't buy cows. You can, but they'll cost you ten dollars a head, and there won't be many two-year-old steers. As for riders, I can't say. Might pick up a few that's sold their cows or can't afford a trail drive. Try the saloons and pool halls."

"Thanks," Story said, and not until they reached their horses did he speak to his companions. "We'll find us a hotel, get some grub under our belts, and look around some."

"This hombre York didn't seem too anxious to help us," said Tom Allen.

"He's partial to Texans," Story said. "We'll have to expect that. It's hard times here, and a man selling his cows for ten dollars a head makes no sense, if there's a chance he can do better."

"Wal, hell," said Coon Tails, "ever'body in Texas ain't got enough cows fer a drive, an' if'n they did, they wouldn't have the cash fer their outfits. After supper, when the saloons an' billiard parlors commence t'fill up, why don't we split up, circulate, an' listen?"

"I think we'll do exactly that," Story said. "When a man's needin' cash, ten dollars a head *now* is worth fifty at the end of a trail he can't afford to ride."

They reined up before the Fort Worth House, a two-story hotel constructed of lumber, and it bore evidence of once having been painted. A porch ran all the way across the front of the building, and above that a balcony, with a single roof covering both. On the lower porch a bench ran the length of the wall from either side of the double front doors. Half a dozen men sat there watching the newcomers approach. Several of the locals were chewing plug, spitting over the porch railing. Numerous stains attested to their inaccuracy. Story and his men nodded to the observers, entered the hotel, and Story took a pair of rooms.

"I ain't one fer beds," said Coon Tails. "Jist gimme room t'spread my blankets on the floor."

"You can have my floor, then," Story said. "I reckon Bill and Tom are used to one another's snoring."

They climbed the stairs. The rooms were nothing fancy, but they seemed clean. There was a chair, a four-drawer dresser, and attached to the wall above it, a small mirror. On the dresser there was a washbasin and a porcelain pitcher. An iron bed stood next to the only window, and the fire escape consisted of a length of rope, one end of which was tied to a leg of the bed. Story and Coon Tails took the first room, which was on their left, while Bill Petty and Tom Allen took the second room, across the hall. Story removed his boots and hat, stretching out on the bed. Coon Tails spread his blankets.

"Should of brung my saddle, 'stead o' leavin' it at the livery," the old mountain man said. "Makes a dang good piller."

"There's two pillows on the bed," said Story. "You're welcome to one of them."

"Thankee," said Coon Tails, "but they's too soft. I'll make do."

Nelson Story wasn't a man to lie abed in the afternoon. In less than an hour he was up, sitting on the edge of the bed, looking out the window. Coon Tails got up, rolling his blankets, reaching for his battered old hat.

"It's a mite early t'hit the saloons," Coon Tails said, "but I purely got t'do somethin'. These fancy hotels is passable fer sleepin', I reckon, but I can't see much need fer 'em in the daytime, less'n a man be crippled."

Story laughed. "I was thinking the same thing," he said, reaching for his boots. "Let's roust Bill and Tom and go find us some steaks with plenty of potatoes, onions, and hot coffee."

"A mite early fer supper," said Coon Tails, "but I kin always eat ag'in."

Petty and Allen were eager and ready to leave the hotel, and the four of them headed for a cafe they had passed earlier. The place had no name. The entire front of the slab-sided building had been decorated with a black-painted likeness of a longhorn bull. Beneath that, in ragged red letters, was a single word: GRUB.

"With a front like this," Bill Petty said, "if they ain't got steak, we oughta pull our irons and shoot up the place."

Since it was well past the dinner hour and much too early for supper, they had the place to themselves. There were tables, but they took the stools along the counter. The cook looked like what he probably was, an ex-cowboy too stove up to ride. Without being asked, he sent four mugs of coffee sloshing down the counter.

"Steak, spuds, onions, coffee, an' apple pie," he said. "Two bits."

"My God," Tom Allen said, rolling his eyes, "in New Orleans a feed like that only costs a dime."

"Then mebbe you'd best hit the trail fer New Orleans," the old cook growled.

Story and his companions howled with laughter, and seeing the humor in the situation, their host managed a grin.

"Relax, pardner," said Story. "Your prices are fair. We're here from Montana to buy Texas longhorns, and we're findin' out there's a shortage."

"Shortage, hell," said the old cook. "Texas is cow poor. They's cows aplenty. They must be a hunnert ranchers what ain't got a prayer of drivin' a herd t'market. 'Course they'll stick you fer as much as yer willin' t'pay. Texans is broke, an' them that ain't is terrible bent."

"I'll be needing riders too," Story said. "Do you know of any men who might be willing to go up the trail for wages?"

"They's plenty that needs the money an' got no hope of anything else, but I got t'live here, an' I ain't namin' no names."

Story said no more. It was a matter of pride. If a man got hungry enough, he might sell his saddle, but it had to be his decision. Finished with their meal, Story and his companions left the cafe. Suddenly there was the roar of a gun, and before the echo died, Nelson Story had a pistol cocked and was running toward the narrow space between two buildings where a cloud of white smoke lingered. His Colt roared twice without effect. The would-be killer had escaped. Blood reddened the upper sleeve of Story's shirt, dripping off his left elbow.

"He burned away some hide," said Story when his companions had reached him, "but missed the bone."

"Damn," Bill Petty said, "we ain't been in town but two hours. How did anybody get a mad-on that quick?"

"He wasn't after you gents," said Story. "He was gunning for me, and I'm just almighty lucky his aim wasn't better."

The shooting had attracted others, one of them a heavyset, unshaven man who wore a badge. A pair of Union soldiers were double-timing toward them, and the man wearing the badge spoke loudly enough for everybody to hear.

"Here, now," he shouted, "I'm the sheriff, an' we don't hold with strangers comin' in an' shootin' up the town. You hombres better have a damn good excuse."

"Somebody tried to gun me down from ambush," Story said coldly. "Is that good enough?"

"Mebbe not," said the arrogant lawman. "I dunno you from Adam's off ox, an' what've I got, 'sides yer word? Anybody see what this gent's claimin' took place?"

"Damn right," Coon Tails said angrily. "The four o' us was walkin' down the street mindin' our own business. Why don't you git over yonder an' nose around betwixt them two buildings where the bushwhackin' varmint was holed up?"

The belligerent lawman glared at Coon Tails, and found himself facing Bill Petty and Tom Allen as well. The pair of Union soldiers were already at the place where the gunman had been hiding, and as much for the saving of face as anything else, the sheriff turned away and joined them.

"Some sheriff," Tom Allen muttered. "Who'n hell elected him?"

"He wasn't elected," said an old fellow wearing range clothes. "That's old Lot Higgins, and when the Yankees took over, he was appointed."

"He won't find anything," said Bill Petty. "Soon as that varmint hit the alley behind them buildings, his tracks could be anybody's."

"Hell," said a disgusted cowboy, "old Higgins ain't never been nothin' but the town drunk. My daddy called him Lot the sot. My God, he couldn't find the depot if you set him on the track and let him foller the train."

"If the sheriff has further need of us," Story said, "I'd appreciate one of you gents tellin' him we have rooms at the Fort Worth House. Now can one of you point me toward a doctor?"

"Doc Nagel," said a cowboy. "Take a right down yonder, like you was goin' to the unfinished courthouse. When you come to the Masonic hall, there's a shack next to it. That's where doc lives."

Dr. Nagel wasn't a talkative man, and he asked no

questions. Story paid him two dollars for dousing the wound with disinfectant and bandaging it.

"That throws a new light on things," Bill Petty said when they had left the doctor's place. "Unless you got some idea who this hombre is that's after you, and can smoke him out in the open, we'll have to put as much time into lookin' for him as for cows."

"He has an edge as long as we're in town," said Story. "Once we're on the plains, there'll always be sign. We've paid for a night at the hotel, but tomorrow we'll buy some grub and find a safer place to hole up. I'm not as aggravated with the bushwhacker as I am old Higgins. He could chuck us into the hoosegow on trumped-up charges, and he'd have the backing of the Union army."

"That's disgusting," Bill Petty said, "takin' away a man's right to vote, and then stickin' him with a shiftless old buzzard like Higgins. It's like the Union wasn't satisfied by beatin' the Rebs to their knees. They're aimin' for total humiliation."

"I expect you're right," said Story, "but it's a wrong that may never be corrected. There's nothing we can do, where the military is concerned. Let's make the rounds of the saloons. We'll split up. Do a lot of listening and not much talking, and use your own judgment as to when you let it be known we're looking for cows and riders."

Story entered a saloon called the Broken Spoke. It was still early and there were few patrons. Story ordered a beer. There was only one bartender, and he eyed Story curiously, but western etiquette forbade him asking questions. His knowledge of strangers was limited to what they willingly shared with him.

"I'm from Montana," Story said conversationally. "I'm looking to buy some cows and hire some riders."

The bartender continued polishing glasses, saying nothing, so Story tried again.

"Seems almighty warm, for this time of year."

"Been a mild winter," said the man behind the bar, "but don't let it fool you. I've watched the grass start to green in March, and then seen a good foot of snow laid over it."

Story's conversation with the bartender was getting him nowhere when a cowboy pushed through the batwing doors. Story recognized him as the man who had referred to Sheriff Higgins as "Lot the sot." He nodded, and Story saw no animosity in him. They desperately needed a friend among the locals who could put them in touch with ranchers willing to sell cows, and with riders who would hire on for the trail drive.

"Pardner," Story said, "I'm buying. Will you join me?"

"Much obliged," said the stranger. "I reckon you got a bad impression of our town. With old Higgins in the sheriff's office, and a Yankee on every corner, that's about all we have to offer." His laugh was bitter.

"So far," said Story with a grin, "I've run into a wall of distrust that'd put the Rockies in the shade. I'm Nelson Story. I came from Montana to buy Texas cows and hire some riders for a drive north."

"I'm Calvin Snider," said the cowboy. "My friends call me Cal. I spent four years with the Rebs, joinin' 'em when I was twenty-one. Pa died while I was gone, and he was the only family I had. Our neighbors rustled our cows. Took every damn thing we had but the corral fence. I'd hire on in a minute, if you could get me past the Yankees. I ain't even got a horse. I'm ridin' the mule that I rode back to Texas after the war ended."

"I've already spoken to Captain Clark, the Union commander," Story said. "You'll be allowed to leave Texas, but you'll have to sign papers agreeing not to take up arms against the Union again."

"I'll sign," said Cal. "Anything to get a good hoss under me and to feel like a man again. How many riders you got in mind?"

"I'd figured on twenty-five," said Story, "because I look for us to have to fight Indians. I have three men with me now, one of them a scout who says he's familiar with Indian Territory. All of us are making the rounds of the saloons, hoping to find riders for the drive and some ranchers with cows to sell. Maybe you can be of some help to us."

"I reckon I can help you with both," Cal said. "I tell you, Texans has been stripped of ever'thing but their pride, and they ain't anxious to part with that. It'll take a right smart of riding to get the cows. Mostly it's a few here and a few there, and likely not a steer in the bunch."

"That won't bother me," said Story, "after I've bought some bulls. I aim to sell part of the herd and keep the rest for breeding stock. I'm willing to pay ten dollars a head in Yankee greenbacks. Forty dollars and found for every rider, with a hundred dollar bonus at the end of the drive."

"Let me do some talkin'," Cal said. "There's men with no ties that would jump at the chance to hire on, if only to get away from the Yankees. There's some ranchers with just a few cows and no hope of ever takin' 'em up the trail. Right now, a hunnert dollars would be like a thousand."

"One more thing," said Story. "We'll be needin' cow horses. I figure every rider will need at least three. Can we find and buy that many?"

"Of that I ain't sure," Cal said. "For grub and a place to sleep, I work three days a week at the York and Draper barn, and we almost never have any good hosses. A few mules, plenty of oxen, but no hosses."

"Meet me in the lobby of the Fort Worth House tomorrow at first light," said Story. "We'll have breakfast and decide where we go from there. Like you said, we haven't been made to feel exactly welcome here, and I aim to find a more hospitable place to hole up until we're ready to begin the drive."

Story followed the young cowboy out of the saloon and they each went their separate ways. Story met Coon Tails as the old mountain man emerged from a billiard parlor.

"Too damn early," Coon Tails said. "Them that has payin' work can't come in, an' them that don't is too broke t'come in."

"I hired one cowboy," said Story, "and he'll be spreadin' the word among ranchers and riders he knows. Let's find Tom and Bill."

Tom Allen and Bill Petty hadn't done any better than Coon Tails had, and they brightened considerably when Story told them of hiring Cal Snider.

"Maybe we'd better just let this cowboy see what he can scare up," said Petty. "Some of these hombres around here, I reckon they'd gut-shoot a man for the price of a drink. This Snider will likely be particular who he's talkin' to, and I'm in favor of that. If word gets out that we're buying cows and hirin' riders, somebody's bound to get the idea we're carryin' cash."

"I'd considered that," Story said, "even before I learned somebody's gunning for me. I mentioned to Cal we'll be leaving the hotel tomorrow, and this being his home range, he may know of someplace we can head-quarter until we're ready for the trail north."

There was a rumble of thunder and the wind had begun to rise, coming out of the southwest.

"Mighty lot o' rain in these parts," said Coon Tails. "More comin', and the ground's still muddy from the last one."

"It'll be rain here," said Tom Adams, "but it'll be snow in the high country."

"It's been a mild winter in Texas," Story said, "and that could be bad news. We could have rain in February and a blue norther in March."

They reached the hotel before the storm broke, and within minutes the wide dirt streets were awash with mud and high water. It was impossible to open the windows, for they were on the west side of the building and the rain came in slashing torrents. The heat was almost unbearable.

"Come on," said Story, "and let's set on the porch until it slacks. Then we can at least open the windows."

But the downpour didn't slack. The thunder and lightning abated, but the rain continued.

"Tarnation," Coon Tails said, "we got t'cross five rivers that I know of, startin' with the Red. If'n this is a sample of what's t'come, they'll be backwater fer ten mile."

Story lay awake far into the night listening to the wind fling gusts of rain against the side of the hotel. While it did nothing to lessen his resolve, there was no denying the logic of old Coon Tails's prophecy. Of all the dangers that lay ahead, swollen, treacherous rivers might be the most formidable.

"She ain't let up enough t'make no diff'rence," said Coon Tails, peering out the fogged up window. "We'd best git our slickers ready."

"We don't know where we'll be going," Story said, "until we've talked to Cal Snider. He should be waitin' for us downstairs."

Snider was waiting, and he wasn't alone. The two young cowboys with him hadn't even begun to shave, and they shifted from one foot to the other as Cal introduced them.

"This here's Hitch Gould and Arch Rainey," Cal said. "They been deprived somethin' terrible. They was too young for the war, so they don't know how to do nothin' but wrassle cows."

The cowboys glared at Cal, furious with him for the

less than flattering introduction. Story sensed their unease and spoke quickly.

"Welcome, gents. There's a pile of work and a long trail ahead of us. Let's find some hot coffee, some breakfast, and then we'll talk."

The water was up to, and in some places over, the boardwalk, as they donned slickers and sought a cafe. Finding one, they trooped in and took a large round table that accommodated the seven of them. Thanks to the still early hour and the pouring rain, the place wasn't crowded. When the waiter arrived, Story ordered for them all.

"Bring us a couple platters of fried eggs, plenty of ham, potatoes, and black coffee. When we're done with that, bring us the whole thing, all over again."

"By God," Coon Tails said, "I purely admire a outfit that don't skimp on the grub. They ain't nothin' a man can't do when his belly's full."

"Cal," said Story, "we're needin' a place to hole up while we gather a herd. You know this country. Where can we sleep dry and not be bothered while we're buyin' cows?"

"There's a canyon maybe twenty miles south of here," Cal said. "It's on the Brazos, near Thorp Spring. Hitch and Arch used to work that range, and I reckon they'll be more familiar with it than I am."

It was Snider's way of drawing the uncomfortable newcomers into the conversation, making them part of the outfit. Story turned to them.

"Yeah," said Hitch, "it's a long canyon with plenty of graze, and there's considerable overhang beneath the west bank. We slept there, keepin' dry through many a storm."

"There's an almighty lot of water comin' down out there," Bill Petty said. "Won't it flood us out durin' heavy rains?"

"Never has yet," said Arch, "and this ain't the first

rainy spring we've had. It's the kind of place you could hole up for months, with nobody knowin' you was there."

"I hear the Comanches have been raisin' hell in East Texas," Tom Allen said. "Can we defend this canyon hideout without losin' our scalps?"

"Till hell freezes," said Hitch. "Nobody can get at us, 'cept from the east wall of the canyon, and from there they can't get a clear shot. Mostly the Comanches is farther south, botherin' riders that's wrasslin' cows out of the brush. Charlie Goodnight and his outfit's ropin' 'em out of the brakes along the Brazos, somewhere south of Waco."*

"We'll load up on supplies, then," Story said, "and head for this canyon on the Brazos. From there we go looking for cows."

"I know where we can pick up maybe two hundred," said Cal, "but like I said, they'll come a few at a time. Hitch and Arch can get us some more, but it'll still be a few here and a few there."

"If you're needin' a cook," Arch Rainey said, "you can get old Sandy Bill. Grouchiest old varmint in East Texas, but there ain't a better range cook."

"Get him," said Story.

---

* Trail Drive Series No. 1, *The Goodnight Trail*

2

"Calvin Snider, what'n tarnation do you think you're doing?"

Story and his men were barely out of the cafe when she confronted them, a bundle of female fury in riding boots, denim shirt, and Levi's pants. She had red hair, blue eyes, and was a good three years shy of being out of her teens.

"If you must know, Lorna," said Cal, embarrassed, "I've hired on with Mr. Story's outfit. I'll be riding north on a trail drive."

"You've quit your job with York and Draper," she said accusingly. "The whole town's talking about it."

"Some job," Cal said hotly. "One meal a day, and sleepin' in the hayloft. It's none of the town's business what I do, no more than it's any of yours."

"Well, I don't want you going," she snapped. "I . . . I'll make Daddy give you a job in the bank."

Hitch Gould and Arch Rainey had been grinning, obviously familiar with what had been a tempestuous relationship. Finally they gave in to their mirth, slapping their thighs with their hats. It was more than poor Cal could take. His face aflame with embarrassment, he turned to Story.

"This here's Lorna Flagg," he said desperately. "She's

follered me her whole damn life, and I swear to God, I ain't done nothin' to encourage her."

"That's a lie, Calvin," said Lorna. "You went to war when I was thirteen and a half, and you were gone four years. Ever since you came back, you've been avoiding me. Now you're going away again. Please, please don't go."

She moved closer to Cal and a big tear rolled down her cheek. Cal seemed mesmerized, and when he became aware of her intentions, it was too late. She threw her arms around his neck, sending his hat tumbling along the muddy boardwalk. It was too much. Cal's companions were roaring, even Story. Worse, despite the rain, others had been attracted by the commotion. Cal tore loose, grabbed his hat out of the mud, and was almost to the next cross street before Story and the rest of the riders caught up to him.

"Lord," said Hitch Gould, rolling his eyes, "I wisht I had Cal's problem."

"God, I reckon," Arch Rainey said. "I'd sleep in the hayloft and fork horse apples for the rest of my life."

"You possum-faced bastards," Cal gritted.

It was cowboy humor at its worst. Even Story got into the act.

"Cal," he said, eyes twinkling, "I wouldn't want to lure you away from a career in banking."

"Aw, hell, Mr. Story," said Cal pleadingly, "old man Flagg hates my guts. He's always looked at me like I was some hairy-legged varmint that crawled out from under a rock."

"If old Cal was to haul down his Levi's," Hitch laughed, "I bet we'd find that little gal's got her brand on both his flanks."

"Wisht she'd dab her loop on me," Arch mourned. "Why, I'd worship the ground her daddy's bank sets on."

"Mr. Story," said Cal, "I'll do anything you ask of me,

but I ain't about to come into town again 'fore we move out with the herd."

Mounted, Story led the way to the livery, where he bought two pack mules. From there they went to the mercantile for provisions.

"Arch," Story said, "were you serious about finding us a cook?"

"Yes, sir," said Arch. "His name's William Sandifer, and he's called Sandy Bill. A hoss rolled on him and he's got a bad back, but he can cook. He's lookin' to hire on, but money's mighty scarce. None of the outfits that went up the trail last fall had a cook. The riders took turns, and wasn't none of 'em liked it. Sandy's got a wagon and a team."

"Why don't you go and get him, then," Story said. "There'll be extra pay for the use of his wagon and team. Have him bring the wagon into town and buy what he'll need in the way of cooking pots, pans, skillets, and eating tools. Here's some money."

"If'n that wagon ain't got 'em, he'd best mount a water keg on each side," said Coon Tails. "Don't look like it'll ever quit rainin' here, but we might hit a dry stretch north o' here."

"Good thinking," Story said. "Now, Hitch, if you and Cal will lead us to that canyon on the Brazos, we'll set up camp."

The rain continued and visibility was limited to a few hundred feet. Arch Rainey rode west to the shack where William Sandifer lived, while Story and the rest of the outfit headed for the canyon on the Trinity. But their departure from town didn't go unnoticed. Once they had vanished into the gray of the steadily falling rain, a single rider followed.

"This is ideal," said Story when they reached the canyon.

"There's already a bunch of dry firewood under that

overhang," said Hitch. "You don't never know what the weather's goin' to do in Texas. You ride out at daylight, and it's warm, maybe rainin', and before you ride in at sundown, it's cold enough to freeze the tail feathers off a paisano."

"I think we'll need a place to conceal Sandy Bill's wagon until we're ready to begin the drive," Story said. "The fewer people who know we're here, the better off we'll be."

"After we've unloaded and toted ever'thing to camp," said Hitch, "there's a thick bunch of willows upriver a ways. They'll hide the wagon, I reckon."

By midday the rain had slowed to a drizzle, but the sky was still overcast and a southwesterly wind had a raw edge to it. It was late afternoon before Arch Rainey rode in ahead of William Sandifer's wagon. There was easier access to the new camp from the canyon floor than from the rim, and Arch had wisely guided the wagon along the west bank of the Brazos into the canyon. Story and his companions made their way down the embankment to the wagon. William Sandifer's hair was mostly gray, and he had keen gray eyes. He walked in a stilted manner, unable to bend his left knee, his back stiff.

"Good, solid wagon," Story said. "Watertight?"

"Sealed her myself," said Sandifer. "New canvas too."

"Good," Story said. "I'm Nelson Story, and these two gents are friends from my bull-whacking days, Bill Petty and Tom Allen. You know the rest of these hombres, I reckon."

"I do," said Sandifer. "I can doctor knife wounds, bullet wounds, snake bite, hangovers, and busted bones. I'm the best damn cook in Texas, and you can call me Sandy, Sandy Bill, or just Bill. I don't answer to Greasy Belly, or Biscuit Shooter, and I don't feed nobody between meals."

"Sandy Bill," Story said, "welcome to the outfit. We'll

help you unload whatever you'll need for temporary camp, and then I'd like for you to hide the wagon in that stand of willows upriver until we're ready for the trail."

There was an ample supply of firewood under the overhang, proof that it had long been a convenient shelter from the elements. The shelf was forty feet long, a dozen feet to the rock above their heads, and of a depth that wind, rain, or snow couldn't penetrate. The horses, along with Sandifer's mules, were loosed to graze along the river within sight of their hole-in-the-wall camp.

"Tomorrow," said Story, "we'll begin buying cows. Coon Tails, I want you here in camp with Sandy Bill. Cal, you'll ride with me. Hitch will ride with Bill, and Arch will ride with Tom. Keep in mind that we're needing horses and riders, as well as cows."

"With the goin' rate ten dollars a head," Tom Allen said, "I can afford two hundred."

"I'm figurin' on that many for myself," said Bill Petty.

"Then we'll shoot for a herd of thirty-four hundred," Story said.

As darkness drew near, there was a faraway rumble of thunder, and the rain intensified from a drizzle into a downpour. Sandy Bill proved himself to everybody's satisfaction by treating them to a supper of Dutch oven biscuits, fried ham, beans, hot coffee, and dried apple pie.

February 3, 1866. On the Brazos.

By dawn the rain had slacked, but not much. There was a chill wind out of the northwest. Story and his friends from the high country donned their mackinaws and gloves, the Texas riders watching enviously.

"Buy whatever cows you can," Story said, "but arrange to leave them where they are, at least for a day or two. There's a chance we may not be able to buy enough cows here. After we've bought all we can, we'll run a tally. If we're short, we'll have to move farther south. I can't see driving a herd of cows with us, only to have to drive them back again."

Story and Cal rode east, Hitch and Bill rode south, while Arch and Tom rode west.

"First two hombres we'll be talkin' to is Russ Shadley and Mac Withers," said Cal, "and I reckon I'd as well tell you they ain't too well thought of around here. They laid back in the brush durin' the war, not takin' sides, but they *did* take ever' damn cow they could get a loop on. Mine included, I reckon."

"Rustlers?"

"No," Cal said, "I can't rightfully call 'em that. In Texas, unbranded cows are mavericks. Fair game for any hombre with a fast loop and a running iron."

"Even if they're two, three, or four years old?"

"Even then," Cal sighed.

"They ought to have a considerable herd by now," said Story. "You reckon they'll sell?"

"Oh, they ain't got that many now," Cal said. "They didn't fight against the Union, and when the Yankees needed beef, who do you reckon they bought it from? They'll sell. Better to you than to the damn Yankees."

The place, when they reached it, was as much a raw-hide outfit as Story had ever seen. The shack was built of logs, with a shake roof and a mud-and-stick chimney. A tattered cowhide anchored somewhere above the jamb served as a door. Cal reined up, Story following suit.

"Hello the house," Cal shouted.

"Turn around," said a voice somewhere behind them. "Do it slow, and keep your hands where I can see 'em."

Cal and Story reined their horses around until they were facing a stand of scrub oak fifty yards from the shack.

"I reckon this ain't a social call," said the voice from the thicket, "so whadda you want, Snider?"

"Shadley," said Cal, "this is Nelson Story, and he's buying cows. Are you selling?"

Shadley came lumbering out of the thicket. He was maybe five-eight, long unshaven, heavily muscled. He wore a denim shirt, faded Levi's, run-over boots, and a used-up flop hat. In his right fist he still clutched a cocked Colt.

"Yeah," he said, only a little less hostile, "I've got a few cows. Git down." He eased the Colt off cock and holstered the weapon.

"How many cows?" Cal asked.

"I ain't dealin' with you, Snider," Shadley growled. "While you was off playin' sojer, your daddy called me a rustler, the old son of—"

Cal moved like a striking rattler. His right fist slammed into Shadley's jaw, lifting the heavier man off his feet. Shadley came down on his back in ankle-deep mud and lay there a moment, shaking his head. Then he went for his gun, but his hand froze on the butt of the Colt. He hadn't seen Nelson Story move, but the big man had him covered.

"In the high country," Story said, "we don't draw on an unarmed man. If that's not the custom in Texas, it should be."

"It is," said Cal angrily, "but I joined the Rebs. I ain't allowed to have a gun, while this Yankee-lovin' bastard—"

"That's enough," Story said. "We're here to buy cows, if we can. Get up, Shadley."

"Thirty head," Shadley gritted, getting to his feet. "You'd ought to watch the comp'ny you keep, Mr. High Plains. That'll be fifteen dollers a head, cash."

Cal Snider was so angry, words failed him. He just stood there fisting his hands and gritting his teeth. Story didn't even consider it worthy of a response. He nodded to Cal and they were mounting their horses when a rider approached. He reined up and dismounted. He was slender and clean-shaven, almost the exact opposite of Russ Shadley, although he was dressed no better. He looked from Cal to Shadley, his eyes lingering on the swelling of Shadley's jaw. Finally he turned to Story, and Story spoke.

"I'm Nelson Story, in Texas to buy cows. Cal's one of my riders, and he brought me here. We were just leaving."

"I know Cal," said the young rider. "I'm Mac Withers. I'm pardners with this unsociable varmint, Shadley. God only knows why. We got cows to sell, but you don't look like a man that's made a deal."

"Not at fifteen dollars a head," Cal said angrily. "It's a poor excuse for a man who'd fall back on his dislike for me to cheat Mr. Story on a cattle deal."

"I agree," said Withers, his eyes on Shadley. "We got thirty head, and the fifteen that's mine are for sale at ten dollars a head."

"We'll take them," Story said, liking this young rider. "I'm hiring cowboys for a trail drive. Forty and found, with a hundred dollar bonus at the finish."

"You just hired yourself a cowboy," said Withers. "Come on. We'll cut out the cows and take 'em with us."

Russ Shadley looked from Withers to Story. All this was happening too fast for him. With poor grace he turned to Story.

"All right," he said, "I was wrong, usin' my mad for Snider agin you. Take all the cows at ten dollars a head, and if you can use another rider, I'll hire on."

"You're hired," Story said, "on one condition. Leave your old grudges behind. I'll tolerate no differences among the riders that can't be settled with fists. Save the gunplay for Indian attacks. Don't you ever pull a gun on one of my riders unless you're ready to draw against me, and if it ever comes to that, you'd better be fast. Almighty fast. *Comprender?*"

"Yeah," said Shadley. While he refused to look at Story, he eyed Cal Snider with anything but tolerance, and Cal glared back. They backed away with all the wariness of a pair of hounds temporarily separated, each as determined as the other that this conflict would resume at some better time and place.

Hitch Gould and Bill Petty rode south, Hitch leading the way. As they rode, Hitch talked and Petty listened.

"The old gent we're goin' to see is Shanghai Wolfington," Hitch said. "Tough old bird. He went to sea when he wasn't more'n a kid. Shanghaied the first time, went back twice more on his own. Missin' his left eye, and he's got scars all over him, mostly from knife and saber. I reckon he's at least fifty now, and tough as whang leather, but the Federals have done what the sea, the Comanches, and the rustlers couldn't do. They've broke him. Come the first of March, they're takin' old Shanghai's ranch. For taxes, they say. I'm takin' you to see him so's he can sell off his stock and come out with somethin'. He's spent thirty years buildin' his Anchor brand, and he's killin' mad."

"Maybe he can sell enough stock to pay the taxes," said Petty.

"No way," Hitch said. "He ain't got more'n five hundred cows and four or five bulls. Sell off all his breedin' stock to satisfy this year's taxes, and what's he gonna do next year? I tell you, them Yanks is smart. There's already talk that next year's taxes will be even higher, so's the banks can foreclose on them that's managed to hang on."

"By God," said Petty angrily, "I never heard of such. Why don't he just leave Texas and drive his stock to Colorado, Wyoming, or Montana territories?"

"He can't," Hitch said. "Texans can't leave the state

without permission of the Federals. They'd just grab his herd to satisfy the taxes."

"I reckon you're right," said Petty. "All he can do is sell off the stock. That'll be better than seein' thirty years shot to hell. But when that bunch takes his spread for taxes, won't they be expectin' some cows?"

"I reckon," Hitch said, "but what can they do? I'm thinkin' old Shanghai and his riders might throw in with the trail drive and just get the hell out of Texas for good."

"They're bound to have some good cow horses," said Petty. "How many riders?"

"Two," Hitch said. "Smokey Ellison and Oscar Fentress. Smokey was just a boy when Comanches kilt his folks. Shanghai took him in, and he's been there ever' since. Oscar Fentress is a black man—a Negro—and he's been with Shanghai more'n twenty years. Now he's bein' told he's free, that he's got to go off on his own. Hell, Oscar ain't wantin' to leave Anchor. It's the only home he's ever had."

Shanghai Wolfington had only a little fringe of gray hair above his ears. He was at least fifty or more, and his old hat with its uncreased crown made him seem taller than he was. His Levi's, flannel shirt, and boots were well worn. He was unarmed. Bill Petty found Shanghai to be all that Hitch had claimed, and more. Hitch introduced Petty, explaining the purpose of their visit.

"Last tally," Shanghai said, "we had five hundred an' ten head, four of 'em bulls. There's a hundred or so two-year-old steers, an' the rest is cows. Gonna be a good calf crop too, not that it'll make any difference to me. I reckon you've heard the Federals is takin' the place for taxes."

"Yeah," said Petty, "Hitch told me. My stake in this trail drive ain't all that big, and I'd like for you to talk to Nelson Story. I kind of feel like we're taking advantage of your misfortune. Besides, Story's hiring riders for the drive north, and I think he'll be very interested in talking to you and your men about joining the drive."

Two men left the barn and approached the house. From the description Hitch had provided, Petty recognized them as Smokey Ellison and Oscar Fentress. Wolfington introduced the riders and told them that Hitch and Petty were interested in buying cows.

"Lawd," said Oscar, "Ah hates to see them cows go. This was goin' t'be the best calvin' we ever had. Why them damn Yankees have t'come an' take ever'thing we worked for?"

"If we had guns and grub," Smokey Ellison said, "I'd say we take the herd and head north, Yankees be damned."

Ellison and Fentress wore range clothes similar to Wolfington's, and even though they were unarmed, Petty admired their defiance. It was to his faithful riders that Shanghai spoke.

"Oscar, you an' Smokey might as well run another tally. I'm ridin' t'meet Story, the gent that's buyin' cows. He's hirin' riders for the drive north, an' if I like him and the looks of the outfit, maybe I'll hire on. With the stock gone, they ain't nothin' keepin' me here."

The trio had been together for so many years, Oscar and Smokey understood what Shanghai was proposing. He was offering to take them wherever his trail led, but he could not—would not—commit them without their approval.

"If this outfit suit you," said Oscar, "see if they hire this old black man what ain't got no home."

"If it's good enough for you and Oscar," Smokey said, "put in a word for me. I don't care where we're goin', long as it ain't neck deep in blue bellies and scalawags."

Hitch rode out, Bill Petty and Shanghai Wolfington following.

* * *

Arch Rainey and Tom Allen rode south along the Trinity until the country grew wilder and the brakes along the river became thicker.

"This is some wild territory for ranching," Allen observed.

"We ain't headin' for a ranch," said Arch. "It's a cow camp, and you're about to meet four of the wildest young hellions that ever forked a hoss. I doubt there's a one older than fifteen. The leader of the bunch is Wes Hardin, and he's quick as forked lightning with a pistol. There's his pard, a quiet hombre called Slim. Greener— and that's all the name I ever heard—carries a sawed-off shotgun. Then there's a hoss-crazy Injun, a tame Comanche called Quickenpaugh."

"A *tame* Comanche?"

"Tame as a Comanche ever gets." Arch grinned. "Wild as Texas jacks, the four of 'em. They're the kind who'll die at the business end of a rope, unless somebody shoots 'em first."

"They purely don't sound like the kind who'd rope wild cows out of the brakes at ten dollars a head," said Allen.

"They're doin' it mostly to gain favor with the Federals," Arch said. "They sell beef to the Unionists, maybe fifty head at a time. Fast as the Federals can buy cows, they git rustled. There's rumors that these four cow wrasslers we're goin' to see is rustlin' them cows, drivin' 'em to another Federal camp, and sellin' 'em all over again."

Allen laughed. "No proof, I reckon."

"No proof," Arch agreed. "The cows are right out of the brakes, and all unbranded. Texans is broke. It'll be almighty important for Mr. Story to get a signed bill of sale and to take the time for trail brandin' before we start the drive. But it ain't my place to go tellin' him how to run the outfit. Maybe you can mention it to him."

"Thanks," said Allen. "Maybe I will."

They found the camp when Arch's horse nickered and a distant horse answered.

"Hello the camp," Arch shouted. "This is Arch Rainey and a friend, and we're lookin' to buy cows."

There was no response, and they rode cautiously on. They came upon four horses grazing along a bend in the river where the grass grew high and the willows hung low. The only evidence of a camp was a burned-out campfire.

"We'll shuck our saddles, give our horses a rest, and wait," said Arch. "They rope longhorns, riders workin' in pairs, and they'll have a holding pen somewhere downriver. Ropin' longhorns is hell on horses, and they'll likely be ridin' in to change mounts at noon."

When the four brush poppers rode in, Arch and Allen were in plain sight, getting to their feet as the riders dismounted. They nodded a greeting to Arch, but eyed Tom Allen with suspicion. They relaxed a little as Arch explained the purpose of their visit. He then introduced the four riders to Tom Allen.

Quickenpaugh, the Comanche, wore moccasins and buckskin pants, and nothing more. Near his left hand the haft of a knife protruded above the waist of his buckskins, while on the right there was the butt of a Colt. His torso, arms, and face were burned almost as black as his hair. He acknowledged the visitors with an almost imperceptible nod and no change of expression. The other three men responded as had the Indian, with nods. They were dressed in well-worn range clothes, run-over boots, and hats that had seen more than their share of rain and Texas sun. Tom Allen noted that they went considerably beyond being well-armed. Quickenpaugh, Slim, and Hardin each carried a saddle gun, while Greener had an ugly sawed-off shotgun behind his saddle, thonged to his bedroll. Greener and Slim each wore a tied-down Colt, while Wes Hardin sported two, in a buscadera rig. They looked more like a band of outlaws or killers than cowboys, Tom Allen thought. Wes Hardin had a horse face, uneven teeth, and pale eyes as cold as blue ice. It was he who finally spoke, not to Tom Allen, but to Arch Rainey.

"Forty head," said Hardin. "No brands. We'll have 'em to your camp at daylight tomorrow."

"Fifteen mile upriver," Arch said. "Camp's under the west rim overhang."

Nothing more was said. The four watched in silence as Arch Rainey and Tom Allen saddled their horses. Only when they were well away from the camp did Tom Allen speak.

"The Federals stripped the rest of you of guns, while them four's got enough weapons to put down an Indian uprising."

"Yeah," said Arch. "There ain't nothin' fair about this Reconstruction. Them four ain't in violation by keepin' their guns, because they didn't fight against the Union. 'Cept for the Comanche, they'd have joined the Rebs if they'd been old enough. Me and Hitch ain't armed 'cause every damn gun in Texas went to war, and the Yanks have went to some pains to see that we don't get our hands on any new ones. Not that we could afford 'em."

"Nelson Story's going to arm the outfit before we take the trail," Allen said. "Do you reckon those cows Hardin and his amigos will be bringin' have been sold to the Federals, rustled back, and are bein' resold to us?"

"I dunno," Arch grinned, "and it'd be a damn unhealthy question to bring up. When a Texan sells you cows and you get a bill of sale, it ain't polite to ask if the brutes have been rustled."

Allen laughed, appreciating the droll cowboy humor. "I reckon not. A bill of sale will cover us, and Nelson Story won't deal without one."

"You forgot to mention to them four that Story's hiring riders for the drive," said Arch.

"I didn't forget," Allen said. "It's up to Nelson, if he wants to gamble on that bunch. I doubt we'd ever get them out of Texas, anyhow. They look like the kind who'd get their enjoys out of selling cows to the Union army, rustling them, and selling them back to the Federals."

"All the more reason the Unionists might welcome the chance to be rid of them," said Arch. "Except for the Indian, all of them lost family or friends during the war. Since this Reconstruction started in Texas, there's been carpetbaggers, scalawags, and some soldiers killed. Some gunned down, some strung up. Wes and his *companeros* have been suspected, but there's been no proof. Even the Union army can't convict a man on suspicion."

"Compared to that," Allen said, "selling cows to the military and then rustling them back is child's play. I think we'd better warn Story. I know he wants men with the bark on, hombres who'd tackle hell with a bucket of water, but he might draw the line at renegades, thieves, and killers."

"I wisht you'd leave me out of it," said Arch. "I reckon I done talked too much, sayin' things that can't be proved. You've knowed him longer than I have, but Mr. Story strikes me as bein' the kind of hombre, if he's wantin' advice, he'll ask for it."

"I think we'd both better keep our silence," Allen said, "and let Story reach his own conclusions."

"You trust his judgment, then."

"As much or more than I'd trust my own," said Allen. "If the world was afire, Nelson handed me the loose end of a rope and said it was the only way out, I'd start climbing."

3

Story and Cal were the first to return to camp, followed by Shadley and Withers, driving their thirty cows. Once the cows were grazing along the river, Story introduced the two new riders to Coon Tails and Sandy Bill.

"We gonna be a while buildin' a herd," Coon Tails said, eyeing the few grazing longhorns.

"I figure a month," said Story. "Maybe longer."

"Shadley and me hired on for a trail drive," Wither said. "Until then, you got any objections to us ropin' more cows?"

"No," said Story. "I'll pay you for the thirty you just drove in, and I'll buy as many more as you can gather. Consider yourselves part of the outfit, starting today."

"That's mighty generous," Withers said. "We'll drive in our gather ever' Saturday, and you'll need a holdin' pen. Them critters we just drove in has been penned awhile, but this new bunch will be fresh out of the brakes an' wild as hell."

"By the time you get the new gather here, I'll have a place for them," said Story.

"That'll keep them busy," Cal said when Shadley and Withers had ridden away, "but what about Arch, Hitch, and me?"

"The three of you will continue riding with Bill Petty, Tom Allen, and me," said Story. "I think we'll wait for Bill, Hitch, Arch, and Tom to return. I want to see how successful they've been. Maybe then we'll have some idea as to how long we'll be here."

"More rain comin'," Coon Tails predicted. "This keeps up, water'll be belly deep all the way acrost Injun Territory."

Thunder rumbled down the canyon and new torrents of rain began pounding the already sodden earth. Bill Petty, Hitch Gould, and Shanghai Wolfington rode in at the height of the storm. While Sandy Bill didn't feed between meals, he kept a pot of coffee on the fire. The three riders left their horses grazing by the river, and shouldering their saddles, made their way up the steep trail to the sheltered camp.

"Gather 'round the fire and have some hot coffee," Story invited.

Hitch introduced Shanghai, inviting the old rancher to tell Story as much or as little as he wished. Shanghai began with his need to sell cows, but found Story sympathetic to his predicament. Three cups of coffee later, the big man from the high plains slammed his tin cup down on a rock shelf and got to his feet.

"Legalized robbery," said Story angrily, "and this is just the start. Meet their demands now, and next year they'll raise the ante."

"That's it," Shanghai said gloomily. "Good range, and the finest breedin' stock a man ever had, gone."

"How many steers?" Story asked.

"Hundred and some," said Shanghai. "Four bulls an' four hundred cows, at least half of 'em calvin'."

"Shanghai," Story said, "that's exactly what I'm looking for. I aim to sell some stock, but what I'm most interested in is breeding stock. There's range in Montana Territory that'll make your mouth water."

"God, what I wouldn't give t'be goin' there with cows of my own," said Shanghai.

"Then why don't you? I'll buy a hundred steers and a hundred cows. That'll leave you with three hundred cows and a two thousand dollar stake."

"Story," Shanghai said, "you're the whitest man I ever met, but I'm up agin' a stacked deck. I can't leave Texas with nothin' but the clothes on my back. The Federals would just take my cows for taxes, an' likely chunk me in the *calabozo* for tryin' t'sneak out with 'em."

"When you leave Texas," said Story, "you'll be taking nothing with you. Far as the Federals are concerned, I'm buying your entire herd. Then when we reach Montana Territory, I'll make you a bill of sale for all or as many of those three hundred cows that survive the journey. I'll hire you and your riders at forty and found, with a hundred dollar bonus as the end of the drive."

For a while the old Texan said nothing. Head bowed, he seemed intently interested in his half-empty coffee cup. He swallowed hard a couple of times before he finally spoke.

"Story, I . . . great God, man! It's like I'm bein' strung up, an' you cut the rope. I'm acceptin' your offer and thankin' God for the opportunity. You just hired three grateful Texas cowboys, an' we'll side you till hell freezes."

"Once you get the herd here," Story said, "I'll draw up a bill of sale from your tally. I'd suggest you not waste any time rounding them up and driving them here."

"You're almighty right," said Shanghai. "Closer it gits t'that tax deadline, the more likely that some scalawag will come sniffin' around. It looks like we'll have rain at least through t'morrow, and that'll cover a lot of tracks. You want us t' hide the herd in some canyon till you're ready for the drive?"

"They're branded, aren't they?"

"Anchor on the left flank," Shanghai said.

"Bring them here," said Story, "and we'll graze them along the river. I don't hide and I don't run."

"That Anchor could be a problem," Cal said when Shanghai had ridden away. "When them tax people discover all they're gettin' is a shack, a barn, and a few acres of mesquite and sage, the blue bellies might come lookin' for cows with the Anchor brand."

"Maybe," said Story, "but I never stomp a snake till he tries to bite me."

When Arch Rainey and Tom Allen returned, Allen told Story of young Wes Hardin and his questionable companions.

"I don't question a man's honesty without cause," Story said. "If the cows are unbranded and there's a bill of sale, that's as strong a claim as I'd want or expect."

"They'll be here at first light with forty head," said Tom Allen. "Where did that bunch of cows come from that's grazin' along the river?"

"Russ Shadley and Mac Withers brought them," Story said. "I hired them for the drive, and they've gone to rope more cows. Did you tell Hardin and his bunch we're needing riders for the drive?"

"No," said Allen, "I'm leavin' that up to you. They're a wild bunch, and not a one more than fifteen or sixteen."

"I'll look forward to meeting them," Story said. "This is the frontier, and a hard land breeds men the equal of it."

Lorna Flagg was accustomed to having her own way, if not through persuasion, then by tantrum. Her father, one of the town's bankers, was affluent, socially prominent, and profoundly boring. When Lorna was sixteen, her mother had gone East for a visit and hadn't bothered returning. Following Lorna's encounter with Cal

Snider, there was a stormy confrontation with her father, Amos Flagg.

"Calvin Snider is trash," Flagg shouted, "and I
wouldn't have him in my office long enough to sweep
the floor, assuming that he knows how."

"He's been to war," said Lorna defiantly, "and he's a
man. I've wanted him since I was twelve, and I still do.
Now he's going away on a cattle drive."

"Good riddance," Flagg said. "Now perhaps you can
begin conducting yourself like a young lady, instead of
the town whore. You're so much like your mother, I
suppose I should be thankful you haven't been sleeping
with this . . . this stable hand."

"How do you know I haven't?" she taunted. "I fault
my mother only for not taking me with her when she
left. And you. You're enjoying this damned government
occupation, aren't you? You're a big, fat buzzard, feed-
ing off the misery of others. Just two more months and
I'll be eighteen. Then, thank God, I can leave here, and
you can't stop me."

"But until then," Flagg said ominously, "I can take a
razor strap to your backside."

"You'll have to take your pleasure some other way,"
Lorna said. "You come after me with a strap or anything
else, and I'll scratch your eyes out."

In her room the girl looked wistfully at a calendar. It
was only the fourth day of February, and not until the
fifth of April would she be eighteen. She untied the
bandanna and counted the money she'd managed to
save. She thought of Cal Snider. Suppose she followed
him to Kansas, Missouri, or wherever this trail drive was
going, and the stubborn cowboy *still* wouldn't have her?
Damn him, he refused to see her as anything but a
gawky, freckled twelve-year-old. Angrily she ripped off
her clothes, and standing before a mirror, regained her
confidence. She'd show Cal Snider a thing or two. . . .

* * *

February 4, 1866. On the Brazos.

The day dawned gray and wet, the rain subsiding just long enough to take a new start. The Trinity ran muddier, deeper, wider. Wes Hardin and his companions rode in, driving the promised forty head of longhorns. Arch Rainey climbed down to the river and led the four young riders to camp. He then introduced them to Story, Bill Petty, and Coon Tails. Cal, Hitch, and Sandy Bill they apparently already knew. There was a prolonged silence as Nelson Story appraised the newcomers, and they seemed not in the least ill at ease. In fact, there was a cockiness about them, and Story liked that. Their horses, still saddled, grazed with the longhorns along the river.

"There's coffee," Story said. "You're welcome to unsaddle your horses and dry out. I'll want a bill of sale."

"We get our money, you get the cows," said Hardin shortly. "No more."

"Wrong," Story said, his eyes meeting Hardin's. "I get the cows, along with a bill of sale, and you get your money. Anything less, and you ride out the way you rode in, taking your cows with you."

Strangely enough, it was the Comanche—Quickenpaugh—who laughed. The others glared at him, and he seemed not to care. Hardin turned back to Story, and when he spoke, it was without emotion.

"If you got pencil and paper, I'll write out a bill and sign it."

Without comment Story took a stub of pencil and a notebook from his coat pocket. He turned to a blank page in the notebook, passing it and the pencil to Hardin. When he had completed and signed the bill of sale, Story read it. Satisfied, he drew out his wallet and from it took four hundred dollars. The eyes of Hardin's companions followed the money as Hardin shoved the bills into a Levi's pocket. Without a word he turned to go, his three riders following.

"Just a minute, Hardin," Story said.

The four of them turned, suspicious, hands near the butts of their Colts.

"We'll be here another month or so," said Story. "When you've gathered some more cows, I'll buy them. I'm hiring cowboys for the long drive north. Men. Men with the bark on."

The four said nothing, making their way carefully down the embankment to their horses.

"Hell," said Tom Allen, "the Indian's the most civilized of the bunch. You reckon they'll join the drive?"

"Maybe not the Comanche," said Story, "but the others will."

"Damn right they will." Coon Tails laughed. "Way you put it to 'em, they'll git to thinkin' on it an' figger you don't think they got the sand. The Injun knows who an' what he is, but the others is jist itchin' t'show the world what *malo* hombres they be."

"They'll be ropin' more cows too," said Bill Petty. "That'll give 'em a reason for ridin' back."

"We want them roping more longhorns," Story said, "and as many others as are willing, such as Shadley and Withers. Time is our enemy. With more and more Texans taking herds up the trail, eventually there'll be little or no graze."

"With the two hundred head Wolfington's promised, and with what we already have, that's two hundred and seventy," said Bill Petty. "Not bad for the first couple of days."

"We won't do that well every day," Story said, "and it's a far cry from the herd we need. We still have most of the day ahead of us. Unless somebody's got a better idea, we might as well split up into the same teams we had yesterday. Cal, we're depending on you, Arch, and Hitch. Can you lead us to some more cows?"

"I don't know of any dead-sure sales," said Cal, "but there's plenty of small ranchers that ain't got enough cows for a drive, even if they had the money."

"Last fall," Hitch said, "a dozen of the little spreads throwed their cows together and come up with fifteen hundred head. Amongst them, they managed enough grub and riders to get the herd to Sedalia. There's a bunch of others aimin' to do the same thing this spring."

"That's driving the price up," said Story. "When I first heard of the wild Texas longhorns, they were going for two or three dollars a head."

"But that combinin' herds for a drive ain't caught on everywhere," Arch said. "I'd say we got a better chance of buyin' cows if we ride farther south, toward Waco. 'Course we don't know nobody there, and we'd just be takin' pot luck."

"Then we'll need a third pack mule," said Story. "We'll split up into three teams and take enough grub for a week. That means we can't start until tomorrow. I'll take one mule with me, buy another in town, and load them both with grub."

"I'm almighty tired of hunkerin' in camp," Coon Tails said.

"I can understand that," said Story, "but I need a man in camp with a quick eye and a quicker gun. Nobody in the outfit's more qualified than you."

"By God, that's right," the old mountain man cackled. "Jist go on an' hunt yer cows. T'won't nothin' nor nobody bother the camp whilst yer gone."

Loading a mule with its packsaddle, Story headed for Fort Worth. The rain slashed in from the northwest, and the fierce wind snatched at Story's thonged-down hat.

"Hoss," said Story, "I've never seen so much rain, but I'm not complaining. On the high plains all this would be snow, and it'd be neck deep by now."

It came against the wind, and Story felt the slug rip through the crown of his hat before he heard the faint sound of the shot. Story had his Henry rifle out of the boot when the second shot came, and it wasn't even close. But there was a scream from the mule, and the animal reared, fighting the lead rope. Story loosed the rope and dismounted. Resting the Henry across his saddle, he blasted four shots into the swirling gray curtain of rain. The storm at his back, he waited in vain for a muzzle flash, for return fire. But there was none, and he pondered the motive of a bushwhacker who had tried to kill him with visibility so limited. He poked his thumb through the hole in the crown of his hat. Whoever the bastard was, he was no slouch with a rifle. Story found the mule, his back to the storm, drifting. There was a burn along the animal's left flank that still oozed blood. When he returned to camp he would attend to the wound, applying sulfur salve.

Story rode on toward town, the Henry across his saddle, cocked and ready. If the bushwhacker tried again and came close enough to be a threat, he would likely be near enough for Story to see the muzzle flash. But Nelson Story rode unmolested into Fort Worth, and it seemed like darkness was approaching. Lamps flickered dimly behind closed windows and through partially open doors. Story had dismounted before the York and Draper livery barn when five riders trotted their horses along the street. They had entered town only minutes behind him. The fifth rider had a horse on a lead rope with an ominous canvas-wrapped bundle lashed to the saddle. Conscious of its macabre burden, the led horse was skittish, fighting the rope. On the off side a pair of boots dangled from beneath the canvas wrap. As the five drew closer, Story recognized the lead rider as the belligerent sheriff, Lot Higgins.

"Hold it," Higgins shouted, drawing his Colt. "Stay where ya are."

Story remained where he was, and when the five had dismounted, Higgins again spoke.

"Raise yer hands," Higgins said, "an' keep 'em up till I say you can let 'em down. Danvers, have a look at his saddle gun. Now, mister, you jist turn around, keepin' yer hands up. I aim to take a look at them Colts. Lift the tail of her coat."

"You expect a lot of a man with both his hands in the air," said Story angrily.

One of the sheriff's men laughed, and Higgins turned on him with a snarl.

"You findin' all this so damn funny, Elmo, git over there and break them pistols, see if they been fired. Danvers, what about the saddle gun?"

"Four loads gone," Danvers said.

"Wal, now," said Higgins, turning to Story, "mind tellin' us what—or who—you been shootin' at out on the prairie in a pourin' rain?"

"Somebody fired at me," Story said, "and I fired back."

"By God," said Higgins, "I never seen a hombre with so many folks after his hide. You got any proof you was shot at, besides yer word?"

"A hole in the crown of my hat and a nasty burn on my mule's flank," Story said. "Unless you figure that was caused by wind and rain."

"Don't git smart with me, pilgrim. I'm the sheriff, they's a dead man on the led hoss, an' till somebody better comes along, the only suspect I got is you. I can throw you in the *juzgado* an' keep you there."

"His pistols ain't been fired," Elmo said. "Does he get 'em back?"

"Shut up, Elmo," said Higgins. "I'll tell you what to do an' when to do it."

"Sheriff," Story said, "if it's not asking too much, who *is* the hombre you're accusing me of killing?"

"Sol Abrahms," said Higgins. "The government-appointed tax collector."

"Sheriff," Story said patiently, "I'm from Montana Territory, here to buy Texas longhorns. Today I'm in town only to get another pack mule and more grub. What possible reason would I have for shooting your federally appointed tax collector?"

"He's right," said one of the sheriff's men. "It don't make no sense. We might as well let him go."

"When I want advice," Higgins snapped, "I'll ask fer it."

"It's good advice," said Story, "and you'd better take it. Otherwise, I'll hire a lawyer, demand a trial by jury, and make you prove me guilty."

Higgins had talked himself into a position from which there was no graceful escape. Several of his men, including Elmo, were grinning behind his back. Higgins had but one choice, and he turned back to Story with a growl.

"Git on about yer business."

Higgins mounted, the others following, except Elmo. He winked at Story, returned his pistols butts first, mounted his horse and rode after the others. Story went on into the livery barn and bought a third mule. On his way to the mercantile, he rode past the Cattleman's Bank just in time to meet Lorna Flagg emerging from it.

"Mr. Story."

Leading his mules, Story trotted his horse as near the boardwalk as he could. He found it difficult to believe that Cal Snider had shown no interest in this girl, and he was more than a little certain that she had hailed him for information about Cal. There was a protective roof over the entrance to the bank, and Story dismounted, thankful for the temporary shelter from the storm. He tipped his hat to Lorna and waited for her to speak. She did, not beating around the bush.

"Mr. Story, please tell Cal I'd like for him to ride in to see me before . . . before he leaves Texas."

"I'll tell him," Story said uncomfortably, "but he told me after that last meeting with you, he wasn't coming to town again."

"Oh, damn him and his Texas pride," she said. "It's not my fault my daddy's a highfalutin, stingy old banker who—"

"Lorna," said Amos Flagg from the bank's doorway, "I'll not have you consorting with riffraff. Come inside immediately."

"I won't," Lorna said defiantly. "Mr. Story, you tell Cal if he won't come to see me, then I'll ride out to see him. I know where the camp is, and—"

Amos Flagg grabbed her arm, but Lorna broke free, tearing the sleeve of her shirt. Flagg swung his right fist and it smashed into Lorna's jaw just below her left ear. The girl was lifted bodily off the boardwalk and splashed into the muddy street on her back. Furious at such blatant brutality, Story snatched a fistful of the portly banker's boiled shirt and laid a thundering right on the arrogant man's chin. Flagg somersaulted over a hitch rail, flopped belly down in the mud and lay there snuffling and grunting like a hog. Story was helping a dazed Lorna to her feet when Amos Flagg sat up. He wiped the mud off his mouth and began cursing Story.

"You cow-nursing bastard," he bawled, "I'll see you in prison. I'll have you locked in irons and thrown in Huntsville to rot."

But there had been a witness to the shameful scene. Emma Baird, owner of the dressmaker's shop across the street, waded the mud until she stood facing Amos Flagg. Emma was a slender gray-haired woman who couldn't have weighed more than a hundred pounds, soaking wet. But when she spoke, it was with such withering contempt, even the furious old man flinched.

"Amos Flagg, you're a filthy, contemptible beast. I

saw you strike that child, and what you got wasn't nearly
what you deserve." With that, she turned to Lorna and
Nelson Story, and it was to Story whom she spoke.

"I saw it all. Bless you, Mister . . ."

"Story. Nelson Story."

"I'm Emma Baird. I saw what you did, and God bless
you for being man enough to do it. If that old fool goes
to the law—Lot Higgins, God help us—then you come
to me. I'll tell the truth of what happened. Lorna, are
you all right, child?"

"I'm all right," Lorna said. "It was no worse than I've
had before. Thank you," she said, turning to Story.
"You will give Cal my message, won't you?"

"Yes," said Story, "I'll give it to him. But will you be
safe here?"

"Yes," Lorna said. "Emma saw what he did, and I can
go to her if I have to. I'll be eighteen in two more
months, and then I can go away. I thought I . . . Cal
. . . please tell him I need to see him, but he must not
come to the bank. He'll know where to find me."

Amos Flagg had gotten to his feet and stumbled back
into the bank. Emma Baird had returned to her little
shop, and Nelson Story watched Lorna hurry along the
boardwalk, unmindful of the storm. Story rode on to the
mercantile, and despite Lorna's assurances, he was concerned for her. There was something about the girl—a
strength of character—that appealed to him, and he
found himself wishing Cal wasn't so hell-bent on washing his hands of her. There was more to this situation
than met the eye, for Lorna had said, ". . . he'll know
where to find me."

But Story needn't have been concerned for Lorna
Flagg's safety. She returned to the house, to the seclu-
sion of the room that was hers, stripping off the torn
shirt, the muddy Levi's, the sodden boots. She poured
water from a porcelain pitcher into a matching basin
and washed the mud from her hair. That done, she

bathed the mud from her body and stood naked before the long mirror attached to her closet door, studying the nasty bruise that had already begun to purple her jaw. How many times had he hit her, hurt her? She had lost count, but she had never pleaded with him, nor had he ever seen her cry. But Amos Flagg was a vindictive man, and she had little doubt that he would find a way to make her suffer, if she permitted it. Reaching a decision, not even bothering to dress, she went to the room that had been her mother's. She lifted the mattress. Resting on the springs was a pistol. A .31 caliber Colt. She removed it, pressing the coolness of its muzzle to the painful bruise on her jaw. She broke the Colt, found it was still fully loaded, and took it to her room. She placed the weapon under her pillow with a silent vow that Amos Flagg had beaten her for the last time. . . .

4

*I*t was near dark when Story returned to the camp on the Brazos with his loaded mules. Cal, Hitch, Arch, and Coon Tails climbed down the embankment to the river, preparing to unload the mules.

"Coon Tails," Story said, "the mule I took to town with me needs some doctoring. Bullet burn on his left flank."

"I'll see to it," Coon Tails said. "That got anything t'do with that ventilation in yer hat?"

"It has," said Story. "I'll tell you about it after the mules have been unloaded."

The rain continued, and the outfit was thankful for the dry camp. When supper was over and they were down to final cups of coffee, Story told them of the ambush attempt and of his run-in with the sheriff.

"Hell," said Cal, "if he's needin' suspects, he can go after any Reb in Texas. Nobody likes a bloodsuckin' tax man. Trouble is, folks that'd most like to see him dead ain't got a gun and can't get one."

"I'm not sure the killing of the tax collector isn't the result of somebody's attempt to gun me down," Story said. "It was raining so hard, I couldn't really see anything to shoot at. Whoever was shooting at me wouldn't have been able to see much better. I'm wondering if this tax collector wasn't gunned down by mistake, by some-body who thought he was me."

"It's possible," said Bill Petty, "if he was near here."

"If this hombre that's gunnin' for you rides around in a storm, what won't he do in good weather?" Tom Allen said.

"I'd welcome a chance to settle this grudge," said Story, "whatever's the cause of it. How do you identify a man in pouring rain? That tells me that whoever's after me may gun down any one of us."

"Thanks to the Federals taking our guns," Cal said, "some of us can't even defend ourselves."

"After what happened today, I'm going to change that," said Story. "I'm going to arm every man in the outfit. I'm not a Texan, and I don't come under the jurisdiction of the Federal government, insofar as gun ownership is concerned."

"There's bound to be some law against armin' disen-franchised Texans," Arch Rainey said. "If there ain't, them Federals will make up one."

"We'll take our chances with the Federal authorities," said Story. "Captain Clark told me I could hire cowboys for a trail drive, and that riders would be allowed to leave Texas provided they sign papers swearing not to take up arms against the Union. If a man swears not to fight the Union, why shouldn't he have a gun to de-fend himself against hostile Indians, outlaws, and kill-ers?"

"Makes sense to me," Bill Petty said. "If there's any to be had, every one of our riders ought to at least have a pistol."

"It's my intention that every rider be armed with a Colt revolver and a repeating rifle before we begin the drive," said Story. "After what happened today, it ap-pears that bushwhacker's not all that particular about who he kills. I can see now there's some urgency in arming the outfit. Tomorrow we'll ride back to Fort

Worth for weapons and ammunition. Sandy Bill, we'll need a wagon and team. May we use yours?"

"On one condition," said Bill. "When you buy them guns, don't forget me."

February 5, 1866. On the Brazos.

Dawn brought yet another day of rain, and along with it, Shanghai Wolfington's herd. Story climbed down to the river to greet them.

"Five hundred an' fifteen," Shanghai said. "Four hundred an' five cows, hundred an' six steers, an' four bulls."

"Leave them here along the river," said Story. "You and your riders come on up to the camp and dry out. You're in time for breakfast."

Reaching the camp, Wolfington introduced Smokey Ellison and Oscar Fentress. Ellison's most distinguishing feature was a carefully groomed longhorn moustache. Oscar Fentress removed his hat, revealing a completely bald head.

"Smokey's got more hair on his upper lip than Oscar's got on his head," Wolfington said.

"Please t'meet you all," Fentress said, shaking their hands and flashing each man a grin.

"Shanghai," said Story, "since you were here, there's been a change in our situation. Perhaps a dangerous change. Since the three of you are joining the outfit, I want you to know what you're up against."

Story told them of the attempted ambush in town, and of the second try during the storm the previous afternoon.

"I'm taking the wagon into town today," Story said. "I aim to buy or make arrangements to buy enough weapons to arm the outfit. At least a Colt for every man who doesn't have one, if I have to order them from St. Louis or Kansas City."

"We're Texans," said Wolfington, "an' we ain't afraid of no man with a gun, long as we can shoot back. Right, boys?"

"Right," Smokey Ellison agreed. "Hand me a Colt and some ammunition and I'll side you till hell freezes."

"That be true for me, suh," said Oscar Fentress. "I fight for my brand."

"You're the kind of men I'm looking for," Story said. "I'll arm each of you with a Colt and with a repeating rifle, when they can be had."

"Reckon we got 'nough hombres here t' watch the camp an' the cows," said Coon Tails. "Way that bushwhacker's follerin' you, I reckon I'd best ride along t'town an' watch yer back."

"Thanks," Story said. "I'll appreciate your company."

"We're gonna be a mite uneasy, just hunkered around doin' nothin'," said Shanghai.

"I want all of you close to camp until you have weapons," Story said. "Once you're armed, I promise you we'll be plenty busy. Come on, Coon Tails, and let's harness the mules. I want this trip to town behind us."

They were well on their way to town when Story remembered he hadn't delivered Lorna's message to Cal.

For a long time after leaving Story's camp, neither Shadley or Withers spoke. When Shadley finally broke the prolonged silence, there was a sulky bitterness in his voice.

"Fine pard you turned out to be. Throwed me down and stood up for that bastard, Cal Snider."

"Oh, for God's sake, Russ," Withers said wearily, "if you're goin' to walk on your hind legs like a man, start actin' like one. If you hadn't had a gun, Cal Snider would of stomped hell out of you."

"I ain't done with Snider, not by a jugful."

"I ain't surprised," said Withers. "You hired on with Story's outfit so you can fight with Cal Snider. By God, this Story hombre's no short horn. He's a *malo salvaje* from the high lonesome, and I'd bet my saddle he can tie a knot in your tail with one hand. If you're of a mind to cause trouble on this drive, don't look for me to side you."

"I ain't lookin' for you to do nothin'," said Shadley. "We'll work this cow gather, but far as Story's outfit's concerned, you ride your trail and I'll ride mine."

"Bueno," Withers said. *"Bueno."*

Wes Hardin and his companions rode in silence until they were well away from Story's camp. When they reined up to rest their horses, it was Greener who spoke.

"I thought you was a reg'lar catawampus, Hardin. This big bastard wants a bill of sale, an' you fold like a wore-out Injun blanket."

Hardin twisted in his saddle, his horse face a mask of fury, his hands on the butts of his Colts.

"Damn it," said Slim, "pull in your horns, the both of you. Wes done the right thing. This Story hombre ain't no dumb Yank. Me, I wouldn't slope back into that canyon after them cows for a thousand pesos."

"By God," said Hardin, his cold blue eyes still on Greener, "anytime you reckon you're man enough to face me down, I'm ready." Greener said nothing, and Hardin turned on Quickenpaugh. "You're almighty quiet, you savage varmint. Ain't you got nothin' to say?"

"Dinero," Quickenpaugh said, with no change in expression, extending his hand.

It struck Hardin as funny, and he slapped his thighs and laughed. From his Levi's pocket he took the money he had received for the cows and removed a hundred dollars. This he passed to the Indian. Wordlessly he handed an equal share to Slim and Greener, and the four rode on.

When Story and Coon Tails reached town, Story drove the wagon directly to the York and Draper store.

"I reckon you ain't goin' through the army," Coon Tails said.

"Not unless I'm forced to," said Story. He climbed down from the box, Coon Tails following, and they entered the store. York knew Story by now, and nodded a greeting.

"I need weapons for my riders," Story said bluntly. "Pistols at least, rifles as well, if you have them. What do you have?"

"Nothin' I can sell to you," said York.

"I'm from Montana Territory," Story said. "I'm not a Texan."

"No," said York, "but I am, and I'll be here when you're gone. I don't aim to get on the bad side of the Federals by armin' a bunch of Rebs."

"You'll be selling to me," Story said patiently, "and that relieves you of any responsibility."

"Responsibility for what?" Lot Higgins demanded. The troublesome lawman had come in unnoticed, and stood with his thumbs hooked in his pistol belt.

"This gent's wantin' guns, Sheriff. He's hirin' Reb cowboys, and I don't aim to be responsible for the violation of Federal law."

"He's no Texan," said Higgins, "so he's within his rights, buyin' whatever he's got money t'pay for. Anyhow, when did you git so almighty law-abidin'? I hear it was you that sold Colts an' rifles to Wes Hardin an' that bunch he rides with, an' by God, one of them's a cutthroat Comanche."

"I was within my rights," York protested. "They didn't fight against the Union."

"Neither did I," said Story, "and I'm not a Texan.

Besides, me and my riders will be leaving Texas once we've gathered a herd. Now I need two dozen Colt revolvers and an equal number of rifles, if you have them." The sparks in Story's eyes belied the gentleness of his words.

"All right," York said weakly, "I have the Colts."

"You got in eight cases of them new Winchester repeaters jist last week," said Higgins. "As picky and law-abidin' as you are, you can't of sold 'em all."

"I have them," York said uncomfortably, glaring at Higgins.

"Two dozen Winchester repeaters, then," said Story, "with five thousand rounds of ammunition. Similar amount of ammunition for the Colts too."

Higgins hung around, watching Story and Coon Tails carry the wooden cases of Winchesters out to the wagon. The ammunition was next, and when they were ready for the Colts, Story turned to York.

"I don't suppose you'd be generous enough to include a holster with each Colt, would you?" Story asked.

"No," said York, "I wouldn't. Not even if I had them."

"Hell," Coon Tails said, "we'll skin a cow, tan the hide, an' make our own. Let's git outta here. I purely don't like the smell o' this place."

Lot Higgins laughed, watching them go.

"I doubt we'll be welcome in there after this," Story said, laughing, "but we have the guns we need."

"I never reckoned that big-mouth Lot Higgins would do nothin' t' help us," said Coon Tails. "Why you reckon he spoke up fer us?"

"He didn't," Story said. "He was mostly hoorawing York, and using us to do it. Whether he intended to or not, he did us a good turn. I'd like to build a herd and leave Texas without ever coming back to this town. I'm a tolerant man, but I've had about enough of this Federal domination of Texas."

As Story and Coon Tails drove back to their camp on the Brazos, the clouds shifted, allowing the sun to peep through.

"Look up yonder," said Coon Tails. "What'n hell is *that*?"

"The sun does shine in Texas," Story said, laughing, "but I wouldn't get too excited. Those thunderheads back yonder to the west are a sure sign of more rain, and I look for it by morning."

There was jubilation among the outfit when Story and Coon Tails drove into the canyon. Story reined up the team, positioning the wagon beneath the overhang that secured their camp.

"Drop me the end of a pair of ropes," Story said. "We have some crated Winchesters, Colts, and ammunition. Get ready to hoist it up."

Story and Coon Tails sent the Winchesters up first, securing one end of a rope to each end of the crates. When the Colts and all the ammunition had been hauled up, Story and Coon Tails returned the wagon to its place of concealment among the willows and loosed the mules to graze. By the time they reached the camp under the overhang, the riders had broken open the wooden cases and were into the new Winchesters.

"My God," said Cal, "they're beauties."

"They're supposed to replace the Henry," Story said. "Brand new, and they'll shoot seventeen times. I want each of you to have one, as well as a Colt revolver. We're lacking holsters and pistol belts, though."

"We don' be lackin' for long," said Oscar Fentress. "Gimme some good leather, some tools, an' some idee of what you wants. I makes anything from belts an' holsters to leather shirts an' britches. I make pistol belts an' holsters fer ever'body what wants 'em."

"We can use some fresh beef," Story said. "We'll kill a cow and tan the hide. Tomorrow, six of us will ride south on a week-long cow hunt. We now have enough cows to

stir up some temptation. Coon Tails, I want you, Shanghai, Smokey, and Oscar to remain here, guarding the
camp and the herd. Shanghai, I'm leaving you in charge
of the stock, and Coon Tails, you're in charge of the
camp. Shanghai—Shadley and Withers may ride in with
a few head of stock before I return. I'll leave you some
money to pay them. If Wes Hardin and his bunch drives
in some cows, pay them as well, but only if you get a bill
of sale."

"Comprender," said Shanghai. "No bill of sale from
Shadley and Withers?"

"No," Story said. "They're already part of the outfit. I
have reasons for wanting a bill of sale from Hardin and
his riders."

"I been hearin' talk," said Shanghai, "so I respect
them reasons."

February 6, 1866. On the Brazos, north of Waco.

Story's prophecy proved itself, and when they arose before first light, they could hear the scream of the wind
and the sound of rain pounding the eastern rim of the
canyon.

"Good day for ridin'," said Cal. "In Texas, the only
other choice you got is havin' the sun bake your brains
and burn you the color of an old saddle."

"I was bawn the color of a old saddle," Oscar said. "I
go downhill fum there."

"Cal, you'll ride with me," Story said. "Hitch will ride
with Bill, and Arch will ride with Tom. We'll return here
no later than a week from today. Remember, you're
only asking for commitments. We'll pay for the cows
when we go after them, or when the ranchers deliver
them to us, and in either case that will be sometime
after February twelfth. Whether or not you're out for
the week depends on circumstances. We'll fan out, like

we did the first time, but we'll swap directions. Cal and me will ride south, toward Waco. Hitch and Bill will ride west, while Arch and Tom ride east. Avoid trouble if you can. Especially gun trouble. Now let's ride."

Cal and Story followed the Brazos, riding wide of the area where they believed Wes Hardin and his riders had established their cow camp. If the hard-bitten young riders chose to join Story's outfit, he intended for it to be their decision. The last thing he wished to have them believe was that he was pursuing them. Once they were well on the way, Story told Cal of his meeting with Lorna Flagg. He mentioned none of the violence surrounding their meeting, conveying only the message the girl had sent. They rode in silence for a while. It was Cal's turn to speak, if he chose to. When he did, it came as a question.

"Mr. Story, what do you think I should do? About Lorna."

"I don't know, Cal. That's a decision only you can make, and I doubt you'll be able to make it by avoiding Lorna. I think you should ride in and talk to her, find out what she wants."

"Hell, I *know* what she wants. She wants me."

"She's a pretty girl," Story said. "She could drop a loop on any cowboy from the Rio Grande to the Yellowstone. Can you honestly say you don't want her?"

"No, sir," Cal said, "if things was different. Before I come back from the war, Lorna's mama left. Went back East, and that's the last anybody's seen of her. Old Amos Flagg branded her a fast woman, a whore, and by the time I got back to Texas, he was treatin' Lorna the same way. He's a powerful man in this town, always suckin' up to the Reconstructionists, and he's down on everybody and everything that was part of the Confederacy. Suppose—and I'm just supposin'—I tried to make a go of it with Lorna, how far do you reckon I'd get? I got no money, no stake, and Amos Flagg hatin' the very ground I walk on."

"So for Lorna's sake, you're avoiding her."

"What choice have I had?" said Cal bitterly. "Was I to be seen with her, old man Flagg would give her hell at home, and he'd figger some new way of gettin' at me."

"From what I've seen and heard, he's giving her hell already," Story said. "Lorna told me she'll be eighteen in two more months, and she'll be leaving. You'll be leaving Texas too, and she wants to talk to you before you go. If the two of you moved farther west, to the high plains, would that help?"

"Just gettin' out of a town dominated by Amos Flagg would help, if I was sure that wasn't her only reason for goin'. How do I know Lorna ain't takin' a leaf from her mama's book, just lookin' for a way out? Hell, she'd foller a sheepman just to get away from her iron-fisted old daddy, and I'd not blame her."

"I think she's pretty enough, woman enough, to have any man she wants," said Story. "When we return to camp, why don't you ride in and talk to her?"

"And tell her what? That she's welcome to give up a roof over her head, decent grub, and fine clothes? For months on the trail with cussing, bitching cowboys, a chance to drown during a river crossing or stampede, or scalping and mutilation by hostile Indians?"

"That's questions I can't answer, Cal. Only Lorna can, and I think you owe her the opportunity. Will you talk to her before we leave Texas?"

"Yeah," said Cal with a sigh. "I'll talk to her."

Hitch Gould and Bill Petty rode west a good thirty miles before seeing evidence of cattle ranching. A cow and calf vanished up a brushy draw ahead of them, and tracks in the mud indicated the presence of others. The rain had diminished to a drizzle when they topped a hill overlooking a run-down cabin and sagging log barn. Beyond the barn was a creek, and beside it a pair of roan horses grazed. There was no other sign of life. From the dirt-and-stick chimney of the cabin a tendril of smoke rose, only to be whipped away by a rising wind.

"If they got even one cow," Hitch said, "it's well hid. Won't hurt if we ride in and ask, though. If they got nothin' to sell, maybe they can head us toward somebody that has."

They rode on, and before they reached the cabin, one of the horses that grazed along the creek nickered. A man stepped out on the porch, and his most prominent features were a high-crowned Mexican sombrero and the Henry rifle in the crook of his arm. He said nothing, waiting for Hitch and Petty to ride closer. A hundred yards distant they reined up.

"We're lookin' to buy cows," Hitch shouted. "I'm Hitch Gould, and this is Bill Petty with me."

"We have no cows, senor, but you are welcome to ride in." He lowered the muzzle of the Henry just a little.

As Hitch and Petty rode closer, it appeared their host was Mexican or Spanish. He wore the tight-legged trousers of a vaquero, and over a white shirt he wore a short open-front jacket. His black riding boots were anything but new, and a thin moustache graced his upper lip. His hair, black as a crow's wing, was over his ears and down to his collar. Hitch and Petty reined up near the porch, and Petty further explained the nature of their visit.

"I am Manuel Cardenas," he said, "and I regret that I cannot ask you in. The Senor Wells returned from the war with lung fever. He is very sick."

"Sorry," said Petty. "Is there anything we can do?"

"Nothing, senor," said Cardenas in a softer voice. "He is dying. I think he will leave us before this time *mañana.*"

So suddenly and silently did the boy appear in the

doorway, Bill Petty had his hand on the butt of his Colt.
Cardenas was swift with an introduction.

"This is Curly," he said. "Curly Wells. He is Senor
Hiram's *hijo.*"

Curly Wells was young, maybe fifteen, with eyes as
black as his hair. He was a good half a foot shy of six
feet, his Levi's were faded and patched at the knees,
and a too-big flannel shirt had the sleeves rolled up
to free his hands. He had dark crescents under his
eyes and worry lines well beyond his years. Bill Petty
spoke.

"I'm Bill Petty, and this is Hitch Gould. We're lookin'
to buy longhorn cows. Sorry about your pa. Is there
anything we can to do help?"

"No," said Curly bitterly, "unless you can take us
back four years, keep my pa out of that damn war, and
run them Yankees the hell out of Texas."

"Nobody can change that," said Petty. "It's nigh dinner time. You and Manuel are welcome to join us, with
somethin' for your pa."

"No," said Curly hastily. "No, thanks."

"The feeds on us," Petty said. "Hitch, unload the
pack mule."

Curly said no more, retreating into the cabin. Manual
Cardenas spoke quietly.

"It is his pride. We are very poor and have little to
offer."

"The war's been hard on us all," said Hitch. "That's
why me and my pard, Arch Rainey, jumped at the
chance to sign on with Mr. Story's trail drive. When we
reach Montana Territory, we'll have some money in our
pockets, and we won't have to answer to Yankees and
carpetbaggers."

"As we was ridin' in," Bill Petty said, "we saw a cow, a
calf, and tracks of others. If they're not yours, whose are
they?"

"Ike Hagerman's, I think," said Cardenas. "His ranch is to the west of us. We have only the horses near the creek, so we do not object when his cows graze our range."

Despite the gravely ill Hiram Wells, Cardenas led Hitch and Petty into the cabin and down a hall to the kitchen. They passed a door that was closed, and from behind it came the painful dirge of consumptive coughing, the sound of a man coughing his life away. Cardenas stirred up the fire in the old stove, adding wood.

"You are generous to supply the food," he said. "I will prepare it."

When the meal was ready, Cardenas knocked on the door to the sick room. Young Curly Wells swallowed resentment and pride, eating as though he hadn't had a decent meal in his life. In fact, he seemed ashamed of his voracious appetite, returning to the sick room when he had finished.

"Manuel," Petty said, "I reckon this is a hurtful time to be thinkin' of it, but there ain't much hope for you and Curly, after . . ."

His voice trailed off, but Cardenas understood. With a sigh, he spoke.

"*Si*, senor, I have thought of it."

"Mr. Story's hiring riders for the drive north," said Hitch. "Men who can rope, ride, and shoot, if need be."

"*Muchos gracias*," Cardenas said. "Curly and me, we do these things, but we cannot leave while the Senor Wells lives."

"We'll be a month or more buyin' enough cows for the drive," said Petty. "Hitch and me will be ridin' back this way in three or four days, and we'll stop by again. We'll leave you some grub too."

Cardenas watched them ride out. They left without seeing Curly again, and when they had ridden a mile or more, it was Hitch who spoke.

"We'll be ridin' back to camp a hell of a lot sooner than next Monday," he said. "Half our grub's gone."

"Well, damn it," Petty said, "they were starving. What would you have done?"

"Exactly what you done." Hitch grinned. "Give 'em half our grub."

5

Arch Rainey and Tom Allen rode southeast, into Navarro County.

"There's some lakes out this way," Arch said. "Waxahatchie Creek runs into one of 'em, and maybe twenty miles east of Corsicana we'll cross the east fork of the Trinity. Corsicana ain't that big of a town, but it's the county seat. There's three or four saloons, and if there's cows for sale anywhere within thirty miles, somebody ought to know of 'em."

"What's beyond Corsicana?"

"More prairie and more little towns," said Arch. "There's Malakoff, but it ain't more'n a wide place in the trail. Beyond that there's Athens, but it ain't nothin' to get excited about. There's a Masonic hall, a hotel, a Presbyterian church, a mercantile, and some saloons. Malakoff's maybe thirty mile beyond Corsicana, and Athens is ten mile east of Malakoff."

"If we don't have any luck at Corsicana, then we might as well ride on to Athens," Allen said. "Even if we don't learn anything in town, we ought to find some ten cow spreads somewhere on these plains."

The rain had intensified by the time they reached Corsicana, and the town appeared deserted. They reined up before an imposing saloon called the Trinity and shouldered through the bat-wing doors, thankful for a respite from the incessant rain. Half a dozen coal-oil lamps cast a dim glow as they swung like pendulums from the ceiling, guttering in the gust of wind through the door. Two men sat hunched over a checkerboard, not even bothering to look up. The barman said nothing, raising his eyebrows in question.

"Couple of beers," Tom Allen said.

The barman brought their beers, collected the money, and said nothing.

"We're lookin' to buy some cows," said Allen.

Still the man behind the bar said nothing.

"Pardner," Allen said, an edge to his voice, "we're here to buy cows. Do you know of any spreads with longhorns for sale?"

"No," said the barman sullenly.

Allen said no more. He finished his beer, waited for Arch, and the two of them left the saloon.

"Unsociable varmint," said Arch. "If the rest of the town's anything like him, we're wasting our time."

"We'll ride down to the courthouse," Allen said. "I reckon they'll have a sheriff."

The courthouse was of brick, and the bench that ran the length of the porch was deserted. There were deep puddles of water in the street, and a rain barrel at one corner of the courthouse had overflowed, creating a minor waterfall. Arch and Allen reined up, looped their horses' reins about the hitch rail, and went inside. They had no trouble finding the sheriff's office. It was the first door they came to, and across the upper third—which was frosted glass—they read: J. WILLOUGHBY, COUNTY SHERIFF.

"It ain't locked," said a gruff voice from behind the door. "Come on in."

Allen opened the door and stepped inside, Arch following. The sheriff dragged his boots off the desk, his swivel chair groaning. He was a big man, gone to fat, his sparse hair gray under his old hat. He wore Levi's, a gray flannel shirt, and a black leather vest to which a tarnished star was pinned.

"Jerome Willoughby," he said. "Sheriff, I reckon, until the Federals appoint some hombre more to their likin'. What kin I do fer you gents?"

He listened while Tom Allen explained the purpose of their visit. There was an agonizing groan from his swivel chair as he again leaned back and rested his scarred boots on an equally scarred desk.

"With most of the men at war," he said, "folks ain't had time to round up many cows. The Comanches has been raisin' hell to the south, near Waco. Nearly ever'body that had cows t'sell sold 'em last fall, mostly fer what they could git. Them few drives that went north near 'bout took all the cows that was ready fer market, and it'll likely be fall b'fore there's any more. Nobody in these parts is got a decent herd, 'cept Spur, and you'll have some trouble there."

"Tell us about Spur," Allen said.

"Spur was built lock, stock, an' bunkhouse by Tobe McDaniels," said the sheriff. "Then the war come, an' Tobe lost his riders, includin' his son, Bud. Fer four long years old Tobe hung on, just him an' his young daughter, Jasmine. When Bud come home from the war, Tobe aimed to take a drive north. Bud come home in the summer of 'sixty-five, an' he wasn't worth a damn to nobody. Laid around and drunk rotgut whiskey an' picked fights with anybody that'd fight him. He was twenty-one, a year older'n Jasmine. It was more than old Tobe could take. He died last year, three days before Christmas."

"The herd should be for sale, then," said Allen.

"It ain't," said Willoughby. "The girl—Jasmine—swears she's takin' the herd up the trail, if she has to boss it herself. But she's got no help, no hope, an' no money. Her no-account brother's back there in a cell, sleepin' off a drunk. Been here since las' night. Sooner or later, Jasmine will come lookin' fer him."

"Does he have a horse?" Allen asked.

"Over t' the livery," said Willoughby.

"Unless you have some objection," Allen said, "we'll take him with us. How do we find Spur?"

"Take the little varmint, an' welcome," said Willoughby. "Keep ridin' toward Malakoff an' you'll ride right into Spur."

Arch brought the horse from the livery, and Sheriff Willoughby revived the sleeping Bud by drenching him with a bucket of water from the overflowing rain barrel. McDaniels came out of it coughing, choking, and cursing. He stumbled to his feet and took a wild swing at the sheriff, but Willoughby stepped aside, and McDaniels collapsed in an ignominious heap on the floor.

"Behave yourself, Bud," said the sheriff. "These gents is takin' you home."

"Don' wanna go home," McDaniels mumbled. Tom Allen helped him to his feet and McDaniels spat in his face. With his left hand Allen grabbed a fistful of McDaniels's shirt, and fisting his right, he slugged McDaniels just below the left ear. McDaniels went limp, breathing raggedly.

"Take his feet, Arch," said Allen.

They carried McDaniels to his horse, flung him across the saddle, and lashed his wrists and his feet together under the horse's belly. The horse glared at them resentfully, unused to this disgraceful arrangement. Without further ado, the duo mounted and rode away, Arch leading McDaniels's horse. Tom Allen and Arch Rainey had ridden almost twenty miles before they began seeing longhorns with the Spur brand on the left flank. The continuing rain had revived Bud McDaniels, and by the time they reined up before the Spur cabin, he was cursing them more viciously than ever. Suddenly the front door opened and a girl stepped out on the porch. Dark curly hair flowed down over the collar of her red flannel shirt. She was trim in Levi's riding boots, and a flat-crowned hat was thonged under her chin. In her right hand she held a Colt.

"What have you done to him?" she demanded.

"Brought him home," said Tom Allen. "Since he didn't want to come, and got a mite nasty, we had to make some arrangements."

"Thanks for bringing him," she said coldly. "Get him off the horse, and the two of you get the hell out of here."

Tom Allen cut the rope, gave the still-cursing Bud a shove, and he slid off flat on his back in the muddy water that had pooled in the yard. The girl splashed through the mud and water to help him, and he dragged her face down in the mud beside him. It was the kind of thing a cowboy couldn't possibly ignore, and Tom Allen and Arch Rainey roared with laughter. By the time the girl sat up, the half-drunken Bud had joined in the laughter. She swung the Colt as hard as she could, and the muzzle of it caught him just above the eyes. His wild laughter ceased and he went down on his back, the rain pinking the blood from the gash above his eyes. Tom Allen took the girl's left hand, helped her to her feet, and was rewarded when she took a vicious swing at his head with the muddy Colt. He caught her wrist, forcing her to drop the Colt, but her left hand was free. She slapped him across the nose and mouth. Hard. Abruptly he let go of her wrist, and, caught off-balance, she fell face down in the muddy, knee deep water.

"You little catamount," Allen said, "I ain't one to argue with a lady, but where I come from, you purely don't qualify."

"Damn you," she squalled, lifting her head from the mire, "help me up."

He rolled her over on her back and helped her sit up. Hostility gone, she tried to get up, but could not. Allen helped her, and this time met no resistance. She staggered over to where her unconscious brother lay, and when she turned to Tom Allen, there was a pleading when she spoke.

"Please take him into the house," she said.

"How far are we from Waco?" Story asked as he and Cal rode south along the Brazos.

"Sixty miles, at least," Cal said. "There's a couple of things that may hurt our chances of buyin' cows down this way. Remember what Hitch was sayin' about Charlie Goodnight's outfit? They're somewhere south of Waco, roping and branding longhorns. Anybody else of the same mind, them that might sell to us, won't find that many cows."

"The other thing, I reckon, is the Comanches," said Story.

"That's it," Cal said. "Just ain't many folks willin' to risk their hair for ten dollars a cow. You'd need a hell of a big outfit, some of 'em to rope cows and the rest to fight Comanches. But even that don't always work. The Comanches stampeded Goodnight's first herd, and he lost 'em ever' damn one."*

"Whatever we accomplish, then," said Story, "will have to be somewhere between our camp and Waco."

"I'd say so," Cal said. "We can ask around Waco. Goodnight's gatherin' cows, not buyin' 'em, so anybody that's of a mind to sell, we ought to have a fair shot. I reckon if Goodnight and his outfit can rope a herd of wild cows out of the brakes, escape the Comanches and get the longhorns to market, he'll be the richest man from New Orleans to San Francisco."

"I reckon he will," said Story, "and I wish him luck, but I'd rather do it my way. It's worth ten dollars a head

* Trail Drive Series No. 1, *The Goodnight Trail*

not to have to fight the Comanches. We'll get our fill of Indian fighting along the Bozeman Trail."

"Do you aim to ride straight to Waco, or will we be lookin' for ranches along the way?"

"We'll be watchful along the way," Story said, "but unless we come upon something promising, I think we'll ride on to Waco. It'll be far quicker if we can get word of ranchers with cows to sell, rather than shotgunning around looking for them."

The rain continued, and the only evidence they found of small ranchers was abandoned spreads. They rode past two such rawhide outfits, the second being only a forlorn copy of the first: log houses with sagging doors and crumbling chimneys, fallen pole corrals, and barns with sagging or collapsed shake roofs.

"The men rode off to war," said Cal, "and while they was gone, Indians or starvation caught up with them that was left behind. In some cases, like with my pa, they just give up and died. Sometimes it's the easy way out."

It was still daylight when they rode into Waco, but because of the continuing rain, it seemed darkness was approaching.

"We'll be spending enough nights out in the mud and rain for the next few months," Story said. "Let's find us a hotel and dry out."

They found an unpretentious one-story affair called the River Bend, more a boardinghouse than hotel. Their horses and the pack mule had been left at the livery, where the jovial liveryman had locked their saddles and grub in a tack room. Across the muddy street from the hotel was the Brazos, which appeared to be the busiest saloon in town.

"We'll mosey over there," said Story, "when we've dried out and rested some. We'll do a lot of listening and very little talking."

"Smart move," Cal said. "Once word gets around that

we're buyin' cows, every thief and no account in East Texas will know we're carryin' *dinero.*"

While their hotel room wasn't fancy, it was clean, and there were dry towels. They shucked their sodden clothes and spread them out on the floor to dry.

"God," said Cal, "I never knew dry socks could feel so good."

They used one of the towels to dry the insides of their boots as best they could, donned dry clothes, and stepped out onto the hotel's porch. The rain had slacked a little, and they took advantage of it, crossing the street to the Brazos Saloon. From inside there came the less than harmonious jangle of a piano and the clink of glasses. Next to the saloon was a cafe from which came the tempting odor of frying steak.

"We'll let the saloon wait another hour," Story said. "We can't spend any time in there without buying a beer or two, and I can't stand the stuff on an empty stomach."

Two cowboys were seated at the counter when Cal and Story entered the cafe, and all conversation stopped. Cal and Story took stools at the opposite end of the counter.

"Steak, spuds, onions, an' coffee, two bits," said the cook, "or you kin swap that fer fried chicken, gravy, an' biscuits, jist a dime more."

"I'll have the fried chicken," Story said, "and bring me a double portion of it."

"Repeat that for me," said Cal.

Cal and Story were finishing their coffee when one of the cowboys got up and looked out the window. "Here they come," he said.

The second man got up, and the two left the cafe. Story set down his coffee mug and turned to the window. A dozen bluecoats were marching down the muddy street.

"By God," breathed the cook, "all hell's a-fixin' t'bust loose."

"Who are they after?" Story asked.

"Them two riders that jist went out, Quanah Taylor and Gus Odell, an' their pards, Virg Wooler, Dutch Mayfield, an' Jules Dyer. When they come back from the war, they commenced ropin' wild longhorns from the brakes. Now they got near fifteen hunnert head, an' the scalawag bastard that's been appointed tax collector fer the county has assessed the herd at a dollar per cow. Quanah an' his boys ain't gonna pay. They couldn't pay if'n they was willin', 'cause they ain't got the money. They're holed up over there in the Brazos, an' they got guns. The blue bellies is usin' that fer a excuse t'go after 'em, callin' it a violation of the Reconstruction Act. Them boys is gon' be shot dead fer no reason."

"Maybe not," said Story. "Come on, Cal."

They had only to step outside the cafe to see the Union soldiers in position before the Brazos Saloon. At that very moment a challenge was flung at the five men inside. The piano was silent.

"This is Sergeant Loe. You men—Taylor, Odell, Wooler, Mayfield, and Dyer—are under arrest. Come out with your hands up."

"Like hell," shouted a voice from inside the saloon. "Come and get us, you bastards."

"Sergeant," said Story, "I'm from Montana Territory, in Texas gathering longhorns for a drive north. I'm Nelson Story, and those are my men. There is a misunderstanding here, and I believe I can resolve it without violence. But I'll need to go inside and talk to them."

"They're still under arrest," Sergeant Loe insisted, "and nothin' will change that."

"Not even if they surrender their weapons?"

"Not even if they surrender their weapons."

"Let me talk to them, then," said Story. "When

they've given up their weapons and surrendered to you, I'm going to ask that the charges be dropped."

"We just follow orders," said Sergeant Loe. "Any appeals will be up to the post commander and the appointed sheriff."

"You men in the saloon," Story shouted, "this is Nelson Story. I have permission from the sergeant to come in and talk. I can resolve this without shooting."

"Come on," shouted the voice from within the saloon, "but if you're part of some Yankee slick-dealin', you won't be around to crow about it."

"Cal," said Story, "move out to the middle of the street. When I bring them out, watch these soldiers. If any man makes a hostile move, kill him."

"You can't do that!" Sergeant Loe shouted.

"The hell I can't!" Story snapped. "Stand your ground, Cal."

Without a backward look, Story shouldered through the bat-wings into the saloon. The bartender was kneeling behind the bar, easing up just enough to see Story enter. Four tables had been turned over, their tops providing a barricade that faced the door. Five riders hunkered down behind it, every man with a Colt cocked and ready.

"Put your guns away," said Story calmly. "I can get you out of this alive, unless you feel there's some kind of glory in dying against impossible odds."

One of the men Story had seen in the cafe got to his feet. "I'm Quanah Taylor," he said. "If you're not with the blue bellies, what's your stake in this?"

"I'm from Montana Territory," said Story, "and I'm buying cattle for a trail drive. I told Sergeant Loe the five of you are working for me. If we play our cards right, I can get you out of this alive. But not if you gun down Union soldiers."

"You still ain't answered my question. What's your stake in this?"

"I'll buy your herd, arm you with Colt revolvers and Winchester repeating rifles, and take you to Montana Territory as part of my outfit. Besides paying you for your cattle, I'll pay forty and found, with a hundred dollar bonus for each man at the end of the drive."

They didn't respond immediately, conversing among themselves, and when they appeared to have reached a decision, Taylor again faced Story.

"We agree on one thing, Story. We ain't got a hell of a lot of choices. If we accept your offer, how do you aim to get us out of here, an' what's gonna happen to us afterward? Who're you that them blue bellies will live up to your promises?"

"I have already spoken to Captain Clark, the commander at Fort Worth," said Story, "and I have permission to hire Texas cowboys for a trail drive north. All that's required is that you sign papers agreeing not to take up arms against the Union again. You don't aim to fight another war, do you?"

"Hell, no," Taylor said, "we're havin' trouble enough tryin' to survive the one we was just in. We seen enough gun-totin' blue bellies to last us a lifetime. We'll sign them papers."

"Those soldiers outside can't make decisions," said Story. "You'll have to give up your weapons and submit to arrest. Then we can go to the appointed sheriff and the post commander. Once these charges against you are dropped, we'll go from there."

"No way I'm givin' up my gun," said one of the riders. "Dud Byler's the appointed sheriff, and he hates our guts."

"There's nothing I can do for you, then," said Story.

There was more talk, and Story waited. When the men had reached their decision, Taylor again turned to Story.

"You got us by the short hairs, Story. We'll do what you say."

"Let me have your guns," Story said, "and I'll take them out with me. One of my riders is waiting outside, and if any soldier pulls a gun, you have my word that he'll die. I'll go with you to the courthouse, or wherever they aim to take you. Just remember, you're all part of my outfit, and the cows you've been gathering are mine."

Each man surrendered his Colt, and Story shouldered his way out the swinging doors. Cal still stood in the street, his Colt cocked and ready. Sergeant Loe eyed the Colts Story presented him, unbelieving.

"How do we know they don't have sleeve guns?"

"There are no hideout guns," said Story. "They have given their word, and I've given mine. These men are unarmed, and I'll kill any man pulling a gun on them. Where are you taking them?"

"To the courthouse," said Sergeant Loe. "That's where the jail is."

"Come on out, boys," Story shouted.

Quanah Taylor came out first, his hands shoulder high. The rest of them followed, careful to make no hostile move.

"We're going to the courthouse," said Story, "and you'll have to spend a little time in jail, until I straighten this out. Sergeant, who is the officer in charge here?"

"Lieutenant Goode."

"Let's go, then," said Story. "I want to talk to him immediately."

Hitch Gould and Bill Petty rode almost ten miles to the west before sighting the outbuildings to Ike Hagerman's ranch. It was anything but a rawhide outfit, and Hagerman came out of the barn as they approached. Petty explained the purpose of their visit.

"I got near 'bout a thousand head," said the rancher, "and I aim to take 'em to market myself."

"We can't fault you for that," said Petty. "Do you

know of anybody else in these parts who might sell to us?"

"Nobody with enough to make any difference," Hagerman said. "You might ride over to Comanche and ask around."

Hitch and Petty rode out, heading east, but once out of sight of the Hagerman ranch, they reined up.

"I got the feeling he was just trying to get rid of us," said Petty, "and I wonder why. Others have only a few cows, or none at all, while he's got a thousand head."

"Somethin' about him didn't ring true," Hitch agreed, "but there ain't no proof. More'n one respectable cattleman got his start with nothin' but a hoss, a saddle, an' a runnin' iron."

"How far is it to Comanche?"

"Few miles," said Hitch. "We can make it 'fore dark, easy."

"We'll ride that far, at least," Petty said. "If we don't have something to show for our efforts by tomorrow night, we'll consider returning to camp. When word gets around that Hagerman's making a drive, there's a possibility that lesser herds will throw in with him."

"I expect we'll know by the time we reach Comanche," said Hitch. "Let's ride."

Tom and Arch managed to get the drunken Bud McDaniels into the cabin and stretched out on the floor. The cabin was surprisingly homey, with Indian rugs on the floor and curtains at the windows. There was an enormous fireplace in which a fire roared as the wind swept down the chimney, sucking at the flames.

"You'd best fix a bed for him, ma'am," said Allen, "while we get him out of these wet clothes. That gash on his head needs tendin' to."

It was good advice, and she left them alone, going into another room.

"She hit him hard," Arch said. "He's breathing, but he's out cold."

They peeled McDaniels down to the bare hide and were astounded at the scars that dominated his body.

"God," said Arch, "no wonder he come back and hit the rotgut. He must of been through hell."

"No doubt," said the girl from the doorway, "but that's no excuse for what he's done. Not so much to me, but to his daddy. The bed's ready."

"Take his feet, Arch," said Allen. They got him into the bed, covering him to his chin. They stepped aside as the girl brought a basin of water, and watched as she bathed the wound she had inflicted. She doused it well with disinfectant and emptied the basin of water out the front door. When she returned to the bedroom, she managed a weary smile, and then she spoke.

"I'm Jasmine McDaniels. I should thank you for bringing Bud home, and apologize for my actions. He . . . well, he sometimes brings drunken friends home, and I . . . I'm stuck with them until they're sober enough to ride. Come to the kitchen and I'll put on some coffee. Then, if you'll excuse me, I must get into some dry clothes."

The coffee was ready before the girl was, and Arch found cups in an oak cupboard behind the table. The fire crackled in the stove, and the warmth of the kitchen was pleasant. The riders drank the hot, black coffee with appreciation. When Jasmine McDaniels returned, they set their cups down and caught their breath. She had changed into an ankle-length dress of Indian design, and had exchanged her boots for moccasins. Her long hair had been brushed, and the smile she wore was genuine.

"Now," she said, "since you're not a pair of Bud's undesirable drinking pardners, what is your business with me?"

Quickly Tom Allen explained the purpose of their visit.

"We have more than a thousand head of longhorns ready for market," she said. "Daddy worked hard during the war, vowing that when Bud came home, we would take the herd to market. Now . . ."

Her voice faded and she looked out the window, into the dismal, blowing rain. Her eyes were so brown they were almost as black as her hair, and in their depths was untold pain, frustration, and despair.

"Ma'am," Tom Allen said, "we have the riders to take a drive north, and the money to pay you for your cows."

"But I want more than that," she said. "I want what Daddy wanted. To go where the grass is up to a horse's belly, to the high plains, where the sky goes on forever. I'll sell the herd on one condition. I'm going with the drive, and I'm taking Bud with me. He's going to become a man his daddy could be proud of, by God, if it kills him."

6

As they marched down the muddy street ahead of the Union soldiers, Story studied the five cowboys. Their boots were rough-out, run-over, their hats battered and used up, their Levi's and denim shirts faded. Not a man of them was more than twenty-one or -two, and but for their empty holsters, they were Texan to the bone. Cal and Story walked behind the soldiers. Reaching the courthouse, the five Texans halted while Sergeant Loe went inside. Within minutes he was back, accompanied by a tall, sandy-haired man with lieutenant's bars on the epaulets of his blue coat. The rain had ceased.

"This is Lieutenant Goode," said Sergeant Loe.

"Pleased to meet you, Lieutenant. I'm Nelson Story, from Virginia City, Montana Territory. This is Cal Snider, one of my men. These five riders the sergeant has under arrest are also my men, and they've been gathering longhorn cattle for my trail drive. These men —Quanah Taylor, Gus Odell, Virg Wooler, Dutch Mayfield, and Jules Dyer—have voluntarily surrendered their weapons for the sake of resolving this misunderstanding. When I reached Fort Worth, I immediately met with the post commander, Captain Clark, and told him of my intention to hire Texas cowboys. He has no objection to that, provided the men sign the necessary papers agreeing not to take up arms against the Union. These men have agreed to sign those papers, and since they won't be taking up arms against the Union, that should entitle them to carry weapons for their own protection. With that in mind, I am asking you to drop any and all charges against them."

"I see nothing unreasonable about your request," said Lieutenant Goode, "but we didn't prefer those charges. That was the doing of appointed sheriff Dud Byler. He can dismiss the charges, or insist that you go before the judge. Sergeant Loe, ask Sheriff Byler to come out here."

When Byler appeared, he impressed Story as being of about the same caliber as Lot Higgins. He wore polished boots, a boiled shirt, a blue serge town suit, and a pearl-gray Stetson. His gun rig was inlaid with silver, and his tied-down Colt had a fancy pearl handle.

"I ain't accustomed to conductin' business outside in the muddy street," he said by way of greeting.

Swiftly Story repeated what he had just told Lieutenant Goode. He then requested that the charges be dropped, since the men could in no way be considered a threat to the Union.

"They was in violation of the law when them charges was made," Byler said. "You can't go back an' undo the violation of the law by promisin' not t'do it agin."

"Sheriff," said Story, "nobody's denying there was a violation of the law. These men have agreed to abide by the legal procedure the Union requires, and that should entitle them to carry weapons for their own protection. If you want to go before the judge, then so be it, but it'll be a waste of your time and ours."

"He's right, Sheriff Byler," said Lieutenant Goode. "Judge Paschal has already ruled that it's not the intent and purpose of this antigun law to punish a man once he has taken an oath not to take up arms against the Union."

"Consider the charges dropped, then," said Byler, with poor grace, "but that don't mean the tax agin' them cows is bein' dropped. The tax has been paid, an' the herd forfeited to the gent that paid it."

"I'm going to disagree with you again, Sheriff," Story said. "That herd is mine, and I'm not a Texan. I'm going to ask you to show me, chapter and verse, where this Reconstruction Act entitles you, or anybody, to impose a tax on a man's herd."

Story's five newly acquired riders were grinning. Byler turned to the lieutenant, but the officer raised his eyebrows and said nothing.

"Well, Sheriff? If you're having trouble making up your mind, we can take this question before the judge," said Story.

"Take the herd," Byler said sullenly, "if you can, but you'll have to settle with Raney Huffmeyer an' his outfit. It was him that paid the taxes an' took the herd on forfeit."

"Then I reckon he'll be looking to you and the county for a refund of his money," said Story, "because we are taking the herd. Lieutenant, if you'll return the weapons belonging to my riders, we'll be going."

"Sergeant," said Lieutenant Goode, "return the weapons taken from these men." He said no more, but there was just a hint of satisfaction in his eyes as he watched the disgruntled Sheriff Byler stalk toward the courthouse. When Lieutenant Goode and his soldiers had departed, Story turned to the five cowboys.

"Now," Story said, "tell me about the herd and this Raney Huffmeyer."

"He's the sheriff's brother-in-law," said Quanah Taylor, "and he's killed a man or two. Fancies himself a real bull of the woods, with a pair of tied-down Colts. Our herd's on his spread, ten miles east of here. He's got nine riders, and they always have money, but they never seem to work. If you get the drift. Our cows is all branded too. Circle Five."

"I get it," Story said. "In the morning we'll go after the herd. Where are your horses?"

"Tied behind the Brazos Saloon," said Taylor.

"We'll take them to the livery," Story said. "Then we'll get you gents a bed for the night and some supper."

"You been straight with us, Mr. Story," said Gus Odell, "and we're obliged. It shames me to say it, but amongst us, we ain't got the price of a cup of coffee."

"You're part of my outfit," Story said. "Besides, I'm going to owe you a pile of money for those fifteen hundred cows at ten dollars a head."

"You ain't got the cows yet," said Virg Wooler. "This Raney Huffmeyer reckons he owns 'em legal, and he's a real sonofabitch."

"We'll get the herd," Story said. "I'll reason with Mr. Huffmeyer in a way that he can understand."

"Hell," said Cal, "there'll be ten of them and seven of us. I reckon that makes it about equal."

When the horses had been led to the livery, Story led the group back to the River Bend Hotel, where he paid for another three rooms for the night. From there they returned to the cafe next to the Brazos Saloon.

"I recommend the fried chicken," Story said. "I reckon Cal and me can use some more coffee."

Story ordered double portions for the five men, and they ate as only cowboys can. By the time they were finished, darkness had fallen, seeming all the more intense because the wind was whipping gray sheets of rain against the cafe's windows. They could barely see the dim glow of a lamp in the hotel's window, just across the street.

Unmindful of the rain, Sheriff Dub Byler left his office for the day. Mounting his horse, he rode eastward, his motivation being the fifteen hundred dollars that he had no intention of returning. It would be far simpler for Raney Huffmeyer to kill this troublesome bastard, Nelson Story. . . .

Hitch Gould and Bill Petty reached Comanche, took a room for the night, and had supper. The weather was such that there were few patrons in the saloons, and they learned nothing that was of any use to them.

"Tomorrow," said Petty, "we'll visit the courthouse and the county sheriff's office."

"I hope the others are havin' better luck than we are," Hitch said, "or we'll never have enough cows for a drive."

When the courthouse opened at eight the following morning, Hitch and Petty were waiting. As yet there had been no Federally appointed lawman, and the sheriff was a gray-haired old fellow in his fifties, Eli Stearn.

"I reckon you could ride the whole of Comanche County," said Stearn, "and not buy ten cows. Ike Hagerman's takin' a drive north, an' he's struck some kind of deal with other ranchers. He'll add their cows to his herd, and split the money."

"Beats selling for ten dollars a head, I reckon," Hitch said.

"For a fact," said the sheriff. "Some of the outfits that took drives up the trail last fall sold for thirty-five dollars a head. Some of the early ones for more'n that."

Discouraged, Hitch and Petty left the sheriff's office.

"We don't know how far this Hagerman hombre's reachin' out," Hitch said. "We could ride another fifty miles and still not buy a single cow. Already we're more'n a day's ride from camp. Do we ride on, or ride back?"

"From what Sheriff Stearn's told us," said Petty, "I think we'll ride back the way we came. Given the same information, that's what Story would do. I'd kind of like to ride back by the Wells place."

"I hope this Curly Wells is good on a horse and quick with a rope and gun," Hitch said. "He don't impress me much otherwise, and he's kind of scrawny to be a cow wrassler."

"He's young," said Petty, "and with his pa dying, it was a poor time for us to ride in. This Manuel Cardenas is a *bueno* hombre, and I reckon he can talk some sense into the kid."

When they rode up to the squalid cabin, Cardenas again met them at the door. He wasted no words.

"The Senor Wells sleeps by the creek. The *hijo* does not take it well."

"I didn't reckon he would," Petty said. "Have you spoken to him about the two of you joining our trail drive?"

"*Si,*" said Cardenas, "but he does not hear."

"We're not quite a day's ride from camp," Petty said. "We'll leave you the rest of our grub, and you'll have until that runs out to convince the boy of the need to move on. I'll tell Mr. Story about you, and if you decide to throw in with us, just follow the Brazos north and look for our camp under the west rim."

"*Si,*" said Cardenas. *"Muchos gracias."*

Cardenas watched them ride away. With a sigh he turned back into the cabin, where young Curly Wells sat slumped in a chair.

"You reckon they'll ride in and talk to Mr. Story?" Hitch asked.

"They'll come. Curly's young and grieving, but Cardenas is a practical man, and he'll be a credit to our outfit. Curly will have to prove himself."

"Ma'am," Tom Allen began, "I—"

"Damn it," the girl interrupted, "stop talking to me like I'm your mother. My name's Jasmine."

"Jasmine," said Allen, regaining his composure, "I'm not sure Nelson Story would ever agree to you joining the trail drive."

"And why not?" she flared. "I can shoot, rope, and ride as well as any man, and better than some."

"It ain't us you got to convince," said Arch, coming to Allen's defense. "Why don't you ride up and tell Mr. Story what you've told us?"

"I'll do that," she said, her anger diminishing, "but not until tomorrow. Bud will need a day to sober up."

"He's had a nasty whack on the head too," Arch said slyly.

"No more than he deserved. I've had enough of his drunken foolishness."

"We should ride on, I reckon," said Allen. "Do you know of others who might have cows to sell?"

"No," she said. "Last fall, just about everybody gathered their cows into a common herd and drove them north, and they're gathering now for a second drive this fall. We couldn't go last time, because Daddy was sick."

"But you aim to go next time," Allen said.

"Yes," she said, "unless your Mr. Story can overlook the fact I'm not a man. I realize our herd will be worth four times as much in Sedalia or St. Louis, but I'm not greedy. I just want to move on, and not just to Sedalia or St. Louis. Frankly, we don't have riders or money for our own outfit."

"I hope you'll talk to Nelson Story," said Allen. "He's straight."

"I'll talk to him tomorrow," said Jasmine, "and I'll take Bud with me. Since you're not going to find any more cows around here, what's the sense in riding farther? The rain's only going to get worse. You're welcome to stay the night. You can sleep in Daddy's room."

Arch said nothing, looking at Tom.

"I think we'll accept that offer," said Allen. "If we're able to buy your herd, we'll have accomplished what we set out to do, and if there's no more cows to be had, once we leave here, all we're likely to get is wet."

"Good," said Jasmine, and she bestowed a smile on Allen that sent a herd of chills stampeding up his spine. "Take your horses to the barn and fork them down some hay."

They waited until the rain slacked a little, then headed for the barn, Arch leading the pack mule. They found some old saddle blankets and rubbed their animals down. Arch climbed to the loft and forked down some hay. When he climbed down, he was grinning.

"What'n hell's got into you?" Allen asked.

"Just thinkin'," said Arch cheerfully. "Ever since you spanked that gal's behind, she's been lookin' at you like a lost calf that's just discovered its mama."

The rain had gotten harder, but Tom Allen plunged into it, heading for the house. Arch Rainey slapped his thighs and roared with laughter.

February 7, 1866. Waco, Texas.

Story and his riders arose at first light, thankful to find that the rain had slacked to a drizzle. Again they crossed the muddy street to the cafe, where Story ordered platters of ham, eggs, and fried potatoes. Before they were finished, the cook had to boil a second pot of coffee. From there they went to the livery, saddled their horses, and Cal loaded the pack mule. They rode east, Story's five new riders leading the way. Stopping once to rest the horses, within an hour they were seeing cattle, many of them with Circle 5 brands.

"They'll be lookin' for us," said Quanah Taylor, "and we ain't got rifles."

"Rein up short of rifle range," Story said, "and hail the house. Cal and me have rifles, if that's how they aim to greet us. If there's killing, we'll let them open the ball, but we won't fight unless we have to. Invite Huffmeyer out to parley."

"Cut him down to size," said Dutch Mayfield, "and the rest of 'em will light out like scared coyotes."

The ranch house was long and low, surrounded by oaks, and more imposing than any Story had seen since arriving in Texas. It was built of logs, and men armed with rifles could stand off an army or a tribe of Comanches. They reined up far enough from the house that they were in no danger from anything less than a buffalo gun.

"Huffmeyer," Taylor shouted, "come out. We need to parley with you."

"Git off my spread," came a voice from the cabin. "We got nothin' to parley about."

"The rest of you stay where you are," said Story. "I'll get his attention and we'll take it from there."

Story trotted his horse fifty yards closer, until he was well within rifle range. He dismounted, and taking his Henry rifle from the boot, fired four rapid shots toward the cabin. The distant tinkle of breaking glass was testimony to his accuracy. He mounted his horse and rode back to join his riders. He didn't wait for a response from the house, but shouted a challenge of his own.

"Huffmeyer, this is Nelson Story. Quanah Taylor and his friends work for me, and the cattle you're claiming belong to me. With or without your approval, I'm taking the herd, unless you think you're man enough to stop me."

"I'm plenty man enough, bucko," came the voice from inside the house, "but I don't trust that bunch you got sidin' you. Come closer to the house and I'll meet you. By God, we'll see who's a man an' who ain't."

"You talk like a fool and a yellow coyote, Huffmeyer," Story shouted. "Your men have rifles, and they'll be shooting from cover. Only one of my men has a rifle, and he's going to be covering the house, in case some of your *companeros* try to sneak out with mischief on their minds. Now if you've got the guts, amigo, you come out that door alone, and it'll be my gun against yours."

"Hell, he ain't got the guts," said Jules Dyer.

"Maybe not," Story said, "but he's got pride, and that's been the death of better men. He'll be coming."

It was a prophecy that was quickly fulfilled. The door opened and Huffmeyer stepped out. Slowly he crossed the porch, descended the steps, and began a slow walk. Story went to meet him, coat unbuttoned, his hands near the butts of his Colts.

"God," said Quanah Taylor in awe, "I've heard of this kind of thing, but I never seen it. This Nelson Story's some kind of man."

Nobody else spoke. Cal Snider stood aside from the others, his eyes on the distant house, the Winchester cocked and ready. Huffmeyer walked slowly forward, and as Story approached him, the gap closed. Huffmeyer wore a brace of tied-down pistols, and it was he who drew first. He drew both guns, and in the rain-washed stillness there was a single shot. Huffmeyer's pistols began to sag, and he fired two shots into the muddy ground. Nelson Story holstered his right-hand Colt as Huffmeyer toppled backward, splashing into the water and mud.

"Lord God," said Gus Odell, "he done it with one shot, and Huffmeyer drawed first. Did anybody see Story make his move?"

"I didn't," said Virg Wooler, "and I was lookin' right at him."

"Gents," said Quanah Taylor, "we just throwed in with a man that's nine feet tall and a yard wide. I'd of give up my share of the herd 'fore I'd of missed this."

Cal Snider had moved forward with his Winchester, lest the Huffmeyer outfit had cut loose with rifles, but there was no activity at the house. Story waited until Cal reached him. Then he again challenged the men in the house.

"We're taking the herd," Story shouted. "If you men in the house want to pick up the fight where Huffmeyer left off, now's the time to do it. If any of you come coyotin' around while we're gathering the herd, we'll take it you're up to no good and gun you down. *Comprender?*"

"It ain't our fight," shouted one of the men from the house.

"Come on, Cal," Story said. "Let's round up those cows and head them upriver. I have a feeling Sheriff Dud Byler's not going to like this."

The cattle had been out of the brakes long enough that they weren't completely wild, and before dark Story and his riders had the herd gathered. There was more rain, and there was no way they could begin the drive north until the following day.

"Without a stick of dry wood and no shelter, I think we'll pass on grub tonight," said Story. "I'd hoped we could get off this range and on our way upriver before dark. Now we'll have to make the best of it. I want every man in the saddle. We'll move out at first light and get as far from here as we can. Tomorrow we'll keep our eyes open for shelter and a place that's dry enough to cook some grub."

Hitch Gould and Bill Petty were the first to return to camp, with nothing to show for their search.

"I ain't surprised," said Shanghai Wolfington. "Them few outfits that was able t'git a herd t'market last fall got a taste of success, an' this year the others is aimin' t'go. There may be some real trouble findin' enough cows fer this drive."

"With Nels and Cal to the south, and Hitch and Tom to the east," Bill Petty said, "we still have a chance."

* * *

February 8, 1866. Malakoff, Texas.

Bud McDaniels awoke with a wretched hangover, a thundering headache, and absolutely no intention of getting out of bed. When Jasmine confronted him with her plan for the two of them to join Nelson Story's trail drive, Bud looked at her incredulously for a moment before he exploded.

"By God," he bawled, "you've lost your mind, whatever little you had. I ain't goin' on no trail drive, and neither are you. Half them cows is mine, and they ain't goin' nowhere."

"Good," Jasmine snapped. "You'll need them for company, because I'll be taking my half of the herd north. You're all the family I have, but I don't aim to wet-nurse you all the way to Montana Territory."

McDaniels began cursing the girl in a manner that would have shocked a bull whacker. Arch and Tom left the kitchen and, reaching the doorway, stepped into the bedroom.

"Jasmine," said Tom, "go on back to the kitchen."

Surprisingly, the girl obeyed, and Allen closed the door behind her.

"Who'n hell are you?" McDaniels demanded.

"I'm Tom Allen and this is Arch Rainey. We brought you home last night."

"Thanks for nothin'," said McDaniels sullenly.

"I've seen some poor excuses for men in my time," said Allen, "but by God, you're the lowest of the lot. No man cusses a woman like you just did. If I thought it'd do any good, I'd haul you out of there and stomp hell out of you."

"Well, damn my eyes, it's Sir Galahad hisself," McDaniels sneered. "So it's you that's lurin' her off on this fool trail drive. Why'n hell don't you mind your own business?"

He had dark eyes and dark hair, like the girl, but the whiskey had already begun to ravage his face. Allen tried a new approach.

"Look, we're part of an outfit that's buying cows for a trail drive to Montana Territory. We're interested in buying your herd, but your sister has refused to sell unless she can go north with the drive. It's her idea, not ours, and it's her idea to take you along. Personally, I don't think you've got the sand, and I don't want you on the drive. Have you ever forked a hoss like a man, or do you do all your ridin' belly down, dog drunk?"

The taunt had the desired effect. McDaniels came out of the bed fighting, but Allen was ready for him. He ducked the blow, caught McDaniels's arm and flung him back on the bed.

"If you're of a mind to go with us," Allen said, "get up, and if I ever hear you cuss your sister like you just did, I'll beat your ears down to your boot tops."

"I'll get up when I'm damn good and ready," McDaniels snarled, "and I ain't ready. Now get the hell out of here."

Arch and Tom went out, closing the door behind them. Jasmine was waiting in the kitchen.

"The only reason I hate to leave him here," she said, "is that by the time I get back, he'll likely be piled up in jail, drunk again."

"Nelson Story won't put up with that," said Tom, "and I don't blame him. This is going to be one hell of a drive, and we'll need every rider. Besides, there won't be any whiskey along the way. What do you aim to do about him?"

"Exactly what I told him I'd do," said Jasmine. "If he can't or won't be a man, then I'll go without him. If you'll saddle the horses, I'll start breakfast."

Arch and Tom had saddled their own horses, one for

Jasmine, and had loaded the pack mule by the time the girl had breakfast ready. Bud McDaniels made good his threat not to get up until he was ready, and when the three had finished breakfast, Jasmine made good her threat to leave without Bud. They rode west, Arch leading the mule.

"How far are we from your camp?" Jasmine asked.

"About seventy-five miles," said Tom. "We'll ride due west, through Corsicana, and ride north when we reach the Brazos. We can be there before dark, but I don't know if Story will be back by then. He's somewhere near Waco."

"I hope he is," Jasmine said. "I need to get back to our place as soon as I can. Bud's worse than a child. God knows what he's likely to do, just to spite me."

Dawn broke, after a night of chill wind and drizzle, as Story and his riders got the herd moving north.

"They're trailing well," Story said.

"Some of 'em have had more'n a year to settle down," said Quanah, "and that'll have some influence on the others, I reckon. You think we'll get out of here without more gunplay?"

"I think so," Story said. "When you gun down the leader of the pack, the rest of the coyotes generally head for the tall timber. I reckon it'll take another three or four days to get the herd to our camp. I'm thinking of leaving Cal with you and riding on ahead. I'll send one of the outfit back to meet you. He can bring another pack mule with more grub, and five Winchesters."

Story found Cal riding drag, and left him in charge of the drive. He then rode north, almost facing the rain that was again blowing out of the northwest. He was only a few miles south of camp when a horse nickered and his own answered. Story reined up, drawing his Henry from the boot. He was in the brush, along the river, and as the three riders approached the Brazos from the east, he thought he recognized Tom Allen's roan. That the third rider was a woman, he was certain. Reassured, he rode on. Tom Allen shoved his rifle back into the boot and the three of them galloped their horses to meet Story.

"Nels!" Allen shouted. "Where's Cal?"

"Headin' this way," Story replied, "bringing us five new riders and fifteen hundred cows."

"Nels," said Allen, "this is Jasmine McDaniels. She's got a thousand head, and they're for sale if we can work out some differences."

7

*W*ell before they reached the camp on the Brazos,
Nelson Story had heard what Jasmine McDaniels
had to say.

"Jasmine," said Story kindly, "I can appreciate the
problems you're having with your brother, but I'll be
honest with you. I'd not want him on the trail with me
unless he's ready, willing, and able. From what you're
telling me, I'm not sure he qualifies at all."

"I feel the same way," Jasmine said, "and I'm dead
serious when I say that I'll leave him behind to go to hell
if he can't be changed. In fact, if you'll see that he's
paid for his half of the herd, I think we can take them
all."

"Stay the night with us, then," said Story. "Tomorrow we'll take some riders with us and return to your
place."

"Does that mean you'll allow me to ride with the trail
drive?"

Story grinned. "I'll go further than that. If you can
ride, rope, and shoot, as well as holding your own with
brawling, cussing cowboys, I'll pay you the same as I'm
paying them. Forty and found, with a hundred dollar
bonus at the end of the drive. But I must warn you.
There will be swollen rivers, and some of us may send

our clothes across in the wagon. We'll be crossing in our drawers, at best, or maybe nothing at all."

"Mr. Story," said Jasmine, "if you're trying to scare me away, you're wasting your time. I've had almost two years of Bud bringing his drunken friends home. You wouldn't believe how many times I've awakened to find them three to a bed or piled on the floor, naked as jaybirds. Your cowboys won't be a problem. Of course, I may be somewhat of a problem to them."

Story grinned. "I daresay you will."

They reached the camp on the Brazos well before dark. Sandy Bill outdid himself with supper. Story listened as Bill Petty told of the difficulty he and Hitch had encountered, and of the possibility that Curly Wells and Manuel Cardenas might be seeking to hire on as riders. Without mentioning Jasmine's drunken brother, Story introduced her to those of the outfit she hadn't met, telling them of the herd that he hoped to buy.

"In the morning," said Story, "here's what must be done. Cal Snider and five other cowboys are driving fifteen hundred head of longhorns from Waco. They have only what's left of the grub Cal and me took with us. They're still maybe three days away, and I want to take them another pack mule with grub, and five Winchesters for the new riders. Bill, I want you and Hitch to ride south, taking the extra grub and Winchesters, and join that drive. I'll take Arch and Tom, ride back with Jasmine and fetch her herd."

Story was amused at the change that came over the cow camp after Jasmine McDaniels arrived. Swearing was cut to a minimum, and any man who forgot was promptly reprimanded by his comrades.

"By God," said Coon Tails after a while, "it's onnatural quiet in here. This is Thursday. Come Sunday, I reckon we'll be ready fer Sunday school."

It was too much. They all laughed, Jasmine McDaniels the loudest of them all.

* * *

February 9, 1866. On the Brazos.

Story and his companions rode south at first light, and
for a change there was no rain, not even a drizzle. There
were two pack mules laden with provisions. One of
them Hitch Gould and Bill Petty would take with them
as they rode south to meet Cal Snider and the five new
cowboys. Carefully wrapped in canvas were five new
Winchesters. The second pack mule would go with Story
as he, Tom, Arch, and Jasmine returned to her spread at
Malakoff. The Brazos was swollen from the continuous
rain, and they rode south along the west bank, seeking a
place shallow enough to cross. There was no wind, and
the blast seemed unusually loud in the early morning
quiet. The pack mule Arch was leading dropped in its
tracks, shot through the head. Story was out of his saddle in an instant, taking his Henry with him. The others
were quick to follow.

"He's somewhere on the east bank," said Bill Petty,
"and usin' a Sharps .50 at least. Our rifles can't touch
him from here."

"He'll be long gone before we can get over there,"
Story said, "high as the water is. Arch, ride back to
camp and bring one of the extra horses."

"I could bring one of Sandy Bill's mules," said Arch.

"No," Story said, "I won't risk his animals. We'll
make do with a horse."

"This is another of the hazards of joining my outfit,"
said Story when Arch had ridden away.

"What a foolish, cruel thing to do," Jasmine said.
"You mean this has happened before?"

"This is the third time," said Story, "but this is the
first time he's killed. The first and second attempts, he
was shooting at me. I think now he's trying to worry me,
to remind me that my time's coming."

"But why?"

"I'm not sure," Story said, "unless it's to avenge the thieves and killers the vigilantes hanged in Montana Territory, back in 'sixty-four and 'sixty-five. I was captain of the miners' vigilance committee, and I know some of the gang escaped. So I don't know if this bushwhacking is the work of one man or two or three. I'm also not sure that he's just gunning for me. He may be the vindictive kind who'll kill anybody in the outfit. That's what bothers me most."

"It's a cowardly way to seek revenge," Jasmine said, "stalking a man and shooting from cover. I appreciate your warning me, but I'm still going with you."

"Curly," said Manuel Cardenas, "it is time to go. It is only through the kindness of Senor Story's riders that we have had food. There is no more."

"Must we go, Manuel? I . . . I hate to leave him here. Him and Mama."

"They have gone to a better world," Manuel said, "and that is what we must do. We have no food, no money, no stock, and except for the Senor Story's trail drive, no hope. The trail will be hard, but no harder than this. You can rope and ride as well as I. We must go before the Senor Story has hired the riders he needs."

They rode east, toward the Brazos, reining up for a last look at the desolate cabin and the two graves beside the creek.

"Vaya con Dios, senor and senora," said Manuel.

Things were not going well in Wes Hardin's cow camp. In four days they had roped but four cows, and as the young riders sat beneath a rock overhang eating beans, they bitched among themselves.

"We ain't got but one choice," said Greener, "and

that's to ride farther south. Either the cows is all movin'
downriver or they been roped out."

"We don't find any betwixt here an' Waco," Slim said,
"we can just purely forget the Brazos. Goodnight an' his
outfit's workin' downriver from Waco, an' they won't be
leavin' doodly for nobody else."

"It don't matter whether they leave any cows or not,"
said Hardin. "This Goodnight's got enough riders to
fight the Comanches. We ain't."

"Him right," Quickenpaugh said. "Comanch' kill
dead lak hell."

"Well, by God," said Greener, "we decided we can't
foller the river south, an' we ain't doin' no good here.
What *are* we goin' to do?"

"I've had 'bout enough of the way things is in Texas,"
said Hardin. "We been gettin' around this Reconstruction thing, but there'll be more and more blue bellies,
and sooner or later they'll start lookin' slanch-eyed at
us. I'm of a mind to hire on with this trail drive Story's
got planned."

"Damn him," Greener said, "he talked to us like we
wasn't dry behind the ears, like we wasn't man enough
even to be considered."

"One more reason to go," said Hardin. "No man
talks down to me, without regrettin' it."

"Hell," Slim said, "I ain't got nothin' to prove to nobody. I say let's give it another week. If we don't do no
better'n we done this week, then I reckon it's time we
rode some other trail."

"*Bueno,*" said Quickenpaugh. "We wait."

Cal and his riders slept little their first night on the trail.
Except for an occasional coyote, they heard nothing.
The rain ceased during the night, and come the dawn,
they even found enough dry wood for a fire. Hot coffee
and food lifted their spirits considerably.

"Mr. Story was right," said Gus Odell. "Gun down

one coyote, and it puts the fear of God into the rest. If anybody was comin' after us, they'd of been here by now."

"Still," Cal said, "we'll ride careful and keep our guns handy. Sometime today we'll have more grub, and you gents will have new Winchesters."

Bill Petty and Hitch Gould proved him right, riding in late that afternoon. Cal introduced the new riders, and the men were jubilant as they got the feel of the new Winchesters.

"Fifty rounds of ammunition for each of you," Bill Petty said. "That'll be plenty to get us back to camp, unless we run into a tribe of Comanches."

Petty then told them of the thousand head of cows Story hoped to buy from Jasmine McDaniels, and that Story, Arch, and Tom were on their way to the girl's ranch, near Malakoff. He also told them of Jasmine McDaniels's intention of joining the drive.

"God," said Cal, "I got the feelin' this trail drive's goin' to be something for the history books."

He didn't know how right he was. . . .

"We might as well stop in Corsicana," Jasmine said. "If Bud's piled up in jail again, drunk, I'll know what I have to do."

But the girl was in for a surprise. Bud wasn't there, nor had Sheriff Eli Stearn seen him. It was late afternoon when they neared the house and a rider rode in from the east, meeting them.

"It's Bud!" cried Jasmine.

Jasmine dismounted and stood there speechless. Bud McDaniels not only looked like a working cowboy, he was cold sober. Story, Arch, and Tom had dismounted, and the girl regained enough of her composure to introduce them.

"Howdy," said Bud. "If we're sellin' the herd, I

reckon we ought to know for sure how many we got. I been runnin' a tally."

Jasmine looked from Story to Arch to Tom, wondering, in view of all she'd told them about Bud's unsavory habits, how they'd react to this change in him. Story was the first to respond.

"Good thinking," said Story. "If we start the gather in the morning at first light, we can start the drive north before dark."

Arch and Tom, following Story's lead, were cordial to McDaniels, and Jasmine flashed them grateful looks.

"Bud," Jasmine said, "help them unload the pack-horse and stable and feed all their animals. I'll get supper started."

As the night wore on, Arch Rainey and Tom Allen found themselves liking Bud McDaniels. He was as out-spoken as his sister, and told them harrowing tales of his days with the Confederacy. It had a profound effect on Story, and Jasmine could see his doubts diminishing. When Tom Allen caught her eye and winked, she blushed, and Arch Rainey just sat there grinning.

"We'd better call it a night," said Story. "Tomorrow will be a long day."

"Mr. Story," Jasmine said, "you can sleep with Bud. Arch and Tom can have the room that belonged to Daddy."

Story closed the bedroom door and turned to find Bud easing a whiskey bottle under the bed with the toe of his boot.

"Don't bother," said Story. "I know about it."

"I ain't proud of it," said Bud, "if that makes any difference."

"We've all done things we're not proud of," Story said, "but a man puts them behind him and rides another trail."

"That's what I aim to do," said Bud.

"*Bueno,*" Story said. "Now blow out that lamp and let's get some sleep."

February 10, 1866. Malakoff, Texas.

The rain started again sometime during the night, but it didn't slow the gather, which began right after breakfast. Story was elated to find a large number of steers in the gather, most of them two-year-olds and older. He had an opportunity to observe Bud and Jasmine and their handling of the longhorns, and wasn't disappointed. The ground was muddy, slippery, and a steadily falling rain added to the hazard. Jasmine's horse went down, and the girl slid out of the saddle, remounting when the animal regained its feet. Story nodded approvingly. This pair would do. The gather went well, but because of the rain, they didn't finish in time to take the trail.

"We'd as well spend the night here," Story said, "and start tomorrow at first light. No point sleeping in the rain if you don't have to. Besides, the herd shouldn't scatter, being on home range."

"Tomorrow we ought to reach the canyon where our camp is," Cal said.

They were driving the herd along the west bank of the Brazos. With the high water, the river acted as a natural barrier, keeping the herd on course with a minimum of effort.

"Tell us again where this trail drive's goin' and where it's gonna end," said Virg Wooler.

"From what Mr. Story tells me," Cal said, "we're going to Quincy, Illinois. He aims to sell part of the herd there, and take the rest on to Virginia City, Montana Territory."

"I've heard a little about that high country," said Quanah. "It sounds like the place where a man can make some big tracks, without nobody botherin' him."

"I can't say I won't never come back to Texas," Cal said, "but it'll be a while. I got nothin' here."

"That reminds me," said Bill Petty. "Nelson said you've got unfinished business in Fort Worth, and that when you get the herd back to camp, you can ride on into town."

"You'd better," Hitch said, "or that unfinished business will come lookin' for you."

February 11, 1866. Cow camp on the Brazos.

As Nelson Story and his riders took the trail north, Manuel Cardenas and Curly Wells arrived at Story's camp on the Brazos. When the pair had dismounted, Cardenas spoke to Coon Tails, who had climbed down to the river to greet them.

"I am Manuel Cardenas and this is Curly Wells. We have come to speak to the Senor Story. We wish to hire on as riders for the trail drive."

"Story ain't here," Coon Tails said, "an' we ain't lookin' for him fer maybe five days. He's bringin' a herd of cows from south o' here. We been expectin' you. Unsaddle yer hosses, shoulder yer saddles, an' come on up t' the camp. We was about t'have breakfast."

When the pair reached the camp, Coon Tails introduced them to Sandy Bill, Smokey Ellison, Oscar Fentress, and Shanghai Wolfington.

"Jist make yerselves to home," Coon Tails said. "Ain't a damn thing t'do 'cept watch the river rise, or watch Oscar a-cuttin' an' a-lacin' whatever the hell he's makin' outta that cowhide."

"I make rifle boots fer them what needs 'em," said Oscar.

"Yeah," Coon Tails said, "that reminds me. Mr. Story's got Winchesters an' Colts fer them that needs 'em. How you fixed fer guns?"

"We have only the Henry rifle, senor," said Cardenas, "and we have almost no shells."

"Mr. Story carries a Henry," Coon Tails said, "an' we got shells. We got extry Colts too, an' enough Winchesters so's you both kin have a long gun."

"Gracias," said Cardenas, "but let us wait until the Senor Story returns. Until then we do not know that he wants us."

February 12, 1866. On the Brazos.

Late in the afternoon, Cal Snider and his seven riders scattered the fifteen hundred head of longhorns along the Brazos, within the canyon where Story's camp was.

"We're gettin' enough cows that we're gonna have to do some nighthawkin'," Cal said. "Some of these brutes might get homesick and go skalleyhootin' down the river. I reckon a pair of us ought to ride this canyon ever' night, at least until Mr. Story gets back and tells us different."

"That's smart thinking," said Bill Petty. "There's enough of us to take it in three four-hour watches, two riders at a time."

When Cal, Petty, Hitch, and the five new riders had loosed their horses along the river, they all climbed up to the shelf beneath the overhang. Cal introduced the new riders to the rest of the outfit, and Petty introduced Curly Wells and Manuel Cardenas to the five newcomers. Young Curly seemed shy, saying little, while Cardenas fitted in almost immediately.

* * *

February 13, 1866. Following the Brazos north.

"I'd say we've come at least forty miles," Story said at the end of their third day on the trail. "In the morning, we'll head slightly northwest, and we shouldn't be more than two days' drive from our camp on the Brazos."

In Story's absence, Cal Snider assumed the role of segundo. He chose himself and Quanah Taylor for the first watch, Bill Petty and Hitch Gould for the second, and Tom Allen and Arch Rainey for the third.

"The rest of you keep your rifles and Colts handy," Cal said, "and if you hear a commotion, come a-runnin'. Those of you that ain't on watch tonight can take a turn tomorrow night."

But the night passed uneventfully. The rain let up, but before dawn it came again, accompanied by thunder and some distant lightning.

"I have some business in town," said Cal, "and I have Mr. Story's permission to ride in and take care of it. I should be back before dark. The rest of you stay close to camp, keep your eyes open and your guns ready."

February 13, 1866. Following the Brazos north.

Their fourth day on the trail, Story and his riders reached the Brazos a dozen miles south of their camp. The rain had continued most of the day, and darkness was coming early.

"We might as well bed them down for the night," Story said. "We'll reach our camp tomorrow, but for tonight it's more ridin' wet and going hungry."

"That's the worst part of all this rain," said Arch. "When it's time for grub and hot coffee, they ain't a stick of dry wood anywhere in Texas."

Story could only agree. It had been a perfectly miserable drive, but not a word of complaint had he heard from Jasmine or Bud McDaniels. They rode hard, driving occasional bunch quitters back to the herd, and kept their silence. Story caught Bud's eye a time or two, and the young rider grinned at him through the rain. It was as though the pair welcomed the incessant rain, the mud, and the lack of food as a means of proving themselves.

"Some lightning back yonder to the west," Story said when they'd bedded down the herd. "Tom, you and Jasmine take the first watch. The rest of us will take it from midnight to dawn."

Arch Rainey grinned in the gathering darkness. Nelson Story was no fool.

February 14, 1866. On the Brazos.

As Nelson Story and his riders got the herd on the trail a dozen miles south, Cal Snider rode out, bound for Fort Worth. He'd rather take a beating with a blacksnake whip, he thought dismally, than face Lorna Flagg. What was he going to say to her? He mulled over in his mind what Nelson Story had said. Story liked the girl, but damn it, she wasn't going to be Story's responsibility. Lorna was strong-willed, could ride like an Indian, and she wouldn't be intimidated by a bunch of hell-raising cowboys. So what was he, Cal Snider, afraid of? Her daddy? In a little more than six weeks the girl would be eighteen, and old man Flagg couldn't touch her. Suppose she ran away before she was legally free, would Flagg send the law after her? Who would he send, or would he even bother dragging the girl back to Fort Worth, when she would only leave again within days? From what Cal had heard, the drive would cross the Red River about eighty miles north of Fort Worth.

Once they were into Indian Territory, all they'd have to worry about was what lay ahead. Amos Flagg, vindictive old bastard that he was, wouldn't go to all that trouble to find a rebellious daughter and drag her home.

"By God," said Cal to himself, "I could do worse. I'll take her with me, and we'll take our chances with the rivers, the damn Indians, and whatever else we got to fight."

He rode on feeling better, grinning to himself as he thought of how the girl would respond. Lost in his thoughts, amid the wind and rain, he didn't even hear the shot. The slug ripped into him just below his right collar bone, flinging him over the rump of the horse. The wind caught his hat, sending it flying, while the blood from his wound mixed with the steadily falling rain. . . .

Story and his riders were in the saddle by the time it was barely light enough to see. Breakfast was out of the question, for they had no shelter, and the rain continued.

"Push them hard," Story shouted, "and let's bring this to a finish."

It was their fifth day on the trail, with almost continuous rain and little food. But nobody had complained, Story noted with satisfaction, and what they were experiencing might be only a small part of what they would face on the long trail to Virginia City, Montana Territory, by way of Quincy, Illinois.

Their diligence paid off, and at what Story calculated was an hour past noon, they drove the herd into the south end of the canyon, a mile or two south of their camp.

"Come on," Story said, "and leave them to graze. We're long past due a good meal, hot coffee, and a chance to dry out."

Coon Tails, Bill Petty, and Arch Rainey came down

the steep trail to help them unsaddle their horses and to unload the provisions that remained on the packhorse. Then, amid the sound of wind and rain, came the patter of hooves. The horse came downriver, from the north, and there was no rider. Coon Tails caught the trailing reins.

"It's Cal's horse," said Bill Petty. "I told him what you said, and he was riding to town."

"Bill," said Story, "you and Coon Tails saddle your horses."

The three of them rode out at a fast gallop, Story leading Cal's horse. Having no idea where they might find him, Story took the most direct route toward town. Cal had fallen into what had once been a buffalo wallow, and was almost entirely submerged in water when they found him.

"God," said Petty, "if the wound don't kill him, the exposure will. That water's cold as ice."

"We'll take him on to town," Story said. "He's going to need a doctor."

They wrapped him in what blankets they had, and although would soon be soaked, they would protect him from the chill wind that continued to blow from the northwest. They had to ride slowly, and it seemed hours before they saw the dim outlines of the buildings through the driving rain.

"We'll take him to the hotel," Story said, "and bring a doctor to him."

They reined up before the Fort Worth House, and while Petty and Coon Tails eased Cal down from the horse, Story went into the hotel to arrange for a room. Story wasted no words.

"One of my men's been shot and he needs a room. I'll guarantee payment for as long as he needs it. How much?"

"Three dollars a night," said the clerk.

"I'm going for a doctor," Story said. "We'll need lots of hot water."

"But we don't have—"

"Then by God," said Story, leaning across the counter, "send out for some, but have it here when I get back. *Comprender?*"

"Y-Yes, sir," said the frightened clerk.

Story held the door open as Coon Tails and Petty carried Cal inside.

"I've arranged for a room," Story said. "When you've taken him to it, one of you wait in the lobby for the doctor."

Story rode at a fast gallop until he reached the Masonic hall. Reining up, he was out of the saddle and running toward the little shack where Doc Nagel lived, where Story had gone to have his own wound tended following the attempted ambush. He found Doc Nagel going through some papers on his desk.

"Doc, one of my riders has been shot. He's at the Fort Worth House. One of my men will be waiting for you in the lobby."

The doctor grabbed his hat with one hand and his satchel with the other. Story mounted his horse and rode until he reached Emma Baird's sewing shop, across the street from the bank.

"Mr. Story," said Emma as Story stepped through the door.

"Emma," Story said, "Cal Snider's been shot. Where can I find the Flagg house?"

"Take a right at the bank," said Emma, "and it's four doors down. White house with a picket fence. Do you need me?"

"Maybe later, Emma," Story said. "Thanks."

Reaching the house, Story pounded on the door. It wasn't the time of day Flagg was likely to be home, but Story didn't give a damn. He beat on the door until it finally opened, Lorna staring at him in amazement. She wore Levi's and a shirt, and her hair was uncombed. Not until later would he discover that her feet were bare.

"Lorna, Cal's been shot. He's at the hotel. Will you come?"

She was out the door in an instant. Story boosted her up to the saddle, mounted behind her, and set off at a fast gallop for the hotel.

8

Russ Shadley and Mac Withers sat in their cabin and listened to the rain pound the shake roof. The fire hissed as water found its way down the old chimney and there was a leak in the middle of the rickety kitchen table. In the days since they'd left Nelson Story's camp, their daily search for more wild cows had been spectacularly unsuccessful.

"I got to admit," said Shadley, in a rare burst of candor, "signin' on with Story's trail drive wasn't a bad idea. We ain't catchin' enough cows to keep us in coffee an' beans."

"Too many riders gettin' into the act," Withers said. "We won't do no better without goin' deeper and deeper into the brakes, and that's where the Comanches are."

"Let's give it till Saturday," said Shadley. "That's three more days. Maybe we can rope four more of the varmints. That'll give us ten."

"With what we already drove in, that'd total four hundred dollars," Withers said. "Story's promisin' forty and found, with a bonus of a hundred at the end of the drive. I look for the drive to take six months or more, and when you add the bonus to wages, that's three hundred an' forty dollars. If we can start the drive with two hundred apiece, that's five hundred and forty dollars in our pockets when we git to Montana Territory."

"Like I said," Shadley growled, "ever' once in a while you come up with a good idee."

Coon Tails rode into the canyon, to the camp on the Brazos, with news of Cal having been shot.

"Bushwhacked," said the old mountain man as the outfit gathered around. "We took him t' the hotel in town. Story an' Petty's with him now, an' so's the leetle gal that's sweet on him. The doc was workin' on him when I rode out. Story says 'cept fer nighthawkin', t'stay close t'camp."

"How hard was Cal hit," Arch Rainey asked, "and where?"

"Plenty hard," said Coon Tails, "jist under the right collarbone. The slug went on through. Doc says if it'd hit a bone, he'd be dead."

"Thank God," Jasmine said. "Then he has a chance."

"I reckon," said Coon Tails, "if'n the peemonia don't git him. When we got t'him, he was layin' in cold water up t'his chin."

The five cowboys who had ridden with Cal from Waco had taken a liking to the young rider, and Quanah Taylor spoke for all of them.

"Somehow, somewhere," said Quanah, "we'll find the skunk-striped varmint, and he's goin' to die slow. The five of us ain't knowed Cal but a few days, but he's been a damn good friend, a man to ride the river with."

It was a sentiment shared by every rider in the camp, and there was anxiety in every face, but they could only wait. They were under orders from Story, and they knew why. A killer rode the plains, and they now knew what they had only suspected. Not only did he have a killing grudge against Story, he had enough hate for every rider in the outfit. . . .

* * *

Dr. Nagel allowed nobody in the room while he worked on Cal. Story, Bill Petty, and Lorna waited in the hall. When Dr. Nagel came out, he closed the door behind him, and Lorna's face went white.

"He'll make it," the doctor said, "but he'll need rest. I'll look in on him again tonight. He'll be in some pain, and someone should be with him at all times. There's laudanum on the table beside the bed, and it'll help him to sleep."

"Please let me stay with him," said Lorna.

"For a while, then," Story said, "but only in the daytime. Bill and me will take turns at night."

"This came at a bad time," said Petty, when Lorna had entered the room and closed the door. "He'll be laid up a good two weeks, maybe longer."

"No help for that," Story said. "The bushwhacker's out to hurt me in whatever way he can, and that includes gunning down my riders. So far he's holding all the high cards. We don't know who he is, and with this never-ending rain, it's impossible to trail him. The only thing we have going for us is that we may be able to move out sooner than we've planned. One more good cattle buy could complete our herd."

"And there's a possibility the bushwhacker won't follow us."

"That's what I'm hoping," said Story.

They heard somebody coming up the stairs, and it proved to be Sheriff Lot Higgins.

"Heard somebody's been shot," Higgins said. "Who, an' why?"

"One of my riders," said Story. "Cal Snider, and we don't know why, unless the bushwhacker was gunning for me."

"By God," Higgins said, "you're bad luck. We never had all this snipin' till you showed up."

"Forgive me, Sheriff, for putting a hex on your town," said Story without humor. "If it's not asking too much, maybe you could look around and perhaps learn if there are any strangers around, men who have been here about as long as I have."

"I ain't seen no strangers 'cept you an' the hombres you brung with you," Higgins said, "an' it ain't my job t' wander around on the prairie lookin' fer bushwhackers." With that, he turned and stomped off down the hall.

"Some sheriff," said Bill Petty.

Their next visitor was Emma Baird. "I won't go in," she said. "I just wanted to know if he's all right."

"He's going to be, we think," Story said. "Lorna's in there with him."

"I thought as much," said Emma, "and when her father hears of it, he may create a terrible scene. His wife left him almost two years ago, and the old fool's been taking it out on Lorna."

"I can't imagine the law allowing that sort of thing to go on, unpunished," Story said. "You have law in this town."

"Lot Higgins? Amos Flagg is a power in this town, Mr. Story, and on the frontier, might makes right. I fear for Lorna's safety."

"Don't," said Story. "I brought her here, and I'll see that no harm comes to her as a result of it."

"Thank you," Emma said. "I'll be ready if you need me."

"I'll walk you back to your place," said Story. "I'd just returned from Waco when I learned Cal had been shot. I haven't eaten in several days, and I'm a mite hungry. Bill, keep watch here until I find some grub."

The big man from the high plains was a striking figure as he and Emma came down the stairs. Wearing a brace of tied-down Navy Colts, Story stood six and a half feet tall in his riding boots and high-crowned, uncreased sombrero. He wasn't surprised that he had accumulated an audience. After the wounded Cal had been carried into the hotel, Dr. Nagel had come, soon followed by Story and Lorna, eventually by Sheriff Lot Higgins, and finally by Emma Baird. It was even less surprising that some nosy bastard had taken word to Amos Flagg, if only for the hell of it.

The rain had subsided as Story and Emma made their way along the boardwalk. Story paused when they were within a block of the Cattleman's Bank.

"I'll be leaving you here, Emma," Story said. "I have some business at the bank."

"If it's what I'm thinking it is," said Emma, "you should have a witness. Take me with you."

"Come along, then," Story said.

They were barely through the door when Amos Flagg confronted them.

"I have no business with you," Flagg said coldly, "and I want none."

"I have some advice for you," said Story, "and whether you have sense enough to take it or not, you're going to listen."

"So you've dragged my foolish daughter to a hotel room with that no good Cal Snider."

"She's in no danger," Story said. "Cal's been shot."

"He's alive, then. That's too bad," Flagg said cruelly.

"Cal Snider is one of my riders," said Story, "and I'll side my men till hell freezes. Don't let me catch you anywhere close to that hotel room."

"I'm going over there and drag that headstrong little bitch home by the hair of her head," Flagg snarled, "and if you lay a hand on me, I'll have the law on you."

"Wrong," said Story. "If you abuse that girl in any way, I'll have the law on you, and I'm not referring to your pet sheriff. I'll go straight to Captain Clark. There are unwritten laws on the frontier, Flagg, and this one's at the top of the list. You do not mistreat a woman. Now here's the advice I promised you. I don't have to see you abuse that girl, Flagg. If I so much as hear of it, I'll drag you out in that street, and before God and everybody, beat you within an inch of your miserable life. You leave Lorna and Cal alone. That's the best advice you'll ever get, and if you value your skunk-striped hide, you'll take it. That's not a threat, Flagg, but an iron-clad promise."

With that, Story turned and walked out the door, Emma following.

"My God," said Emma admiringly, "I wish the entire town could have heard that. If there's anything I can do . . ."

"There is," Story said. "As long as Cal's laid up, one of my men will be with him or close by. If her father lays a hand on that girl, you get word to one of my cowboys. Whoever's with Cal."

Story left Emma at her shop and found a cafe, where he ordered hot coffee, ham, fried eggs, and potatoes. From there he returned to the hotel, finding Bill Petty hunkered down in the hall, outside Cal's room.

"Bill, I'll be here the rest of today and tonight. Send somebody in to relieve me in the morning. Ride careful, and warn the others. Continue the nighthawking, two riders each watch."

When Petty had gone, Story eased open the door and stepped into Cal's room. Lorna sat near the bed, unmoving.

"I've been to see your father, Lorna, and I don't believe he'll object to your sitting with Cal, but I think you should limit it to the daytime. As long as Cal's here, me or one of my riders will be here. He's going to recover, but he'll need some rest."

"I'll stay with him every day, whether Daddy likes it or not."

"He's not liking it," Story said, "but I think he'll accept it. If he hurts you in any way, go to Emma's place. She'll get word to me."

"Thank you," said Lorna, with a wan smile. "Did you . . . give my message to Cal . . . before . . ."

"Before he was shot? Yes," Story said, "I suggested he ride in and talk to you. He was riding here to do just that, when he was shot."

"Who would have shot Cal, Mr. Story?" Story could see suspicion dawning on her, and she stood up to face him, fire in her eyes. "Do you think he—my daddy—had Cal shot?"

"No, Lorna," said Story. "He doesn't like Cal, but he didn't have anything to do with that. Somebody has a grudge against me, somebody from my past. More than once he's tried to ambush me, and now it seems he's trying to hurt me by gunning down my riders."

"That's terrible. What are you going to do?"

"We're going to set a trap for him," Story said, "once the rain lets up. He's used the storm as cover, and it's been impossible to trail him, because of the mud and high water."

"Mr. Story, when Cal's well, what . . . what do you think he'll do about me?"

"I don't know," said Story. "That'll be up to Cal, but I believe he'll do right by you. Just don't push him. I think you'll be surprised."

Not long after, Bill Petty rode into the canyon, finding the rest of the outfit anxious for news about Cal.

"He'll make it," Petty said. "Nelson aims to keep a man in town, close by, for as long as Cal's there. Every morning, one of us will ride in, stayin' a day and a night. Lorna Flagg's sittin' with Cal now."

"That gal's somethin'," said Arch Rainey. "When old Cal comes out of it, he's gonna think he's died and gone to Heaven."

February 17, 1866. Fort Worth, Texas.

For the first three days after Cal had been shot, Dr. Nagel came twice a day. It was past midnight of the second day when Cal awakened to find Arch Rainey beside him.

"How long," Cal muttered, "have I . . . been here?"

"You're into the third day," said Arch. "You caught a bad one. Your hoss come gallopin' into camp just a few minutes after Mr. Story rode in. It was him, Bill Petty, and Coon Tails that found you and brought you to town. The doc patched you up, and we been dosin' you with laudanum regular, so's you'd sleep. There'll be somebody else from the outfit here to relieve me in the mornin'. Lorna's been with you durin' the daytime, ever' day since you was brought in, and I reckon she'll be back in the mornin'. God, but you're one lucky hombre, and I don't mean just because that slug didn't finish you."

"The bushwhacker, I reckon," said Cal.

"That's what Mr. Story thinks," Arch said, "and he vows we're goin' to nail the bastard. But I can't see how, until this damn rain lets up."

An hour after first light, Hitch Gould rode in to relieve Arch, and within minutes Lorna Flagg arrived.

"I think I'll go out and find me some hot coffee," Hitch said, grinning at the girl. "With old Cal all hogtied in them bandages, I reckon you can handle him." He went out and closed the door. Lorna ignored the chair and sat on the edge of the bed.

"I was ridin' in to see you," said Cal, "and I . . . got delayed . . ."

"I know," Lorna said. "Mr. Story told me. He came to the house and got me. I was here almost by the time the doctor was."

"I'm surprised your daddy ain't up here . . . givin' us both hell," said Cal.

"It's because Mr. Story went by the bank and gave *him* hell. Emma Baird was with him, and she said Mr. Story was magnificent. He stood up for you and for me, and he's keeping a rider in town day and night, as long as you have to stay here. He was here himself, the first day and night after you were shot. I've done some thinking, Cal, and I have two things to say. First, I'm sorry that I embarrassed you that day in front of the bank. I acted like I was twelve years old, and I'll never do that again. It hurts me to say this, because you'll be leaving Texas . . . and me, but I believe you've done the right thing, joining Mr. Story's trail drive. He cares about his riders, Cal, and whatever lies ahead—out there on the high plains—has to be better than what you've had here. . . ."

"Lorna," he said, "I . . . I'm so bound up, I can't move anything but my hands. Please . . . come closer. . . ."

She leaned closer until her eyes were looking into his.

"I'll be leavin' Texas, Lorna, but I won't be leavin' you. It won't be easy on the trail, but I'm takin' you with me."

Cal had expected her first reaction, as a big tear spilled from each of her eyes, but what followed changed his mind about a lot of things. Whatever hazards lay ahead, she seemed the equal of them. The freckled, twelve-year-old girl was gone forever, and in her place was all the woman Cal Snider could handle. Her lips met his in a lingering kiss and Cal forgot everything else . . .

February 18, 1866. On the Brazos.

"It's time I was talking to Cal," Story said. "I'll ride in this morning and relieve Tom. There's one idea I aim to pursue in town, which could lead us to the skunk that gunned down Cal, and Coon Tails, I'll need your help. You can ride back to camp before dark."

"Senor Story," said Manuel Cardenas, "you have had much on your mind, and we have been unable to talk.

We do not wish to become a burden. Shall we stay or go?"

"Sorry, Manuel," Story said. "I've been neglecting you and Curly. All I really need to know is can the two of you ride, rope, and shoot?"

"These things we can do, senor, but we have had only the rifle. We have had no *experiencia* with the *pistola.*"

"There are new Colt revolvers here," said Story. "Each of you take one and begin getting the feel of it. You'll have some time to practice before we take the trail north."

"*Si,*" Cardenas said with a grin. "We will be ready."

Story spent a minute or two with the rest of the riders. Since Cal had been shot, Story had hardly spoken to any of them, and he sought to make up for it. Jasmine McDaniels seemed to have a genuine affection for Sandy Bill, and had been helping him prepare the meals. Bud and some of the other riders had begun helping Oscar Fentress fashion needed holsters and rifle boots from cowhide. Inactivity was getting to them, but they were making the best of it.

"Coon Tails," said Story as they rode toward town, "either we're facing two different bushwhackers, or one that swaps rifles. The slug that killed the mule came from a Sharps .50, while the lead that struck Cal came from a Henry or a Winchester."

"Cal's jist damn lucky the bastard didn't git him with the Sharps," Coon Tails said. "That buffalo slug would of cut him in half. If yer askin' my opinion, they ain't but one bushwhacker. The sneaky varmint's jist switchin' rifles t'throw you off'n the trail."

"That's what I'm thinking," said Story. "You don't see many riders with two saddle guns, and I'm ashamed of myself for not having thought of this sooner. I want you to wander around town, paying particular attention to the saloons, looking at saddled horses. Don't be too obvious. Look for a rifle boot with a Sharps. If you find one, position yourself so that you can see the man who claims that horse."

"Damn good idee," Coon Tails said. "Sooner er later, this hombre's got t'come t'town, if'n only t' wet his whistle."

They split up when they reached town, Story taking his horse to the livery and walking from there to the hotel. He found Tom Allen sitting in the lobby.

"He's in good hands," said Allen. "Lorna's with him, and I got a mite tired hunkerin' in the hall."

"You can ride on back to camp," Story said. "Keep to the open plains as much as possible."

"By the way," said Allen, "the bushwhacker ain't the only danger out there. Yesterday evening, a rider come in from western Palo Pinto County with news of Comanche trouble. Somewhere along the Brazos, a rancher and his two sons was murdered and scalped. The wife hid in the brush and escaped to some neighboring ranch. Captain Clark sent some soldiers to investigate. While we don't want to come off like buzzards preyin' on the unfortunate, you could ask around and see if that rancher has cattle. If there's only the wife left, I wouldn't be surprised if she only wants to get the hell out of there."

"You're right, Tom," Story said. "I'd feel like a scavenger, so soon after the poor woman's lost her family. But I'll keep it in mind. Thanks."

Allen rode out, and Story mounted the steps to the hotel's second floor. His hand on the knob, he was about to enter the room when he thought better of it and knocked. It was Lorna who eventually answered, and Story entered. She sat demurely on the chair beside the bed, but Story suspected she hadn't been there when he'd knocked. Her face was flushed, and Cal looked anything but innocent.

"Well," said Story, grinning at the young rider, "besides having been shot, how do you feel?"

"I ain't sure," Cal said, "until I've talked to you. How do *you* feel about havin' a woman on the trail drive?"

"I just hired Jasmine McDaniels as a rider," said Story.

"I thought about what you told me," Cal said, "and I'm taking Lorna with me. We aim to settle in Montana Territory."

"Glad to hear it, Cal. It'll be a hard trail, Lorna, but I believe you can conquer it. If you can ride and throw a loop, I'll put you to herdin' cows and pay you like a cowboy."

Lorna had been listening, wide-eyed, and when she moved, it took Story by surprise. She sprang out of the chair, grabbed him around the neck and kissed him. This time it was Story who was embarrassed. He went red, and Cal laughed. When Dr. Nagel came in, his answer to Story's inquiry was optimistic.

"Give him another week," the doctor said, "and he can get up. But no hard riding, roping, or brawling."

To Story's surprise, he found Coon Tails waiting for him on the boardwalk outside the hotel. For the second day in a row there was no rain.

"By God," Coon Tails said, "the third saloon I goes to, I sees this bay hoss tied outside, an' they was a Sharps in the saddle boot. Reg'lar boot, it was, an' the muzzle of the buffalo gun was stuck out a foot."

"You followed the man who claimed the horse?"

"Shore did," Coon Tails said. "He took a quart o' rotgut with 'im, an' I follered the varmint t' a hotel called the Hondo, over yonder beyon' that unfinished courthouse buildin'. Hoss he's ridin' is got a pitchfork brand on the left flank, an' he ain't ridin' a cowboy saddle. Single rig. I'd reckon he's about t'pile up fer a day o' serious drinkin', so we ain't gonna lose the varmint."

"Now tell me something about the man," said Story.

"Mebbe six feet, black hair down t' his collar, an' a faceful o' whiskers. Wearin' what looked like wool britches, an' a mackinaw coat kinda like yours. Pistol on the right side, tied down, butt t' the front, an' a flat crown hat with a chin strap. Boots wasn't fancy. No spurs."

"*Bueno,*" Story said. "You didn't miss a thing. We have a suspect, but no proof. We'll have to trail him until he makes some hostile move."

"You want me t'stay on his tail, then, I reckon."

"No," said Story, "I want you to ride back to camp and get Bill Petty, and the three of us will take turns watching that hotel. This man's no short horn. He sees the same hombre there all the time, he'll know we're on to him. Tell Tom Allen he's the segundo until I say different, and he's to continue sending in a rider every day, as long as Cal's laid up in the hotel. Tell him that he's not to count on you, Bill Petty, or me, until we resolve this situation with the suspected bushwhacker. I'll watch the hotel until you return with Petty. Where did this gent leave his horse?"

"Kind of barn behin' the hotel," Coon Tails said. "Ain't a livery. You got t'stable an' feed yer own hoss."

"Ride, then," said Story, "and when you and Bill return, I'll be watching that hotel, but don't join me there. I'll be watching for you. Just ride past, so I'll know you're here, and we'll meet here at the Fort Worth House. From then on, one of us will be watching for that hombre's next move."

Coon Tails rode out and Story got his own horse from the livery. Careful not to take a direct route to the Hondo, he followed side streets until he was in a narrow alley that ran behind the place. Concealing the horse was most important. A man being watched would notice a horse as quick or quicker than a man, especially if the horse stayed in one place too long, or was seen there too often. The animal must remain saddled in case the suspected bushwhacker rode out unexpectedly. Story found an abandoned building across the alley from the rear of the hotel, and picketed the animal where it could graze without being seen unless somebody went looking for it. The old hotel where the suspect was holed up was single story and there was a back door, allowing easy access to the barn where the hotel's occupants left their horses. A western man seldom walked anywhere, except to the outhouse, and since Story couldn't watch both the front and back doors, he chose the back. The barn had wide double doors at each end, so that a hay wagon might be driven in and hay pitched to the loft.

Careful that he wasn't being observed, Story entered the barn, found the ladder to the loft, and climbed up there. From his lofty perch he could see the back door of the hotel and the narrow street that ran in front of it, so he would know when Coon Tails and Bill Petty had returned. If he was discovered, he could always pretend he'd had a snootful at one of the saloons and was sleeping it off. If they were forced to watch the hotel for more than a day or two, the loft would prove a welcome shelter, for already a new herd of thunderheads were gathering to the west.

A little more than two hours after Coon Tails had ridden out, he and Bill Petty rode past the hotel. Story waited until they were well out of sight before climbing down from the loft and seeking his horse. By the time he reached the Fort Worth House, Coon Tails and Petty were waiting for him.

"I've been in the hayloft of the barn behind the hotel," Story said, "and it's a good observation point. Nobody left the hotel, at least not by the back door. While you can't see the front door, you can see the street. Not many hombres will walk if they can ride, and the horses are all in the barn behind the hotel. This is going to be almighty boring, especially if it lasts more than a day or two, and that's why three of us are going to devote all our time to it. We'll take it in six-hour watches. You're on for six hours, and off twelve. If this suspected bushwhacker rides out, don't try to trail him alone. Notice the direction he's riding, and the three of us will trail him. We'll take another room here, on the first floor, so that when you're not on watch, you'll have a place to sleep. Bill, you can take the first turn, and one of us will relieve you at six o'clock this evening. Just be sure to leave your horse where it can't be seen from the hotel, and if this hombre rides out, you shag it back here and let us know."

So began what Nelson Story hoped was a showdown with the bushwhacker. He took another hotel room at the Fort Worth House, and leaving Coon Tails there, returned to the room occupied by Cal. Quanah Taylor sat outside the door on a three-legged stool.

"Kind of crowded in there, I reckon," said Story.

"Yes, sir," Taylor grinned, "and I wouldn't wanta get in the way. She's some woman, and Cal Snider's the luckiest son that ever forked a hoss."

9

February 19, 1866. Fort Worth, Texas.

Late that afternoon, Captain Clark's detachment of soldiers rode in, bringing with them the lone survivor of the Comanche attack in Palo Pinto County. The distraught woman was led into the lobby of the hotel, and Story spoke to a grizzled old-timer who had ridden in with the soldiers.

"Anything I can do to help?"

"I reckon not. I'm Whit McCulloch, an' it was my place she come to fer help. She run nearly ten mile, an' time me an' my boys got to her place, wasn't nothin' left but ashes an' dead bodies. We buried her dead. My missus wanted me to ride in with her, so's she wouldn't be amongst strangers. We're puttin' her up here for a few days, hopin' she'll git to herself. She just wants to go back East, to her family, an' she'll need money. Nothin' left but their stock, an' we need to know what she wants done."

"I'm registered here at the hotel," Story said, "and I'm buying cattle and horses. When she's able to talk about it, if she wants to sell, I'll buy the stock. My name is Nelson Story. Will you be here awhile?"

"At least till she's able to talk fer herself, an' can settle her affairs enough to git home to her family. She's got a right smart of a herd, and they was some hosses, but the Comanches took 'em."

"I have Room Six on the first floor," said Story. "If I'm not there, one of my riders will be."

At half past five Story sent Coon Tails to relieve Bill Petty. Story would take the watch from midnight to dawn. No sooner had Petty reached the Fort Worth House, when the storm that had been building since early morning broke. It roared out of the northwest, the wind-driven rain beating against the windows, turning the already muddy streets into an all too familiar quagmire.

"Thank God for that hayloft," Petty said. "If that's our bushwhacker, I doubt he'll be ridin' in this kind of weather."

"We can't count on that," said Story. "It was just about this kind of day when he plugged my hat and grazed my mule, and not much better the day he ambushed Cal. But in a way, it's good that he prefers this kind of weather, because it'll limit him to daylight. In the rain, he couldn't see his hand in front of his face at night."

"Hey," Petty said, "when you think about it, he's followin' a kind of pattern. It wasn't raining that mornin' he killed the mule, but it was just a little past first light. That's about the same time of day he shot Cal. That means he could be ridin' out just before or just after first light."

"That's sharp thinkin', Bill. I'll be watching mighty close that last hour or two before first light, and you'll have to do the same thing, when you take my place in the morning."

The rain had slacked to a drizzle when Story climbed up the ladder to the hayloft.

"Wasn't completely sure that was you," said Coon

Tails, easing down the hammer on his Colt. "Ain't been nobody in er outta that back door, 'cept t'visit the outhouse. Might be a good idee t'git outta this loft an' hide somewheres else b'fore first light. They's six hosses down there, an' somebody's got t'fork down some hay fer 'em."

"I've thought of that," Story said, "and you can always climb out on the roof if you have to disappear in a hurry. There's a wide overhang."

Story made himself comfortable in the hay, preparing for a long six hours, thinking of what Bill Petty had said. It made sense, and combining that with Coon Tails's admonition not to get caught in the loft by owners of the horses coming to feed them, Story decided to leave the loft while it was still dark. There were other points from which he could observe, although he couldn't remain there for long. Besides, if the suspected bushwhacker rode away, minutes would count, and Story knew he could reach his horse much quicker if he wasn't trapped in the barn.

Well before first light Story climbed down the ladder and stood just inside the barn doors, facing the back door of the hotel. Suddenly the door opened and a man stepped out. In the predawn darkness there was only the dim light from the lamp inside the hotel's back door, and that was soon closed. There had been only seconds for Story to glimpse the bearded face, the flat-crowned hat, but his sharp eyes had caught something far more important. Under the man's arm there had been a long canvas-wrapped parcel that almost had to be a rifle. Story hurried to the other end of the barn, and dark as it was, hid himself in an empty stall. He held his breath, fearful that Bill Petty might arrive and enter the barn, unaware that the suspected bushwhacker was preparing to leave. Story heard the unmistakable sound of the man saddling his horse, and finally the creak of the barn doors as the animal was led out into the alley. Story crept through the doors at his end of the barn and ran for his horse. Leading it, he reached the alley in time to see the man ride past a lighted window that bled a little light into the rainy darkness.

"Nels!"

Despite the use of his name, there was a cocked Colt in his hand when Story turned to face Petty.

"I got to the barn in time to see you leave it," said Petty.

"He's ridin' out," Story said. "Come on. Soon as we know what direction, you ride back and get Coon Tails. I'll keep him in sight."

They rode past the unfinished courthouse, past the Masonic hall, and when the pursued man reached the next cross street, he rode south.

"Get Coon Tails and come on," Story said. "I think this is our man."

The rider seemed in no hurry, so Petty and Coon Tails soon caught up.

"The two of you continue following him at a distance," said Story. "He seems to be following the west bank of the Brazos, but I believe somewhere between here and our camp, he'll cross. I aim to cross to the east bank and get ahead of him, so that when he finally takes his position, we can maybe catch him in a cross fire."

"Wisht we knowed if he's aimin' t' use that Sharps," Coon Tails said. "He can cut us down 'fore we git close enough t' even touch him."

"Maybe not," said Story. "The rain's getting harder, and he can't hit what he can't see. I'll be somewhere ahead of him, and he won't be expecting that."

Story found a point on the Brazos where he was able to swim his horse across, and reaching the east bank, set out at a fast gallop. He had no fear that the man they pursued could see him from the west bank. However, he kept half a mile distant from the river. Looking toward the Brazos, he could see nothing, but the wind was from the northwest. Eventually he caught the faint odor of wood smoke and realized he was past their camp on the west bank. He reined up, seeking cover. While the suspected bushwhacker might not see him, Story thought, he might spot the horse. The banks were far above the river, stony, and there was little vegetation. Story had to leave his horse well away from the east bank. Carrying his Henry, he walked close enough to see the west bank of the chasm. There were deep gullies that emptied into the Brazos, where the poor soil had eroded down to bare rock. Story found one deep enough to hide him from an adversary approaching from the north. There was water in the bottom, runoff from the rain rushing toward the Brazos, but Story was unmindful of it. He hunkered down, waiting.

Meanwhile, Coon Tails was saying, "We're so far behind, we can't even see the varmint."

"Best leave it that way," Petty replied. "We get close enough to see him, he can see us. He could always just ride on, and we couldn't prove he was up to no good."

"We'll play hell catchin' him in a cross fire," Coon Tails said, "with him an' Story on t'other bank, an' us over here. Mebbe we oughta cross."

"No," said Petty. "Nels could be wrong. If we cross over there, and this hombre don't, we could lose him. We'll have to depend on Story to catch him at whatever he aims to do."

Story waited, counting on the bushwhacker to take his position somewhere along the east rim before he reached the gully in which he was hiding. If the man rode beyond where he was hiding, Story knew he would be discovered and all would be lost. Story could see a stone parapet along the lip of the canyon. Not only would it provide excellent cover, the stone would offer a convenient rest for the heavy Sharps.

Even with the rain, the ground was flint-hard in places, and Story heard the horse before he could see either horse or rider. The horse slowed before reaching Story's place of concealment, and Story sighed with relief. Taking off his hat, he eased up enough to see. The rider had dismounted and was removing the canvas from the rifle. Indeed it appeared to be the deadly Sharps. He hunkered down behind the upthrust stone, resting the heavy weapon in one position and then another. Finally he found one he liked, the Sharps angled almost vertical, and Story knew who he was gunning for. It had to be one of the cowboys who had been nighthawking, keeping the herd in the canyon. Story climbed out of the gully and was halfway to the bushwhacker when his horse nickered nervously.

"Freeze," Story said. "You're covered."

But that wasn't the killer's way. Unsurpassed for long range killing, the Sharps was heavy and unwieldy up close. It went clattering down the wall of the canyon as the bushwhacker went for his Colt. Story drew his own right-hand Colt and fired twice, the lead slamming into the man just above his belt buckle. He lost his grip on the Colt and lay back, blood soaking the front of his denim shirt. Story holstered his Colt and stood looking down at the dying man.

"Who are you?" Story asked, "and what have you against me?"

"Alder Gulch, you bastard. You didn't get . . . us . . . all."

It was his last words. Story left him there, taking his horse, then recovering his own. He rode downriver until he found a place shallow enough to cross. Troubled, he pondered the dying man's words. "You didn't get us all." Did that mean there were others, that this menace might continue to stalk him and his outfit on the long trail north? When Story reached the west bank, he found Coon Tails and Bill Petty waiting for him. They had heard the shots and Story led the other man's horse, so there were no questions. They rode into the canyon, leaving their horses beside the river and climbing up to the camp beneath the overhang. The rest of the outfit had heard the distant shots and were anxiously awaiting some explanation.

"We caught the bushwhacker in the act," Story told them. "He's dead."

Their relief was such that Story didn't diminish it by telling them of the dying man's words and his own doubts. This might be the end of it, but he couldn't be sure. There might be other killers awaiting him, vengeful men who had escaped the rope on that day of reckoning in Alder Gulch. . . .

Story had breakfast with his outfit and then rode back to Fort Worth. He believed Cal would be recovered enough to take the trail by March first, but they still lacked a substantial part of their herd. Story had a room at the hotel, and he hadn't forgotten the unfortunate woman whose entire family had been murdered by Comanches. If she had stock to sell, then he certainly wouldn't be out of line in bidding for it. Gus Odell had ridden in to take Quanah Taylor's place outside Cal's room, and Story met Quanah riding back to camp.

"Heard you nailed the varmint that shot Cal," Taylor said. *"Bueno."*

"Cal's still on the mend, I reckon," said Story.

"I reckon," Quanah said. "He's rarin' to get up and back to camp."

Story rode on to town, and when he reached the Fort Worth House, he asked about Whit McCulloch.

"He's still here," said the desk clerk. "Room Eight, first floor."

Story knocked on the door and McCulloch opened it.

"I just rode in from my cow camp," said Story. "Have you had breakfast?"

"No," McCulloch said. "I was about to ask the Missus

Hamby if she would join me. We ain't talked yet, an' we need to. I don't care fer this town livin'."

"Why don't you go talk to her, then," said Story. "If she's willing, then I'll buy your breakfast and hers."

Story waited in the lobby until McCulloch returned. With him was a pale, gray-haired woman with lifeless eyes, who probably wasn't as old as she looked.

"Ellie, this is Nelson Story. He knows about your misfortune. He's invitin' us to breakfast."

"Mrs. Hamby, I'm sorry," said Story. "I wish there was something I could do."

"Thank you," she said, her voice breaking, "but there ain't nothin' nobody can do."

Story led them to a cafe, allowed them to order breakfast, and he then ordered coffee for himself. Ellie Hamby only picked at her food. Story felt sorry for her, and was about to suggest they go back to the hotel, when Whit McCulloch spoke.

"Ellie, Mr. Story buys cows, an' if you're up to it, he'd like to maybe talk to you about buyin' your herd."

"Oh, Lord," Ellie cried, "I don't know what to do. All I know is, I don't never want to go back to that awful place. Never!"

"I've talked to Cap'n Clark," said McCulloch, "and the army will see that you get to New Orleans. From there you can take a boat back East, but you'll need money. Why don't you go ahead an' sell the cows to Mr. Story, so's you can go home?"

"Whit, they'll be scattered God knows where, and I don't even know how many they was."

"Ellie," said Story kindly, "do you recall how many head you had at the last tally?"

"Eight hundred, I think," Ellie said.

"I'll pay you for eight hundred head," said Story, "and however scattered they are, we'll round them up. Are they branded?"

"Yes," said Ellie, "they're Boxed H. But that wouldn't

be fair to you. The Injuns may of took some of 'em. Maybe all of 'em."

"Ellie," Story said, "I have an outfit of Texas cowboys. If you'll sell those cows to me, I promise you we'll find them. We're needing horses too."

"We had nine good cow horses," said Ellie. "They was branded Boxed H too."

"Injuns got the hosses," Whit said. "We trailed 'em a ways, but they was too many of 'em."

"Ellie," said Story, "I'll pay you fifty dollars apiece for those horses, whether we recover them or not."

"Ed and my boys gentled them horses," Ellie said, "and it hurts me just knowin' they're bein' rode by them murderin' Injuns. I'll sell you the cows, Mr. Story, but I ain't takin' no money for the horses. If you can take 'em, they're yours, and I hope you kill the murderin' devils that stole 'em. It'll comfort me, just knowin' that Texas cowboys will be ridin' our horses, 'stead of them damn Comanches."

"Story," said McCulloch, "if you'll ride out an' git your boys together, you can ride back t' Palo Pinto with me. While you're gone, I'll help Ellie write you a bill of sale for the cows."

Story saw them back to the hotel. Despite her loss, Ellie Hamby smiled at him as he took his leave. Just the possibility that the Comanches might be made to pay for what they had done had lifted her spirits more than the sale of the cattle, Story thought. When he reached the camp, he found that Wes Hardin's outfit was there, with ten more cows.

"We decided to give you a chance," Hardin said arrogantly. "We'll sign on for your trail drive."

"Thanks." Story grinned. "The Indian too?"

"I said we'd sign on," Hardin growled, "and that means all of us."

"Good," said Story. "You couldn't have come at a better time. I've just bought a herd in Palo Pinto that may have been run off by the Comanches. If that's the case, there may be some Indian fighting. We'll ride in half an hour."

Story thought Hardin, Greener, and Slim received that information with mixed emotions, but when he looked at Quickenpaugh, the Indian laughed. Story then went about choosing the others who would ride with him.

"Some of you must remain here in camp," Story said. "You'll need nighthawks for the cattle here in the canyon, and for another three or four days we'll need a rider outside Cal's door. Jasmine, Bud will ride with me, but I want you here in camp. Shanghai, I want you, Smokey, and Oscar here. Manuel, you and Curly will remain here, and so will Arch and Hitch. I don't know how long we'll be gone. I'm figuring at least ten days, with the time it'll take to return with the herd."

There were groans of disappointment from those being left behind. When Story again rode out, he had with him Wes Hardin, Slim, Greener, Quickenpaugh, Tom Allen, Bill Petty, Bud McDaniels, Quanah Taylor, Virg Wooler, Dutch Mayfield, Jules Dyer, and Coon Tails. Each man carried a rifle, a Colt revolver, and ammunition for both. Tom Allen and Bill Petty led mules bearing packsaddles. They would be loaded with provisions in town. Whit McCulloch was waiting, and he had Story's bill of sale. The rain had ceased, the clouds had broken up, and a meek sun was making occasional appearances. It was almost noon.

"How many miles ahead of us?" Story asked.

"Mebbe fifty," said McCulloch. "We set out now, we can make it 'fore dark."

"Two of my riders are at the mercantile getting provisions," Story said. "When that's done, we can ride."

While they were waiting, Cal Snider stepped out on the hotel porch, with Gus Odell and Lorna following.

"He was threatening to get up and come down here

jaybird naked," Lorna said, "if I didn't fetch his clothes and boots."

"Well, hell," said Cal, "I ain't ridin' *with* the outfit. I just come down to see 'em off. If I wasn't able to be up, I wouldn't be."

"The doctor thought you needed more time," Story said, "and I'll let you argue that with him. At least stay here until he dismisses you. By then, I think we'll have the rest of the herd, and we'll be ready for the trail."

Allen and Petty arrived with the loaded pack mules, but before they were able to ride out, a Union soldier rode up.

"Mr. Story, Captain Clark wants to talk to you."

"Damn it," said Story, "we're ready to ride. I don't suppose it can wait until I return?"

"No, sir," the soldier said.

"Stand fast," Story told the outfit. He rode out, following the soldier, and when they reached Captain Clark's tent, the officer was standing before it, waiting. The soldier saluted.

"At ease, soldier," said the officer. He then turned to Story, who hadn't dismounted. Clark didn't mince words.

"When you arrived here, Story, I believe I told you I wasn't opposed to your hiring Texans, as long as they signed papers promising no further conflict with the Union. That, of course, is to allow them to legally bear arms. Now I am told you have a veritable army of men here in town, armed to the teeth. Nobody has signed the required papers. Until they do, every Texan bearing arms is in violation of the law and subject to arrest."

"We were about to ride out for two weeks," said Story. "I suppose it would be foolish of me to suggest you delay this until we return."

"It would," said Clark.

"I'll get them, then," Story said, striving to hold his temper. "Are you prepared to witness their signatures?"

"I am," said Clark.

Without another word Story rode back to the hotel and spoke to his riders.

"Captain Clark insists that all of you who are Texans sign papers agreeing not to take up arms against the Union. Otherwise, your being armed puts you in violation of the law and subject to arrest. Clark's waiting to witness your signatures. It shouldn't take more than a few minutes."

"Hell," said Wes Hardin angrily, "some of us ain't fought again' the damn Union."

"No matter," said Story. "This is not the time or the place to argue the point. Sign, and let's be done with this foolishness."

"The Injun can't write," Greener said.

"He can make his mark," said Story, "and Clark can witness it. Cal, that includes you and Gus. Let's go."

"I have a gun," Lorna said, "and I'm going with you on the drive."

"Let it wait," said Story. "You might unleash a whole new bunch of Federal dogs we don't know about."

When they reached Captain Clark's tent, he had set up a folding table and chair, with inkwell and quill. Cal signed first, followed by Quanah Taylor, Gus Odell, Virg Wooler, Dutch Mayfield, and Jules Dyer. Wes Hardin, Greener, and Slim signed, leaving Quickenpaugh for the last. Story grinned at the expression on Clark's face when he saw the Indian. It was a paradox, with Comanches having murdered three people in less than a week, while this lone Indian was signing papers to legally bear arms. The significance of it wasn't lost on Quickenpaugh. When he had made his mark and Clark had witnessed it, the Indian's obsidian eyes met those of the military man, and Quickenpaugh had a question.

"Quickenpaugh make mark. Quickenpaugh no kill. Other Comanch' no make mark, kill dead lak hell. Why you no take gun?"

It was an unanswerable, impossible question. Captain Clark's face flamed red with anger, embarrassment, or a combination of the two. Then the Indian added insult to injury. Quickenpaugh laughed, but not as uproariously as the cowboys. Clark looked as though he'd not be satisfied with anything less than seeing the lot of them before a firing squad. Story quickly intervened.

"If that's satisfactory, Captain, we should be going."

"That will be satisfactory," said the officer, striving to recover some dignity. Story rode out, his riders following.

When they reached the rest of the outfit, Cal wasted no time in telling them of Quickenpaugh's quick wit, and the Indian received some admiring looks. It was an enigma Story had never encountered, a Comanche with a sense of humor. As they rode, Whit McCulloch told them something about the country where they would be gathering the Hanby herd.

"It's in northwestern Palo Pinto," McCulloch said, "where they's so many crooks an' turns, the Brazos nearly meets itself a dozen times. When they's lots of rain, like we been havin', they's backwater fer miles. For some reason nobody's ever figgered out, that place is overrun with possums."*

"Sounds like the ideal place to lose a herd of cows," said Story.

"It is," McCulloch said. "Ed Hanby was a mite strange in his thinkin', an' I reckon he had plans fer that herd, but it never made no sense to me. Only thing I can figger, it would of been a hell of a job rustlin' Ed's cows. You'd have to round 'em up first. He did have some

---

* Today, as a result of the Morris Sheppard Dam, there is a twenty-thousand-acre lake with a shoreline of 310 miles, spreading into Palo Pinto, Stephens, Jack, and Young counties, furnishing water for municipal supply, irrigation, and power generation. It is known as Possum Kingdom Lake.

good cow hosses, though. Damn shame the Comanches got 'em."

"You said you trailed those Comanches a ways," said Story. "When they rode out, which way did they go?"

"North," McCulloch said. "Across the Brazos, into Jack County. Ain't more'n seventy mile to the Red. I hear that when things gits a mite hot fer 'em in Texas, they scat across the Red, into Injun Territory."

"It wouldn't be easy trailing them, then," said Story, "as much rain as we've had."

"I dunno," McCulloch said. "Even with all the rain an' mud, you got fifty an' more hosses headin' the same way, there'll be plenty of sign. That wasn't the problem. Like I said, they was a good fifty Comanches, while there was jus' me an' three other hombres."

"Captain Clark sent eight soldiers and a sergeant," said Story. "When they arrived, what did they do?"

"No more'n we did," McCulloch replied. "Hell, not even as much. We buried the dead. When them blue bellies seen how many Injuns they was, them Union boys lit a shuck back the way they'd come, takin' me an' Ellie Hanby with 'em. Few soldiers here an' a few there, ain't enough of 'em in one place to scare even one Comanche, let alone fifty of 'em."

That was about the size of it, Story thought, recalling his very recent experience with Captain Clark. The army seemed more intent on harassing Texans than pursuing Comanches. Story became aware that Wes Hardin was riding behind him and had been listening to his conversation with McCulloch regarding the Comanches.

"You find the need to trail some Comanches," said Hardin, "Quickenpaugh can foller 'em across solid rock, through water, or into Injun Territory."

"I'll keep that in mind," Story said, "if he's willing."

"He's Comanche enough, he ain't scared of nothin' or nobody," said Hardin, "but he ain't Comanche enough to side with the varmints. Way you whip Comanches,

Cap'n, is track 'em down and shoot the bastards dead 'fore they knows you're close by."

Story was forced to take another look at Wes Hardin. Young, arrogant to a fault, but in some ways older than the ages. Fearless young hellion that he was, Story suspected that John Wesley Hardin would end up in trouble with the law, to be hanged, unless somebody shot him first.*

* By the time John Wesley Hardin was seventeen, he had killed seven men. In 1895, in El Paso, he was shot in the back of the head by Constable John Selman. At the time of his death, Hardin had more than thirty notches on the butt of his gun.

10

As Whit McCulloch had predicted, they reached his place before dark, making their camp beyond his barn, near a creek.

"In the mornin'," said McCulloch, "I'll ride with you to the Hanby place."

"The old varmint could of invited us to supper," Wes Hardin said when McCulloch had ridden on to the house.

"You lean almighty heavy on a man's hospitality," said Quanah Taylor. "There's thirteen of us, includin' a Comanche."

"I don't take kindly to nobody criticizin' my manners," Hardin said, with a wolfish grin that held no humor.

"That's enough," Story interrupted. "We have our own grub, and there's plenty of tinned goods. You want anything fancy, somethin' that needs cooking, then it's every man for himself. Bill Petty's boilin' the coffee."

February 21, 1866. Palo Pinto County, Texas.

After a hasty breakfast, Story and his outfit rode north, following Whit McCulloch to the Hanby place. The house and outbuildings had been burned to the ground. Nothing remained standing except the forlorn chimney and a few poles from the corral that had adjoined the barn.

"We buried 'em down there below the barn," said McCulloch. "We're mebbe three miles south of the Brazos. All kinds of brush has growed up in them bends, an' that's where you'll likely find most of the Hanby herd. Over yonder to the west of where the house stood, you can see where them Comanches rode out to the north. Now if you got no more need for me, I'll be ridin' on to the house."

"We're obliged to you," Story said. When McCulloch had ridden away, Story found Quickenpaugh riding along the trail left by the departing Comanches. He trotted his horse, catching up to the Indian.

"Them leave sign like *estupido* squaws. You want Quickenpaugh find?"

"Si," Story said. "Find." Story pointed to one of the pack mules. "Take grub, shells."

Tom Allen and Bill Petty had heard the conversation, and began unloading the pack mules.

"You want I should ride along with the Injun?" Coon Tails asked.

"No," said Story, "I think he'd take offense at that. This leaves twelve of us, and that works out in teams of two, for the gather. When Quickenpaugh takes what he needs, we'll cache our provisions, picket the mules, and head for the Brazos."

When Quickenpaugh rode north, the rest of the outfit rode northwest.

"I ain't never seen no Injun like this Quickenpaugh," Coon Tails said. "The sign he's follerin' is might' nigh a week old. You really think he kin find them Comanche?"

"He thinks he can," said Story, "and that can make all the difference. Whether he does or not, I think he finds the hunt more appealing than roping cows out of the brush."

"If these brutes have been in the brakes too long, we'll need a holding pen," Tom Allen said. "Unless we can find a blind canyon, that'll take some work."

"I can't see them being all that wild," said Story. "Ellie Hanby said they're branded, but we'll have to rope a few and see what happens."

The first half-dozen longhorns proved to be two-year-olds, and to everybody's surprise, they could be driven. It was a revelation that excited them all, for instead of a week of roping wild, unruly animals, they might finish the gather in a day or two. It might also eliminate the need for holding pens, saving them time and much hard work.

"Forget about roping them," Story said, "unless there's some wild ones in the bunch. We'll push them across that rise and try to hold them on the graze beyond."

The first hundred longhorns they drove out of the brakes were two-year-olds, mostly steers, and to Story's satisfaction, they settled down on the grassy swale to which they'd been driven.

"Now if we can just get the rest of 'em out of there," said Tom Allen, "we'll have ourselves a herd."

Elated with their good fortune, they rode the brakes continuously until darkness was almost upon them.

"Tom, you and Bill ride back and get the mules and provisions. Quanah, you and Bud ride along with them. The rest of us will stay here with the herd until you return."

"They ain't no water closer'n the river," Coon Tails observed.

"No matter," said Story. "We have the start of a herd here, and we'll stay with it. Tomorrow, after we've gathered more cows, we'll move nearer the river."

When Tom, Bill, Quanah, and Bud returned, Quickenpaugh was with them. The Indian looked at Story and shook his head.

"Sobre rojo agua," said Quickenpaugh.*

"He lost 'em," Coon Tails said. "They've crossed the Red, into the damn Injun Territory."

"No lose," protested Quickenpaugh. "Them go many suns." He pointed to the east.

"You were right to turn back, Quickenpaugh," Story said. "Since they've crossed the Red and are riding eastward, they're too far ahead of us. We'll finish this gather and start the drive back to our camp on the Brazos."

By the end of the second day, according to Story's tally, they had 475 longhorns.

"Steers, two-year-olds and up, are runnin' almost fifty-fifty," Bill Petty said, "and if I'm any judge, there'll be a pretty good calf crop too."

"Don't need no calves," said Coon Tails. "They'll slow down the drive."

"No matter," Story said. "If need be, we'll slow the drive. I don't aim to lose a one, if it can be helped. Calves grow into cows, and that's what I'm after."

At noon of the third day, Story again took a tally, counting 810 head.

"There may be a thousand of 'em in there," said Bud McDaniels.

"I already have more than I paid for," Story said. "We'll give it the rest of the day, then tomorrow at first light take what we have and go."

The rest of that day, their combined efforts accounted for only fifteen more longhorns. The gather was finished.

---

* Over red water

* * *

February 24, 1866. Palo Pinto County, Texas.

"Our camp bein' on the Brazos," Coon Tails said, "we could just foller the river, if it wasn't so damn crooked."

"At least we don't have to go back through Fort Worth," Bill Petty said.

"We should be able to travel southeast," said Story, "cutting the distance to maybe thirty-five miles. We don't have to follow every crook and turn of the river, but we'll stay close enough to it to water the herd."

The longhorns were well grazed and watered, so there were few bunch quitters. While the sky was overcast and they saw little of the sun, there was no more rain. Story estimated they covered at least fifteen miles that first day.

"These cows ain't no trouble at all," said Virg Wooler. "I thought we was bringin' back a bunch of wild varmints."

"None of us knew what we were buying into," Story said. "This Ed Hanby didn't talk much to his neighbors. I think he aimed to take this herd to market himself, and protected it by having everybody think the cows were wild."

"I think you're right," said Tom Allen.

As Story and the outfit began their drive back to their cow camp on the Brazos, Cal Snider had the same destination in mind. While he had the doctor's permission to go, he was having trouble leaving Lorna behind.

"If I'm going to live with cowboys on the trail," the girl said stubbornly, "why can't I go and live with them now?"

"Because I ain't wantin' to antagonize your daddy until we have to," Cal said. "You settin' by my bed in this hotel is one thing, while you movin' out to the cow camp is somethin' else. Once we move 'em out, we'll be across the Red in maybe five or six days. The more trouble it is to bring you back, the less likely he is to try it. Can't you understand that?"

"I understand," said Lorna. "I just want to be with you, damn it."

"Then you're going to do it my way," Cal said. "Now you listen to me. When I need to get a message to you, I'll leave it with Emma Baird. Every day or so, you talk to Emma, and be decidin' what you want to take with you. Go with what you can tie behind your saddle or what will fit into saddlebags. When it's ready, bundle it up and sneak it over to Emma's. The morning the herd takes the trail, I'll leave my horse behind Emma's place and send her for you. Does your daddy own the horse you ride, or is he yours?"

"Prince is mine," said Lorna. "Mama bought him for me, and I have the bill of sale."

"Good," Cal said. He held out his arms, and when she came to him, he found himself hating to leave as much as she hated having him go. . . .

February 27, 1866. On the Brazos.

When Story and his riders reached their camp, they found not only Cal Snider there, but Russ Shadley and Mac Withers. The pair of down-at-the-heels cowboys had brought ten more cows. Story paid them, then took out his notebook and a pencil and did some figuring.

"Three thousand, seven hundred and fifteen head," Story said. "That's more than we figured on, but we'll lose some. We've done well, amigos, and unless I'm overlooking something we've left undone, we should be able to take the trail at first light tomorrow."

"One more thing needs doin'," said Cal, "if you aim to keep these Yankee blue bellies at bay until we get out of Texas. Way I figger it, there's still eight of us that ain't signed them damn papers that Cap'n Clark thinks is so almighty important. There's Sandy Bill, Russ, Mac, Smokey, Oscar, Shanghai, Manuel, and Curly. Jasmine's the ninth, I reckon, if you think Cap'n Clark's that much of a fussbudget."

"I haven't the slightest doubt that he is," Story said. "We'll be going almost through Fort Worth on our way north. I'd planned to stop there long enough for Sandy Bill to load the wagon with provisions. While that's being done, those of you who haven't signed Clark's papers can ride over to his tent and sign them."

"I'm claiming two hundred head of this herd," said Bill Petty. "Here's my money."

"And mine," Tom Allen said. "I'm paying for two hundred head."

"Somebody can't count worth a damn," said Wes Hardin. "They's more'n any thirty-seven hunnert cows in this canyon."

"Four thousand and fifteen," Story said. "Three hundred of them I haven't counted, because they belong to Shanghai Wolfington."

Shanghai looked uncomfortable, while Hardin looked as though he had more to say on the subject, but something in Nelson Story's eyes changed his mind.

February 28, 1866. The start of the long trail north.

Arch and Hitch led the mules upriver, harnessed them to the wagon and brought it along the west bank, near their camp. The canvas had been removed to make loading easier, and with every rider pitching in, it took but a few minutes to load the wagon.

"Sandy Bill," said Story, "take the wagon and go on to the mercantile. I'll meet you there and pay for the provisions. Get plenty of everything. We don't know what conditions or prices will be farther north. Cal, I want you riding point. We'll swap the other positions around, so nobody's stuck with riding drag every day. If the ground ever dries out, there'll be an almighty lot of dust."

The graze had worn thin in the canyon along the Brazos, and the cowboys had no trouble getting the herd moving. By Story's figures, they had only ninety head of longhorns—those bought from Wes Hardin, Russ Shadley, and Mac Withers—that could be considered wild. The wild ones, being a minority, would eventually be forced to accept the idea they were part of a herd. The whole bunch could have been wild as Texas jacks, Story reflected, and so he was satisfied. Story rode ahead, catching up to Cal at the point position.

"I reckon you had enough time in town to make some plans with Lorna," Story said. "So far, we've complied with all Captain Clark's demands. I'd hate to be arrested for kidnapping before we can cross the Red."

"You know Lorna's daddy," Cal said with a grin, "so I can't promise you that. I'm leavin' my horse behind Emma's place, and sending her to bring Lorna. Unless the old buzzard gets suspicious, with the herd passing so close to town, we'll have the rest of the day before he misses her."

Story halted the herd a mile west of Fort Worth. Those riders who had yet to sign papers were accompanied by Story to Captain Clark's tent. The captain seemed almost jovial, and Story wondered if his elation was a result of ridding himself of so many potentially troublesome Texans. The officer seemed about to smile when Jasmine McDaniels presented herself, but his eyes fell to the butt of the Colt tucked beneath her waistband. Without comment he allowed her to sign. Story sighed with relief when the rest of the outfit had signed, and when they rode back to the herd, he went on to the mercantile. Suddenly he reined up, slapping his thighs in disgust. Sandy Bill hadn't signed.

"Damn it, hoss," he said aloud, "I've had enough of this foolishness. I reckon we'll just take our chances on gettin' old Sandy Bill out of Texas, unreconstructed."

Reaching the mercantile, Story helped load the wagon, anxious to be going.

"We ain't forgettin' nothin', are we?" Sandy Bill asked.

"Nothing we can't get along without," Story said. "Let's go."

"Emma," said Cal as he came through the back door, "we're ready. Will you fetch Lorna?"

"I'll get her," Emma said.

Cal waited, shifting from one foot to the other, nervous. What was he going to do if old man Flagg overtook them, or perhaps sent the sheriff after Lorna? His dire speculations were interrupted by the return of Emma, Lorna at her heels. From the table Emma took a package carefully wrapped in oilskin and tied with string.

"Lorna," said Emma, "this is for you. Keep it dry, and don't open it until you reach Montana Territory. Good luck, child."

The women embraced and wept, while Cal stood there waiting, more nervous than ever. Looking out the front window, he discovered Lorna had tied her horse to the hitch rail, right across the street from the bank! He turned to the girl as she was gathering up the few things she would take with her.

"Why'n hell didn't you leave your horse out back, with mine?"

"Because Daddy knows I come to Emma's three times a week, and I never come in the back way."

With that she stepped boldly out the front door, leaving Cal to go out the back way. He paused at the door.

"Thank you, Emma. Thanks for everything."

He mounted and rode down the alley until he reached the next cross street. Lorna was waiting for him in a post oak thicket, beyond the York and Draper livery barn. They rode south and then southwest, catching up to the slow-moving herd. The riders who had met Lorna waved their hats at her as she approached.

"Mr. Story," Cal said, "I'd better ride drag with Lorna, until she's used to the herd and the trail."

"Find Shanghai, then," said Story, "and tell him to take over at point."

Story had plenty of riders, and he went about positioning them at swing and flank positions, and finally, drag. Cal and Lorna found themselves riding with Curly Wells, Oscar Fentress, Tom Allen, and Jasmine McDaniels. The rest of the outfit was strung out for a mile behind the spiraling herd, while Sandy Bill's wagon was well ahead of it. The longhorns were kept four abreast for easier handling, the steers taking the lead because of their longer stride. While the sky was overcast, there was no more rain. Once they were well past Fort Worth, Story rode ahead, joining Shanghai Wolfington at point. Slowly they turned the herd slightly northeast. Cal anxiously watched the back trail, but as the day wore on, his confidence grew. When they bedded down the herd on the west fork of the Trinity, Story estimated they had traveled more than fifteen miles.

"We're off to a good start," Tom Allen said. "I hope it'll last."

"It won't," said Coon Tails. "See them thunderheads over yonder to the west? Tomorrer there's gonna be rain, and from what I've see of Texas, mebbe a hell of a lot of it."

Jasmine McDaniels quickly made friends with Lorna Flagg, and the two of them found a place to spread their blankets. Story noted with approval that Lorna carried a revolver shoved under the waistband of her Levi's. During supper, Lorna sat cross-legged next to Cal, balancing her tin plate like the cowboys.

"We've got the first day behind us," the girl said hopefully, "and he still hasn't sent anybody after me."

"By the time he missed you, it would have been too late to come after you today," Cal said. "Tomorrow's the day we have to get behind us. If Coon Tails is right, and we're buildin' up to another storm, that'll help."

"I can't imagine what it'll be like," said Lorna, "riding through the wind and rain for months."

"That's the easy part," Cal said with a laugh. "When we come to the river crossings, you may see some cowboys in their drawers, longhandles, or nothin' at all."

"If they can stand it, I can," said Lorna. "Do naked cowboys look all that bad?"

It was a difficult question for Cal. Jasmine McDaniels laughed, while Bud, Tom Allen, and Bill Petty were grinning. Cal went red from his hairline to the collar of his denim shirt.

"I reckon that's somethin' you'll have to judge for yourself," Cal said with a grin, recovering his sense of humor.

"We'll nighthawk in three four-hour watches," said Story. "Cal, you're in charge of the first watch, Shanghai the second, and I'll take the third. There's rain in the air, and the storm may break before morning. If there's thunder and lightning, we could have a stampede on our hands."

An hour before dawn the storm struck, but there was no thunder or lightning. Riders thonged down their hats to avoid losing them to the chill wind that whipped out of the northwest. The herd, almost facing the wind and rain, kept trying to mill, to turn their backs on the storm. Still they moved on, forcing the longhorns ahead. It was a chill, wet, miserable day, but Cal Snider was thankful for it. Sandy Bill had been up the trail before, and with just such a day in mind, he had brought along

an eight-foot-wide strip of canvas, with tie ropes at each
corner. Two of the corners he tied at the very top of the
hindmost wagon bow. Stretching the canvas taut, he anchored the remaining corners to a pair of convenient
cottonwoods. The wagon stood between Sandy Bill and
the wind-blown rain, protecting the cook fire. The over-
head canvas wasn't large enough, so the outfit had to eat
a few at a time, but it kept them out of the rain while
they had their supper. Night came, but nobody slept.
The canvas wrap that was part of every rider's bedroll
offered no protection when the very ground was a sea of
water and mud. Story kept in touch with every rider,
and to his satisfaction, nobody complained. Sandy Bill
kept the supper fire alive, and when the coffee ran low,
he started another pot. Weary of the incessant rain, riders could retreat to the canvas shelter for a few minutes,
enjoying cups of hot coffee. Although the rain had
slacked to a drizzle during the night, it was far from
finished. More thunderheads rolling in from the west
attested to that. After breakfast, Sandy Bill led out with
the wagon, and the herd followed.

"One thing fer shore," Coon Tails said, "we shore as
hell ain't got t' worry 'bout water."

As their third day on the trail came to an end, so did
the rain. For a while, at least. For the first time in many
nights the skies cleared to the extent that a few timid
stars winked down.

"Even with the miserable weather," Story said,
"we've covered at least fifty miles. Two more days and
we should reach the Red."

Sandy Bill had managed to find some high ground for
the night, and the riders who had completed their watch
or had it ahead of them gratefully rolled in their blankets for much needed sleep. Cal spread his blankets
near Lorna, and tired as she was, the girl was awake.

"I'm free of him, Cal," she said.

"I hope so," Cal replied, "but I won't breathe easy till we cross the Red."

March 5, 1866. Red River.

Dark clouds were again rolling in from the west when they first sighted the Red River. So great was the backwater, it seemed an ocean, and they were able to define the north bank only where trees and vegetation grew high enough to be seen.

"God," said Arch Rainey, in awe, "I never seen so much water all at once. Look at them waves."

The wind had risen, and there was the unmistakable feel of more rain in the air. It was then a little past noon, and Story had two choices. He could go ahead and attempt a crossing, or he could wait until the following morning, in the hope that the water might subside. With more rain coming, that seemed a forlorn hope, and Story acted accordingly.

"We'll go ahead and cross," he said, "but I think we'll divide the herd. Cal, you'll take the first half and I'll take the second. You'll take eleven riders with you, and I'll bring the rest with me. When we're done with the herd, some of us will have to come back and float the wagon across. Throw your bedrolls in the wagon, along with your boots and any clothes you want kept dry. Strip down to whatever extent you like, but I'd suggest you not go beyond your drawers or longhandles. There are ladies present. Eleven of you can volunteer to go with Cal, and the rest of you will have no choice."

"We're goin'," said Wes Hardin. He rode forward, followed by Quickenpaugh, Greener, and Slim.

"So are we," Quanah Taylor said. Gus Odell, Virg Wooler, Dutch Mayfield, and Jules Dyer followed him.

"I'm going with Cal," Lorna said.

"I'll go," said Jasmine McDaniels.

"One more," Story said.

"I go," said Oscar Fentress. "I be scairt of dis much water, an' de longer I wait, de scairter I be."

Hardin, Greener, and Slim shucked boots, hats, denim shirts, and Levi's. They wore neither drawers or longhandles. Wearing his buckskins, making no move to follow their example, Quickenpaugh looked at the trio and laughed. Except for Lorna and Jasmine—and Oscar, who wore longhandles—the rest of the volunteers peeled down to their drawers. Several of them couldn't help looking self-consciously at Lorna and Jasmine, who were doing their best not to laugh.

"Well," said Jasmine, "what do you think?"

"I think they look better in their drawers," Lorna said.

The naked and near-naked riders cut out what they considered half the herd, and found the brutes unwilling to enter the seeming endless mass of swirling red water. Longhorns were characteristically reluctant to enter a river when they were unable to see the farthest bank. The leaders had to be virtually stampeded into the water. Even before they got the first half of the herd into the river, the rain started, and this time it was much, much colder. By the time all the cattle were in the water, the rain had changed to hail. Large, painful hail, as large as walnuts. Story and the riders remaining on the south bank took refuge under several cottonwoods, and were showered with small limbs and leaves, as the hailstones took their toll. There was no help for the horses, and Sandy Bill fought to hold the mules as they brayed and fought the harness. But the riders caught in the river suffered the most. Except for Lorna and Jasmine, none of them had even a hat to protect their heads. All they had going for them was that the longhorns were also being pelted by the bruising hail, and every one was imbued with a maddening desire to reach good, solid ground. By the time they were in shallow backwater, nearing the north bank of the Red, the hail had begun to subside. But it was replaced with freezing rain.

"God," said Shanghai, "I never seen such hail. Must be two or three inches deep."

"Come on," Story said. "We have to get the rest of the herd across and come back for the wagon. Without clothes, those riders across the river are hurting."

Shanghai had dipped his hand into the rushing water, and looking at Story, he shook his head.

"Cold, I reckon," said Story.

"Beyond that," Wolfington said. "Hold your hand under for five minutes, and you can't move your fingers. It may have hailed a hell of a lot worse upstream, an' now it's freezin' rain. Run the herd into that, an' you'll drown the whole damn bunch, hosses an' riders included."

Across the river, Cal Snider had just reached a similar conclusion.

"Gents," he said, "that water's just pure ice. The rest of 'em can't get over here, and we can't get back over there."

"Damn," said Greener, "the grub's over there."

"Mah shirt an' britches be over there," Oscar said gloomily. "It take longer to starve den it do to freeze."

They looked at him, their teeth chattering, and nobody laughed.

"Well, damn it," Quanah Taylor said, "let's don't just stand here and freeze in our tracks. We got to have some shelter, if only from the wind."

"You got a point," said Cal. "The damn cows are smarter than we are."

He started toward a distant thicket where the first half of the herd sought shelter from the freezing rain. His comrades followed, yelping in pain. The ground was still littered with hailstones, and beneath that there were rocks and other objects to torture bare feet. Fully clothed, with boots to protect their feet, Jasmine and

Lorna followed the miserable cowboys. Ahead of them was a rise, and near the crest of it, a rocky backbone. There was a stone lip, an overhang, that faced the east. It offered shelter from the freezing rain, and more important, protection from the biting wind. There were ashes from an old fire, some slivers of resinous pine, and most of the log from which the kindling had been cut.

"Now, by God," Hardin said ungratefully, "who's goin' to swim the river and git some matches?" He turned his wolf grin on Cal Snider.

"Mr. Hardin," said Lorna, with as much contempt as she could muster, "you are lucky that women don't have to strip naked to cross a river." Unbuttoning the pocket of her shirt, she handed Cal an oilskin packet that contained a few sulfur and phosphorous matches. Quickenpaugh looked at the naked Hardin and laughed. Despite herself, Jasmine joined the Indian in his laughter, and Wes Hardin looked from one to the other, murder in his pale blue eyes. Cal took a pine sliver and tried to ignite one of the matches against a rock, but the head popped off.

"Rock be wet," Oscar said.

"Well, hell," said Cal, "they'll all be wet."

"Not all," Oscar said. He moved the pine log, revealing a flat stone beneath it. Cal tried another match, and it ignited immediately. He quickly lighted a sliver of pine, and soon had a promising blaze going. But the bulk of the pine log had rotted away, leaving only the heart, and it wouldn't last long.

"Hell," said Hardin, "it's rained ever' day for the last month. Where you reckon we'll find anything dry enough to burn?"

"I don't know," Cal said, "but if we don't come up with somethin', it'll be a long, cold night."

Their eventual salvation was an oak that had been struck by lightning. Some of the limbs, large as a man's leg, had been split off from the trunk.

"Damn it," said Dutch Mayfield, "we need an ax. A bunch of them."

"That's dry, dead oak," Cal said. "An ax would just bounce off. We'll drag some of these big limbs to the fire, put the butt ends together and let 'em burn."

There was much groaning and cursing as sore feet got sorer. Bare arms, legs, and backs were clawed by vicious briars and thistles that seemed to have been waiting all their lives for such a glorious opportunity. But Cal's advice had been good. Once the butt ends of the heavy oak limbs had been dragged together and a fire of resinous pine built beneath them, the heavy oak bark soon dried out enough to catch fire. The hard wood underneath was already dry, and there was soon a satisfactory blaze. With the stone behind them to deflect the heat, they began to feel better. Once the original fire had created a large bed of coals, Cal used a large flat stone to move some of the coals a dozen feet from the first fire and start another.

"Thank you," said Jasmine. "Now Lorna and me can stay warm without being surrounded by naked cowboys."

"You'd better enjoy this naked cowboy while you can," Gus Odell said. "The next river we cross, I ain't partin' with a damn thing but my Colt. There's worse things than wet britches an' boots, and *that's* no britches and no boots."

"Amen, brother," said Virg Wooler.

11

On the south bank of the Red, Story and the rest of the outfit could see the glow of the fire.

"God knows how they got it started," Story said, "but they have a fire. This freezing rain can't last forever, and soon as the temperature of the Red rises enough, we'll take the rest of the herd across."

The rain did end during the night, and by dawn the water was still cold, but not unbearably so. The remaining longhorns, as had their comrades the day before, had to literally be driven into the water. Once started, however, they crossed without difficulty. The sky was still overcast, and while there was no immediate threat of rain, the promise of it was in the wind. Cal and his comrades were waiting when Story and the rest of the outfit rode out on the north bank.

"I reckon," said Story, his eyes on Jasmine and Lorna, "you hombres have had a hard lesson. What I want to know is how in tarnation you started the fire."

"Lorna had an oilskin of matches," Cal said, with a sheepish grin.

"Except for Lorna and Jasmine," said Story, "you all look pretty well used up. The rest of us will bring the wagon across, so's you can get decent while Sandy Bill's gettin' breakfast."

Hitch Gould and Arch Rainey unhitched the mules and drove them across first. Tom Allen, Bill Petty, and Smokey Ellison secured their lariats to the upriver side of the wagon, so the force of the water wouldn't topple it or sweep it away. Bud McDaniels and Shanghai Wolfington tied their lariats one to each end of the doubletree. Sandy Bill sat on the wagon box. When Bud and Shanghai pulled the wagon beyond the backwater, the swift current almost toppled it, despite four horsemen attempting to steady it. But the lariats held fast, and the riders regained control. The very instant the wagon rolled up on the north bank, there was a mad scramble for Levi's, shirts, boots, and hats. Breakfast was a hurried affair, but Manuel Cardenas made a discovery that would delay them even more.

"Calves, Senor Story," said the Mexican. "Three of them, from the cows that first crossed the river."

"Are they able to stand, Manuel?" Story asked.

"*Si,*" Cardenas said, "but not so well."

"We'll give them a while, then," said Story.

"Give 'em four hours from when they was dropped," Shanghai said, "an' they can git along pretty good."

"Since we'll be here awhile," Jasmine said, "Lorna and me are going up the river a ways and clean up."

"Not too far," Story cautioned. "We're in Indian Territory now."

"Heavens," said Jasmine as they made their way along the Red, "this river is dirty. I have mud in places I can't even decently talk about."

"So do I," Lorna said. "I'd change clothes, but what's the use? Before the day's over, it'll be raining on us again."

"Quiet," said Jasmine, taking Lorna's arm. "I heard something."

The backwater from the Red had reached some post oak thickets, and it was from one of these that the riders emerged.

"My God," Jasmine whispered, "Indians!"

They rode two abreast, and their stealth indicated that they were well aware of the riders and the herd.

"Run," Jasmine whispered. "They haven't seen us yet."

But the backwater was far beyond the river's natural banks, and there was little vegetation for cover. Jasmine and Lorna were still far from the herd when the Indians discovered them. There was no shouting or screeching, just the patter of hoofs drawing closer.

"Damn it," Jasmine panted, "they're after us. We'll never make it."

There was a windblown pine whose entire top was submerged in backwater. It was the only cover in sight, and once it was between them and the pursuing Indians, Jasmine pulled Lorna down behind the trunk. To their surprise, only two Indians rode after them, uncoiling lariats.

"The bastards aim to take us alive," said Jasmine, "while the rest of them attack our riders."

"I have my pistol," Lorna said, "but I've never shot anybody before."

"Neither have I," said Jasmine, "but it's us or them, and our shots will warn our riders. If they're taken by surprise, some of them could die."

And one of those who died might be Cal. Lorna drew the Colt, cocked it, and steadied the weapon with both hands. Jasmine had done the same, and she turned to Lorna with a final word.

"Don't let them see the gun until they're within range. You take the one to your left, and I'll try for the other one."

Jasmine held her breath, fearful that they'd hear the sounds of attack before their shots could warn the rest of the outfit. On the Indians came, and the roar of Lorna's Colt startled Jasmine. But it had a devastating effect on the Indian. Lorna's aim had been true, and he was thrown backward over the rump of the horse. Jasmine fired, but she hadn't been swift enough. The surviving Indian kicked his horse into a fast gallop, clinging to the offside, using the animal to shield himself. Jasmine fired again, but only hoping to warn the rest of the riders. To her satisfaction, rifles began to roar until it sounded like a war in progress.

"Somebody got surprised," Lorna said, "but I don't think it was our riders."

"We warned them in time," said Jasmine. "Good shooting."

Lorna still gripped the Colt with both hands, and they began to tremble. Her face went white and she sat down on the trunk of the fallen pine.

"My God," she said in a whisper, "I . . . I killed a man."

"Lorna," Jasmine said, "this is the frontier. It's shoot or be shot, and that's the way you have to look at it." She sat down beside Lorna and they listened as the gunfire diminished. When they next heard the sound of hooves, it was from the direction of the herd. The riders were Tom Allen and Cal Snider. They dismounted.

"You had us worried," said Tom, "because we didn't know how many of them might be after you."

"Just two," Jasmine said, "and Lorna shot one of them. I wasn't fast enough to get the other one."

"No matter," said Cal. "The shots warned us, and we got ten of them, without a one of us gettin' a scratch. By God, with them seventeen-shot Winchesters, our outfit could fight a war."

"Come on," Tom said, "and let's get back to the outfit. That bunch was Comanche, and we picked up some pretty decent horses. I'd like to have a look at 'em."

When Story's riders gathered the ten scattered horses, they were in for a surprise. Four of the animals were bays and were branded with a Boxed H.

"It's the same bunch that murdered the Hanby family," said Story. "The Comanches took nine horses, and it looks like we've recovered four of them."

"We could take a day and go after them," Bud Mc-Daniels said, "and likely get the rest of those horses."

"We could ride into a Comanche ambush," said Coon Tails, "an' git our ears shot off. It cost 'em eleven braves, but them varmints is learnt somethin'. They know we got some God-awful firepower, an' if they fight us agin, it'll be from ambush."

"Coon Tails is right," Story said. "It's one thing to defend ourselves, and something else to split our outfit and go off Indian hunting. Even if they didn't ambush us, they could double back and attack the riders who were left with the herd."

"They know we're headin' north," said Shanghai. "Comanches is vengeful bastards, an' they might be somewheres ahead of us, layin' in wait."

"That's something we have to consider," Story said, "and even if we don't run into this bunch again, there may be others ahead of us. Cal, I want you and Shanghai to swap out on the point riding. Starting today, I aim to scout ahead. We have the guns and ammunition to hold our own in a fight, but not if we're taken by surprise. I aim to see that doesn't happen."

"Comanch' kill *en obscuro*," said Quickenpaugh.

"He be right," Oscar Fentress said. "De Comanches rides through de dark like debils from hell. Dey kills you in de dark er in de daylight."

"There may be bands of renegades as well," said Story. "I think we'll eliminate the third watch and change at midnight. That'll have half the outfit in the saddle from sundown to first light. The rest of you can decide whether you want the first watch or the second, but leave a place for me on the second. We'll have to be prepared for trouble at any time, but if there are surprise attacks, I look for them between midnight and dawn."

Story rode out ahead of Sandy Bill's wagon. He would scout as far ahead as he expected the herd to travel that day, seeking any sign of potential trouble. As much rain as there had been, he doubted they'd lack for water, and his optimism was justified as he found streams running bank-full. Many of them were strictly wet weather, and come July and August, they'd be bone dry, but for now there was water aplenty. He rode warily, his Henry across his saddle, the early morning Comanche attack still strong on his mind.

Cal still rode drag, helping Lorna become accustomed to the herd. Jasmine McDaniels had taken to riding with Lorna, creating a friendship, for there was not that much difference in their ages. Riding drag wasn't unpleasant, for with almost continuous rain, there was no dust, and the wildest of the longhorns were being kept more to the middle of the herd. Young Curly Wells rode flank, with Wes Hardin at swing, and it was from these positions that the most unruly longhorns were apt to quit the bunch. An old brindle cow broke away, with Curly in pursuit, Wes Hardin following. Hardin uncoiled his lariat, and when he cast the loop, it dropped over Curly's head. Hardin's horse slid to a halt, the rope went taut, and Curly was jerked out of the saddle. Hardin laughed as the young rider came down on his back in a pool of muddy water. Curly was on his knees, pulling his Colt, when Hardin back-stepped his horse. Curly went facedown in the mud, and Hardin laughed all the harder. Shanghai Wolfington hadn't seen it all, but he'd seen Curly hit the ground. He rode up as Curly was again getting to his knees. Before Hardin could back-step the horse a second time, Shanghai spoke.

"This is a cattle drive, Hardin. We got no time for games."

"Well, hell," Hardin said, "I throwed a loop at the cow. Wells got in the way." He grinned at Wolfington, knowing Shanghai knew it to be a lie, daring him to do anything about it.

But the confrontation with Shanghai had allowed Curly Wells to get to his feet. Seizing the rope, he flung the muddy loop over Hardin's head, dragging him from the saddle. Hardin came off facedown in the mud, his boot caught in the offside stirrup. Shanghai caught the reins of the startled horse before it could run, and had his hand on the butt of his Colt by the time the furious Wes Hardin got to his feet. But he ignored Shanghai, turning his killing look on Curly. But Curly held his Colt steady, its muzzle unwavering. When the young rider spoke, his voice trembled with anger.

"Damn you, I ought to kill you."

"You'd best do it while you got the chance," Hardin snarled.

"This ain't the time or the place t'settle differences," said Shanghai. "Put the gun away, kid."

Slowly, reluctantly, Curly eased down the hammer of the Colt, returning it to the holster. Without a word, he went stomping off after his grazing horse.

"Now," said Shanghai, passing Hardin the reins, "git back to your position with the herd."

The errant brindle cow, galloping down the back trail, had been headed by the drag riders. Cal returned the animal to the fold, wondering why the flank and swing riders had allowed it to escape.

Nelson Story rode what he estimated was twenty miles, and was about to turn back, when he struck a trail that bothered him more than all the Indians in the territory. It was a wide, well-defined cattle trail that came from the south, angling northeast. Story followed it a ways until he found where one of the herds had bedded down for the night. The cattle and horse droppings were days old. In a somber mood, Story rode back to meet the herd and around the supper fire he told the outfit what he had discovered.

"There's a crossin' near Doan's store," Shanghai said, "mebbe forty mile east of where we crossed the Red. Most any herd bein' drove from East Texas would of gone due north. Us goin' northeast, our trail wouldn't run into theirs until we was well across the Red. There must of been a hell of a lot of cows, leavin' such a trail after all the rain we've had. I wouldn't of believed there'd be so many herds goin' north this early."

"There's no way of knowing how many herds are ahead of us," said Story, "but from the sign, I think there'll be enough to make a difference in prices at Sedalia, Quincy, and maybe beyond."

"It won't help the graze none either," Quanah Taylor said. "I ain't sure how it is to the north, but the grass don't start to green in Texas till the first few days into April."

"That's another thing I'll have to watch for as I ride ahead," said Story.

Most of the riders sat cross-legged around the supper fire. Some of them had finished eating, and since it wasn't yet time for the first watch to begin, they were enjoying a last cup of coffee. Wes Hardin tilted the blackened pot, suspended from an iron spider, filling his tin cup. When Hardin turned away, he stumbled, spilling the coffee. If Curly Wells hadn't moved his head forward, the scalding brew would have caught him in the groin. As it was, it splashed onto the crown and brim of his hat. Snake-quick, Curly flung himself backward, driving hard into Hardin's legs. Hardin fell across Curly, facedown into the hot ashes that surrounded the fire. Hardin came up squalling, probably more in anger than in pain, half blinded by the ashes. Riders scrambled out of the way as Hardin got to his knees. He went for his

Colt, but lost all interest in that when Curly drove a
boot heel into his groin. Hardin tottered, almost fell
backward into the fire, and then went belly down. He lay
there gagging and heaving. It had all taken place in a
few furious seconds, and Curly was aiming a boot at
Hardin's head when Story intervened. He grabbed the
collar of Curly's shirt, turning the young rider around
till they were facing.

"You don't kick a man when he's down," Story said.
"Now what in tarnation is this all about?"

Unrepentant, Curly looked Story in the eye and
spoke not a word. Story turned to Hardin, who had
again gotten as far as his knees. Story waited until he
had staggered to his feet.

"Well," said Story, "do you have anything to say?"

"This is pers'nal," Hardin panted, "an' you'd best say
out of it."

"I aim to," said Story, "to the extent that I can. Fight
with your fists all you like, as long as you don't get so
stove up you can't rope and ride. But the first time you
or anybody else pulls a gun on one of my riders, you'll
run headlong into me. I'm not just picking on you and
Wells. This is for the benefit of every one of you. I don't
have many rules, and I don't spout them every day. I'll
warn you once, and then when you step over the line, I
get mean. *Patada asno bueno pronto."*

It was time for the first watch to saddle up. It consisted of Cal Snider, Hitch Gould, Arch Rainey, Russ
Shadley, Mac Withers, Shanghai Wolfington, Curly
Wells, Manual Cardenas, Jasmine McDaniels, Lorna
Flagg, and Tom Allen. Story had been pleased to discover that Cal Snider had the makings of a first-class
segundo, while Shanghai Wolfington had the sand and
the savvy to boss the drive, if need be. With Cal and
Shanghai in charge of the first watch, and Story himself
overseeing the second, security seemed more than ade-

quate. Once the riders began circling the herd, Manuel Cardenas sought out Curly.

"The Senor Hardin is a dangerous man," Manuel said. "There is death in his eyes."

Curly rode on, saying nothing.

"While the Senor Wells was yet alive," said Manuel, "I promised him that I would take care of you. How am I to do that when you antagonize men who are willing and eager to kill you?"

"Hell's fire, Manuel," Curly said bitterly, "I was minding my own business when Hardin started pickin' at me on the trail. Tonight he deliberately doused me with hot coffee."

"You do not know that it was deliberate," said Manuel. "Perhaps it was accidental."

"Accidental, hell," Curly said. "You can think what you like, but I know better."

"You are no match for him," said Manuel. "The Senor Story has forbidden the use of the *pistola*, and for that I am thankful, but neither are you equal with your fists. Your father, the Senor Wells, feared for you."

"And now he watches me from the grave, through you," Curly said. "Damn it, Manuel, turn me loose. I either ride to the finish or I get throwed and stomped, but I got to do it myself. Stop cluckin' around after me like an old hen with one chick. You want to be of some real help, keep one eye on Hardin, so's the varmint don't shoot me in the back. He's heavier, and he may beat my ears down, but he'll know he's been in a fight."

Manuel Cardenas shrugged his shoulders and said no more. Privately he believed Wells had been overly protective of Curly, but it had been none of his business. Now, despite his misgivings, he suspected Curly might be made of stronger stuff than the father had thought. In the days to come, Manuel Cardenas would see revealed a new Curly, and would better understand the fears of the departed elder Wells.

* * *

March 7, 1866. Indian Territory.

Story estimated they were thirty miles into Indian Territory when the drive reached the beaten trail Story had discovered the day before.

"We might as well just foller their trail," Shanghai said, "unless the grass plays out."

"I think so," said Story, "but I still aim to scout ahead. These tracks are several weeks old, at best. Circumstances may have changed up ahead since then."

Story rode out, wary as ever, but there were things on his mind. One of them was the unexpected brawl between Wes Hardin and young Curly Wells. Curly had proven adequate on the trail, and while the young rider had little to do with the rest of the outfit, that certainly wasn't a fault. Story suspected the spilling of the coffee was no accident, but what had Curly Wells done to provoke Hardin? Curly was on the first watch and Hardin on the second, so it was unlikely there would be conflict as the riders circled the drowsing herd.

Nelson Story was the kind to look ahead, seeking out potential trouble before riding headlong into it. For the past several nights, during the second watch, Story had noted a growing friendship between Wes Hardin and Russ Shadley. It seemed all the more unusual because neither man had ever been overly friendly to anybody. Quickenpaugh, Greener, and Slim said little or nothing to Hardin, although they had hunted wild cows together. A similar alliance had existed between Russ Shadley and Mac Withers. But that too had changed, and Withers seemed to be avoiding Shadley, spending his time with Hitch Gould and Arch Rainey. Story had only his suspicions, but he saw no good coming of the growing friendship between Shadley and Hardin. Collectively or individually, they were potential trouble.

More than once Story had caught Shadley looking at Cal Snider with what could only be described as hatred. Once that hatred had festered to a certain point, violence would erupt.

"There's another hour of daylight," Story said, "but we might not have a good, clear-running creek as handy as this. We'll bed down here for the night."

Thunderheads were again moving in from the west, painted crimson and pink as the sun crept toward the horizon. After supper, despite disapproving frowns from Jasmine, Bud McDaniels broke out a deck of cards. Bud folded a blanket for the stakes, and soon there was a poker game under way. There was Bud McDaniels, Cal Snider, Wes Hardin, Russ Shadley, and Quickenpaugh. Twice Shadley shuffled and dealt, and twice he won. After Shadley had taken a third pot, Quickenpaugh said what the rest of them were thinking.

"Him cheat," said the Indian, looking Shadley in the eye.

Shadley went for his Colt, but Cal's hand was quicker. His right fist exploded on Shadley's chin, and he went over backward. Everybody scrambled out of the way as Shadley got to his knees. Cal was already on his feet. Story stepped up behind Shadley and took his Colt.

"Cal," Story said, "shuck your Colt. I reckon this has been brewing long enough. Go ahead and settle it."

Cal removed his rig, passing it to Bud McDaniels. Lorna said nothing, biting her lower lip, dreading what lay ahead. Shadley was on his feet, and came charging at Cal like a bull. It was a crude attack, and Cal stepped aside, burying a fist in Shadley's belly. Shadley stumbled back, the wind going out of him. He outweighed Cal, and he stood there clenching and unclenching his big fists, but Cal didn't wait for him to catch his breath. But Shadley blocked the blow, caught Cal's arm and flung him facedown on the ground. Shadley aimed a kick at Cal's head, but Cal caught the foot and threw Shadley

on his back. In an instant Cal was on him, driving his
fists into Shadley's beefy face. But Shadley humped Cal
off, got astraddle him and began slamming Cal's head
against the ground. Shadley's big hands were around
Cal's throat, thumbs crushing his windpipe, and Cal's
vision had begun to dim. With the very last of his failing
strength, he smashed Shadley's nose with a driving right.
The pain was enough to loose Shadley's grip on Cal's
throat, and Cal heaved the heavier man off. Cal got to
his knees and staggered to his feet, only to find Shadley
lumbering toward him with all the determination and
fury of a grizzly. Shadley was flexing his big hands, again
coming for Cal's throat. His starved lungs were still
sucking in air, and he dared not allow Shadley another
opportunity at his aching throat. Cal stood there unmoving, and so intent was Shadley on getting his big
hands on Cal's throat, he forgot everything else. When
he was near enough, Cal drove his right boot into Shadley's groin. It was a blow no man could have survived,
and when Shadley's head came down, Cal was ready.
Holding both his fists together, he brought them down
on the back of Shadley's head like a club. Shadley went
down and lay there groaning, but made no attempt to
rise.

"That's enough," said Story. "This is not a fight to the
death."

For just a moment Story's eyes met Lorna's, and they
shared a similar thought. One day these two would
meet, and only one would walk away. . . .

12

The rest of the outfit left Shadley alone, allowing him to rise if and when he was able. Even Hardin shied away from him. While Shadley had until midnight before his watch began, Cal had to saddle up, ignoring his hurts.

"There's enough of us without you," Lorna said. "Can't you take just this one night and rest?"

"No," said Cal, "I can't. There ain't no bones broke, and I won't give that sonofabitch the satisfaction of thinkin' he's hurt me."

"But he has," Lorna said, "and what I'm most afraid of is that he'll shoot you in the back."

"I'll make it a habit not to turn my back on him," said Cal.

The conversation ended when they met other riders circling the herd from the opposite direction. Lorna fell in with Jasmine McDaniels, and they rode together. Jasmine sensed Lorna's fears and misgivings, and sought to reassure her.

"Cal's a man," Jasmine said, "and there's always some risk. It just goes with the territory. He's proven he can handle himself in a fair fight, and like he said, he'll have to be careful not to turn his back. You have a gun and you can use it. If he's ever in real danger, and can't watch his back, then do it for him. Naturally, you don't breathe a word of this to Cal."

"Naturally," Lorna said, laughing. There was the unspoken recognition of Cal's pride.

"I'll be twenty-three in August," said Jasmine, "and I've been around cowboys all my life. I think, ride, rope, shoot, and cuss like a cowboy, and there's not a hell of a lot they can do that bothers me, but this Hardin and Shadley are a pair I wouldn't trust as far as I could flap my arms and fly. They're the kind that seem to have a mean streak a yard wide."

"As many riders as there are in the outfit," Lorna said, "I suppose we should be thankful there's only one Shadley and one Hardin. What do you think happened between Hardin and Curly Wells that led to their fight yesterday at suppertime?"

"I'm not sure," said Jasmine, "but there was some disagreement. Remember that brindle cow that broke loose and made it all the way back to drag? I think that was somehow the start of it, because Curly and Hardin were ahead of us, at flank and swing."

"We know what Hardin is," Lorna said, "but what about Curly? He rode in with this Manuel Cardenas, and now you almost never see the two of them talk or even ride together."

"Bill Petty told me a little about Manuel and Curly," said Jasmine, "and Curly's an orphan. Manuel kind of took over when Curly's daddy came down with lung fever, and now Manuel feels some responsibility for Curly. I'd say Curly wants to grow up and Manuel's standing in the way."

"Curly's awful small and thin," Lorna said. "I was afraid Hardin would kill him."

"So was I," said Jasmine, "but the little varmint's snake-quick and hits considerably below the belt. Mr. Hardin may have lost some parts down there."

"Unless things have changed since he stripped to

cross the river," Lorna said, "he didn't have much to lose."

Their combined laughter drew Cal's attention, and he caught up to them.

"I ain't seen a hell of a lot to laugh at since we left Texas," Cal said. "What's so funny?"

"We were just talking about how fast Curly Wells moves," said Lorna, "and wondering what kind of shape old Wes was in, down there south of his belt buckle."

Cal said nothing. Lorna and Jasmine laughed, sensing his embarrassment.

"Sorry, Cal," said Jasmine. "I've corrupted her."

"And it only took a week," Cal said. "By the time we get to the end of this drive, she'll be so rough around the edges, we can hire on to punch cows, and she can sleep in the bunkhouse."

"No, thank you," said Lorna. "I'll sleep out in the brush, like civilized people. I've seen enough naked cowboys to last awhile."

"Don't judge us all by Wes Hardin and that scroungy pair ridin' with him," Cal said. With that, he rode away, leaving them to discuss things he dared not even ponder. Secretly, though, Cal was pleased. Not only had Lorna adapted, she had become a credit to the outfit, for while she had been concerned about him during his fight with Shadley, she had kept her silence and allowed him to do what he had to.

March 8, 1866. Indian Territory.

The day dawned dark and dreary, and there was an ominous quiet. Not a breath of air stirred, and there was a distant rumble of thunder that seemed to reverberate from one horizon to the other.

"We're in for a bad one," Story said. "We'll leave the

herd bunched and try to finish our breakfast before the storm breaks."

Like golden fingers of fire, lightning leaped from one horizon to the other. The riders circled the herd, but there was no calming the longhorns. They lowed like lost souls as the first few drops of rain came on the wings of a rising wind. Thunder had become almost continuous, but the lightning seemed to have diminished.

"She's gonna give us billy hell," Coon Tails shouted. "They's gonna be ground lightnin'."

When it came, it was worse than any of them had imagined. Great balls of blue and green fire literally rained from the heavens. They bounded about like crazed tumbleweeds, some of them the size of a man's hat, while the others seemed as large as wagon wheels. Lightning danced on the tips of cows' horns, while the manes and ears of the horses seemed afire with blue, green, and gold flames. A huge ball of lightning struck a pine and it exploded like a cannon. The horses went crazy and took to frog-walking just as the longhorns began to run. Bawling in terror, they lit out toward the east like hell wouldn't have it. Not a rider was able to pursue the herd, and three—Oscar Fentress, Gus Odell, and Tom Allen—were bucked off and left afoot. By the time the horses had been calmed, the worst of the storm had passed, except for the rain. It hit them in wind-whipped waves, and the riders took what shelter there was beneath oak and poplar trees.

"God," said Coon Tails, "I never seen such a storm. She's likely t'blow like this fer half a day."

"Let's hope not," Shanghai said, "or them cows will be drinkin' out of the Mississippi 'fore we catch up to 'em."

"Maybe not," said Story. "They're mostly trailwise. This was the first really bad thunder and lightning we've had, and that's what spooked them. I think they'll soon tire themselves out."

"They drift before the wind and the rain," Manuel Cardenas said, "but we soon catch up to them."

Eventually the force of the wind diminished and the rain became just a steady downpour. Story studied the lead-gray sky and judged they might wait the rest of the day without much change.

"Let's ride," said Story. "We're not likely to get any wetter, and the longer we wait, the farther they'll drift. Oscar, Gus, and Tom, just stand fast. Soon as we catch up your horses, one of us will bring them to you."

The rest of the outfit rode out, and within two or three miles they saw the three runaway horses. The animals didn't resist when the riders went after them, and Bill Petty led them back to the trio of riders who had been left afoot. Petty, Tom, Oscar, and Gus soon caught up to the rest of the outfit. As Story had predicted, the herd had soon begun to tire, and within five miles most of the herd was found grazing. One cow wandered about, bawling disconsolately.

"That's one of the three that dropped a calf," said Virg Wooler. "It's been lost or trampled."

The wind had died, and it wasn't difficult to get the herd moving west. Along the way they discovered the remains of the calf, trampled in the stampede. Story rode ahead, roped the bloody mess and dragged it well out of the path of the herd. Many a herd had stampeded at the smell of blood. When they reached the wagon, Sandy Bill was ready. Story rode out ahead of the wagon, and when he had traveled less than ten miles, was brought up short by the bawling of a cow somewhere ahead. It seemed highly unlikely they had caught up to one of the herds ahead of them, but that seemed the case, unless a bunch quitter had made good its escape. Story rode on, discovering not one cow, but three of them. They stood looking southward, as though undecided as to where they wished to go. Story continued on, and the three ran ahead of him.

"Rein up, pilgrim," said an unseen voice, "and keep your hands where I can see 'em."

Story did as bidden. A few yards ahead a grizzled rider rode out of the brush, a Winchester across his saddle. When he spoke again, it was with a question.

"You drivin' my cows, or followin' 'em?"

"Following them," Story said. "I have a herd of my own down the back trail, and I'm scouting ahead. Your cows came as a total surprise."

"You may be in fer a lot of surprises. I got twelve hunnert of the bastards scattered from hell to breakfast. Worst storm I ever seen. Damn herd split three ways. Some run north, some run east, an' the rest lit out to the south. This purely ain't a good time to bring another herd up the trail."

"I agree," said Story, "but I don't aim to go back to Texas. I'm Nelson Story, and if any of your herd mixes with mine, you're welcome to them. Are yours branded?"

"Yeah," he said. "D-M connected. I'm Dillard McLean, from San Antone."

"With your herd split three ways," said Story, "you're likely to be here awhile. We'll move on. You're welcome to ride in and look over our herd at any time, and you can cut out any cows wearing your brand."

"That's fair," said McLean. "I'm obliged."

Story turned his horse and rode back the way he'd come. This was an entirely new development, one he didn't like. There was no help for it, of course, for nobody wanted a stampede. Now he had to consider the possibility that, if the storm had been far-reaching, some or all the other herds on the trail ahead might have stampeded. Any delays would further diminish the graze on which they all must depend. When he told the rest of the outfit of this new development, they were equally dismayed.

"Maybe we can get ahead of some of them," Shanghai said.

"I doubt it," Story replied. "They may be pretty well strung out from here to Sedalia, and the longer they're delayed, the less graze there'll be for our herd. We'll just have to move on and see what happens."

But when trouble came, it was from a source nobody expected. The herd was strung out for a mile. The sky was still overcast, and there was almost a certainty of more rain. Cal, Lorna, Jasmine, Oscar, and Bud were riding drag. Suddenly, from somewhere ahead, there was a single shot.

"Trouble," said Bud McDaniels.

"Bud, come with me," Cal said. "The rest of you stay with the drag."

Cal and Bud rode at a fast gallop along the right flank, and by the time they could see the riderless horse, they saw Nelson Story riding hard. The three of them arrived at the same moment, their eyes on the rider who lay on his back in the mud. It was Curly Wells, and blood had already soaked the left side of his shirt to his belt. In his right hand was his Colt.

"That bastard Hardin," said Cal.

"I'll ride ahead and stop the herd," Story said. "Cal, you and Bud bring him to the wagon."

Before Cal and Bud got the wounded Curly to the wagon, Story had circled the leaders, and the herd had begun to bunch. Aware that something was wrong, the rest of the riders rode to the wagon, arriving just as Cal and Bud appeared with Curly. Wes Hardin was the only rider missing, leaving no doubt as to who had shot Curly.

"Let's take a rope and go after the bastard," Quanah Taylor suggested.

"No," said Story. "Curly had his gun in his hand, so it must have been an even break. When we've taken care of Curly, maybe we'll go after Hardin."

Sandy Bill had let down the tailgate of the wagon, and Curly Wells was of such short stature, they stretched him out on it, on his back. Manuel Cardenas had pushed his way as near as possible. Swiftly Cal unbuttoned Curly's too-big shirt, while Bud unhooked the belt and unbuttoned the Levi's. When the clothes were peeled away, they all caught their breaths in shock. Not at the extent of the young rider's wound, but because Curly Wells was a woman!

"Great God Almighty," Shanghai Wolfington said.

As shocked as the rest, Story said nothing. Instead he turned to the Mexican, Manuel Cardenas, who seemed more dismayed than anybody else.

"I did not know, Senor Story," Manuel pleaded. "I swear by the blessed virgin, I did not know."

"All of you get the hell out of the way," said Jasmine McDaniels, "and I'll see to her."

Surprisingly, they did. Even Story.

"Sandy Bill," Jasmine said, "bring the medicine chest."

"I've never done anything like this before," said Lorna, "but I'll help if I can."

"Get some blankets," Jasmine said. "While we're deciding what to do, the poor girl shouldn't have to lie here naked before everybody."

Sandy Bill brought the medicine chest, and Lorna placed it on the ground, beneath the wagon's tailgate. Sandy Bill looked doubtfully at Jasmine.

"You ever done this before, ma'am?"

"No," said Jasmine, "but when I was fifteen, I drove a Comanche arrow on through my daddy's hip, and nursed him through three days of fever."

There was a cowhide slung under the wagon in which Sandy Bill carried dry wood. He soon had a fire going, with a pot of water on to boil. Cal Snider, Bud McDaniels, and Quanah Taylor went to Story with a request.

"Mr. Story," said Cal, "we'd like to trail Hardin for a

ways, at least far enough to find out which way he went. There'll be rain before dark, washing out all sign."

Story saw the anger in their eyes, understood their need to do something, for their feelings were his own.

"Go on," Story said, "but ride careful. He's the kind who might welcome pursuit, then hole up and gun you down from cover. You'll never catch him in the dark, so don't try it."

When they had ridden away, Story sought out Greener, Slim, and Quickenpaugh.

"I'm not blaming the rest of you for what Hardin did," said Story, "but you've ridden with him for a while, and I'd like to know your feelings."

"He had the sand to sell wild cows to the blue bellies," Slim said, "and there wasn't no money anywheres else. You told us how it was when we hired on. I don't aim to go gunnin' for nobody, unless they come after us first."

"That goes for me," Greener said.

Finally Story turned to the Indian, who had listened solemnly to the exchange between his companions and Story.

"*Dinero,*" said Quickenpaugh. "Quickenpaugh want much *dinero.*"

It was an all-inclusive statement that might cover anything from robbing banks to holding up stages, but Quickenpaugh said no more. As Story turned away, the Indian laughed.

Jasmine covered Curly to the hips with a blanket and covered her upper body with a second blanket, leaving bare only the angry wound in the side. Lifting the girl, she felt for an exit wound, sighing with relief when she found one.

"Bad?" Lorna asked.

"Lots of blood," said Jasmine, "but the slug went on through. If we can clean it, stop the bleeding, and disinfect it, she'll make it. Is there any whiskey in that medicine box?"

"Quart," Sandy Bill said, from inside the wagon. "That water oughta be boilin' by now. You'll be needin' cloth for cleanin', and for bandages. I got a bolt of white muslin in here."

"Thank you," said Jasmine. "Cut me some pieces a yard long, to bathe the wound. Then I'll need a piece four or five yards long, to go around her middle, to bind the wound."

Lorna returned with the pot of boiling water, and Sandy Bill provided the requested muslin to bathe the wound. Curly groaned as the hot cloth was applied. As one cloth cooled, Jasmine dipped another in the hot water. Lorna raised the girl just enough for Jasmine to bathe the exit wound. Finally, Lorna handed Jasmine a bottle of evil-smelling disinfectant, and Jasmine doused the wound with it. Curly's groans became more pronounced.

"Stuff burns like hell," Sandy Bill said helpfully, "but it's doin' some good."

Jasmine made two thick pads of the muslin, soaking them both with the disinfectant. A pad was placed over each wound, and with Lorna lifting the wounded Curly, Jasmine repeatedly wrapped the muslin around the girl's thin middle.

"Now, Sandy Bill," said Jasmine, when the bandage had been tied securely in place, "I need one more favor of you."

"What?" Sandy Bill asked.

"Fix a bed in the wagon for Curly."

"They purely ain't room in here," Sandy Bill complained.

"Make room," said Jasmine. "She won't need that much room. You aim to leave her lie on this wagon tailgate, with a storm on the way?"

"I reckon not," Sandy Bill said, and began re-arranging things behind the puckered canvas.

Jasmine and Lorna took all the blankets and wrapped Curly from her feet to the tip of her chin. When Sandy Bill was ready and had loosed the canvas pucker, Jasmine and Lorna lifted Curly inside. Sandy Bill had made a bed of blankets, and small as Curly was, there was barely room for her. It meant Sandy Bill would be out in the rain with the rest of them, if he slept at all, but the grouchy old cook said nothing. Seeing Curly being taken inside the wagon, the rest of the outfit again surged forward, Story among them.

"It's a clean wound," said Jasmine. "The slug went on through, and if we can keep down the infection, she'll be all right. But I'd suggest you not count on her riding for a while."

"Had I known she was a young girl," said Story, "she wouldn't have been riding at all."

"She has no family in Texas," Bill Petty said. "What do you aim to do with her?"

"I don't know," said Story. "I suppose that will be up to Manuel."

"It is what the Senor Wells wished of me," Manuel said, "but he is dead, and I have been told by the Senorita Curly that it is no longer my business."

"I suppose I can't consider myself part of this drive," said Lorna, "but when Curly's well, why can't she just go on to the end of the drive? She rides and ropes as well as any of you, and she even bested Hardin in a fight. Is it her fault she wasn't faster with a gun?"

"Those are questions I'd like to hear answered," Jasmine said.

"Those are decisions that will have to be made when Curly's well enough to talk," said Story, "but whether she continues as a rider or not, I won't send her away."

Cal, Bud, and Quanah rode in before dark, just ahead of the storm.

"Hardin rode south," Cal said.

"I expected him to," said Story. "He knows he's not likely to encounter any of us in Texas. Sooner or later, somebody will shoot Hardin, and he'll be just as dead as if one of us had done it. Curly should be all right. The slug didn't hit any bones or vital organs."

The outfit barely managed to get through supper before the storm struck. There was thunder, but none of the devastating lightning, and while the herd was restless, they didn't run. The rain finally slacked, and Jasmine and Lorna escaped the worst of it by taking shelter beneath an oak.

"I hope Mr. Story allows Curly to continue as a rider," said Lorna.

"I suspect he will," Jasmine replied. "She took her beatings like a man, and he can't help admiring that."

"Curly has some Spanish blood," Lorna said. "Fix her up some, and with those big dark eyes, she'll have cowboys fighting over her. And I won't be too surprised if your brother Bud's right in there among them."

"You're probably right," said Jasmine, with a laugh. "It was his idea to go after Hardin, and the minute he returned, he wanted to know how Curly was. But ever since Curly joined the outfit, she went out of her way to avoid the rest of us. When she comes out of this, she'll have friends, but only if she responds to them."

"She couldn't risk getting close to us while she was supposed to be a man," said Lorna. "When she recovers, she won't have to worry about keeping that secret anymore. That will make a difference."

When Jasmine and Lorna left the first watch at midnight, they stopped at the wagon and found Curly's face hot to the touch.

"There's no way both of us can get in there," Jasmine said, "and she's got to swallow some of that whiskey."

Jasmine climbed over the wagon's tailgate, careful not to step on the feverish Curly. Sandy Bill was asleep under the wagon, snoring. Jasmine found the quart of whiskey in the dark, and cramped as she was, managed to get Curly to swallow some of it. She heard voices, and by the time she got out of the wagon, Bud McDaniels was there.

"Tell him Curly's all right," said Lorna. "He wants to hear it from you."

"She's all right," Jasmine said. "What's the matter with you? You've only known she's a girl for twelve hours."

"Long enough," Bud said, undaunted, and Lorna laughed.

March 10, 1866. Indian Territory.

Before breakfast, Lorna and Jasmine again visited the wagon, finding Curly's fever unchecked.

"I didn't get enough of the whiskey down her last night," said Jasmine.

"I'll let the tailgate down," Sandy Bill said helpfully, "and you can bring her out so's you got room."

"Please do that," said Jasmine, "and we'd better do the same thing at suppertime."

Again the herd took the trail, and again Story rode ahead, wondering if he would encounter even more stampeded cows. But the thunder and lightning was long past, and any outfit worth its salt would have gathered its herd by now. While Story saw no more stampeded longhorns, he found the graze along the much-used trail woefully lacking. Reaching a creek, he rode half a mile upstream before he found decent graze. He then rode downstream for twice the distance. Outfits ahead of his had been forced to leave the trail, driving along the creeks until they found graze that hadn't been picked over. It didn't look promising, but he could only press on.

Returning to the outfit, Story rode a ways with Shang-hai, at point. The old cattleman shook his head when Story told him of the lack of graze.

"Don't make no sense," Shanghai said. "How can the graze be that used up, when the outfits are beddin' down for just one night? Hell, we ain't used *all* the graze nowhere we've stopped."

"I don't understand it myself," Story replied. "From the looks of it, the herds ahead of us have been bedded down two or three nights in a row. That tells me there's some kind of trouble at Sedalia, and maybe beyond."

"Could be the beef prices," Shanghai said. "When prices goes down, you got two choices. You sell fer what you can git, or you hang around fer as long as you can, hopin' the prices will rise. Them little herds last fall done all right, 'cause there wasn't too many cows, an' that kept prices up. This spring, they's more an' bigger herds, an' it's just natural fer buyers to beat you if they can. I ain't sayin' that's what's happenin' up ahead, but they's somethin' goin' on, an' it ain't good news fer us."

Shanghai was dead right, and that evening at supper-time they were faced with the ugly truth. A dozen men rode in from the north, leading two pack mules whose packsaddles were almost empty. Story and his riders were ready, hands near the butts of their Colts, but the incoming riders raised their hands.

"Step down and rest your saddles," said Story when the riders were close enough.

"Thanks," said the lead rider. "I'm Chug Sherrill, from Beaumont."

"Nelson Story, from Montana Territory. I reckon you've sold a herd. What's it like in Sedalia and beyond?"

"Hell, we never even seen Sedalia," Sherrill said. "Time we got within a few miles of Baxter Springs, Kansas, herds was ever'where, and there wasn't no graze for miles. Prices is down, and renegades from both sides of the war's demandin' a dollar a head to let herds through. We couldn't pay, if'n we'd wanted to. Our grub was played out, and there wasn't no graze, so we sold to a speculator for eight dollars a head."

"Great God," Story said, "you could have sold for ten in Texas."

"They's a time in ever' man's life when it's neck meat or nothin'," said Sherrill. "We got eight dollars. When you git there, it'll be six. Mebbe four."

The dozen Texans stayed for supper, and it was a somber affair. They didn't wish to discuss their defeat, and Story's outfit had heard enough to sicken them. Story's riders, their eyes wide in unbelief, looked to him for answers, and, for the first time in his life, the big man from the high plains had none. . . .

13

$\mathcal{A}$fter the unfortunate Texans had ridden away, Story spent an hour going over the less-than-adequate maps on which he had to rely. Before they took the trail again, he wanted some answers, as much for himself as for the outfit. As best he could tell, they were within a day or two of crossing the Arkansas River, just east of its confluence with the Canadian and the North Canadian. From there, he figured three days until they'd be approaching the Kansas line. Safe to say, then, that within a week they would be in the same untenable position as those who had gone before them. The more he studied his intended route to Quincy, Illinois, the more impossible it seemed. It was one thing to brave the elements, turbulent rivers, and fight Indians or renegades; and something entirely different when there was no graze, and there were hordes of opportunists demanding a dollar a head. Story reached a decision. Folding the maps, he replaced them in the oilskin pouch.

"This is what we're going to do," Story said when the outfit had gathered for breakfast. "First we're going to get off this beaten path by moving our drive a mile west. Second, we're going to avoid those dollar-a-head thieves who are blocking the way to Sedalia and Quincy. Third, we're taking the old Oregon Trail at Fort Leavenworth, Kansas, and driving to Montana Territory."

It was what they wanted to hear, and their Rebel yells frightened some of the horses.

"I'm almighty glad we ain't got to deal with them blood-suckin' renegades in Missouri," Shanghai said, "even if they was plenty of graze. How many miles you figger from here to Fort Leavenworth?"

"I estimate two hundred and fifty miles," said Story. "We're at least a hundred miles south of Baxter Springs, Kansas, and I figure a hundred and fifty miles from Baxter Springs to Leavenworth. We should be reaching the Arkansas tomorrow or the next day."

So involved had Story become in this change of direction, he had all but forgotten the wounded Curly Wells. He sought out Jasmine McDaniels.

"Her fever's down some," Jasmine said. "Another day, I think, and she'll be on the mend."

"I never properly thanked you for seeing to her," said Story. "We'd take care of a cowboy who'd been shot, and think nothing of it, but . . . this was different. Curly never really took to any of us, and I think she'll feel a mite better, knowing you saw to her needs. When she comes out of it, perhaps you shouldn't tell her. . . ."

"That we learned she was a girl by stripping her before the entire outfit?" Jasmine laughed at Story's embarrassment. "I hadn't intended telling her that," Jasmine said. "Maybe later, when she feels more comfortable with us."

When the herd took the trail, Story again rode ahead, more confident now that he had set a new course. His hope was that by trailing due north, they might slip through to the east of Baxter Springs, traveling along the eastern border of Kansas to Fort Leavenworth. Story had fond memories of Leavenworth, as well as friends there, for it was at Leavenworth that he'd talked his way into his first job since leaving Ohio. It had been hard work, bull whacking, but it had made him a man of the plains. Story had ridden almost twenty miles before reaching the Arkansas. While it didn't seem quite as forbidding as the Red, it looked treacherous enough. Backwater was such that he couldn't choose one place over another when it came to crossing. He rode back to meet the outfit.

March 11, 1866. The Arkansas.

The outfit spent a perfectly miserable day on the trail. Rain began before they were finished with breakfast and dogged them all the way to the Arkansas River.

"Damn," Tom Allen said, "it's as bad or worse than the Red. Do you aim to cross today?"

"No," said Story. "Everybody's pretty well give out. It's already so out-of-bank, the rain that falls between now and in the morning won't make any difference."

They made camp, the riders taking turns eating their supper beneath Sandy Bill's stretched canvas. The first watch was already circling the herd when the Indians rode in. There were fifteen of them, the leader wearing the headdress of a chief. Thumbs to his head, he wasted no time making the buffalo sign. Pointing to the grazing herd, he raised both hands, spreading his fingers.

"Kiowa," Shanghai said. "They'll ask for cows first, then they'll ride back and stampede the herd if'n they don't git 'em."

"It might be worth a few cows to get rid of them," said Story, "but they don't get ten." He turned to the chief and held up his right hand, spreading all the fingers.

"Nnngh," the Indian grunted, shaking his head. "Much hungry."

"Not that hungry," said Coon Tails. "Who you be?"

"Be Lone Wolf," the Indian said.

Story raised his right hand, spreading his fingers, and then raised one finger on his left. He pointed to Lone Wolf, then toward the herd. The riders who would take the second watch now stood behind Story and Coon Tails, their Winchesters ready. The show of strength wasn't lost on Lone Wolf. He raised the five fingers on his right hand and one finger on his left.

"Lone Wolf take," he said.

"Coon Tails," Story said, "ride out there and tell Cal to cut out six cows, but none of those about to calve."

The Indians drove their six longhorns downriver, and as it grew dark, Story and his riders could see the glow of a fire.

"They're havin' supper," said Arch Rainey. "I hope they ain't here in the mornin', wantin' six more cows for breakfast."

"That's the risk you take when you buy 'em off," Shanghai said. "They's just likely to show up wantin' more."

"That's the end of it," said Story. "We'll cross the Arkansas at first light and be on our way."

But Story hadn't counted on a change in the weather. Just before midnight a new storm moved in, bringing with it thunder and lightning. With every rider in the saddle, they tried to calm the herd, but the longhorns refused to bed down. First there was the uneasy lowing of a single cow, then a dozen, and finally, most of the herd. They didn't even wait for the lightning. There came a clap of thunder that vibrated the very earth, and the herd was off and running, the wind and rain at their backs. They were stampeding along the river, Story and his riders galloping to head them. But the leaders were long-legged steers, and while they had no idea where they were bound, they had no intention of being detained. Story rode alongside them firing his Colt, and it only seemed to make the brutes run all the faster. Story reined up, aware that the cause was lost. Bill Petty and Oscar Fentress were right behind him.

"Nothing more we can do tonight," Story said.

The outfit was strung out along the river, having tried to head the stampeding longhorns, and it was a while before they all came together.

"I've seen this happen before," said Shanghai. "Herd start out bein' calm, an' nex' thing you know, they's runnin' at the drop of a hat. It's their nature to run, fer any reason or no reason, an' that's what's gettin' into this bunch. That clap of thunder wasn't near as fearsome as all that ground lightnin'."

In the morning, Jasmine and Lorna went to the wagon and found Curly awake but hostile.

"How do you feel?" Jasmine asked.

"Like hell," said Curly sullenly. "How am I supposed to feel?"

"We're only trying to help you," Lorna said.

"I ain't asked for your help."

"Curly," Jasmine said, "you have friends here. We know all about you, and we like you. Can't you accept that?"

"Everybody knows that I . . . I'm . . ."

"That you're a girl? Yes," said Jasmine, "everybody knows."

"Oh, damn it," Curly cried.

"There was no help for it," said Jasmine. "You were hurt and—"

"Leave me alone," Curly said. "Just leave me alone."

Jasmine and Lorna turned away from the wagon, aware that something was amiss. Sandy Bill wasn't snoring, and they suspected the old cook had been lying under the wagon listening.

"What's going to become of her?" Lorna asked.

"I don't know," said Jasmine. "She has to reach out to somebody, and until she does, nobody can help her."

After a hasty breakfast, the outfit set out along the Arkansas, seeking the herd. The rain had let up, but the sky was still overcast, and the wind from the northwest promised more rain, and soon.

"Ain't but one thing in our favor," said Dutch Mayfield. "They had to run east or south. It ain't likely they went chargin' across that overgrowed river."

"They nearly always run with their tails to the storm," Shanghai said. "I figger we'll find 'em scattered along the river."

Back at the wagon, Sandy Bill filled a tin cup from the still simmering coffeepot. Careful that nobody was observing him, he dipped corn mush onto a tin plate, to which he added three sourdough biscuits and a slab of fried ham. He placed the food and coffee on the wagon's lowered tailgate and spoke through the canvas pucker.

"Kid, you must be hungry, 'cause you ain't et for three days. I brung you some breakfast, some coffee, an' eatin' tools."

There was only silence from the dark interior of the wagon.

"I know you ain't sleepin'," the old cook persisted, " 'cause I heard you givin' them gals hell. They been here two er three times a day, doin' ever'thing they could to keep you alive."

There still was no response from within the wagon.

"There's more rain comin'," said Sandy Bill, "so I got to close this tailgate. I'll set your grub an' coffee inside, an' you can take it or leave it. I got nothin' else to say, kid, 'cept this. You'd likely git treated like you was growed up if you took to actin' like it."

With that, he placed the food and the coffee behind the canvas and raised the wagon's tailgate.

* * *

"There they are," said Shanghai with satisfaction as they sighted the first bunch of grazing longhorns. "I look to find ever' blessed one of 'em strung out along the river."

"We'll ride on and get the farthest ones first," Story said, "and pick these up on the way back."

"Look yonder," said Tom Allen. "More calves."

"They been dropped long 'nough t'be on they feet," Oscar Fentress said. "All our luck don't be bad."

Most of the longhorns had become trailwise to the extent that they did not resist efforts to gather them into a herd. The rain started again at mid-morning, hampering their efforts, and it was past noon when they had what appeared to be most of the herd. There were five new calves. Shanghai and Cal ran a quick tally.

"We got 'em all," said Shanghai, "an' three extry. Three of 'em is branded D-H Connected."

"Part of Dillard McLean's stampeded herd," Story said. "We'll take them with us. I invited him to ride back, in case we found any of his cows."

Sandy Bill saw the herd coming and prepared to hitch up the mules. But first he went to the rear of the wagon and fumbled around inside until he found the tin cup, the plate, and the eating tools. He grinned to himself, for the cup and the plate were empty. At least the cantankerous little varmint had been hungry, and that was a good sign.

"If we don't accomplish anything else today," Story said, "at least we can cross the Arkansas."

"If what I think means anything," said Cal, "I think we ought to take the herd across all at once."

"We already soaked to de hide," Oscar said, "an' I think we oughts to keep our britches an' boots on. I be goin' to."

"We'll cross the herd all at the same time, then," said Story, "and come back for the wagon."

It seemed they were going to cross the herd without difficulty, but as the drag steers were about to enter the river, disaster struck. Tom Allen, Oscar Fentress, Hitch Gould, Jasmine and Lorna were riding drag. The last few longhorns were some of the wildest, and for some reason—or no reason—they spooked. Bawling in confusion, they turned on the riders, determined to hit the back trail. The drag riders scrambled to get out of the way, but a steer flung its massive head and a horn raked Jasmine's horse. The animal screamed, began to pitch, and the girl was thrown headfirst from the saddle. The horse broke into a fast gallop down the back trail, dragging its unconscious rider, her left boot caught in the stirrup.

"Jasmine!" Lorna cried.

With doubled lariat, Tom Allen fought his way through the plunging steers and kicked his horse into a fast gallop. The fleeing horse had a good lead and Tom gritted his teeth as Jasmine was dragged through brush and bare red earth as hard as stone. Jasmine's horse slowed, allowing Tom to ride alongside it. He seized the bridle, forcing the trembling animal to a halt. In an instant he was out of the saddle, freeing Jasmine's boot from the stirrup. She lay face down, and he held his breath as he turned her on her back. Her breath came in gasps. Her shirt was in tatters, her face a mass of scrapes and cuts, and a livid bruise above her eyes. Oscar Fentress rode up, dismounted, and knelt beside Tom.

"You mount up," said Oscar, "and I lift her up to you."

Tom leaned from the saddle, taking the girl in his arms. She was a dead weight, unconscious. She might have broken bones or internal hurts, but there was no choice except to get her across the river. Story and some of the other riders had come back across the river and were taking the wagon across. They were waiting on the farthest bank to greet Tom when he crossed bearing Jasmine. Oscar followed, leading Jasmine's horse. Story himself took the girl from Tom, placing her on a blanket. Before anybody could make a move, Tom was out of the saddle, kneeling beside Jasmine. Suddenly she opened her eyes and the first face she saw was that of a concerned Tom Allen.

"Thank you, Tom," she said. She spoke so softly that Tom doubted anybody had heard her except himself, and something in her eyes told him that was her intention.

"Get her to the wagon," Story said. "We'll stay where we are for the night."

The rain had become more intense, and the sky had become so dark, it seemed that night was approaching. There was no shelter for Jasmine except the canvas that Sandy Bill had stretched behind the wagon. She lay partially under the wagon, her head on a saddle. While it seemed no bones had been broken, she hurt all over, and there was little that could be done for her. Lorna had folded muslin into pads, dipping them into a pot of cold water, continually applying them to the terrible bruise above Jasmine's eyes. Tom Allen stood anxiously by, and the entire camp was in a somber mood. When it was time for the first watch, Story spoke to Lorna.

"Stay here with her," he said. "She may have a concussion."

It was to Sandy Bill's credit that he was able to keep enough dry wood for a fire. On miserable, rainy nights, when nobody slept except in the saddle, the old cook kept the coffee hot. This night was no exception, and each time Tom Allen rode in for coffee, he spent a few minutes with Jasmine McDaniels. As her pain lessened, Lorna discontinued the cloths dipped in cold water, and when Tom came off the first watch at midnight, Jasmine was able to talk.

"I thought you were a goner," he said, hunkering down beside her.

"So did I," Jasmine replied. "It all happened so fast. I

thought I'd had everything done to me a cow could do. I reckon I was wrong."

"It was somethin' that could have happened to any of us. Who'd have expected those unruly varmints to turn on us and try to go back the way they'd just come?"

"What happened to them?" Jasmine asked. "Did we lose them?"

"No. They're grazing along the other side of the river. Nelson said we'll round them up in the morning. When we do, I think they'll all be going to the head of the drive. I own a couple hundred of those brutes, and I'm tempted to claim those troublesome varmints across the river. Then, come daylight, just ride over there and shoot the whole damn ornery bunch."

She laughed. "I'm flattered, Tom, but I wouldn't want that. I think Mr. Story had his doubts about me, and I don't want any partial treatment because I'm a woman. I feel guilty already, lying here under shelter while the rest of you were out there riding in the rain."

The pleasant interlude with Tom ended as the rest of the riders from the first watch came by for a final cup of coffee.

"Jasmine," Bud said, "Tom's sweet on you, and I think you done that a purpose, just so's he could tote you back across the river."

"That's exactly what I had in mind," said Jasmine. "Just be glad it wasn't you that got throwed and dragged, little brother. Is there anybody in this outfit that's sweet enough on you to save your hide and tote you across the river?"

It was a perfectly foolish conversation, but they all laughed, including Bud. It had been an absolutely wretched day, and they needed to laugh. Mercifully, the rain had let up, and the riders from the first watch began seeking high ground to spread their bedrolls. Lorna remained with Jasmine, and when they were alone, they went to the rear of the wagon to find out how Curly was.

"Curly, are you feeling better?" Jasmine asked.

"Yes," said Curly, "and I'm sick of this damn wagon."

"We've neglected you," Jasmine said. "I suppose you're starved."

"No," said Curly. "I had breakfast, and there was water in here, but God, I'm a mess, and these blankets are ruined. I've got to get out of here and clean myself, but I'm jaybird naked. Where are my clothes?"

"In there somewhere," Jasmine said, "but if you're that much of a mess, just wrap yourself in one of the blankets until you've washed. We'll need to dress your wound again. If I let down the wagon's tailgate, can you get out here so that we can help you?"

"I think so," said Curly. "I'm awful sore and weak."

On her back, Curly slid onto the tailgate and managed to sit up. "See if you can find my boots," she said.

Fumbling around in the dark, Lorna found the boots, and it was a real struggle getting them on, for Curly hadn't the strength to help. The fire had burned down to a bed of coals. Curly was even weaker than they had expected, and it took both Lorna and Jasmine to keep the girl on her feet. They kept losing the blanket in which Curly had wrapped herself, and finally Jasmine flung it aside.

"Nobody's going to see you," Jasmine said. "It's dark as the inside of a cow's gullet. Once we get you to the river, Lorna can fetch some cloth for you to wash, some clean blankets, and your clothes."

"That river water's going to be awful cold," said Lorna.

"I don't care," Curly said. "I stink, and I just want to be clean again."

The backwater from the Arkansas had reached a mass of upthrust stone, and they eased Curly down on the edge of a huge flat rock near the water.

"That will be rough and cold on your bare backside," said Lorna, "until I can get some blankets."

"I don't aim to mess up any more blankets," Curly said. "I can wash right here."

When Lorna had gone after the cloth for washing and for dry blankets, there was a long silence. Finally Curly spoke, and the words didn't come easy.

"I . . . heard all that went on after you were hurt, and after that you still thought of me. I'm truly sorry for the way I talked to you before. I was an *asno,* an ungrateful *perra.*"

"You were," Jasmine agreed, "but you were hurt and scared, and that puts the best of us on the defensive. Somewhere beyond that, I believed there was someone I could like. I still do."

"Thank you," said Curly. "I've never had a friend, except for Manuel, and he didn't know . . . about me, because I was thirteen when he came to us. Mama died when I was seven, and I think Daddy wanted a boy, and all he got was me."

"So you tried to become the boy he wanted," Jasmine said.

"I tried, but I was small, and I didn't have the strength."

Lorna returned with several blankets, some yard-long pieces of muslin, and a large bar of Sapolio soap.

"Sandy Bill sent the soap," Lorna said.

"Good," said Jasmine. "We'll need it."

"He brought me breakfast yesterday morning," Curly said, "and give me hell for the way I talked to you. I felt rotten all day."

Curly's teeth were chattering by the time they were finished with her.

"Here," said Lorna, "wrap yourself in this blanket until we get back to the wagon. Sandy's built up the fire so we can see to tend to your wound and bandage it again. Then you can get back into your clothes."

When they reached the wagon, it took only a few minutes for Jasmine to disinfect Curly's wound and apply a clean bandage. She got dressed without help and was able to stand. Sandy Bill had discreetly stayed out of the way, but suddenly he appeared with a tin plate of food, eating tools, and a tin cup. He spoke to Curly.

"You ain't et but once in three days, kid. Just so's nobody gits the wrong drift, I don't feed between meals. This was left from supper. Some cold ham, beans, an' biscuits. Fresh coffee on the fire."

"Thank you," Curly said, "and thank you for the breakfast yesterday. I was awful hungry. I'm trying to take your advice too."

"It's becomin'," said Sandy Bill gruffly, "an' yer welcome."

14

March 12, 1866. Indian Territory

*U*nder leaden skies the herd again took the trail north. Despite Curly's protests, Story wouldn't allow her to ride for another day or two, but at least she was able to sit upright on the wagon box with Sandy Bill. Story again rode out ahead of the herd, anxious to know what lay ahead, hoping to avoid any unpleasant surprises. He had ridden half a dozen miles when he topped a ridge and saw the horsemen crossing the valley below. He counted seventeen riders, and they were heading due south. On the frontier it was seldom that men rode in so large a number, unless they were soldiers. Or renegades up to no good. While these seventeen were well-mounted, they were definitely not soldiers. Story whirled his horse and galloped back to meet the drive. At least they wouldn't be taken by surprise. When he was within sight of the herd, he removed his hat, held it high, and brought it down. He repeated the signal two more times. Cal and Shanghai headed the leaders, halting the drive. Story reined up when he reached the wagon.

"Turn around, Sandy Bill, and get back to the herd,"

Story said. "We've got company comin', and I don't like the looks of them."

By the time Story reached the milling herd, the riders were all there, wondering what had caused the delay. Story waited until Sandy Bill arrived with the wagon, and then he spoke.

"Seventeen riders coming," said Story, "and I don't think they're cowboys returning from a drive. If I'm wrong and they're friendly, then there's no harm done. But if they're what I suspect they are, we'll need the show of force. Keep your weapons handy."

"Yonder they come," Coon Tails said, "an' all they got is the hosses they're ridin'. If'n they was cowboys, they'd have a pack mule er hoss."

As the seventeen drew near they fanned out, with a single rider taking center. Story stepped forward, his Henry in the crook of his right arm, his thumb hooked in his pistol belt near the butt of his left-hand Colt. While a man didn't question another's business on the frontier, this was probably the one exception where it was permitted. Story and his riders were in hostile territory, and so large a number of unfamiliar horsemen were open to suspicion. Observing this unwritten law, the leader spoke.

"I'm Cap'n Paschal Stewart, recently of the Union army, an' these are some of the men from my outfit."

"All right," Story said mildly, "but what does that have to do with us?"

"Jist wanted you to know we wasn't no riffraff, that we fought fer Mr. Lincoln. We've went into business fer ourselves, an' we're here to offer you our services. Fer a dollar a head, we'll git you an' your herd clean through to Sedalia without no trouble."

"We're not going to Sedalia," said Story.

"Don't make a damn *where* yer goin'," the arrogant leader said. "You flat gonna have trouble gettin' there without protection."

"There's no graze from Baxter Springs to Sedalia," Story said. "Will you take care of that too?"

"Haw haw," said Stewart, "this peckerwood's got a sense o' humor. All we're offerin' is protection against yer herd bein' stole or stampeded. The graze is yer problem."

"We can protect ourselves," Story said. His left-hand Colt spoke, and Stewart's hat went flying. The man to Stewart's right had his Colt half out of the holster when Cal Snider shot him out of the saddle.

"Now the rest of you ride," Story said, "and if you bother us again, it'll be you needing protection."

One of them caught the dead man's horse and they rode out, leaving their comrade where he had fallen.

"A couple of you rope that carcass and drag it far enough away so the smell of it won't spook the herd," said Story.

"Get the herd moving again," Story said when the renegades had ridden away. "I'm riding ahead to find us a secure camp for the night."

Story offered no explanation, nor did he need to. He fully expected the remaining men to return, to at least stampede the herd, and he aimed to be ready for them.

"Good shootin', son," said Shanghai as he trotted his horse alongside Cal's. "You'd best keep your iron handy, 'cause that bunch will be back."

Before returning to his swing position, Bud McDaniels rode over to the wagon to see Curly.

"You're lookin' better and lots prettier," Bud said.

"Thank you," said Curly. She blushed, unaccustomed to being spoken to as a female, and not used to compliments. "I'd feel better if I was riding my horse."

"If you're feeling up to it," Bud said, "I'll get him for you."

Sandy Bill scowled at Bud, and Curly looked undecided. But only for a moment. "Get him for me," she said.

Bud rode back to drag. Lorna, Jasmine, Bill Petty, Quanah Taylor, and Mac Withers were the drag riders.

"I need one of you to cover for me at swing," said Bud. "I got somethin' important to do."

"We saw you riding toward the wagon," Jasmine said. "Would that 'something important' involve Curly?"

"It would," said Bud. "She wants her horse, and I'm takin' it to her."

"Mr. Story didn't think she was ready for the saddle again," said Jasmine.

"Curly don't feel that way," Bud said. "Is one of you gonna cover for me or not?"

"I'll do it," said Quanah Taylor.

"I wish Bud hadn't done that," Jasmine said after Bud and Quanah had ridden away.

"Curly's daddy can rest in peace, and Manuel Cardenas can sleep nights," said Lorna. "Curly's got somebody to look after her."

Curly's saddle had been stored beneath the wagon bed with Sandy Bill's supply of dry firewood, while her horse had been running with the longhorns. Bud caught the animal, and Sandy Bill stopped the wagon long enough for him to retrieve Curly's saddle. Bud saddled the horse and led it alongside the wagon. When Curly got to her feet, Bud lifted her bodily off the wagon and into the saddle. Suddenly he felt her stiffen, and as she settled into the saddle, her face was pale.

"Are you sure you're all right?" Bud asked anxiously.

"I . . . I'm all right," she said. "I will be."

"You'd better ride with the drag," Bud said. "I wouldn't want anything to happen to you."

"You never even looked at me," said Curly, "until I'd been shot."

"That was before . . ."

"Before you knew I was a girl," Curly interrupted.

"Well, hell," said Bud, "I ain't the kind to ride around givin' cowboys the eye. But it was me helped tote you to the wagon after you'd been shot."

"When did you discover I wasn't just another cowboy?"

"Well, uh . . . when . . ."

"When they took my clothes off?"

"Well . . . yeah, I reckon." He looked away, embarrassed.

"So when you saw me stripped, even with a bloody hole in my gut, you decided you liked my looks," Curly said, enjoying his discomfort.

"Yeah . . . no . . . I . . . damn it, Curly, we wasn't tryin' to take advantage of you. We was tryin' to see to your wounds, and it wasn't our fault . . ."

"That I was a girl," Curly finished.

"No," he said, "and I . . ."

When he dared look at her, he could see the merriment in her eyes, and when she laughed, he laughed with her. Mostly in relief.

"I've never had anybody interested in me before," said Curly. "Not a cowboy, anyway. What am I supposed to do with you?"

"Be patient with me. Hell, Curly, I growed up on the plains of East Texas, and I spent my time with men. There wasn't any girls around except Jasmine, and she cussed me and walloped hell out of me till I was sixteen."

"All without cause, I reckon."

"Well, there was a few things," Bud said sheepishly, "like the time I sneaked down to the creek and watched her takin' a bath. . . ."

Again Curly laughed, and he felt more at ease with her, but they were coming to the drag, and the interlude ended.

*   *   *

Nelson Story rode on until he found what he was seeking. The canyon was deep, with ample graze for the herd and a fast-flowing creek. While it would take them a little out of their way, it might well be worth the detour. Story rode back to meet the oncoming herd, and when he reached the wagon, he turned his horse, riding next to Sandy Bill.

"Where's Curly?" Story asked.

"Ridin' her hoss," said Sandy Bill.

"There's a canyon six or seven miles ahead," Story said, "and that's where we'll bed down the herd. By the time we get close, I'll be back to guide you in. It's a little out of our way."

Story rode back to drag, not surprised to find Curly Wells there. He seldom reprimanded anybody, but there was something about him that got to those who had disobeyed an order. Curly kept her head down, but when Story spoke to her, there was no condemnation in his voice.

"Curly, I reckon you're feeling better."

"Yes, sir," Curly said. "I just had all I could take of that wagon."

Story rode on around the herd and back toward the point. He would reveal his plans for the night when the outfit came together in the canyon.

A dozen miles north, Paschal Stewart and his fifteen followers were making plans for their return visit to Story's outfit.

"Rest of you stay here till I git back," Stewart said. "When I see where they're beddin' down, I'll ride back an' we'll figger when an' how to go after 'em."

Stewart rode out, and when he judged he'd ridden half a dozen miles, he reined up on a ridge. There was only clumps of sage and stunted oak, so he was able to see the next rise, almost a mile distant. Beyond the far rise was a deep canyon, with water and graze. It had some overhang that would provide shelter for cowboys, if there was rain, and a hasty look at the gray sky assured him there would be. He rode on toward the next ridge, and reaching it, reined up in a thicket. Stewart knew that if the herd bypassed the canyon, he and his men would have no trouble keeping ahead of them, and he had no doubt the herd would travel at least this far before bedding down for the night. Eventually he saw the wagon coming, a lead rider ahead of it, and he sighed with anticipation. The horseman turned into the canyon and the wagon followed. That was all Paschal Stewart needed to see. Wheeling his horse, he rode back the way he'd come.

Story rode down the canyon a mile, and when the herd got within sight of him, he had no trouble heading them. The graze was abundant and there was water. Story rode through the grazing longhorns. It was time to tell the outfit of the reception he had planned for Paschal Stewart's bunch, if they were foolish enough to return.

"I look for us to have visitors sometime tonight," Story said, "and I chose this canyon for a reason. The walls are high enough that they can't pick us off from the rim, so whatever they aim to do, they'll have to ride into the canyon. Since we don't know which end of the canyon they'll try to enter, we'll stake out both ends. Shanghai, you'll take half the outfit and cover the east end. I'll take the others, and we'll cover the west end. We'll take our positions well before dark, although they may not arrive until past midnight, or even in the small hours of the morning."

"We're shootin' to kill, I reckon," said Shanghai.

"After a call to surrender," Story said, "but these men aren't the kind to surrender, because they'd only end up facing a rope. I look for them to answer our challenge with their guns. When they do, cut them down."

"Who's goin' to decide who takes which end of the canyon?" Shanghai wanted to know.

"You'll cover the east end," said Story, "and you'll take the riders who ride the first watch. I'll cover the west end, taking with me the riders who stand the second watch. *Comprender?*"

Nobody disagreed. Shanghai's defenders consisted of Cal, Jasmine, Lorna, Curly, Manuel, Tom, Bill, Oscar, Smokey, Mac, and Bud. With Story were Hitch, Arch, Slim, Greener, Quickenpaugh, Quanah, Gus, Virg, Dutch, Jules, Coon Tails, and Shadley.

"Remember," said Story as they split up, "you don't have to answer to anybody. There's not enough of them to divide their forces, so they'll be coming in one end of the canyon or the other. Shanghai, if they enter at your end, it's all up to you and the eleven riders with you. Forget about us, because we'll be at the far end with the herd between us. Likewise, if they enter at our end, there'll be nothing you can do except hold fast where you are. Don't, under any circumstances, come charging down the canyon, because we'll be shooting at anything that moves. We can come out of this without a scratch, but only if everybody obeys orders. Are there any questions?"

"No questions," Cal said, "but a suggestion. If they hit us first, let us give you an all-clear before any of you head down our way. If they hit you instead of us, we'll wait for your all-clear. Otherwise, some of 'em could be layin' there playin' possum, waitin' to gun some of us down."

"Good thinking, Cal," said Story. "The rest of you, consider what Cal suggested as being added to our procedure. No smoking, no talking, and no moving about. Remember, sound carries at night. Be listening for the sound of a hoof against stone, or even for the creak of a saddle. Anything to alert us that they're coming. Make every shot count, because you won't get that many chances. Once the command has been given for them to drop their guns, allow them a few seconds to react, because you won't have a target. Force them to shoot first, if you can, and then fire at their muzzle flashes."

Time dragged. There was adequate cover at both ends of the canyon, and despite the low-hanging gray clouds, the rain held off. Although Story had forbade talking, Bud had settled down next to Curly and they whiled away the hours in quiet conversation. At the upper end of the canyon, Story had his riders positioned on both sides of the entrance. Quickenpaugh, his Winchester ready, had settled down near Story. While Quickenpaugh's attitude toward the rest of the outfit was mostly irreverent, he seemed to have genuine respect for Story. Story had begun by developing a tolerace for Quickenpaugh's unconventional ways, and had begun liking the young Comanche. It was almost midnight, and Story hadn't heard a sound.

"Them come," said Quickenpaugh quietly, getting to his knees.

There was no way Story could warn the rest of his men, for they were scattered on both sides of the canyon mouth. He would have to depend on them being alert and following his lead. It was important that nobody fired too soon, allowing the renegades to gallop away. Eventually Story could hear the creak of saddle leather and the clop-clop-clop of hooves. Finally, even in the darkness he could see the dim shapes of the riders. It was time.

"You're covered," Story shouted. "Drop your guns!"

The response was what he had expected. While the renegades had no targets, they had nothing to lose, and they began firing at the sound of Story's voice. But Story was belly down, his Henry roaring, the thunder of other rifles seeming like an echo. Horses reared, screaming, and there were anguished cries from men who had been hit. It lasted but a few seconds, the silence that followed seeming all the more intense. The horses had fled into the canyon to escape the conflict. Story waited a few minutes before his first cautious inquiry. He remained belly down, lest some of the renegades be alive, awaiting a target.

"This is Story. Lay low for a little longer."

His words drew no fire. Thunder rumbled in the distance, and a chill wind brought the unmistakable feel of more rain. Convinced the renegades were dead, Story got to his feet, the Henry in the crook of his arm.

"They're finished," Story said. "Let's move into the canyon ahead of the rain. We can use the overhang for shelter. We'll have a look at these varmints at first light. Shanghai," he shouted, "the rest of you come on in."

Suddenly, from the lower end of the canyon, there was a single shot. Story and his men waited, but there was only silence until there was a shout from Shanghai.

"Caught one of the coyotes at this end," the old rancher bawled. "He was gut-shot, an' we put him outta his misery. We're comin' in."

By the time they all reached the wagon, Sandy Bill had a fire going. He had the wagon beneath the canyon's overhang, a welcome shelter from the rain, which had gotten harder.

"Anybody hurt?" Story asked.

Nobody was. They hadn't lost a rider, and Story sighed with relief.

"Unless they got away at this end," Tom Allen said, "we picked us up some horses. This bunch won't be needin' 'em."

"We can use them," said Story, "but I think some of them may have been hit. We'll have to wait until first light to find out. We might as well take advantage of this bit of shelter. Shanghai, you and your riders take three hours for sleep, while the rest of us stand watch. Then you can relieve us and we'll sleep three hours. Come first light, I want us out of this canyon. This bunch we gunned down may or may not have fought for the Union. I don't care to argue the point when they're discovered."

Come first light, Story discovered the ambush hadn't been as complete as he'd thought. They had accounted for only fifteen of the renegades. The leader, Paschal Stewart, was not among the dead.

"The biggest buzzard of the bunch flew away," said Bud McDaniels. "I'd not be surprised if he shows up somewhere along the trail."

"He does," Quanah Taylor said, "and we'll pluck the bastard."

Tom Allen, Bill Petty, and Cal Snider had ridden down the canyon to look for the horses ridden by the renegades. They returned with some good news.

"Fifteen of them," said Allen, "but four have some bad lead burns. Doctored with sulfur salve, and they'll heal."

"Get the salve from Sandy Bill," Story said, "and take care of their wounds. Are they branded?"

"Some of them," said Allen. "No brands I've ever seen, though."

"We'll gamble on them," Story said.

After breakfast the riders were forced to drag the dead renegades away from the canyon, lest the smell of death spook the longhorns.

"We have enough horses to require a pair of wranglers," said Story. "Arch, you and Quickenpaugh bunch the horses, keeping them between the herd leaders and Sandy Bill's wagon."

They took the trail, traveling north, the wind-driven rain still dogging them. Story rode ahead, more wary than ever, following their experience with Paschal Stewart and his renegades. He believed they were not more than three days' drive south of Baxter Springs, Kansas. Finding no Indian sign and nothing else to arouse his suspicion, Story rode back to meet the herd. But before

they bedded down the herd for the night, they met yet
another group of disconsolate Texans who had sold their
herd for a pittance and were on their way back to Texas.
It was disturbing news, despite Story's decision to drive
on to Fort Leavenworth, and from there to Montana
Territory. Mercifully, the rain ceased before dark, and
by the time the first watch began circling the herd, the
riders were in dry clothes.

Lorna was riding with Cal, Curly with Bud, and Jasmine McDaniels found herself riding alone. But not for
long.

"You seem to be alone," said Tom Allen. "Is it all
right if I ride with you?"

"Ah reckon," she said.

"I don't stir up a hell of a lot of excitement, do I?"

"I just had an awful wallop on the head," Jasmine
said. "Who *are* you?"

His stirrup was touching hers. Suddenly he leaned
over and kissed her hard, on the mouth. When she
didn't resist, he did it again.

"Am I the first cowboy you ever kissed?" he asked
softly.

"You could be," she said. "You *do* look a mite familiar."

They laughed, comfortable with one another, enjoying the foolish banter.

"What do you aim to do when you reach Montana
Territory?" Tom asked.

"I don't know," Jasmine replied. "Mr. Story owes us
for the sale of our herd, and when we add our wages to
that, Bud and me will have some money. What will you
do?"

"I'll follow Nelson's example, grab me some Montana
graze and start me a ranch. I can't do it on his level, of
course, because I'll have only two hundred cows, but I
figure four or five years of natural increase will set me
up pretty decent."

"You're from Montana Territory," she said wistfully, "and you're going home. I wish I was."

"You could be," he said, leaning close. "What's the use of me becomin' a rich cattlemen if I don't have a beautiful woman to spend the money on?"

"I don't know, Tom. I just don't know. I've got a temper like a stomped-on rattler, and I could unleash more fire and brimstone in a day than you've seen in your whole life."

"You don't have any good qualities, then, aside from being beautiful?"

"I'd question even that," said Jasmine, laughing. "Please don't give up on me. We'll talk again."

On the other side of the herd, Bud McDaniels and Curly Wells had been having a similar conversation, with far less satisfactory results.

"That don't make sense," Bud said. "You must have some idea as to what you aim to do with the rest of your life."

"Damn it, Bud, I *said* I don't know," Curly snapped. "I won't even be sixteen until September, this is the first time in my life I've been out of Texas, and I don't know how I feel about you or any man. How can you go from thinking I was a cowboy to knowing I'm a girl, all just in a few days? For ten years I've tried to think and act like a man. I just purely ain't used to a man . . . messing around with me. Hell, before I have to plan the rest of my life, give me time to get used to bein' a woman."

"You could start," said Bud, "by not swearin' every time you open your mouth."

"I don't aim to become so much a woman that I can't swear when there's somethin' or somebody that needs swearin' at," Curly said.

"I just ain't comfortable with a woman that swears like a bull whacker."

"Well," Curly said, "if your hoss ain't growed roots where he's standin', ride on. Ever' since you saw me with my shirt unbuttoned and my Levi's down, you been followin' me like I was the last female west of the Mississippi."

"Well, by God," said Bud, "with you actin' like a damn ignorant cowboy, I wouldn't have you if you *was* the last female west of the Mississippi."

He reached for her, but she was too quick and caught his wrist. His horse, startled, sidestepped, leaving Bud off balance. He slid out of the saddle on the offside, and the skittish horse trotted away, Bud's right foot caught in the stirrup. Curly caught the reins, halting Bud's horse.

"You're lucky there was a damn ignorant cowboy handy to catch your hoss," Curly said. "You'd have had a sore backside in the morning."

March 16, 1866. Baxter Springs, Kansas.

"Git," said the farmer with the shotgun. "You ain't wanted in Kansas. You Texans an' yer damn tick-infested cows has done enough damage."

Story led the herd slightly to the northeast, veering back again once they were past the human blockade.

"We in Kansas er Missouri?" Shanghai wondered.

"I'm not sure," Story said. "We'll stay as much on the line as we can, gambling that we don't hit a blockade on the Kansas side and the Missouri side at the same time. As we travel farther north, away from the Sedalia trail, the less opposition we should meet. If there are no more delays, I figure we're five days out of Fort Leavenworth."

"When we get to Fort Leavenworth," said Cal, "then how far will we be from Virginia City?"

"The way we'll be going, about twenty-two hundred miles," said Story. "When I came West in 'fifty-four, I took a job bull whacking, west out of Fort Leavenworth.

I have some business there, and we'll be laying over a few days."

"I need clothes," Lorna said. "I brought almost nothing with me, and I'll be in rags before we reach Montana Territory."

"I think we can arrange for everybody to have a day in town," said Story "Just about everybody's needin' his ears lowered, if nothing else."

Story seemed more at ease with Jasmine, Lorna, and Curly at drag, and that's where they remained. The men alternated, two at a time, to keep five riders at drag, so at no time were the three women there alone. When Bud was there, he had little to say to Curly, and their lack of communication didn't go long unnoticed by Lorna and Jasmine.

"Curly," said Jasmine, "you and Bud are avoiding one another. Has he done anything . . . improper?"

"Not what you're thinkin'," Curly said. "He said I'm more of a damn ignorant cowboy than a woman."

"Why, damn him," said Jasmine, "what does he expect? You've been a cowboy all your life, and you've had just a few days of being a woman. Just let me get hold of him—"

"No," Curly said, "I don't want you forcing him to do anything. If his feelings toward me change, let it be because he wants them changed. I'm just . . . well, new to these feelings, and after trying to be a man most of my life, I'm not comfortable havin' a man followin' me around. Bud is . . . can be . . . nice, but I reckon I'm not ready for him."

"Men don't feel the same about much of anything, as women do," said Lorna. "Cal was ready to leave Texas without me until he was shot. While he was lying there in that hotel room, he—"

"Took you to bed with him," finished Jasmine.

"Oh, no," Lorna protested. "He was a gentleman. Besides, he'd been shot. I'd been mad about him since I was twelve, and he kept treating me like I was *still* twelve, until he was shot. Then he seemed to notice me, not as a pest of a kid, but as a woman."

"He'd have had to be blind as a bat not to see the change," Jasmine said, looking her over.

"I don't know if I want to be a woman," said Curly. "Maybe when this drive is over, I won't be. Maybe I'll ride to a new range where nobody knows . . . what I am."

March 21, 1866. Fort Leavenworth.

Story and the outfit followed the Kaw River to Fort Leavenworth, then, driving northwest half a dozen miles, they bedded down the herd in a grassy valley along the Smokey Hill River. The day of their arrival, Story gathered the riders around the supper fire.

"I have many friends in Leavenworth," he said, "most of them bull whackers. Since we're going to Virginia City anyhow, I aim to buy some wagons, load them with provisions and trade goods, and hire some drivers to take them on to Virginia City."

"I ain't faultin' you fer that," said Coon Tails, "but they'll slow us down, an' they'll be mighty damn temptin' to them Sioux along the Bozeman."

"No slower than we're likely to be anyhow," Story said, "with these cows dropping calves. As for the Sioux, with or without the wagons, we'll have to contend with them. I'm allowing myself three days to buy wagons, load them with goods, and hire drivers. I want at least half of you here with the herd at all times. This is a major fort, and there'll likely be a pretty good force of Union soldiers here. I'd suggest none of you go about crowing too much of Texas. You could end up with your neck on a chop block. Wet your whistles if you like, but know when to back off. I can advance a month's pay to anybody that's broke. Sandy Bill, I'll want you to take the wagon in as I go, and we'll load up on provisions."

"When are you aimin' to go?" Shanghai asked.

"In the morning," said Story. We'll also be bringing back enough shoes to reshoe every animal needing it. We'll see to that while we're laying over here. Cal, I'm leaving it to you to see that it gets done."

"My stars," Jasmine said, when Story had ridden away, "is there no limit to his money? He'll need a fortune."

Tom Allen laughed. "He has one. He came out of the gold fields of Montana with forty thousand in gold. Now you keep that under your hat. Nelson Story knows exactly what he's doing."

"I won't mention it," said Jasmine. "It's just that, after four long years of war, with nothing to buy and no money to buy with, what he's done and what he aims to do leaves me breathless. What *could* he buy, with the wealth he has?"

"Just to give you some idea," Tom replied, "in New Orleans you can order steak, potatoes, onions, bread, pie, and coffee for ten cents."

"Then why in tarnation is he risking his life to drive a herd of Texas cows to Montana Territory?"

"Because he's Nelson Story," Tom said.

15

" *I*'ll be conducting some of my business at the fort itself," Story said, "but the rest of you have no business there. Confine your visit to the town, and don't volunteer any information about the herd. We'll be heading into Sioux country, and the military may try to stop us. The less they know of our affairs at the fort, the better off we'll be."*

When Story rode in, he purposely started an hour ahead of the riders who would visit the town. Sandy Bill took the wagon, followed by Hitch Gould, Arch Rainey, Russ Shadley, Slim, Greener, Quickenpaugh, Quanah Taylor, Gus Odell, Virg Wooler, Dutch Mayfield, and Jules Dyer. Upon reaching the town, everybody except Quickenpaugh and Sandy Bill headed for the barbershop. Sandy Bill drove on to the mercantile, as Story had instructed, while nobody knew what had become of Quickenpaugh. Leaving the saloon, Shadley, Greener, and Slim went in search of a whorehouse. Hitch Gould, Arch Rainey, Quanah Taylor, Gus Odell, Virg Wooler, Dutch Mayfield, and Jules Dyer found a cafe and or-

---

* Fort Leavenworth was built in 1827 to protect those who traveled the Santa Fe Trail. The town of Leavenworth, settled in 1854, flourished as a supply point on westward travel routes.

dered an enormous meal of steak, potatoes, onions, dried apple pie, and coffee. Finished, they set out to find some means of amusing themselves. There were saloons in abundance.

"Hey," said Jules Dyer, "they got billiards."

They made their way into the Broken Bow Saloon, only to discover it had but one billiard table, and that was monopolized by four Union soldiers.

"Let's have a beer," Dutch Mayfield said, "and wait till they're done."

But it soon became obvious the game wasn't going to end. Another pair of soldiers came in, taking the place of two of those who were already there. The two who were no longer playing went to the bar and ordered beers. For a while they watched the game in progress, and then turned their attention to the seven cowboys who were obviously waiting for the billiard table.

"By God," said one of the soldiers at the bar, "somebody's left the gate open and the stock's got loose."

"By God," Dutch Mayfield said, "with Injuns raisin' hell, you'd think the damn bluecoats would have somethin' better to do than drape their carcasses across a billiard table."

"Maybe we have, cow stink," said one of the soldiers at the bar. "How'd you like to have *your* carcass stretched across a billiard table?"

"I won't say it can't be done," Dutch said, "but you'll need help. I reckon we can wait, while you go wake up the rest of the troops."

The billiard ball narrowly missed Dutch's head, smashing the mirror behind the bar. A second ball smashed a tier of bottled whiskey, and the bartender came across the bar, a bung starter in his hand. A speeding billiard ball smacked him between the eyes, and he went back over the bar, falling with a crash. Gus Odell was knocked senseless with the heavy end of a cue stick, while the soldier responsible was felled by a smashing right to the chin by Hitch Gould. A flung chair missed its mark and went through the front window onto the boardwalk. Their supply of billiard balls had been exhausted, and the players were swinging cue sticks when the sheriff stepped through the front door.

"That's enough, damn it!" His Colt roared, and that got everybody's attention.

The bartender had revived to the extent that he could stand by leaning on the bar. "Arrest them, Sheriff," he croaked. "The bastards wrecked my place."

The seven cowboys were locked in one cell, and their soldier adversaries in the adjoining one. The sheriff was a gray-haired, grim-faced old codger who looked as though he'd as soon gut-shoot the lot of them as not. First he turned his attention to the six battered soldiers.

"I've sent word to the commandin' officer that you varmints is in here," he said. "You won't git no payday fer a while. Yer eight dollars a month's goin' to pay fer damages. Now, as fer you hell-raisers," he said, turning to the cell with the seven hapless cowboys, "you better have some money in yer pockets, or by God, I'll sell yer hosses an' saddles."

But Story's riders had an ace in the hole of which they were unaware. Quickenpaugh had been to the mercantile and was seeking the rest of the outfit when he saw them and the soldiers being herded toward the jail by the grim old sheriff. Behind the jail there was a creek, its banks lined with aspen, briars, weeds, and brush. Quickenpaugh circled around, coming in behind the jail. From a large sack he took some of the items he had purchased, and lighted a match. . . .

The sheriff had just finished his fiery speech to his newly acquired prisoners when all hell broke loose somewhere behind the jail. It sounded like an Indian uprising, or perhaps a major battle of the recent war being refought. It became a veritable fusillade, a continuous roar. The sheriff, in fear of his life, was out the door in an instant, but that was as far as he got. Quickenpaugh cut off his wind with an arm around his throat and knocked him senseless with the muzzle of his Colt. Quickly, the Indian found the jail keys and ran toward the front of the building. The roar from along the creek had begun to die away, but the jail being at one end of the town, nobody had yet come to investigate. Quickenpaugh burst through the door, the keys in his hand.

"Quickenpaugh!" the cowboys shouted.

The Indian said nothing, but began trying the keys. The third one turned the lock and the door swung open. Quickenpaugh headed for the door, his comrades on his heels.

"Hey," one of the soldiers bawled, "what about us?"

"No time," Arch Rainey shouted. "We got to get back to that billiard table 'fore some more blue bellies grabs it."

"God," Hitch Rainey panted, "why couldn't he of let us ride our hosses down here?"

But Quickenpaugh had moved the horses, bringing them as close as he dared, concealing them behind an abandoned store. Gratefully, the riders mounted on the run, and Quickenpaugh took the lead. Not until they were far from the town did they stop to rest their horses.

"Quickenpaugh," said Quanah Taylor, "you're one *bueno* Injun. But how in tarnation did you manage all that shootin' behind the jail?"

"Chinee cannon," Quickenpaugh said. From a sack he pulled a yards-long string of firecrackers.

While Story had instructed his riders not to talk of the herd and to avoid the fort, he knew it would be impossible to keep the military out of his affairs. He wished to be as tactful as possible, to secure whatever help they were willing to provide, and the best means of accomplishing that was by going through the post commander. But the man was on leave, and the acting post commander, Captain Ferguson, was aghast at Story's proposed drive along the Bozeman Trail.

"Mr. Story," Ferguson said, "this has to be the most reckless proposal I've heard in my career as a Union officer. Are you not aware that Red Cloud, the Sioux chief, walked out of the Laramie Peace Conference?"

"I am," said Story, "and your superiors in Washington gave him all the cause he needed. The army made a treaty with the Sioux and immediately started building forts in Wyoming and Montana. Red Cloud considers that a violation of the treaty, and now he's taken the warpath. I can't say that I blame him."

There came a knock on the door, and Captain Ferguson granted permission to enter. An aide came in, looked questioningly at Story, and saluted the captain.

"At ease," Ferguson said. "Now, what is it?"

"Someone from town to see you, sir," said the private. "Six of our men were in a brawl with some civilians. They wrecked a saloon, and the sheriff has them in jail."

"Show this party to the orderly room, private," said Ferguson, "and I'll see him shortly."

When they were again alone, Ferguson said, "Mr. Story, your empathy for Red Cloud and his bloodthirsty savages is touching, but it is neither my place nor my desire to debate military policy with you. While I cannot forbid you to take the Bozeman Trail, I feel I have done the next best thing, and warned you of the danger. If you proceed, and you and your men are slaughtered, then I have done my duty. Good day, sir."

Story was neither surprised nor disappointed. If the military couldn't or wouldn't help him, then the next best thing was having them leave him strictly alone. Since most of the freight that went west from Fort Leavenworth was of a military nature, the army had set up a freight depot for the teamsters. Story went to the agent in charge, inquiring of some of the bull whackers with whom he had once worked.

"Buckalew ain't with us no more," the agent said. "Sioux got him. I reckon Holden and Lemburg is in town. Try the Plains Hotel. Puckett an' Summers won't be back till next Monday, the twenty-sixth."

These were men Story hoped to hire to drive his wagons to Virginia City. They were friends, tried and true, and it would be worth waiting for them to return. While he waited, he could track down Holden and Lemburg, buy four wagons, and begin loading them with goods that would bring premium prices in Virginia City. He left the fort and rode toward town, thinking of the soldiers who were in jail for having busted up a saloon. The military could make it hard on men living near an army town, and for that reason, civilians weren't anxious to brawl with soldiers. Story had a sneaking suspicion he knew who these particular civilians were. When he had gone to the mercantile and settled for Sandy Bill's wagonload of provisions, he would visit the jail. When Story arrived, Sandy Bill was still waiting for the wagon to be loaded.

"The Injun, Quickenpaugh, was in the store," said Sandy Bill, "but I ain't seen the rest of 'em. They's been a passel of shootin' this mornin'."

Story changed his mind about visiting the jail, until he had some better idea about what had taken place. Instead he went to the Plains Hotel and found that his bull-whacker friends, Jubal Holden and Handy Lemburg were there. The hotel was imposing enough to have a dining room, and he found the pair having breakfast. Story pulled out a chair and sat down, and their conversation began as though they had parted only hours ago, instead of years.

"Reckon you heard about Hez Buckalew," Jubal Holden said.

"Yes," said Story. "The agent at the fort told me."

"Red Cloud's bunch," Handy Lemburg said. "Long as that varmint's alive, the Bozeman's goin' to be hell with the lid off."

"I know," said Story, "and I need to hire four men I can trust. I have twenty-five riders and four thousand Texas longhorns half a dozen miles west, along the Smokey Hill. We're bound for Virginia City, Montana, and I aim to take along four wagonloads of trade goods."

"By God, Nels," Holden said, "I ain't doubtin' you can do it, 'cause you lead a charmed life. But I ain't sure I do."

They took the time to laugh at that, and then Nelson Story got serious.

"Gents," said Story, "I want you on two of those wagon boxes, and when Levi Puckett and Waddy Summers roll in, I'm hirin' them. There's danger, I'll admit, but every one of my riders is armed with a Colt revolver and a Winchester rifle."

"Too bad they ain't the new Remington breechloaders," Handy Lemburg said. "They got the range of a Sharps, take metal shells, an' with some practice, a man can load an' shoot ever' four seconds."*

"My God," said Story, "that's what we need for the Bozeman. Where do I get these Remingtons?"

"We got ours through the agent at the fort," said Jubal, "because all our runs is smack through Red Cloud's stompin' grounds. You might try some sweet talk at the fort. The troops here at Leavenworth is testin' them new Remingtons right now. Come on up t' our room an' have a look at one of 'em."

Story followed his friends up the stairs to their sec-

---

* The Remington rolling block rifles were the first modern breechloaders made, and were manufactured virtually without change from 1866 to 1933.

ond-floor room, and was handed one of the new Remingtons.

"She's a .50–.70," Jubal said. "Ain't near as heavy as a Sharps, but she'll down a buffalo at a thousand yards."

Story handled the weapon with reverence. Both the hammer and breech blocks rotated on heavy transverse pins in the receiver. When the hammer was brought back to full cock, the breech block could be thumbed back, exposing the chamber so that the fired shell could be extracted. The breech was then flipped back to closed position after a fresh cartridge had been inserted into the chamber. When the hammer fell in firing, the two blocks locked into a solid steel breech, Remington's guarantee there would be no backfire.

"If there are thirty of these weapons to be had," said Story, "I'll get them. Armed with these, we won't need the army."

"Speakin' of the army," Handy said, "they was one hell of a fight up to the Broken Bow Saloon this mornin'. Six soldiers got into it with a bunch of cowboys, an' the sheriff, old Webb Hankins, throwed the lot of 'em in jail. You dead sure all them cowboys of yours is out there on the Smokey Hill?"

"No," said Story, with a sigh. "Some of them rode into town. I reckon I'll have to ride over there and pay them out."

"I reckon you won't," Jubal laughed. "That ain't the end of it. Somebody set off a hellacious bunch of firecrackers behind the jail. Sounded like a war goin' on. Old Hankins lit out the door, an' somebody buffaloed him, took his keys, an' let them cowboys loose. Left them soldiers in there, an' the sheriff swears they'll pay fer that saloon if it takes their paydays fer ten years. Tickled hell out of the town, though. Some of them soldiers thinks their blue britches makes 'em better'n anybody else, like they're up there next to God."

"That may be the case," said Story, "but it couldn't

have happened at a worse time. Those soldiers in jail are part of the same army I'll have to sweet-talk into selling me thirty Remingtons."

"I reckon we'll ride with you to Virginia City," Jubal said, "whether you get the Remingtons or not, but they shore make a man's hair feel better."

"You gents didn't spend much time in town," Cal Snider said. "Where's Shadley, Greener, and Slim?"

"Still in town somewhere," said Arch Rainey. "We got some town grub, had our ears lowered, and there wasn't much else to do."

Some of those who had remained with the herd looked curiously at the big sack Quickenpaugh had, but the Indian didn't enlighten them. The day dragged on, and Story didn't ride in until almost suppertime. Before he even dismounted, he discovered Greener, Slim, and Shadley were missing.

"Greener, Slim, and Shadley aren't here," Story said. "You didn't leave them in jail, did you?"

Quickenpaugh laughed, but the rest of them had trouble looking Story in the eye. They knew that he knew the three missing riders weren't in jail, that he had asked the question only to see how they would respond to it.

"No, sir," Arch said, "we ain't seem 'em since they left the barbershop. The rest of us, 'cept Quickenpaugh, went to a saloon to shoot some billiards, and we . . . well, by God, some soldiers jumped us, and . . . and we defended ourselves."

"A hundred and twenty-five dollars worth of defense," Story said. "I paid for the damage to the saloon and had the sheriff release the soldiers."

"You didn't have to do that," said Dutch Mayfield. "We escaped."

"You don't escape from anything, where the army's involved," Story said. "You only delay things until they catch up with you. By tomorrow, a company of soldiers would have been looking for you. I have important business here that will involve the army, and I can't very well negotiate with them if they're filing charges against half my outfit."

"Damn it," said Cal, glaring at the escapees, "you've ruined any chance the rest of us had for getting into town."

"Not necessarily," Story said. "They won't be going in again, but the rest of you can go tomorrow. Just stay out of trouble with the law and with the military. The rest of you end up in the *juzgado,* you'll have to escape, because I aim to leave you there."

It was after dark when Greener, Slim, and Shadley finally rode in.

The following morning, the second half of the outfit headed for town, with the exception of Coon Tails, who declined to go.

"I'll stay here an' keep this bunch from gittin' in trouble," said the old mountain man.

"Damn," Hitch said, "we ain't never gonna live that down."

"We knowed better," said Arch, "but Mr. Story's right. He went to a hell of a lot of trouble, gettin' us out of Texas, for us to get in trouble with the Unions over a damn saloon fight."

"Maybe it was a fool thing to do," Gus Odell said, "but it was almost worth it, seein' Quickenpaugh pull that trick with the fireworks."

Story rode back to the fort, knowing better than to approach Captain Ferguson with his request for the Remington rolling-block rifles. Instead he appealed to Jenks McCarty, the civilian freight agent.

"Thirty? My God, Nels, I ain't got that many drivers," said McCarty.

"Does the army actually know how many bull whackers you have?"

"No," McCarty said, "but—"

"You can get the Remingtons, then," Story said.

"Well, yes, but some of my teamsters still don't have one."

"But all your teamsters aren't on the trail," said Story, "and my men are going to be. You have some time, and I don't. If the army's testing this weapon, it means they've ordered a bunch."

"Ten thousand, I hear," McCarty said.

"Damn it, Mac, I need those rifles. I'll make it worth your while. Do you have any freight for Virginia City?"

"Some. Nothin' even close to a full load. It'll have to wait till I do."

"No it won't," said Story. "You get me those rifles, and you can load your Virginia City freight on one of my wagons."

"Check with me tomorrow," McCarty said. "I'll see what I can do."

When the second half of Story's outfit reached town, the men reined up at the barbershop.

"Lorna, Curly, and me are going to the mercantile," Jasmine said.

"It's near dinnertime," said Cal. "When we're lookin' human again, let's find a fancy place and get some town grub. One of us will come and get you."

"You reckon they'll look any better?" Lorna asked as the three of them rode away to find the mercantile.

Jasmine laughed. "Probably not, but it makes them feel better."

When they entered the huge store, Lorna and Curly followed Jasmine to the area that featured women's clothing.

"I aim to have some muslin for that bad time of the month," said Jasmine. "The three of us can share a bolt."

"What—" Curly began, and then recognition hit her. "Hell's fire, they sell stuff . . . for *that?*"

"God, Curly," Lorna said, "you *was* better off bein' a man."

The ladies' dresses were long and flowing, their hems sweeping the floor. Jasmine held one of them in front of her, and Curly swore.

"You get all gussied up in that, and you're naked under there. Just how in tarnation do you aim to squat or sit down, without—"

"Pantaloons," said Lorna, snatching up a pair. "You wear them under the dress, to cover your bottom."

"Levi's cover my bottom," Curly said. "I wouldn't be caught dead in . . . in that thing."

"Then if you ever wear a dress," said Jasmine, "be careful how you sit, and don't *ever* squat."

Curly had stopped to look at a pile of flesh pink corsets in varying sizes, displayed on a table.

"Looks like somebody scraped a bunch of hogs," Curly said, "gutted 'em, and then laced their bellies up again."

"When you get old—maybe thirty—and you've had too many younguns," said Lorna, "you tie yourself up in that, and it keeps you from looking so big."

"I don't aim to get old or have younguns," Curly said, "and if I did, I'd take a Colt and shoot myself 'fore I'd stuff my carcass into somethin' like that."

"Well," Jasmine sighed, "we've ruled out all the finery. What are we actually going to buy?"

They had attracted the attention of a female clerk who had begun to wonder the same thing. Hearing Jasmine's words, she approached.

"I want some denim shirts and Levi's pants," said Lorna.

"In what size?"

"My size," Lorna said.

"We have nothing like that for ladies," the woman

said primly. "You'll have to go to the men's department."

Curly found that hilariously funny, and when the three of them headed for the other side of the store, the mystified clerk seemed relieved to be rid of them. Lorna bought two shirts and two pairs of Levi's pants, and from there Jasmine led them to the bolted cloth and sewing goods.

"Needles, thread, buttons, and some shears," said Jasmine. "I reckon the rest can wait until we reach Montana Territory."

"Let's ride back to the barbershop," Curly said. "I don't like the way this bunch in here keeps lookin' at us."

Story found a wagon yard and made arrangements to buy four wagons. From there he went to a livestock dealer and bought four team of oxen, to be picked up when he had hired his teamsters. Neither could he load the wagons until he had drivers for them. He rode back to the Plains Hotel and had dinner with Jubal Holden and Handy Lemburg.

"I knowed you'd git them Remingtons if they was to be had," Lemburg said, laughing, "and you won't be sorry."

Story had just stepped out the hotel's front door when a slug slammed into the doorjamb, just inches from his head. The shot had come from across the street, and before he could make a move, a freight wagon had driven between him and the position from which the bushwhacker had fired. By the time the wagon had gone, there was nobody in sight. Angrily, Story recalled the trying days on the Brazos, a killer stalking him, and finally the fateful, stormy day when the bastard had gunned down Cal Snider. If this one was of the same stripe as the man he had shot on the Brazos, Story thought, then this bushwhacker might make their lives miserable along the trail until the man stopped playing games and killed him or one of his riders. The solution was simple, Story decided. His bull-whacker friends, Levi Puckett and Waddy Summers, wouldn't return until the twenty-sixth. His only defense against the bush-whacker was to catch him in the act and gun him down. The gunman had tried once, and given the opportunity, he would try again. While he waited for Puckett and Summers, Story thought, he would make himself a target, but not the kind of target the bushwhacker would expect. A rattler-swift target, with a blazing Colt in each hand . . .

There were only two barbers, and it seemed forever before the riders were out of the barbershop. Cal Snider and Tom Allen were the last to leave, and when they came out, except for Bud McDaniels, the rest of the men were gone.

"We should have eaten first," Jasmine said. "For the time it took, none of you look that much better."

"Thanks," said Tom. "It always makes a man feel nine feet tall, blowin' six bits tryin' to look human, only to be told he's wasted his money. Does anybody else aim to insult me, or can we go eat?"

"Let's go eat," said Lorna. "We can insult you anytime."

"Let's try the hotel dining room," Cal said.

They mounted their horses, but Curly hadn't made a move.

"Come on, Curly," Bud begged. "Let's go with them."

"Come with us, Curly," said Jasmine. "If Bud gets smart with you, I'll spank him."

Bud reddened but said nothing, for it had won Curly over. Laughing, she mounted her horse, Bud mounted his, and they rode off toward the Plains Hotel.

16

*T*he day before Puckett and Summers were to return, Story spent another day in town. He hadn't told the outfit of this new ambush threat, nor did he intend to, unless he was forced to leave Fort Leavenworth with the man still on the loose and stalking him. In the past several days, he had ridden out of town occasionally, hoping he would be followed, but the bushwhacker hadn't taken the bait. His kind preferred to kill from cover, taking the victim by surprise. One of the inherent problems of stalking a man in daylight was the possibility that the hunted might lay an ambush of his own, thus becoming the hunter. So if the bushwhacker were to be tempted, he must be made to feel safe, to believe that ultimately he would have an opportunity to waylay Story in darkness.

Story decided to make it appear that he intended being away overnight, perhaps for several nights, and alone. He went to the livery, rented a mule and packsaddle, and rode from there to the mercantile. There, he loaded the mule with trade goods he would later transfer to one of the wagons. With the mule fully loaded, Story tarried around town until the day was well-spent, knowing that the bushwhacker must have time enough to become aware of his intentions.

When Story eventually rode out, it was to the south. If his adversary stopped to try and make any sense of the move, he likely wouldn't follow, but if he had a reason for wanting Story dead, he would get no better opportunity than this. Story kept to the plains, where there was little or no cover, knowing this wouldn't antagonize his pursuer. If the killer was following, he wouldn't make his move until he felt secure in darkness. An arroyo with a creek and some sheltering willows provided exactly the setting Story sought, and he stopped there, supposedly for the night. He unsaddled, picketed his horse, and unloading the mule, picketed the animal near his mount. He then started a fire, put on some water to boil, and made coffee. He presumed that the odor of coffee and the smoke from the concealed fire would enable the bushwhacker to find him.

Once it was dark enough to conceal his activity, Story arranged his blankets and bedroll in such a way that it appeared he was sleeping, head on his saddle, hat over his eyes. Moving back into the shadow of the arroyo's overhang, he settled down to wait. The fire had burned down to a bed of coals, and with the starlight, it was enough. It was exactly the kind of setting that appealed to a western man, and Story dozed to the sound of the horse and mule grazing.

He was instantly alert when the grazing abruptly ceased. The bushwhacker—or something—was approaching. In the starlight the killer would be skylined, but Story didn't need even that. Once the killer fired into his bedroll, Story knew he would have all the target he needed. The horse snorted, and Story held his breath. If the animal became too alarmed, only a fool would expect a frontiersman to sleep through that. But the horse and mule again began to graze, and Story settled back to wait. But the wait was short, and he sensed the man's presence before the shots came.

Story had his Colt cocked and ready, and when two

shots blasted out of the darkness, Story fired. Once at
the muzzle flash, and a second time to the right of it.
The horse nickered, the mule brayed, and then there
was only the sound of the animals grazing as they again
settled down. Story got to his feet, and when there was
no response to his movement, he walked to the point
where he could climb the bank of the arroyo. A pale
quarter moon was on the rise, and by the time he
neared the bushwhacker's position, he could see the dim
outline of the man. He lay on his back, both arms flung
above his head, and there was no sign of a gun. Story
hunkered down, lighted a match, and found himself
looking into the dead face of Ken Tanner.

"You escaped the rope at Alder Gulch," Story said.
"You were a damn fool not to quit while you were
ahead."

With a sigh, Story got to his feet. Surely this would be
the end of it. He turned Tanner's horse loose, loaded
the mule, and rode back to town. It was still early, and
the night man let him into the wagon yard, where he
transferred the load of goods from the mule into one of
his wagons. He then returned the mule and the packsaddle to the livery, left his horse there for the night, and
took a room at the Plains Hotel. He was suddenly tired,
but having had only coffee for supper, his belly was lank.
It being Sunday night, the hotel dining room was open,
so he had steak, potatoes, and coffee. He returned to
his room, blew out the lamp, and went to bed.

Dinner in the Plains Hotel dining room was an event to
be remembered, especially for Curly. She laughed,
talked, and didn't swear even once. Bud McDaniels was
encouraged, while Cal, Lorna, Tom, and Jasmine were
amazed.

"Maybe we can do this again, a kind of celebration,"
Jasmine said, "when we reach Virginia City. That is, if

Virginia City has a hotel with such a fancy dining room."

"Of course Virginia City has a hotel with a dining room," said Tom, with a laugh. "Having you imply that we're not at least as good as Leavenworth wounds me deeply. Fortunately, though, I heal quickly."

"You talk like that slimy lawyer my daddy's always meeting with," Lorna said.

"Well, thanks," said Tom. "If one of you will lift my rock, I'll crawl back under it."

Around the same time, leaving the barbershop, Manuel Cardenas, Bill Petty, Oscar Fentress, Smokey Ellison, Mac Withers, and Shanghai Wolfington began looking around for something to occupy them. The town had an abundance of saloons, but it seemed there was little else.

"After a man gits a bath and his ears lowered, there ain't nothin' left but the saloons," Smokey said.

"There's whorehouses," said Mac. "Shadley, Slim, and Greener spent the day in one yesterday."

"They must've rented a room and slept there," Bill Petty said. "Otherwise, I doubt the three of 'em would have been there more'n ten minutes."

"I stays outta dem places," said Oscar. "I 'fraid I git somethin' I don' pay fer."

"There are the saloons," Manuel Cardenas said. *"Riesgo."**

"That's likely safe enough," said Shanghai. "It's early in the day, but there's more'n enough of us fer a good poker game."

They chose a likely looking place called the Bullwhip. There were plenty of tables, for the saloon was empty, except for a sleepy bartender. The six riders went to the bar and ordered beers, and the bartender came to life long enough to serve them.

* Gamble

"Business kind of slow, ain't it, hoss?" Shanghai observed, in the way of conversation.

"Too damn early for drinkin'," said the bartender. " 'Cept for them that likes drinkin' early," he added hastily.

The riders pushed a pair of tables together and sat down. Manuel had a deck of cards, brand new. He broke the pack, pouring the cards from one hand to the other in graceful spirals.

"No wonder he wants to gamble," Smokey said. "He's a damn cardsharp."

They all laughed, but before they'd played the first hand, two men came into the saloon that brought all play to a halt. One of them was Paschal Stewart, the renegade who had escaped the canyon ambush.

"We don't want no trouble," said Shanghai quietly. "Ignore the varmint."

But Stewart wouldn't be ignored. Once his eyes became accustomed to the dim interior of the saloon, he stood with his back to the bar, openly staring at the six men seated at the table. Glass in hand, Stewart walked over to the table and stood there facing Bill Petty.

"I've seen you somewhere before, pilgrim, and it wasn't a happy meetin'."

"I doubt it," Petty said coolly. "I'm choosy about the company I keep."

Stewart leaned across the table and deliberately poured the remainder of his beer on Petty's poker hand. Bill Petty moved like chain lightning. He snatched a fistful of Stewart's shirt, dragged him across the table, and drove a hard right to his chin. He then took Stewart by the back of his belt and dropped the renegade facedown, raising a cloud of dust.

"Hey," bawled the bartender, "no fighting in here."

"Who's fighting?" Petty asked. "This hombre's lackin' in manners, and I just showed him the error of his ways. If he comes to and wants a fight, we'll do it outside."

Stewart's companion still stood at the bar, making no move, saying not a word. It was Shanghai who spoke, and his voice seemed loud in the stillness.

"He's lookin' fer trouble, Bill. Mr. Story ain't gonna like this. Maybe we oughta ease out, while we can."

"I've known Nels since vigilante days in Alder Gulch," Petty said, "and he wouldn't run from this. Neither will I. I'm my own man, and I'll take responsibility for whatever I have to do. The rest of you back off, and when this varmint's able to stand on his hind legs, it's his move. But if there's any runnin' to be done, he'll be the hombre doin' it."

The bartender was easing toward the door, and Petty stopped him.

"If you're goin' for the sheriff, don't bother. I want you here, with your eyes and ears open, when this coyote wakes up. If he needs some more education, we'll go outside, but I want you to witness his intentions."

Stewart's companion hadn't moved from his position at the bar. Shanghai stood up, facing the man.

"Friend," said Shanghai, "are you buyin' chips in this game?"

"No way," the stranger said hastily. "It ain't my fight."

"He's likely drunk," the bartender said as Stewart began to stir.

"His problem," Petty said. "I've shot troublesome drunks when they insisted on it."

Stewart rolled over and sat up, eyeing Petty with all the hate he could muster.

"You can get up and get out of here," said Petty, "and that'll be the end of it. The choice is yours."

"Nobody does that to me and lives to talk about it," Stewart hissed. "Nobody. If you're man enough to meet me in the street, I'll kill you." There was a strange look in his eyes that bordered on insanity.

"I'm man enough," said Petty. "I'll meet you outside."

Stewart got unsteadily to his feet, backing toward the door. Reaching it, he stepped outside, his eyes still on Petty.

"Except for watching my back," Petty said, "the rest of you stay out of it. You heard what he said, and I'm taking him at his word."

Everybody, including the bartender and Stewart's unnamed companion, followed Bill Petty outside. Stewart stood in the middle of the dirt street, a hundred yards away. It was early enough in the day that nobody else was in sight. Petty stepped into the street, waiting. There was intimidation in the act itself, forcing Stewart to come to him. But Stewart did, walking slowly, his hand near the butt of his Colt. Petty waited, his thumbs hooked in his pistol belt. His very nonchalance was intended to unnerve Stewart, for a nervous gunman was tempted to rely more on speed than accuracy. Such was the case with Paschal Stewart. Compared to Stewart's, Bill Petty's draw seemed painfully slow. Stewart got off two shots, both of them over Petty's head. Bill Petty fired once, and Stewart took a step backward. Then his knees buckled and he fell on his back, unmoving. But the shots had aroused the town, and before Petty had holstered his Colt, men came on the run. One of them was Sheriff Webb Hankins. He took just one look at Bill Petty and his cowboy companions and broke out his string of profanity.

"I might of knowed it," he said bitterly. "You varmints has got to be the rest of that damn Story outfit. Has anybody got anything t' say, 'fore I chunk the lot of you in jail?"

"He drew on me, and I defended myself," said Petty. "Does a man go to jail in Kansas for that?"

"He's right, Sheriff," the bartender said. "This gent comes in lookin' for a fight. He was give a chance to back off, but he wouldn't have it. I was asked to be a witness, which I was. This hombre ain't done nothin' he wasn't forced to do."

Clearly that didn't go according to what the sheriff wished to believe, but half the town had heard the bartender's speech. It was too convincing to be ignored, so Sheriff Hankins did the sensible thing. He backed down.

"Self-defense is legal," he said grudgingly, "but nothin' else is, damn it, an' don't none o' you fergit that."

He turned and walked away, leaving Stewart's body where it lay. Let somebody else plant the varmint.

"I think I'll ride back to the herd," said Petty. "I've had enough of town for a while."

"I be goin' with you," Oscar said.

Nobody wanted to stay, so they all rode out. They rode in silence, but to a man they were proud of Bill Petty. Not only was Nelson Story a man with the bark on, his friends were of the same measure.

Story's outfit had all had their time in town, and had time on their hands. Story had spent all day Saturday and Sunday away from camp, and when he didn't return at all Sunday night, they began to wonder. He had told them only they would likely be taking the trail west on Tuesday, the twenty-seventh. They knew only that he intended to buy wagons and trade goods, and that he would be hiring drivers. He had purposely said nothing about the Remingtons, choosing to wait until Fort Leavenworth was far behind. One word falling on the wrong ears could ruin his friend at the fort, and destroy his friend's chances of replacing the rifles he had sold to Story. And Story knew his drivers would need those rifles in the months to come, as Red Cloud and Crazy Horse began their rampage along the Bozeman.

* * *

Story slept poorly in his hotel bed, and was up before first light on the morning of the twenty-sixth. He had breakfast with Jubal Holden and Handy Lemburg, and spent the rest of the day impatiently awaiting the arrival of his friends, Levi Puckett and Waddy Summers. When they rolled in, part of a six-wagon train, it was almost dark. When they had howdied, Story wasted no time.

"Supper's on me, amigos. Then I have a proposition for you."

"Excuse me if I don't git too excited," Waddy Summers said. "Ever'time I fall for one o' your porpositions, I end up bein' shot at, or with some bastard wantin' to cut my throat."

"I was just thinkin' the same thing," said Levi Puckett, "but you said it lots better."

Story laughed, and then took them to the Plains Hotel dining room, where they joined Jubal Holden and Handy Lemburg.

"Whatever he's got in mind," Waddy said, "I can see he's already roped and branded these gullible old varmints."

When the waiter had taken their order and they waited for their steaks, Story told them of his plans and what he wished of them.

"Nels," said Levi, "before the year's done, you're goin' to see the Bozeman runnin' red with blood. White man's blood. Them damn forts the army's got strung out acrost Wyomin' an' Montana is a two-edged sword. Fer starters, compared t' Red Cloud an' Crazy Horse, they ain't got enough fightin' men t'sneeze at. Second, not only is the forts not helpin', the damn things is hurtin' the cause, bein' a violation of the treaties with the Sioux."

"You don't have to convince me," Story said. "I agree with your every word. Not only are the forts likely a violation of the government's treaty with the Sioux, they're only a temporary solution. They're for protection of whites on the Bozeman Trail until the Union Pacific finally completes the transcontinental railroad. That's supposed to eliminate the need for the Bozeman, but there have been setbacks for the railroad, such as graft, corruption, and under-the-table deals in Washington. The rails won't be reaching Wyoming until God knows when. Predictions are for 1868."*

"Hell," said Waddy, "that's two more years of Sioux hell-raisin' along the Bozeman."

"You're dead right," Story said, "and that gets us back to my proposal. Everytime you roll out of here, you're taking your life in your hands. I have an outfit of twenty-five riders, and every one will be armed with the new Remington rolling-block rifles and a Colt revolver. Besides, there'll be the four of you, with the same arms. How many times have you driven the Bozeman with that kind of defense?"

"I reckon the answer t'that's obvious," said Levi. "By God, I knowed he'd rope us in. When are you aimin' t'move out?"

"Just as soon as the two of you are willing," Story said. "Tomorrow?"

"Hell, no," said Waddy. "Wednesday maybe. We been out there near six months, an' there ain't been a night I didn't hear them war whoops in my nightmares. Now I aim to have a couple nights without 'em, just so's I don't ferget what it's like."

"Wednesday, then," said Story. "I'll meet you at first light, at the wagon yard. I'll have the wagons loaded tomorrow."

March 28, 1866. The Oregon Trail.

Story was already at the wagon yard when his four bull whackers arrived. First they went to the livery, where

* Trail Drive Series No. 2, *The Western Trail*

each man had awaiting him a team of oxen on lead ropes.

"Waddy," Story said, "you hitch up and lead out. There's room in your wagon for some freight you'll be picking up at the fort. When you're done there, just follow the Smokey Hill west until you see the herd."

Not all the freight Waddy was to pick up would be legitimate. Included would be the wooden crates containing thirty Remington rolling-block rifles, with an ample supply of .50 caliber shells.

When the four loaded wagons rolled into the valley where the herd had been gathered, Story introduced his riders to the bull whackers, and the drive took the trail. A dozen new calves had been dropped during the week near Fort Leavenworth. That, plus the four loaded wagons, slowed the drive, and they covered less than ten miles.

"We'll be traveling more slowly the rest of the way," Story said that night around the supper fire, "but the danger won't be any greater. Jubal, Handy, Levi, and Waddy will be on watch with the rest of us. Besides that, I've evened the odds some. Waddy, you and Levi break out those gun crates."

The two teamsters unloaded the heavy crates from Waddy's wagon, and with a crowbar Waddy began breaking them open. Quickly Story explained the new Remingtons, and the riders gathered around as he demonstrated their features.

"It'll be a mite crowded in our saddle boots," Coon Tails said. "We still got them Winchesters."

"There's room for them in Waddy's wagon," said Story. "I want all of you armed with these new Remingtons. When you have the time for it, practice ejecting the spent shell and reloading. This weapon has a range of a good thousand yards. Learn to use it, and Indian arrows can't even come close."

While the trail drive was slowed to accommodate the

loaded wagons, there were benefits. The calves were able to keep up with the herd, and the longhorns began to put on weight. The animals had become trailwise, and with the slower pace, there were no bunch quitters. During their first days on the trail there was almost constant rain. Now the situation seemed to have reversed itself, and there was no rain. The drag riders wore their bandannas over their faces to avoid some of the dust. Time dragged, and one night during the first watch, Lorna trotted her horse alongside Cal's.

"You know what day this is?" she asked.

"No," said Cal. "They kind of run together. Friday?"

"It's April fifth," she said, irritated. "It's my birthday. Today I'm eighteen."

They were stirrup to stirrup, and he leaned over, kissing her hard. "Happy birthday," he said. "Now you're a woman."

"I've been a woman for a long time," she said. "I thought you discovered that back in Fort Worth, in the hotel."

"I did," said Cal, "but it didn't do me no good. I was all trussed up and couldn't move."

"Cal, when we get to Virginia City, what are we going to do . . . first?"

"Find us some bunks where they ain't a damn cow nowhere in sight, and sleep for a month." There was a long, painful silence. Awkwardly, Cal spoke again, and only made it worse. "Well," he said, "I reckon we won't spend *all* our time sleepin'."

"Calvin Snider," she cried, "you're a damn crude, ignorant, unromantic cowboy, without the slightest notion of how to treat a woman."

She rode away, leaving him pondering his ignorance, wondering how to get back on the good side of her. He didn't know Bud McDaniels was anywhere near until Bud spoke.

"Shake, brother," Bud said sympathetically. "I've had

the same brand slapped on me, except she left out unromantic."

"I ain't wantin' to talk about it," said Cal sullenly.

"Then let's talk about me and Curly," Bud said. "She
swears at me, and Jasmine laughs at me. What'n hell
does a woman expect of a man anyhow?"

"Maybe she just wants to be left alone," said Cal.

"Hell of a lot of help you are," Bud said. "I could of
got that out of Curly. She's acted like a man for so long,
she can't get out of the habit, I reckon."

He rode on, leaving Cal to his own thoughts. He wondered how Tom Allen got along so well with the fiery
Jasmine. The girl swore like a bull whacker when she
was angry, and had a temper like a sore-tailed bobcat.
Yet she shared all her meals with Tom, and they rode
together during their nightly watch. When Jasmine had
a siege of temper, Tom usually said something perfectly
foolish, and the two of them ended up laughing together. But when he himself tried a similar tactic, Cal
thought, Lorna rode off and sulked. He wished the girl
could be more like Jasmine, and wondered what in tarnation he was going to do with her once they reached
Montana Territory.

Again Story took to riding ahead of the drive, often
seeking water. He consulted with the bull whackers he
had hired, for they were now more familiar with this
route than he was, having driven it for the many years
since Story had given it up. While other landmarks had
grown dim in his memory, he still remembered the rivers and where they would eventually parallel the trail.
Once they crossed into Nebraska, the drive could follow
the Deshler River almost until they reached the Platte.
It flowed west from Omaha, running nearly parallel with
the old Oregon Trail the last two-thirds of the way to
Fort Laramie. It was a sure source of water. Each day,
usually at the supper fire, Story added their day's travel

to his previous total. His "calendar" was a yard-long strip of rawhide, with a knot for each day and a double knot for Sunday. When one strip was used up, he'd start another. Shanghai watched him tie the first knot in a new thong.

"First day of the month," said Shanghai. "Which month?"

"May," Story said.

"How many miles we come since leavin' Fort Leavenworth?" Shanghai asked.

"A little over two hundred," said Story. "We're about four hundred miles from Fort Laramie."

The drive was more than a month west of Leavenworth before there was rain, and it rode in on a screaming, vicious wind that threatened to rip the canvas from the wagons. Mud and water was hub deep, and the efforts of the oxen were in vain. The heavy wagons wouldn't budge.

"Unhitch them," Story said. "We'll have to wait this out."

It was all but impossible to drive a herd into a storm. The longhorns wanted only to turn their tails to the fearsome wind and drift back the way they had come. The best the riders could do was to start them milling and hold them in a bunch. But the rain and high wind proved to be the least of their problems. The thunder rumbled closer, and behind it came the lightning. Long, jagged streaks that danced like demons across the heavens. A cow bawled and others joined in, like a demented chorus, the herd just waiting for something to start them running. It began when lightning flared from one horizon to the other and when a bolt struck somewhere near. The earth shook, and before the shock died, a second bolt struck. The terrified longhorns stampeded to the east, back the way they had come, the oxen that had drawn the wagons running with them. Pursuit of the stampeding herd was impossible, as riders tried to calm their buck-jumping horses and remain in the saddle. When the storm finally blew itself out, darkness had fallen. Story and his riders were chilled to the bone, discouraged, and hungry. But there would be no supper, no sleep, probably no breakfast, and a gather facing them that might take days. . . .

17

Somehow Story and his riders survived the long, miserable night, and Sandy Bill had enough dry firewood for a breakfast fire. The day dawned gray and cold, with low-hanging gray clouds harbingers of rain yet to come. Leaving the four teamsters there to guard their wagons, Story and the outfit set out to gather the stampeded herd. Before they had ridden two miles, they discovered the mangled bodies of three calves trampled in the stampede, and a little farther, the bodies of two of the oxen Story had bought to draw the wagons.

"Lightnin' got 'em," Coon Tails said. "They may be more."

While they found no more dead animals, the live ones proved troublesome enough. This stampede was different from earlier ones, in that the longhorns hadn't regrouped. Many of them grazed alone, or at best, in groups of two or three.

"I dunno what got into the varmints," said Shanghai. "The stampede split an' they just fanned out from hell t'breakfast."

The extra horses and Sandy Bill's mules were found first, and after that, the rest of the oxen. Gathering the scattered longhorns was a slow, painful endeavor, with many of the brutes becoming rebellious. Early in the afternoon there was more rain, and while there was no thunder or lightning, there was an excess of mud and water. Horses slipped and fell, and riders were thrown, saved from injury by the very mire that had spilled them. Cal Snider and Quanah Taylor ran a tally, and the results were disappointing.

"We don't have even half of 'em," Cal said.

They rode on, finding two or three longhorns at a time, driving them back to a slowly growing herd. The low-hanging clouds promised early darkness, and it became apparent to Story that they couldn't finish the gather until the next day.

"We'll take what we have," said Story, "and drive them back to where the wagons are. Tomorrow we'll look for the rest of them."

"I found somethin' we can use back yonder," Mac Withers said. "I'm goin' after it." He galloped away toward a distant brushy draw, and when he caught up, he had hitched his lariat to what was left of a pine log. There was a large, resinous heart studded with pine knots, and it would burn readily.

"I reckon Kansas be a dog's idee of hell," said Oscar. "They be no trees."

"Oscar," Story said, "if there's some of that cowhide left, I want you to make a pair of simple calf halters."

"They be some hide left," said Oscar. "It be in Sandy Bill's wagon."

"Good," Story said. "We're going to replace the two dead oxen with a pair of longhorn cows. Bulls are out of the question. The cows will likely be trouble enough, and that's why I want the calf halters. We'll harness one cow with each team of oxen, and we'll use the cows that have just dropped calves. We'll tie one end of a lead rope to the calf halter and the other end to the cow's harness. I'm hopin', with the calf walking beside the cow, the brute won't fight the harness and make it hard on the oxen."

The rain held off, and by suppertime the riders had dried out. Sandy Bill had a cowboy's intuition, and knowing that everybody's enthusiasm was at a low ebb, made dried apple pies for supper. By the time the riders for the first watch were mounting up, the clouds had parted to reveal a few timid stars.

"Thank God," said Jasmine. "I don't ever remember being as cold, wet, and hungry as I was last night."

After the dinner in the Plains Hotel, when Curly was almost pleasant, Bud McDaniels had left her pretty much alone. It didn't seem to matter to Curly, but it did to some of the other riders. Bud had seen Arch Rainey, Mac Withers, and Dutch Mayfield talking to the girl, and Curly responded to them more civilly than she ever had to Bud. He decided to find out where he stood with her, or if he had any standing at all. The best time to approach her was while they were nighthawking, and he caught up, walking his horse beside hers.

"Curly."

"Leave me alone," she said, "or I'll swear at you."

"I don't care," said Bud. "That's better than having you ignore me."

"What do you want of me?"

"I just want you to be my friend," Bud said, "if you're never anything more."

"I like you, Bud," Curly said, more kindly than she'd ever spoken to him. "It's just . . . too soon for me to think of you as . . . as a woman would think of you. I'm still a cowboy in my mind, and I don't know how long before I can be anything else. Or if I ever can. If you can be . . . my friend, without pushing me, I . . . I think I'd like that."

They rode and talked until it was almost time for their watch to end, and it was the most pleasant time they'd ever had together. There hadn't been a harsh word, and Bud McDaniels silently vowed not to lose the advantage he believed he had gained.

Meanwhile, in the days following her last blow-up, Lorna Flagg had been decidedly cool to Cal Snider. As undesirable as her home life had been, she had left a measure of security for she knew not what, hitching her dreams to those of Cal Snider. But what *were* those dreams? Would he bed her like a squaw or saloon woman, leaving on a whim, returning if and when he wished? She had no reason to believe he would, but she had burned her bridges, and desperately needed some assurance as to what lay ahead. Suddenly she heard voices, and Curly's laugh. Lorna turned her horse, riding back the way she had come. She'd been feeling sorry for Bud McDaniels in his less than satisfactory relationship with Curly, and it now seemed that the two might yet reconcile their differences. Encouraged, she rode until she found Cal. He sat his saddle with his right leg hooked around the horn, hat tipped over his eyes, apparently dozing. But he had heard her coming. He tipped back his hat, waiting for her to speak, if she intended to.

"Cal," she said uncertainly, "I . . . I feel just awful. I . . ."

"You've had enough of the trail, I reckon."

"I can take anything the trail throws at me," said Lorna. "What I can't take is this feeling that . . . that you don't really care about me, that you brought me with you because . . . damn it, because you couldn't sneak off and leave me behind."

He reached for her, but as he caught her arm, her horse sidestepped. Off balance, he slid out of the saddle, taking her with him. They fell in an ignominious tangle of arms and legs as their horses danced nervously away. Lorna was torn between anger and laughter, and laughter won. She laughed, and Cal joined her.

"Tell me again what we're going to do when we get to Virginia City," Lorna said.

"First," said Cal, "I reckon we'll find you some fancy duds. A dress. In all the years I've knowed you, I've never seen you wear nothin' but Levi's pants. What are you hidin' from me?"

"You'll find out, when the time comes." She laughed, and then she became serious again. "A dress will be nice, Cal, but that . . . that's not what I wanted to hear."

"A woman should have a new dress on her marryin' day," Cal said.

"That's what I wanted to hear, you damn ignorant cowboy." Her actions took the sting from her words, and Cal Snider no longer had any doubts as to what he would do with her when they reached Virginia City. . . .

Story and his riders spent all the next day seeking the scattered herd. Despite the lack of trees on the Kansas plain, there were arroyos and thickets in which the longhorns were adept at hiding, and it wasn't all that easy, flushing them out. Especially from the thickets.

"It's that much like Texas," said Gus Odell. "There's aways a thicket so dense a man can't swing a rope, and that's where the cows are."

Story laughed. "We'll cut the cards, and the low man gets to crawl into the thicket and punch them out with a sharp stick."

They all laughed at the cowboy humor, but it wasn't far from the truth. When the end of the day was near and they were forced to end the gather, a tally revealed they were still missing sixteen head.

"That's it," said Story. "We can't devote another day to hunting them."

* * *

When the herd took the trail the following morning, Jubal Holden and Waddy Summers each had an unwilling longhorn cow replacing one of the dead oxen. Trotting beside each cow, secured by the halters Oscar had fashioned, was the cow's newly dropped calf.

"I never would of believed that if I wasn't seein' it," Shanghai said. "We're just almighty lucky all them calves wasn't trampled in the stampede."

As unlikely as it seemed, after three or four days with the longhorns in harness they were making as many miles as they'd been making with only oxen pulling the wagons.

Handy Lemburg laughed. "That's why Nelson Story was such a good teamster. He'd git a wagon through, no matter what. Give him a chance, and he'd of roped the devil, harnessed the varmint, an' had him drawin' a wagon."

The drive reached the Deshler River, and it would answer their need for water until they were within two or three days' drive of the Platte. One morning as they were about to take the trail, there was a rumble that sounded like distant thunder. The wind was from the northwest, and the sound rose and faded with the wind. Coon Tails put his ear to the ground, listened, and sat up.

"Buffalo comin'," said the old mountain man. "One hell of a bunch of 'em. We'd best stay where we are, so's we don't git caught up in that."

"You're right," Story said. "Bunch the herd."

"Mr. Story," said Cal, "some of us would like to try these new Remingtons. When we know where the herd's running, do you care if we shoot some buffalo?"

"Go ahead," Story said, "but not more than two or three. We can use some meat, but I don't believe in killing for sport."

"It's likely one of the last great herds," Coon Tails said. "Bill Cody, Drago Herndon, an' some others is killin' 'em by the thousands t'feed track layers that's buildin' the Union Pacific, out there west of Omaha."*

The thunder grew louder. The horses grew skittish with the vibration of the earth, and the riders circled the herd, lest the unaccustomed sound frighten the longhorns. After a while they could see the ragged edge of the herd as it thundered almost due south.

"God knows how wide a swath they're cuttin'," Shanghai said. "Damn good thing the herd didn't git caught in that."

Cal Snider, Tom Allen, and Quickenpaugh rode out with their new rolling-block Remingtons, reining up at what they considered a thousand yards from the lumbering herd. Cal fired first, bracing the Remington across his saddle. A buffalo staggered, fell, and lay still. Tom Allen fired, and with the same results. Quickenpaugh repeated their feats, grinning his appreciation of the powerful weapon.

"*Bueno,*" said Quickenpaugh. "*Mucho poder.*"*

The trio managed to get close enough to the passing herd to retrieve the three animals they had shot, dragging them near the camp for the skinning. They dared not go too near, lest the smell of blood spook the longhorns. Quickenpaugh viewed the buffalo he had shot with some distaste.

"*Bueno* hunt," said the Indian. "No squaw. *Malo.*"

Tom Allen laughed. "Sorry, Quickenpaugh. You skin your own kill. It's the white man's way."

"Some way *bueno,*" said Quickenpaugh, "some *malo.* This *malo.*"

With little else to do, some of the other riders helped skin the buffaloes, and they took the hump and the tongue.

* Trail Drive Series No. 3, *The Chisholm Trail*
* Much power.

"If we get to it," Tom said, "we'll have time to peg and scrape the hides."

"This herd may be a day in passing," said Story, "which is just as well. Oscar and Manuel says we're about to gain some new calves, and they'll need time to get on their feet."

June 10, 1866. The Platte River.

By the time Story's outfit reached the Platte, some of the dangers of the trail had become all too evident. There were the remains of burned wagons and the bleached bones of horses, mules, and oxen. More sinister were the inevitable grassed-over graves of those whose dreams of the frontier had met with bitter reality.

"But all we've been hearing is the Bozeman Trail," Jasmine said, "and we still have a long way to go before we get there."

"It's some misleadin'," said Coon Tails. "The Sioux is horse Injuns, an' they ain't limited. You hear more about the hell-raisin' on the Bozeman, 'cause that's Sioux stompin' grounds, an' that's where the forts is that's got Red Cloud an' Crazy Horse in a fightin' mood. But that don't mean the red varmints can't ride back along the Oregon, liftin' hair an' lootin' wagon trains. I reckon the forts along the Bozeman is some little pertection, but they ain't nothin' along the Platte to git in the way."

It was grim news, and however quiet the surrounding darkness, the riders no longer dozed in their saddles. Nebraska didn't seem all that different from Kansas, except that there was no shortage of water, for they would virtually follow the Platte River until it flowed south to Colorado, beyond Fort Laramie. But despite the macabre evidence of previous Indian attacks along the trail, Story's drive continued unmolested. But Story wasn't a man to push his luck. He always had the riders bunch the herd a good hour before dark, and when supper was done, Sandy Bill allowed the cook fire to remain no more than a bed of coals to keep the coffee hot. It was a pleasant time, when the outfit came together, and it was during one such interlude that Lorna asked Story about the high plains.

"Well," said Story, "it's at a much higher altitude and it's not all that hot in summer. In fact, the nights are cool, and you'll need your blankets. There's grass, belly high on a horse, as far as you can see. But the winters can be hard, with snow, and temperatures far below zero. I expect it will be late fall before we reach Virginia City, and it'll be almighty cold. When we get to Fort Laramie, each of you will need to buy winter clothes. You'll need a heavy coat, warm gloves, wool socks, a wool scarf to protect your ears, and wool longhandles."

"Longhandles for me?" Lorna asked with a straight face.

"Longhandles for you, Jasmine, and Curly," said Story with an equally straight face, "and I'd suggest you get at least two pair. There'll be days when you'll be wearing them both, and wishing you had a third pair."

July 25, 1866. Fort Laramie, Wyoming Territory.

It was late afternoon when they sighted the fort. Leaving the herd half a mile away, along the Platte, Story rode in. He was shown into the office of Colonel Moonlight, the post commander. Story's trail drive to Montana Territory had met with only hostility from the military, and that's all he had expected at Fort Laramie, but Colonel Moonlight went beyond that.

"What you are attempting, sir, is foolish in the extreme," said Moonlight. "The best advice I can give you is this: sell your cattle to the commissary, and let this foolish endeavor end here. It is civilian activity such as you propose that prevents the army from doing its job."

"I am painfully aware that the army isn't doing its job, Colonel," Story said, "but I wasn't sure why. Thanks for enlightening me. I aim to push on to Virginia City, with or without your blessing."

"You'll go without it," Moonlight snapped. "You'll get no protection from this post."

"I don't want it," said Story. "Before I'd lick any part of your carcass, I'd fight the whole damn Sioux nation, just me and my cowboys."

His riders, when he delivered the colonel's message, expressed opinions even stronger than Story's, and in far more explosive language. Despite the hostility of the post commander, Story decided to spend several days there, allowing his riders to purchase clothing suited to high plains winters, and to learn what he could of the Indian menace ahead. The store, Bordeaux's Trading House, would be their best source of information. Coon Tails was known there, and Story asked the old mountain man to accompany him. They were fortunate to find Black Bill Guthrie in the store. Black Bill, a friend of Coon Tails, also knew Jim Bridger. Black Bill was more than a little contemptuous of Colonel Moonlight, and was willing to talk.

"The colonel's one of them West Point wonders," Black Bill said, "an' you ain't gonna believe what a god-awful mess he's made of things, just in the little time he's been here. 'Fore you leave, walk up yonder an' have a look at the bluff, north of the emigrant campground. You'll find what's left of Black Foot an' Two Face, a pair of Red Cloud's braves. Colonel Moonlight had 'em hung, so he claims, as a warning to all Indians. Turned out, by God, the Injuns wasn't guilty of what he was chargin' 'em with."

"God Almighty," said Story. "No wonder things have

gone to hell between Indians and whites. What were the charges?"

"When the soldiers found Black Foot an' Two Face," said Black Bill, "the Injuns had a white woman an' her baby with 'em. You know the gover'ment's got a standin' reward for the surrender of hostages, an' this woman—a Missus Eubank—an' her baby was bein' brung to the fort fer the reward. This woman an' her baby had been taken somewheres in Nebraska, an' it wasn't Black Foot an' Two Face that stole 'em. They'd bought the captives from hostiles, an' all they wanted was the reward. This Missus Eubank told the story, told it true. She begged fer mercy fer Black Foot an' Two Face, but Colonel Moonlight didn't pay no attention to her. He hung them pore bastards an' then chained their carcasses to the face of that bluff, fer buzzards an' magpies to pick their bones."

It was a gruesome tale. The next morning Story walked to the foot of the bluff north of the emigrant campground. He climbed to where the bodies of the unfortunate Oglala braves hung from a gibbet, dangling from chains. Magpies pecked at the rotting remains, and the stink was such that Story was forced to retreat. Later he learned that Coon Tails had told the tragic tale to others in the outfit, and they too viewed the remains of Black Foot and Two Face, who had received their reward for abiding by government regulations. The tragic event, the deaths of two men who had done no wrong, had a sobering effect on Story's riders. They understood, perhaps for the first time, Indian hostility. Other whites would pay the price for Moonlight's folly, and would not Red Cloud have this strong on his mind when it came time to extract vengeance?

"I don't agree with what the Sioux are doing," Jasmine McDaniels said, "but I understand their reasons for doing it."

"They's goin' to be hell on the Bozeman," Coon Tails predicted, "an' it'll come 'fore the end of this year."

"I'm hoping we'll be in Virginia City before it comes," said Story, "but if we have to fight, then so be it. We'll be ready."

During Story's second day at Fort Laramie, two young men approached his camp.

"I'm John Catlin," said one, "and this is Steve Grover. We'd decided we was goin' to rot, settin' here waitin' for somebody goin' to Virginia City. Somebody that stood a chance against the Sioux. We'd like to ride with you."

"I have no objection to that," Story said, "if you don't mind fighting."

"Mind it or not," said Grover, "we got the experience. We just got done fightin' a war."

"I see you have Colt revolvers," Story said, "and I have extra rifles for you. Rifles such as you've never seen before. We move out in the morning at first light."

When Story's outfit met around the supper fire, he took the opportunity to introduce Grover and Catlin. And he had some final advice for his riders.

"You'll find Virginia City a mite primitive in some ways. That's why I'm packin' in these wagons loaded with goods. With trouble coming on the Bozeman, some things may be in short supply for a while. The other forts along the trail are new, and with the Indian trouble, their stores—if there are any—will have only bare necessities. Anything you need now, or expect to need in Virginia City, go to Bordeaux's and get it now. I'll advance money to those of you needing it. One other thing. Having seen the military's approach to peace with the Sioux, I think it's only fair that I sweeten the pot some. At the end of the trail, every one of you will receive an extra fifty dollar bonus. It's little enough for what lies ahead. The danger is even greater than I expected."

Most of the riders followed Story's advice and spent the evening at the store. Already they had the winter clothing Story had suggested, and these final purchases would be personal items. Even with the danger that lay ahead, it was a happy occasion. Curly and Bud now seemed satisfied with one another's company, there had never been any obvious disagreement between Tom and Jasmine, and Cal Snider resolved forever any doubts Lorna might have had. Fortified with a hundred dollar advance from Story, Cal bought Lorna the ring she would wear when they reached Virginia City. It became a night to remember, and even the garrulous old Coon Tails revealed a sentimental depth nobody had ever suspected. From around his neck he took a slender silver chain from which was suspended a tiny silver dragon. This he gave to Lorna.

"Wear it, girl," he said. "It was my mama's, an' it'll look better on you than on some Sioux brave. I got a feelin' this might be my last trail, er close to it."

"Thank you," said Lorna. Impulsively she stood on tiptoe and kissed the old man on his weathered cheek. He wandered away into the darkness before knuckling his eyes.

In Story's absence the riders were contemplating their wages and the promised bonus.

"Mr. Story's payin' us from the first of February," Hitch Gould said, "and I look for it takin' us maybe ten an' a half months on the trail. That figgers out to at least five hunnert an' fifty dollars. God, I seen my daddy not end up with that much in two or three years."

"Lawd God," said Oscar Fentress, "I have to see it. I ain't sure dey be that much money in the whole blame world."

It was one of those occasions when Sandy Bill, never very talkative, had joined the riders around the fire.

"What will you do, Sandy Bill?" Lorna asked. "Will you go back to Texas?"

There was an uncomfortable silence. It wasn't the western way to inquire more of a man than he'd voluntarily revealed. Cal caught the girl's eye, and she knew she had crossed a line of which she had been unaware. But Sandy Bill saved her with a sense of humor none of them had realized he possessed.

"I ain't got much hair left," he said, "but such as it is, I'd like t'keep it. Maybe I'll go back t'Texas one day. All my kin's buried there, an' they ain't goin' nowhere. Neither am I, till this trouble with the Sioux is finished. Until then, I reckon I'll find me a place an' go on dishin' out grub to half-starved, ungrateful cow wrasslers."

It was the longest speech any of them had ever heard from the usually tight-lipped old cook; and they embarrassed him with a round of applause.

"Bill," said Shanghai, "I got me a stake an' some seed cows. If this new range on the high plains is even close t' what Story claims, you won't be lackin' fer a place t' hang yer hat. You kin bunk with me as long as you want."

"It'll be fine for them that's got cows," Mac Withers said, "but what's the rest of us gonna be doin'? We got enough riders right here to cowboy six ranches, an' half of this herd's gonna be sold for beef."

"There's always work in the mines," said Bill Petty. "I reckon the big strikes are behind us, but nothing's played out."

"That puts us Texans in a bad position," Bud McDaniels said, "because we can't work the mines from a saddle."

It was an undisputed fact, and worthy of the laughter that followed.

"I've got a guarantee of two good riders," said Shanghai, "an' besides Smokey an' Oscar, I reckon I can use two more."

"Tom and me won't have that many cows, just startin'," Petty said, "but I reckon we can each use a couple of riders. I reckon nobody will be left out in the cold."

"Nels has more cows than any of us," said Tom. "He'll be needing riders. Knowin' him, once the challenge of this drive has been met, he purely won't be satisfied ridin' the range and pullin' cows out of bog holes. He'll hire cowboys for that."

"Well, thanks," Arch Rainey said. "That's what my mama always wanted, for me to learn a trade, so's I wouldn't have to work so hard."

"These high plains, if they are truly *pais de alto hierba*,* there will be a place for us all," said Manuel Cardenas.

Quickenpaugh had listened, saying nothing. Only when he became aware that some of the riders were watching him did he speak.

"No cow, no bog hole," Quickenpaugh said.

* Land of tall grass

18

July 28, 1866. The Bozeman.

*T*he last thing Story and his riders saw as they moved north on the Bozeman Trail was the rotting remains of the pair of Sioux that Colonel Moonlight had unjustly executed. Despite the firepower of the new Remingtons, Story had to concede he might be leading twenty-eight riders to their deaths. Short of turning back, he had but one alternative, and he had rejected that. He could have cut back to the southwest on the Oregon Trail, crossed the divide into Idaho, turned north, and then recrossed the divide into Virginia City. But the season was late, and before he could have gotten safely through the two mountain passes, it would have been October. Or even later, with the wagons slowing him down. He would have almost surely lost his entire herd, as well as the wagons, in deep snow. The Bozeman, with the marauding war parties of Red Cloud and Crazy Horse, was the only real choice he had. The Bozeman was at a lower altitude, with less chance of crippling snow, and the route to Virginia City was nearly three hundred miles shorter. Manuel Cardenas and Curly were the horse wranglers for the day, and they quickly moved the extra horses out behind Sandy Bill's wagon. Next came the herd, and following the drag, the four freight wagons. In recognition of the mountain man's years of scouting the high plains, Story had asked Coon Tails to accompany him as he scouted ahead of the herd.

"I hope the post commander at Fort Reno's more civil than the varmint at Fort Laramie was," Coon Tails said, "but I ain't countin' on it."

"Neither am I," said Story. "We'll report in, tell them where we're going, and move on. How far are we from Fort Reno?"

"The army figgers it at a hunnert an' seventy mile," Coon Tails said, "but I'd say two hunnert. Soldiers kin ride hosses where wagons can't go."

Two hundred miles to Fort Reno. They'd had a few good days, traveling ten miles, Story recalled, but they had seen entirely too many other days when they had covered only eight miles, or even less. The month of August would be nearly spent before they reached Fort Reno.

The second day after leaving Fort Laramie, Story and Coon Tails could see puffs of smoke rising from distant buttes to the north.

"Smoke talk," Story said, "and I reckon we know what they're saying."

"White man comin'," said Coon Tails, "bringin' the white man's buffalo, an' wagonloads of doodads to brighten Sioux wickiups."

Their first brush with the Sioux came in the late afternoon of the third day. The tag end of the herd was just topping a ridge when a band of Sioux came screeching out of a draw. The whooping, combined with their sudden appearance, spooked the herd, allowing the Sioux to drive away fifty head.

"They won't get far," Story said. "Cal, take five riders

with you and go after them. You have the range and the advantage with the Remingtons, so don't endanger yourselves. We'll hold the drive here until you return."

Cal chose Smokey Ellison, Quanah Taylor, Bud McDaniels, Quickenpaugh, and Arch Rainey.

"They're nervy bastards," said Smokey. "They left a trail you can foller in the dark, and nobody behind to slow pursuit."

"They got us considerably outnumbered," Cal said, "and they don't know about these Remingtons. Soon as we get within sight of 'em, we'll begin their education."

It took them almost an hour, for the Sioux had retreated to a secluded valley watered by a creek. Cal and his riders were about to top a ridge when they smelled smoke.

"We'll leave the horses here," Cal said, "until we see what they're up to."

They crept over the hill, keeping to cover, until they could see the Sioux gathered below.

"Well, just look at that," said Bud. "They've already killed a cow, and they're cookin' it for supper. They ain't expectin' to be followed."

"Why should they?" Cal said. "They outnumber us two to one, and if the army ain't got the sand to go after 'em, why should they be afraid of a bunch of cowboys? Let's get a mite closer, and we'll change their minds."

Cal led the way, and when he judged they were within range, halted. The six of them readied their Remingtons, and when Cal gave the signal, they all fired. Their first volley dropped six of the Sioux, and a second volley got five more. There was no opportunity for a third, as the remaining Indians scattered like quail. The riders returned to their horses, and with their Remingtons across their saddles, rode cautiously into the valley.

"Looked like seven of 'em hit the brush," said Quanah. "If the varmints is anything like Comanches, they could be bellied down, waitin' for us to get within their range."

"Maybe," Cal said, "but I don't think so. We call 'em savages, and in some ways they may be, but they ain't fools. They've never been hit from so far away before, and they don't know what to make of it. Come on, and let's round up those cows. Maybe we can get back to the drive before dark."

All the cows were recovered except the one the Indians had slaughtered. When Cal and his riders returned to where they had left the drive, they found it had moved on.

"They're lookin' for a place to bed down for the night," said Quanah.

It was after dark when Cal and his riders caught up with the drive, and they wasted no time praising the new Remingtons. Riders became especially watchful as they circled the herd in the darkness. But they weren't disturbed that night or for days thereafter.

"Maybe we'll reach Fort Reno without them coming after us again," Tom Allen said.

"Maybe," said Story, "but keep your rifles handy."

It was good advice, but the continued absence of the Sioux and the nearness of Fort Reno led to a false sense of security, and twenty miles south of Fort Reno, the Sioux attacked. They came storming down a ridge, two hundred strong, yelping like coyotes. Riding hard, they cut in close enough to loose their arrows. When they galloped away, two of Story's riders had been wounded. Slim had an arrow in his left side, while Greener had stopped one with his left shoulder. Again the Sioux had cut out part of the herd and had taken them over the ridge at a fast gallop.

"There'll be a doctor at the fort who can better treat these arrow wounds," Story said, "and the fort should have an ambulance. I'll need one man to ride to the fort for the ambulance, and a dozen of you to ride with me. We'll be going after our cows."

"I'll ride to Reno for the ambulance," said Cal.

"Hit the saddle, then," Story said. "Jasmine, please see what you can do for Greener and Slim. I'll take some riders and go after our cows."

Story rode out with a dozen men: Hitch, Arch, Smokey, Oscar, Quanah, Gus, Virg, Dutch, Jules, Manuel Cardenas, Bud, and Coon Tails. As before, there was difficulty in following the Sioux. This time, however, it seemed they had driven away the cows with the intention of laying an ambush for the riders who followed.

"Lemme git ahead," said Coon Tails. "This looks almighty like they want us t'foller 'em, an' that means they'll be layin' fer us. We got t'flush 'em out without gettin' close enough fer their arrers t'take effect."

Three or four hundred yards ahead was a thicket that from a distance seemed impenetrable. Suddenly a covey of birds dipped toward the thicket, but something within it frightened them, and they flew away.

"They're in there," Story said. "When I fire, cut loose with your rifles. We don't have anything to shoot at, but the Sioux aren't going to know. As many as there are, just firing blind, we'll hit some."

One after another the Remingtons cut loose, and as rapidly as the men reloaded, it seemed like ten times their number. After three barrages of .50 caliber slugs, there was a clatter of hooves beyond the thicket.

"They've sneaked out the other side and lit out," said Virg. "Are we goin' after 'em?"

"No," Story said. "They've seen what our rifles can do, and they won't allow us within range again. I think we'll find our cows on the farthest side of that thicket."

The cows were there, less than a hundred head, and the cowboys rounded them up. They had ridden wide of the thicket, and did so as they rode back the way they had come.

"I wonder if we hit any of 'em in that thicket," Arch said.

"Ain't likely," said Coon Tails, "but them .50 caliber hunks of lead kin make enough wind in their passin' to purely scare hell out of a man. I reckon them Sioux just lit out t' wait for a better time an' place."

When Cal returned with the ambulance, Cal rode behind, while two soldiers rode escort. There had been little Jasmine could do for Greener and Slim. The arrows would have to be driven on through, and it was fortunate they were near enough to Fort Reno for the cowboys to be cared for by a doctor. As it was, in the cumbersome ambulance they were still a long, bumpy ride from the fort. While there was little to be gained by the Sioux attacking the ambulance, Story wasn't one to take chances.

"Arch, I want you and Hitch to accompany the ambulance to the fort, just in case. Report to the post commander and tell him we'll be arriving sometime tomorrow. Just wait there for us."

"Let's move 'em out," Story shouted when the ambulance and its escort had gone. Mac Withers and Quickenpaugh took over as horse wranglers, and the herd again took the trail.

August 25, 1866. Fort Reno, Wyoming Territory.

Colonel Mattingly, the commanding officer at Fort Reno, proved helpful and courteous. He was adamantly opposed, however, to Story's drive to Virginia City. Story listened as Mattingly painted a grim picture of what lay ahead.

"Colonel Henry B. Carrington is in charge up there," Mattingly said. "He's just finished Fort Phil Kearny, and has selected a site for Fort C.F. Smith, in Montana Territory. Somewhere beyond, toward Virginia City, he has plans for two additional forts."

"He's a man who gets things done, then," said Story.

"Not necessarily," Mattingly replied, and Story caught an inflection in the officer's voice he probably hadn't intended. "We're already spread too thin, and I question the wisdom of building more forts when we're unable to adequately man those we already have. This is my personal opinion, and I am speaking unofficially, of course."

"Of course," Story said, inviting him to continue.

"Colonel Carrington has three hundred soldiers," said Mattingly, "while it's estimated Red Cloud has three thousand braves. A hundred and fifty soldiers and civilians have died in that vicinity. The Sioux are killing his men and running off his horses almost daily."

"There's going to be hell on the Bozeman, then."

"There is," said Mattingly, "and I don't know of a damn thing that any of us can do about it. Except," he added hastily, "avoid it."

"Thank you, Colonel," Story said. "Grim as it is, your point of view is refreshing. Up to now, I've been under the impression that the army had it all under control, that if I'd keep my trail drive off the Bozeman, everything would somehow work itself out. From what you've told me, I'd say it's goin' to be hell with all the fires lit, whether I go on to Virginia City or not."

"Since I've been speaking off the record," said Mattingly, "yes, I'd have to say that's a correct assumption. We're in over our heads, Story, and it's going to become worse before it gets better. If it ever does."

Story left Colonel Mattingly's office, and while he was not reassured, he had been profoundly impressed with the man's honesty. While Mattingly had not been openly critical of Fort Phil Kearny's commanding officer, Story had a picture of Colonel Henry Carrington that was anything but promising. He sounded like a "book" soldier, a West Pointer, who would die—or allow others to—before he would deviate from the rigid code that had been drilled into him. Story went on to the post hospital for some word on the condition of Greener and Slim. The young doctor was Lieutenant Marner.

"We drove the shafts on through," Marner said, "and both men are under sedation. The real danger is the possibility of infection, and we can control that, I think."

"Thank you," said Story. "When will I be able to talk to them?"

"Tomorrow afternoon, unless they take a turn for the worse."

That Greener and Slim would have to be left behind, Story had no doubt. Already the cottonwood leaves were disappearing, as the west wind had begun stripping the trees in preparation for the coming winter. There was thin ice along the edges of streams, and the night wind had a bite to it that hadn't been there just a few days ago. By Story's reckoning, they were still four hundred miles from Virginia City, and maybe a hundred from Fort Phil Kearny, with Indians all the way. Once they reached Montana Territory and were across the Yellowstone, it would be Crow country from there on to Virginia City. The Crows were friendly to whites and mortal enemies to the Sioux. But in the high country death didn't always come astride a hard-running pony, to the screech of war whoops. It also came on the wind; silent, deepening snow that could bury a man and his horse, accompanied by temperatures that dropped to forty and below. While the Indian threat was more immediate, it was no greater than that of approaching winter. Story dared not be caught on the trail when snow drifted deep in the mountain passes and moved on to the plains beyond. . . .

* * *

Story had been allowed to bed down the herd near the stockade, while he and his riders had been made welcome at Fort Reno. He felt a little guilty because he had not warned his riders of what might lie ahead at Fort Phil Kearny. After all, most of it was Story's own misgivings, and nothing that he could present as fact. But what other choice did any of them have but to push on? Since they must remain at Fort Reno another night, regardless, Story waited until almost suppertime before returning to the little post hospital. He found Greener and Slim awake, but in less than hospitable moods. He suspected they knew what was coming and resented it, but he had no choice. Story was not a man to hedge, to beat around the bush, and he didn't now.

"I reckon you know we have to move on," he said without preliminary.

The two men only looked at him, allowing their silence to speak their dissatisfaction.

"We'll leave your horses, your saddles, and your weapons here at the fort," Story said, "and when you're able, come on to Virginia City. Probably the Indian threat will be over, and there'll be a place for you, if you want it. I'm leaving each of you ten months' wages, and since it's not your fault you won't finish the drive, I'm adding another hundred and fifty dollars for your bonus."

"I don't want no charity," said Greener sullenly.

"Me neither," Slim said, just as sullenly.

"I don't consider it charity," said Story. "You've earned it. I'll leave it with the doc, and if your attitudes improve, I'll see you in Virginia City. Adios."

Story departed the hospital after leaving the money he had promised Slim and Greener. Thanks to their sullen arrogance, he felt less guilty. Tomorrow, Sioux or not, they would take the trail to Fort Phil Kearny. Story had one last duty before leaving the fort. He stopped by

Colonel Mattingly's office and thanked the man for his courtesy.

August 29, 1866. North on the Bozeman.

"By God, they's waitin' fer us," Coon Tails said.

His words were unnecessary, for they could all see the distant columns of "talking smoke." There was no doubt they were in for it. The unanswered question was when. Again Story and Coon Tails rode well in advance of the herd, while Bill Petty and Quickenpaugh rode behind the last freight wagon, their Remingtons across their saddles. They were still vulnerable. As they had done twice before, the Sioux could strike somewhere along the length of the spiraled herd, for Story's riders were strung out from one end to the other. The best defense against a massive attack was to bunch the cattle and the wagons, allowing the cowboys to concentrate their fire, but that would be possible only if the advance or rear scouts could see the Indians coming. But Story wondered if they could count on such attacks, for twice the Sioux had counted their dead without taking a single scalp. They had accomplished nothing except the wounding of Greener and Slim.

"I'm getting cold chills down my spine," said Lorna, "just knowing they're out there somewhere." Jasmine and Curly rode with her at drag, with Oscar Fentress and Tom Allen there as well.

"Mr. Story's taken all the precautions he can," Jasmine said, "and these Remingtons are light enough for us to fire them. I hate it that Greener and Slim were hurt, but they could have been dead."

"I fired a Sharps once," said Curly, "and this Remington ain't near as heavy. Besides, Bud says he'll kill every damn Sioux in Wyoming Territory if they bother me."

"Bud's always had a habit of biting off more than he

could chew," said Jasmine. "I'd suggest you keep the Remington handy."

The "talking smoke" continued as they rode north, but there was no sign of the Sioux. The Bozeman followed the Powder River for a ways after leaving Fort Reno, and Story bedded down the herd at a bend in the river. It would be their first night since leaving the relative security of Fort Reno, and every rider in the outfit was nervous, except Coon Tails.

"The varmints won't attack in the dark," said the old scout.

"But we've kilt some braves," Gus Odell said. "They might make exceptions for us."

"I 'fraid you be right," said Oscar Fentress. "I keep my rifle cocked."

That seemed to be the thinking of the entire outfit, and Story didn't discourage it. But the night was calm, and the dawn broke without a sign of the Sioux. Still, by the time the drive was again moving north, there was more smoke on the horizon ahead. Waddy Summers drove the last wagon, and the right rear wheel slid off a stone ledge with a sickening crunch. The rim had split, leaving the wide iron tire dangling loose. Bill Petty rode at a fast gallop until he reached Shanghai and Cal, who were riding point.

"Busted wagon wheel," Petty said. "We'll have to replace it."

Shanghai needed to know no more. He waved his hat downward, and then he and Cal began heading the leaders. Petty rode on and caught up to Sandy Bill's wagon, having already spoken to Dutch Mayfield and Jules Dyer, the horse wranglers for the day. Story and Coon Tails were scouting somewhere ahead. When Petty returned to the damaged wagon, he found Waddy shifting the freight to reach the wagon jack.

"In all my years of bull whackin'," said Waddy, "I

never needed that damn wagon jack that it wasn't buried somewhere under the load."

"That raises a question," Petty said with a grin. "Why do you bury it under the load?"

"I didn't," said Waddy. "Story had the wagon loaded before I got back to Fort Leavenworth."

Replacing the broken wheel cost them two hours. The riders remained vigilant, but no Indians were sighted. Story and Coon Tails returned as the drive again took the trail. Story spoke to all the riders, eventually reaching Quickenpaugh and Petty.

"I reckon I missed all the fun," Story said.

"You did," Petty agreed. "Waddy an' me had to shift half the freight in that damn wagon, looking for the wagon jack. Quickenpaugh didn't lift a finger to help us."

Quickenpaugh looked at Story. "Squaw *trabajo,*" he said.*

Story laughed, riding back along the left flank to the point position. The day wore on, and while there was more smoke, there were no Indians.

"They're planning somethin'," John Catlin said. "What gets on a man's nerves is not knowin' when it's coming."

"It's not just Indian attacks," said Story. "That's the way life is. If we knew when the dam was goin' to break, we'd have time to shore it up a mite."

Steve Grover laughed. "I've learned more hard truth on the trail than I'd learned in my whole life, back in Indiana."

"That's how it is," Story said. "I had some college in Ohio, but when I came west, I felt like an ignoramus. Indians will educate a man to the ways of the frontier pronto."

"You have an Indian among your riders," said Catlin,

---

* Squaw work

"and he's as well-armed as any of us. Back East we were told all Indians were ignorant savages."

"I'll let you be the judge of that," Story said. "Quickenpaugh just sat on his horse and watched a pair of white hombres unload and then load a freight wagon."

"The commander at Fort Reno seemed a decent sort," said Grover. "What do you know of the post commander at Kearny?"

"Not much," Story said, "but I suspect he's a 'book' soldier. You know the kind."

"Oh, God, yes," said Grover. "He'll have his troops dodging arrows and doing close order drill on Sunday morning."

If the continual "talking smoke" wasn't enough to keep everybody's nerves on edge, there was daily evidence of Indian atrocities along the trail. One of these was an overturned, partially burned wagon, while others consisted of the rotting carcasses or the bleached bones of mules, horses, and oxen. Then there were the graves —one, two, three, and often more—many of them newly made and not yet grassed over.

"It's so sad," Lorna said. "They must have come this way looking for a new life, and all they found was death. That one little bit of ground is all they'll ever have, without even a marker to say this is where it all came to an end."

"God," said Curly, "hush. You sound like a preacher. All they ever talk about is the grave, dyin', torment, hell-fire, and how the devil's likely got his brand on us all. I reckon he has, but damn it, do we have to waste what time we got, bawlin' about it?"

"Sorry," Lorna said. "I didn't know you were touchy about those things."

"I hate death, even the mention of it," said Curly. "I never really knew my mama, and I lost Daddy when I was fifteen. He had lung fever and seemed afraid for me to be near him. Since I was eleven, all I had was Manuel, and he fussed over me like some old granny."

"An old granny would have known you were a girl," Jasmine said. "Either Manuel didn't know or he put on a good act."

"I kept my britches on when he was around," said Curly, "and I wore one of Daddy's old shirts. Till last winter, I was flat-chested as a barn door."

"All the better for roping cows," Lorna said. "You got nothing to get in the way."

"Something's happened up ahead," said Jasmine. "The herd's slowing."

19

September 10, 1866. Fort Phil Kearny, Wyoming Territory.

A sentry had spotted the drive, and a contingent of soldiers had halted it three miles south of the fort. Story said nothing, and when the sergeant in charge spoke, he wasted no time on introductions or preliminaries.

"Sir, Colonel Carrington sends orders that your animals be brought no nearer to the fort, because the grass is needed for government stock. The colonel feels your stock and wagons will prove a temptation to the Sioux, and endanger the fort, and this garrison does not have the manpower to protect you."

"We've managed so far without the protection of the military, Sergeant," said Story, "and we will continue to do so. As for the herd, they'll be kept well away from the fort for the short time we intend to be here. Does the colonel have any further orders for us?"

"Just one," the sergeant said stiffly. "You—if you are responsible for this caravan—are ordered to report to Colonel Carrington's office at once."

"He's likely to back you up against the stockade wall

and have you shot, Nels," Tom Allen said, "just on general principles."

"Come on, Coon Tails," said Story.

The soldiers waited for Story and Coon Tails to ride on ahead, and they felt like prisoners. They were marched into Carrington's office, and the colonel was formal, spit-and-polish, every inch the "book" soldier Story had expected. He sat tugging at his beard, and when he finally spoke, it was in clipped tones, without a hint of cordiality.

"Suppose you tell me who you are, why you are here, and where you think you are going?"

"My name is Nelson Story, Colonel, and I *know* where I'm going. I'm bound for Virginia City, Montana Territory."

"You are forbidden to continue this foolish trek along the Bozeman," Carrington said, "until this fight with the Sioux has been resolved."

"Colonel," the old mountain man cut in, "I'm Coon Tails, an' Jim Bridger's a friend of mine. Wher' is Jim?"

"Bridger is scouting the foothills," Carrington snapped, "and his whereabouts has nothing to do with this situation. For reasons of which you are aware, your cattle are not to be grazed near the fort. There is a large pole corral on Clear Creek, and you may secure your stock there at night."

Clearly, they had been dismissed, but Story turned on Carrington in a fury.

"From what I hear, Colonel, your stock has been stolen from under your very nose. I won't hold my herd at your whim, to be taken a few at a time by the Sioux."

"You will do as I have commanded," Carrington thundered. "There are three hundred soldiers on this post, and by God, I will use every last one, if I have to. Take the trail in defiance of my orders, and I'll have you and your riders shot out of the saddle."

Carrington's eyes burned with the fire of fanaticism.

Story and Coon Tails left the colonel's office to find the
stockade swarming with excited civilians and more wagons than the limited area could comfortably accommodate.

"What's happened, soldier?" Story asked a private.

"Party of miners attacked by the Sioux," said the soldier. "Bunch of miners killed, and the rest hightailed it
back here."

"These damn blue bellies from back East don't know
doodly about fightin' Injuns," said Coon Tails in disgust.
"You aim to foller them orders?"

"For a while," Story said. "There's no denying those
miners have had a bad time of it, and all that 'smoke
talk' we've been seeing hasn't been for nothing. We'll
give it a few days, but no more. If the Sioux have picked
Carrington clean of riding stock, they won't spare us."

"With er without Carrington's blessin', 'fore we move
out, I'll do some lookin' around. If I kin find Bridger,
he'll know what these Injuns is up to."

Story got the outfit together and told them of Carrington's order. Since they had little choice, they drove
the herd on to Clear Creek, setting up camp in the vicinity of the corral Carrington had mentioned. They were
in the foothills, and to the north, above the black timber
belt, loomed the snowcapped Big Horns. From their
first night on Clear Creek, the Sioux began picking at
the herd and trying to get at the horses. The herd had to
be driven into the pole corral at night, and that helped
some, but not much. During daylight hours, riders had
to constantly circle the herd, as well as the extra horses.
There was no respite, except when the riders were allowed occasional visits to the sutler's store, and then
they could go only two or three at a time. It was on one
such visit that Bill Petty met Alicia Blackburn. The girl
was leaving the store, her arms full of purchases, just as
Petty and Arch Rainey approached the steps. Alicia
stumbled, parcels went everywhere, and she would have

fallen facedown in the dirt street if Petty hadn't caught her.

"Oh, this is so embarrassing," the girl cried as Petty released her.

"Loose board on the porch," said Petty as he and Arch went about gathering the things she had dropped. By the time the fallen articles had been recovered, the girl had a smile for them.

"Thank you so much," she said. "I'm Alicia Blackburn. Mostly just Alice."

"I'm Bill," Petty said, removing his hat, "and this is Arch. We're with the trail drive, on Clear Creek. Wherever you're bound, why don't you let us carry this stuff for you?"

"I . . . I would," she said, "but I fear it wouldn't be proper. You see, I live in one of the officer's cabins, with my husband. He . . . he's a captain."

She took her parcels, and almost dropped them again as she hurried away. Looking after her, Arch sighed and turned to Petty.

"God, did you see them eyes? Black as her hair. She's part Spanish."

"And all married," Petty added.

"Yeah," said Arch. "Why else would a beauty like her be stuck out here, neck deep in Indians?"

Story and his outfit spent a week on Clear Creek, and fed up with the constant harassment by the Sioux, Story again called on Colonel Carrington.

"Colonel," Story said, "I'd be no worse off on the trail to Virginia City. As it is, we're bogged down here, while the Sioux nibble away at our cows and our horses. I'm requesting that you rescind that order and allow us to leave."

"Absolutely not," said Carrington. "I'll place the lot of you under military arrest if I have to. While the Indians are 'picking at you,' as you put it, that brings them out of the hills and canyons, where we have a chance to get at them."

"So that's it, damn it," Story shouted. "You're using my riders, my cows, and my horses to bait the Sioux."

"To some degree," said Carrington, with his maddening smile, "but you are civilians, and in time of war, you are subject to my command. The order stands."

As though to justify his outrageous behavior, Carrington sent a dozen soldiers on a reconnaisance patrol, with Captain Blackburn in command. When the patrol returned, three of their number were tied across their saddles, and one of the dead was Captain Blackburn. A burial detail dug the graves as other soldiers patrolled the area against further attack. Near sundown a bugler climbed to the parapet high inside the stockade walls, and the mournful notes of taps drifted through the evening stillness. Under heavy guard, soldiers bore the three wooden coffins from the fort to the newly dug graves. Some of Story's riders gathered for the brief ceremony, and one of them was Bill Petty. Alicia Blackburn was dressed all in black, including a veil, and Petty was unable to see her face. He wished he could have spoken to her, but he was an outsider, and protocol forbade it. He watched as she was consoled by other officers and their wives. When it came Carrington's turn, he took her hand, but she tensed and withdrew it. Petty took grim satisfaction in that. Even in her grief, Alice Blackburn had sand, and she knew Carrington for what he was.

"Bill," said Arch later, "now that the Blackburn woman's free, you ought to go callin' on her. We may not be here much longer."

"Hell's bells, Arch," Bill exploded, "it wouldn't be proper. Her man ain't even cold in his grave. Why don't *you* go callin' on her?"

"She didn't look at me the way she looked at you. A

woman can be hooked up in double harness, but that don't mean she's satisfied."

Petty shook his head, but found himself unable to dismiss Alicia from his mind. It was said that a single or widowed woman on the frontier took in laundry or took in men. Petty didn't know what military policy was, but he suspected Alicia Blackburn would be lucky if she got a one-way ticket back East, to her family.

"Nels," said Coon Tails after a week of Carrington's high-handedness, "I aim to ride into them hills, an' whether I find Bridger er not, I aim to find out wher' them Sioux is holed up."

"Maybe you're right," Story said. "With or without Carrington's approval, we're leaving here."

The outfit watched him ride away, and it wasn't just Nelson Story who had misgivings.

"I wish he wasn't going," said Lorna. "I have this awful feeling that . . . he won't ever come back."

The old scout had slipped away before first light. The day wore on, and as shadows lengthened and the first stars appeared, Story grew worried. He could think of no reason why Coon Tails hadn't returned, unless he was dead. The outfit had grown close to the garrulous old man, and their minds were on him as they circled the herd. As they came together around the breakfast fire, Story made an announcement.

"I'm taking Quickenpaugh with me, and we're going after Coon Tails. I want all of you in the saddle, circling the herd and the extra horses."

Story had a horse on a lead rope. The Sioux might have shot Coon Tails's horse from beneath him, and the old man might be holed up, fighting for his life. Quickenpaugh rode ahead, having no trouble picking up the trail. They rode with their Remingtons across their saddles, and they had ridden no more than four or five miles when Quickenpaugh reined up. The trail was no longer necessary. In the blue of the Wyoming sky, in the shadow of the grim and everlasting Big Horns, buzzards spiraled earthward. Quickenpaugh kicked his horse into a fast gallop, Story following. Coon Tails lay facedown, literally spiked with arrows. The shafts of a dozen had to be broken before the body of the old scout could be wrapped in blankets and slung across the horse Story had brought. It was a sad occasion when Story and Quickenpaugh rode into camp. The riders forgot the herd, the horses, everything except the blanket-wrapped body tied across the saddle. Most of the riders wept.

"He knew," Lorna cried. "He knew . . ."

It was just the diversion the devilish Sioux had been waiting for. Somehow they had driven some buffaloes into a nearby draw, and whooping like demons, sent the animals charging into the grazing longhorns, horses, and oxen. The horse bearing Coon Tails's body was already skittish, and Story had a time holding the animal. He swung out of the saddle just long enough to lower the body of the old scout to the ground. He then mounted, and kicking his horse into a fast gallop, joined his outfit in pursuit of the Sioux. It was the first time since reaching Fort Phil Kearny that Story's riders had been able to fire at the elusive Sioux. The Sioux, expecting the limited range of the army rifles and the time it took to reload, didn't seem concerned. But that changed quickly as Story's riders cut loose with the Remingtons. They got off three volleys before the Sioux got out of range, and they had to abandon the stolen cattle to do so.

"Cal, Hitch, Arch, Smokey, and Bud, come with me," Story said. "We'll go after these cows. The rest of you hightail it back and start gathering the others."

The charging buffaloes had taken a wedge of about fifty longhorns, but the rest of the herd had soon settled down to graze. The horses and oxen had not been near enough to become spooked by the intruding buffaloes. Story and his riders had some difficulty separating the buffaloes from the longhorns.

"Double your lariats and swat the buffaloes," Story shouted.

There were fewer buffaloes than cows, and they finally managed to separate the beasts from the longhorns. When Story and the riders returned to camp, Tom Allen and Bill Petty were digging a grave for Coon Tails. He would be laid to rest beside Clear Creek. Story's camp was far enough from the fort that the burial went unnoticed, only Story and his riders present. Story took a Bible from his saddlebag and read over the blanket-wrapped body of the old mountain man, and he was soon just another mound of earth that would grass over and become lost in the wilds of Wyoming Territory.

Since Bill Petty hadn't accompanied Alicia Blackburn to her cabin, he had no idea where she lived. The officers' cabins were no more than shotgun shanties built of logs, with an outhouse and a tiny yard in back. Most of the cabins had rain barrels beneath the eaves, and he found her there with a wooden bucket, dipping a bucket of water. She didn't seem surprised to see him. She set the filled bucket on the wooden stoop and waited for him to speak. Now that he had found her, he was more ill at ease than she.

"Alicia . . . Alice . . . I just wanted to tell you how sorry I am. I wanted to speak to you at the . . . service, but I reckoned it wouldn't be proper. . . ."

"Thank you," she said. "You're very kind."

"Well, I . . . I'd better be going. It wouldn't be right for me to be seen here so soon after—"

"I know," she said. "Back east, I'd be in mourning for a year. But Mr. Petty . . ."

"Bill."

"Bill . . . it . . . everything . . . is so different on the frontier. It's been less than a week, and already the men . . . the single men . . . are looking at me, and the officers' wives are talking . . . wondering how long . . ."

"All it'll take, then," Petty said, "is for somebody to see me standin' here talking to you."

"But that's what I *need,*" she cried. "Someone to talk to me."

"The officers' wives . . ."

"The officers' wives are avoiding me like the plague," she said bitterly.

"Alice," he said, encouraged, "if you tell me it's none of my business, then I'll say no more and I'll leave. But what do you aim to do? I know the military must have some policy. . . ."

"They do," she said. "Eventually I'll be sent back to Virginia, but not until there's some kind of peace with the Sioux. There's simply no way for me to get safely away from here. Perhaps when the railroad reaches Cheyenne . . ."

"Alice, that's two years away, maybe longer," said Petty.

"I know," she said miserably.

A back door opened and a woman came out on the stoop of an adjoining cabin. Whatever she intended to do was quickly forgotten when she saw Bill Petty, and she vanished into the cabin.

"Damn it," Petty said, "I'd better go."

"It won't matter now," she said. "Please see me again, before you—"

"I will," said Petty. "Colonel Carrington has ordered us to remain here until he says we can go, but—"

"Oh, damn him," she cried. "I . . . I hate that man. It's because of him . . ."

"Alice," said Petty, "I can't get into the stockade at night. Besides, I'm needed at camp, so I'll have to see you in the daytime, whenever I can."

"I'll be here," she said. "I have nowhere else to go. Please come back."

She held out her hands to him, and he almost took them, but he suspected curious eyes were watching, perhaps from more than one window. He turned quickly away, the fear and desperation in her eyes going with him. . . .

With the start of his third week at Fort Phil Kearny, Nelson Story's patience ran out. He called his outfit together and wasted no words.

"We've been hunkered here two weeks, with the Sioux picking at us night and day. We've lost Coon Tails, and I have to take responsibility for that, for allowing him to ride out alone. Sunday night, after taps, we're moving out. The Sioux will come after us, but we have the firepower. For the next few days we'll go about our business, and not a word of this must reach Carrington. Despite his threats, once we're away from here, I can't believe he'll come after us."

In Bill Petty's mind a plan was taking shape, and at first it seemed as impossible as it was audacious. But there were no alternatives. Anyhow, it all depended on Alicia Blackburn and her trust in him. When he called on her again, he went boldly to the front door. In another week it wouldn't matter. She seemed glad to see him, and invited him in.

"Let's go to the kitchen," she said, "and I'll make coffee."

Petty dragged out a ladder-back chair and sat down at the table. He was at a loss as to how to tell her what was on his mind. In cowboy fashion, he threw caution to the winds and waded in.

"Alice," he said, "if I can get you away from here, take you to Virginia City, will you go?"

She dropped the lid to the coffeepot, and when she turned to him, there were tears on her cheeks.

"I'll go," she said simply. "If there's a way, I'll go."

"We're pulling out Sunday night," Petty said, "defying Carrington's orders. There's no way of getting you out of the fort at night, so we'll have to do it in the day-time."

"Bill, I simply can't let you attempt this. If you're caught, Carrington will have you before a firing squad."

"I don't aim to be caught," Petty said. "I'll see you again on Friday, and I'll tell you what we're going to do. I just want you to be sure this is what you want. For a certainty we'll have to fight the Sioux."

"I don't care," she said. "Carrington is scared to death of them, and I live in fear the Indians will overrun the fort and kill us all. Get me a gun, and I can shoot. But what will your friends say . . . about you taking me?"

"That's the least of our worries," said Petty. "There are already three women with the drive, earning their way as riders. I'll get you a horse, or you can ride in one of the freight wagons. I'll see that the outfit knows that we . . . I . . . have no strings on you. There's a hotel in Virginia City, and I'll see that you reach there safely. I'm not askin' anything of you, but I . . . when you've had time to . . . to think on it . . . I'd like to call on you. If . . . if you think . . ."

"I think I'd like that, Bill. I can't promise when—or if —I'll have feelings for another man, but when I do, if I should, I'd . . . want you to be there. . . ."

His elation soaring, Bill Petty rode back to camp feeling that he could slay dragons with a cottonwood limb. But common sense prevailed. He would have to talk to Nelson Story, because if anything went wrong, it would bring Carrington down on them like the wrath of God. While Carrington wouldn't care a damn for Alicia Blackburn, sneaking her out of the fort would be a violation of military regulations. Nelson Story was the kind of man who saw nothing as impossible. It usually just took a little longer. Story listened as Petty explained Alicia's problem, and finally how Petty proposed to solve it.

"Great God, Bill," Story sighed. "Why couldn't you have come up with a simple thing, such as converting lead into gold double eagles? Since you're involving me in this, there's something else I need to know. Is this Alicia Blackburn's idea, or yours?"

"Mine," said Petty, "from start to finish. She tried to talk me out of it."

"Sensible woman," Story said. "I'd be on the right trail, then, if I said your interest in Alicia Blackburn goes deeper than just wanting to help an unfortunate woman out of a bad situation."

"You would," Petty said. "She's made no promises, and I've asked just one. All I've asked is, once she's safely in Virginia City, that I have the chance to call on her, and I've been welcomed."

"That's a good sign," said Story. "When we move out, we'll be disobeying Carrington's order. I doubt we can do anything that will get us in any deeper than that. Go ahead and make your plans with Alicia, but she isn't to leave the fort until late Sunday afternoon, just before the gates close."

Petty chose a pair of his own well-worn Levi's pants and an equally worn flannel shirt. From his bedroll he took an old black flop hat that had seen more than its share of sun, wind, and rain. These he placed in a large brown gunnysack.

After Petty had gone, Alicia Blackburn walked into the small bedroom and sat on the edge of the sagging bed. The single window looked out upon the parade ground and the weathered log wall of the stockade beyond. Alicia shuddered. "Oh, God, Bill," she sighed, "please, please take me away. . . ."

The Sioux continued to be a problem for Story and his riders. While they didn't dare attack in force, they were a constant source of irritation. Braves galloped their horses as near as they dared, clinging to the offside, firing their arrows.

"The varmints don't give you nothin' to shoot at," Shanghai grumbled.

Only Quickenpaugh managed to strike a blow at the elusive Sioux. The next brave who galloped near had the surprise of his life. No sooner had he loosed the arrow than Quickenpaugh was after him, Bowie knife in hand.

"Ride him down, Quickenpaugh," Quanah Taylor shouted.

Quickenpaugh intended doing exactly that, but he and the pursued were nearing a stand of jackpines from whence most of the Sioux attacks had come. Quickenpaugh kicked free of his stirrups, springing like a cougar upon the Sioux, dragging him from his horse.

"Get your rifles ready," Story said, "and watch those jackpines. Some of the others may buy into this."

The Sioux brave had a Bowie, and five hundred yards away he and Quickenpaugh circled one another like wary lobos. Just as Story had suspected, there were other Sioux among the jackpine, and four of them emerged, galloping their horses toward the conflict. Story and his riders cocked their rolling-block Remingtons. Jasmine and Curly were among those who fired first, and the four Indian ponies galloped away riderless.

"I got one," Jasmine cried. "That one's for you, Coon Tails."

"We ought to go help Quickenpaugh," said Lorna.

"We're givin' him the only help he needs or wants," said Cal, "keepin' the varmints off his back. He can take care of himself. Just watch."

If there were other Sioux in the jackpines, they remained there, and the brave who fought Quickenpaugh was on his own. The pair circled, each seeking an opening. They parried, and there was a clang as blade struck blade. Quickenpaugh thrust, withdrew, and thrust again. He stood for just a moment over the fallen Sioux before driving the blade of his Bowie into the dirt. He then trotted back to join his comrades.

"What a grand, glorious thing to have done," Lorna said.

"All of that," said Tom Allen, "but dangerous as hell. If any of the rest of us had done that, Nels would be chewin' on us into the middle of next week."

"I would," Story laughed, "but I'll have to give credit where credit is due. He killed his opponent, and in so doing, lured four more of the devils out of the brush."

"I've always heard Indians take scalps," said John Catlin.

"Not always," Story said. "They didn't scalp or mutilate Coon Tails, because they considered him a brave man. Quickenpaugh showed them the same courtesy."

20

$\mathcal{D}$uring the next several days, Bill Petty visited the sutler's store, emerging each time with his purchases in a large brown gunnysack. Those who were interested in his coming and going would, he hoped, not consider it unusual when he again left the fort with the large brown gunnysack on Friday. He found himself eager to see Alicia, to tell her that his plan was acceptable to Story, chafing at the delay as he waited for Friday. He entered the fort as casually as he could, hoping nobody would notice that he had somehow acquired the large brown gunnysack without going to the sutler's. Alicia let him in, closed the door, and then impulsively threw her arms around him. Finally she drew away, blushing furiously.

"I'm sorry," she said. "I . . . I shouldn't have done that. But I'm so happy to see you, and I was so afraid something would happen, that I couldn't go."

"You're going," said Petty. "Story says we're in so deep already that taking you from under Carrington's nose won't matter. He can't have us shot but once. Now here's what we're going to do. In the sack there's an old hat, one of my flannel shirts, and a pair of my Levi's. You'll have to work on the shirt and the Levi's, so's they'll fit, but leave the shirt loose in the front so—"

"So I can pass for a man." She laughed.

"At least until we get you safely away from here," Petty said. "Now I want you to think of the things you're going to take with you. Limit them to what you can get into this sack, because I'll be taking it with me. When you leave here, it has to be near dark, and you have to look enough like a cowboy to get you through the gate. Sunday evening, a few minutes before the gates close, light your lamp, so's it can be seen easy. Slip out the back door wearin' these clothes of mine, and pull the hat low over your eyes. I'll meet your at the sutler's store, and I'll have a horse for you. We have to get past the sentry at the gate. How long do you think it'll be until you're missed?"

"I don't know," said Alicia. "Nobody comes around, but they watch me. I suppose, if they don't see me in several days, somebody will come knocking on the door."

"Carrington will know we're gone long before that," Petty said. "I'll wait while you gather your clothes. I'll hide them for you in one of the wagons."

Petty found it necessary to take Arch Rainey into his confidence. He had to get a horse into the fort for Alicia, and he dared not simply ride in, leading the animal. Somebody had to ride it into the sutler's store, so that hopefully no questions would be raised when Alicia rode it away.

"Let me get this straight," said Arch. "You want me to tie my horse at the sutler's store so's this lady can escape, leavin' me afoot."

"Damn it," Petty said, "you won't be afoot. We'll leave your horse in that pine thicket just north of the fort. You and me will ride in before three o'clock, because that's when they change sentries at the gate. When I ride out with Alicia, it won't be long until the gates will be closed. There'll be a new sentry, and he won't remember you. Just walk out the gate, go get the horse we'll be leavin' for you, and ride back to camp."

"You don't think the sentry's gonna wonder why a cowboy ain't got a horse?"

"Let him wonder," said Petty. "He'll be new on the post, and he won't know you didn't come in afoot. If he says anything, tell him your horse got loose, or somebody turned it loose and you're havin' to hoof it back to camp. We'll be in Montana before that bunch figures out what happened, if they ever do."

September 30, 1866. The trail north.

"God, I'll be glad when we git on the trail again," Shanghai said. "It ain't near as hard keepin' them Injuns off'n yer back when you ain't at the same place all the time."

Most of the trees in the foothills surrounding the Big Horns were bare, their dry brown leaves blowing into arroyos and canyons as the chill winds from the mountains swept across the high plains. Sandy Bill broke ice in Clear Creek for water to boil breakfast coffee, and the riders who had just come off watch wore their heavy coats and gloves.

"We owe Mr. Story for having us get those wool longhandles," said Lorna. "I'm going to wear mine until next summer, at least."

"Pore Cal," Hitch Gould said, laughing.

"Summers are short in Montana," said Tom Allen. "There's spring in July, summer in August, fall in September, and the rest is winter."

There was speculation among the outfit when, a few minutes before three o'clock, Bill Petty and Arch Rainey rode out toward the fort, Arch leading an extra saddled horse.

"Can't be a pack hoss," Mac Withers said. "No pack-saddle."

"It's got somethin' to do with us movin' out tonight," said Tom Allen. "I've spent a lot of years with Bill Petty, and I've never seen him act as damn strange as he has this past week. What's bitin' him, Nels?"

"Before suppertime," Story said, "I think old Bill will have a surprise for all of you, and eventually an even bigger surprise for our Colonel Carrington."

Bill Petty and Arch Rainey tied their horses at the rail and went into the store.

"You shouldn't be here more than an hour, Arch," said Petty. "I'll be out front. When we ride away, give us a little while before you leave."

The days had become short, and purple shadows had already begun to dress the Big Horns for approaching night. Alicia's place wasn't far from the store, but she would have to pass half a dozen other cabins to reach the horse he had waiting for her. He wasn't as concerned about getting the girl past the sentry at the gate as having her safely away from the other cabins from which meddling officers' wives might be watching. Even in the chill of evening Bill Petty had begun to sweat. Finally he saw her coming, taking her time, and as she drew nearer, he had to admit she was convincing. Her hair had been stuffed into the old hat, and it was down to her eyes. The Levi's fit, and the shirt had been altered just enough. She had even managed to darken her hands and her face. Over her arm she carried a heavy coat, something Petty had forgotten. Petty mounted his horse, and without seeming to notice him, she mounted the other. The stockade was in shadows when the sentry opened the gate for them to depart. They rode on, Bill Petty half expecting to hear the sentry's order to halt. But it didn't come, and they rode over the hill, past the stand of pines that concealed the horse Arch would ride. Just to be sure, Petty chose a path that would take them near the picketed horse.

"By God," Petty said, "I should have expected that."

"What is it?" Alicia asked.

"The damn Sioux took the horse I left for Arch. I have to get you to camp and ride back with a horse for Arch."

Without difficulty they reached camp, and Petty helped Alicia to dismount. The riders, those who weren't circling the herd, were waiting for the surprise Story had said Bill Petty had in store.

"Nels," Petty said, "this is Alicia Blackburn. Alicia, this is Nelson Story, and this is his trail drive. He knows about you and will introduce you to the riders. Nels, cuss me for a damn fool, if you want. I left the horse for Arch practically within sight of the fort, but the Sioux got it. I got to meet Arch with a horse. He'll have my hide if he has to hoof it from the fort."

"Get riding, pronto," Story said. "With the Sioux out there, it may already be too late. Bud, you and Quick-enpaugh ride with him."

"I'm sorry to be so much trouble," Alicia said.

"Not your fault," said Story. "Bill should have known better."

The rest of the riders had gathered around, and briefly Story told them of Alicia's predicament, and finally of Bill Petty's decision to take her to Virginia City.

"Good for Bill," Lorna said. "Alicia, come with Jasmine, Curly, and me. We'll find us a place to talk."

Story was thankful for Lorna's fast thinking, for he had enough on his mind. His primary concern was for Arch Rainey and the three riders who had gone to meet him. At any moment he expected the hear the crash of gunfire in the direction of the fort. But there was only silence, and Story began to feel better. In a little more than three hours he would give the order to move out the longhorns and take the Bozeman Trail north.

Bill Petty rode hard, Bud McDaniels and Quick-enpaugh right behind him. Petty was furious with him-self. Story was put out with him, and with good reason. Only a damn eastern tenderfoot would have picketed a horse in Sioux country, expecting to find it when he returned. Petty had to admit he had been distracted by Alicia Blackburn and his decision to rescue her, but why hadn't Arch Rainey said something? They reached the pines where the Sioux had taken the horse, and there was no sign of Arch.

"Yonder he is," Bud said.

He had started up the hill and was almost invisible in the approaching darkness and the shadow of the Big Horns. The three rode to meet him, Petty leading the extra horse. Arch mounted without invitation, and the four set out for camp. Story's relief was obvious when they rode in unharmed. Bill Petty went looking for Ali-cia and found her with Curly, Lorna, and Jasmine.

"We're lookin' out for her, Bill," said Jasmine.

"Thanks," Petty said. "Alicia, will you be riding a horse, or one of the wagons?"

"Sandy Bill asked me to ride with him," said Alicia, "and I think I will. At least for a while."

That settled, Petty went in search of Nelson Story. He half expected Story to reprimand him for his foolishness in leaving a horse for the Sioux to steal, but Story didn't mention the incident.

"She's a beautiful woman, Bill," Story said. "Now all we have to do is get her, ourselves, the herd, and these five wagons far enough from Fort Phil Kearny that Col-onel Carrington won't feel safe coming after us."

Story waited until taps sounded from the vicinity of the fort. Then, with Sandy Bill's wagon taking the lead, the horse remuda following, the longhorns again took the trail north. Recalling the times the Sioux had swept away portions of the herd where it was the least pro-tected, Story had designated four outriders. Their sole duty was to continually ride the length of the drive, protecting the wagons and the riders tending the cattle. Cal and Quickenpaugh kept mostly to the rear, should the Sioux single out one or more of the freight wagons. The drive moved slowly, Story scouting ahead, seeking to avoid terrain that wouldn't accommodate the wagons. A sliver of moon seemed to hang suspended from its upper horn, and in the light from millions of stars, the land was deceptively peaceful. With Quickenpaugh and Cal riding near the freight wagons, Story had reduced the drag to four riders. Throughout the drive, except for the incident at the river crossing, Jasmine and Lorna had ridden drag safely and effectively. Now Curly rode with them, and to the trio, Story always added one man. Tonight Quanah Taylor rode with them. Far away a coyote howled, and more distant, another answered.

"I've heard that Indians imitate coyotes," Lorna said.

"They do," said Curly, "but you can tell if it's a real coyote. There's no echo. Them you just heard was real."

Cal caught up to the drag, talked to Quanah Taylor for a few minutes, and dropped back with Quickenpaugh.

"It's getting awful cold, especially at night," Lorna said. "Does any of you know how many more rivers we'll have to cross?"

"Tom says just the Yellowstone," said Jasmine, "but he says we'll have to cross some lesser streams too."

"I dread the river crossings more than the Sioux," Lorna said. "The others were cold enough. By the time we reach the Yellowstone, it may be just solid ice."

"I hope it is," said Curly. "We can just walk across."

The night dragged on. Shortly after first light the drive reached a stream and Story called a halt for breakfast. Sandy Bill kept the fire as small as he could, sheltering it in an old buffalo wallow. The four freight wagons had been brought close, so that the herd, the horses, and all of the wagons could be more easily pro-

tected. The teamsters—Jubal, Handy, Levi, and Waddy
—made no secret of their liking for Sandy Bill's cooking. Story paused for a word with Waddy Summers.

"How far are we away from the fort, Waddy?"

"Not more'n six or seven miles, Nels. You aim to
spend the day here or move on?"

"We're moving on," Story said. "I'd like to get a few
more miles between us and Carrington. Even then the
damn fool may send soldiers after us."

After breakfast they again took the trail, and the
longhorns showed their displeasure by trying to break
loose, to graze. Riders no longer were able to slump
comfortably in their saddles. Instead they swung their
doubled lariats, swatting longhorn rumps, forcing the
brutes back into an unwilling column. The herd trudged
on, bawling, breaking away at the least opportunity. The
longhorns finally settled down only when they became
too exhausted to break away, but that didn't lessen their
mournful lowing.

"Damn," said Bud McDaniels, "we might as well of
sent a rider ahead, blowin' a horn. With this racket,
every Injun in two hundred miles will know we're
comin'."

"The Sioux have known since we left the fort last
night," Manuel Cardenas said. "Those who may not
know already are being told."

Bud looked to the north, where Manuel pointed, and
was barely able to see the dirty gray of the "talking
smoke" against the blue of the early morning sky. He
turned and looked to the south, and there was a second
smoke.

"You're right," said Bud. "What'n hell are they
waitin' for?"

"They seek to wear us down," Manuel said, "until we
are firing at the shadows, at sounds we think we have
heard, perhaps at one another."

After three grueling days, Story estimated they were

still not more than twenty-five miles from Fort Phil Kearny, and while that lessened the chance that Carrington would send troops after them, it did nothing to diminish the frequency of the daily columns of "talking smoke."

There were nights that Alice Blackburn had Bill Petty saddle a horse for her, and she rode with him as he circled the herd. Petty found himself drawn more and more to her, and he believed she felt the same way about him. He waited, not always patiently, for some sign that she was considering making her life part of his own. He told her little about his life, or of his plans when they reached Virginia City. He wanted her to care enough to ask, and finally she did.

"Bill, what will you do when you reach Virginia City?"

"Stake me a claim on as much Montana grass as I can get my hands on, put me up a cabin, and raise cattle. Two hundred of these longhorns are mine."

"Won't that be terribly hard, just you alone?"

"Most of the riders from Story's drive will be needing work," Petty said. "I reckon I can use a couple of them. Just startin', they may be more than I can afford to pay."

"You'll need a cook."

"I can't afford a cook," he said.

"I can cook and keep house. That's about all I can do."

"You're looking for a job, then," said Petty. "I said I'd put you up in a hotel until—"

"Bill," she began, and her voice caught somewhere between a laugh and a sob. She had reined up, and he sidestepped his horse over next to hers.

"When we reach Virginia City, you have nowhere else to go, do you?"

"No," she said softly. "My parents are dead."

"Well," Petty said, seeking to sound as serious as he

could, "I reckon I could sell some of the stock. I could afford to hire you for a while. . . ."

"No," she cried, taking him serious. "I . . . I won't let you do it. I . . . I don't want much . . . no money. Just a roof over my head . . . and a little food. That's all I've ever had. . . ."

"You're not looking for a job, then," said Petty, still assuming his dead serious role. "What you want is a position, and I reckon I can help you there. You do all the cleaning and cooking, cut hay, wrassle cows when you have to, and all the other miserable, low-down things that always need doin' around a ranch that I'll never get done by myself. You get all the beans you can eat, and when there ain't nothin' left to do outside, you'll have a roof over your head. Now this position pays nothin', but you get half of everything. Especially the work. We share everything."

"Even the . . ."

"Bed," he finished

"I want the position," she said, "but please . . . can we not share the bed for a little while . . . until I . . . I feel right . . . about it?"

"I won't push you," said Petty. "I'll wait.

She leaned from the saddle, he met her halfway, and they sealed the bargain. . . .

Their fifth day on the trail began with overcast skies, and two hours before noon thunder rumbled somewhere beyond the Big Horns. The wind had risen, coming from the northwest, and the temperature had dropped. It had all the earmarks of an early winter storm, and Story rode ahead, seeking a measure of shelter. He found a deep canyon with enough overhang to provide some shelter for the riders, with a tree-lined creek for the longhorns, the horses, and the oxen. By the time Story returned to the herd, freezing rain had begun to fall. Sleet rattled off the crowns and brims of

their hats, and a film of ice had begun to coat the cattle
and the horses. The wind blew the rain and sleet almost
into the faces of the plodding herd, and they wanted
only to turn their tails and drift. Riders swung doubled
lariats against bovine rumps, forcing the longhorns into
the growing storm. They were approaching the canyon
on the highest rim, and there was a miserable, time-
consuming drive until they reached a point low enough
for the herd and the wagons to enter the shelter.

"Run the herd along the creek," Story shouted, "and
loose the horses and oxen with them."

Many of the trees within the canyon were pine, and
the foliage did much to dilute the freezing rain and
sleet. The animals quickly spread along the creek, taking advantage of the shelter. Sandy Bill and the teamsters had drawn the wagons parallel to the canyon's
overhang, leaving a generous space between the wagons
and the canyon wall. Whatever came—even if it was
snow—they could survive.

"Everybody start looking for firewood," Story ordered. "With all these pines, there ought to be some
resinous logs. Drag them in, as many as you can find. It's
going to be almighty cold come dark."

The snow began before dark, and by the time the first
watch saddled up, they couldn't even see the cattle for
the blowing snow. Lorna rode with Cal, and little had
been said since the start of the snow. They well remembered Story's warnings regarding snow on the high
plains. For the moment, they had their backs to the
wind, and Lorna spoke.

"From what Mr. Story's said about snow here in the
high country, we may be stuck in this canyon until
spring."

"I reckon not," Cal said. "Won't be enough firewood
to last a week."

Cattle always tended to drift with the storm, and this
was no exception. Some of the herd had begun wander-

ing down the canyon, and Cal was the first to see them.
He kicked his horse into a gallop, Lorna right behind
him. They circled, got ahead of the half a dozen drifting
longhorns, and it took a supreme effort to head the
animals. Finally they were driven back up the canyon,
resisting every foot of the way, for they were heading
into the storm. Sandy Bill kept the coffee hot, and the
riders rode in, one or two at a time. Shortly after midnight the wind died and the snow began to diminish.
Soon there was only the patter of tiny particles of ice,
and in patches of purple sky, stars twinkled.

"I've never seen the like," said Story. "Unless it
clouds over and starts fresh, we'll be able to move out in
the morning."

But the dawn brought a crisis none of them had fore-
seen. Cal Snider was awakened by Jasmine McDaniels
shaking him.

"Cal, Lorna's gone!"

Cal sat up, rubbed his eyes, and flung off his blankets.
He had only to pull on his boots and grab his hat.

"I reckon you got no idea how long she's been gone."

"No," Jasmine said. "I suppose she went to the
bushes."

"Damn it, why didn't she just get behind one of the
wagons?"

"I don't know," said Jasmine. "Curly was going looking for her, but I wouldn't let her. If there's tracks, it
would only confuse things."

"Good thinking," Cal said.

Curly was waiting, Waddy Summers with her. The
teamster had gone back to his wagon for something.

"We'd best get on her trail," said Summers. "Might
already be too late."

Cal was thinking the same thing, and when he made
Story aware of the situation, Story wasted no time.

"The Sioux," Story said. "Take Quickenpaugh with

you. If you're greatly outmanned, don't try anything foolish. One of you ride back for help."

Cal and Quickenpaugh had no trouble finding where Lorna had been taken. First there were only her footprints, then signs of a scuffle, and finally a set of moccasined footprints that led to where an unshod horse had been waiting. Cal allowed Quickenpaugh to take the trail, and he followed. Once out of the canyon, the trail swung back to the north, toward the Big Horns. Eventually Quickenpaugh reined up, and leaning from the saddle, studied the trail. When Cal caught up to him, he learned why the Indian had paused. There now were tracks of four unshod ponies.

"Four of the Sioux varmints," said Cal.

"Tres," Quickenpaugh said. "Squaw ride."

There were now three Sioux, and that was bad enough, but there might be still more. Quickenpaugh rode on, Cal following. Story's warning was strong on his mind, but his concern for Lorna was stronger. Riding back to camp would cost them an hour or more, and he feared Lorna might not have that much time. They were nearing the foothills of the Big Horns. The mountains appeared stately from a distance, but as Quickenpaugh and Cal drew nearer, the peaks looked formidable. While Cal didn't for a moment doubt Quickenpaugh's bravery or his expertise on the trail, the two of them were at a great disadvantage, for this was unfamiliar country. These mountains were the home of the Sioux, however, and they would know every rock and crevice. Again Quickenpaugh had reined up, and Cal could see no reason for it. The trail—that of four horses—continued along the rise, into a stand of pines, and apparently to a first plateau beyond.

"Emboscada," Quickenpaugh said.*

* Ambush

"Damn it," said Cal impatiently, "how are we gonna get to the bastards?"

Quickenpaugh said nothing, but rode on toward the pines at the start of the foothills. Doubtfully, Cal followed. But Quickenpaugh didn't actually enter the stand of pines into which the beckoning trail led. He rode along the rise toward the south, where he couldn't be seen from the plateau above the first stand of pines. A mile to the south the pines thinned out, and it was here that Quickenpaugh began his ascent. The way was steep, rough, and they were forced to dismount, leading their horses. Reaching the shelf—the first plateau above the forested foothills—they rode warily to the north. Reaching the point where the trail they were following should have emerged from the belt of pines below, there were no tracks.

Quickenpaugh pointed to the unbroken snow and then to the stand of pines at the foot of the mountain. "We kill dead lak hell," said the Indian.

21

Nelson Story was torn between his desire to get the herd on the trail and concern for his riders. Especially Lorna. His anger for her having foolishly left the camp had been replaced with a desire only to have her taken from the Sioux before the savages did things to her that couldn't be undone. Cal Snider was normally careful, cool in the face of danger, but with Lorna in the hands of the Sioux, might that not affect the young Texan's judgment? The Indians would have expected pursuit, perhaps welcomed it, and Story suspected the incident had been nothing more than a ploy to lure some of his riders into an ambush. The more Story thought about it, the better he felt about having sent Quickenpaugh with Cal. While Cal's thinking might be muddied by Lorna's predicament, it wouldn't sway Quickenpaugh. The young Indian's sole intention would be to kill Sioux.

At first Lorna Flagg had been accepted by Story's outfit because she was Cal Snider's woman, but Lorna had won acceptance for herself by enduring all the hardships the trail had to offer. Story believed the entire outfit would have ridden to her rescue at the drop of a hat, and more than one of the riders would have been willing to drop the hat. Now most of them rode the canyon, watching the herd. While all of them weren't needed for the task, it provided something for them to do. Even Alicia Blackburn was riding with them, Story noted with approval. Jubal, Handy, Levi, and Waddy were leaning against their wagons, their Remingtons ready.

"It must be terrible, being carried away by Indians," Alicia said. "I used to have nightmares about the Sioux storming the fort and taking me away. How long do they keep a woman before she is violated and ruined?"

"I don't know," said Jasmine. "I've heard they're forced to become the wife of some brave. I suspect one as young and as pretty as Lorna would end up wife to a chief."

"I wouldn't want no damn Indian pawin' around over me," Curly said, "chief or not."

"I don't imagine Lorna wants that either," said Jasmine. "Let's just hope Cal and Quickenpaugh get to her in time."

Cal and Quickenpaugh left their horses on the plateau and crept toward the treeline below. It was hard going, with the snow hiding stones, dead branches, and leaves. Quickenpaugh held up his hand and Cal paused. He had no idea what Quickenpaugh had in mind, but somehow the Sioux must be flushed out without their harming Lorna. Quickenpaugh proceeded down the slope, and Cal remained where he was. There was a chance one of the three concealed Sioux might cut down Quickenpaugh with arrows, but with the odds three against one, it wasn't likely. Suddenly one of the Sioux dropped from the branches of a pine, but Quickenpaugh had sensed his coming and had his Bowie drawn. It had been the intention of the Sioux to drop onto Quickenpaugh's back. Instead he found himself facing Quickenpaugh, and the two of them were equally armed. But the Sioux had no intention of it being a fair fight, as the second one sprang for Quickenpaugh's back. But Cal was ready. Drawing his Colt, he put two slugs in the Sioux, who flopped facedown into the snow. Lorna screamed, and Cal half fell, half slid through the snow, getting to her. She had broken loose from her captor, was on her knees, and the Sioux had her by the hair. Again Cal drew and fired, and Lorna was free. Quickenpaugh had found an opening for his Bowie, and stood over the body of the third Sioux. Lorna clung to Cal, trembling.

"I only went to the bushes," Lorna said.

"While we're in Sioux country," said Cal, "stay out of the damn bushes."

Quickenpaugh had found the four Indian ponies, and Lorna rode one of them back to camp. She immediately came face-to-face with an unsmiling Nelson Story.

"If you *ever* do a fool thing like that on this trail drive again," he roared, "I'll make you sleep in one of the wagons and post a guard. *Comprender?*"

"I'm sorry," said Lorna. "I feel like the drive would have been better off if I'd stayed in Texas."

"Anybody can make a mistake," Story said, a little more kindly, "but where hostile Indians are concerned, you don't often get a second chance. Just remember that."

Half the day had been lost when the herd finally took the trail. The snow slowed them further, the wagons slipping and sliding, and horses were lamed when a hoof plunged unexpectedly into unseen holes. No sooner had they left the canyon than there was more "talking smoke" ahead of and behind them. Story continued to use outriders, whose sole duty it was to protect the rest of the outfit from hit-and-run attacks by the Sioux. But there were no attacks, and they saw no Indians. Story again rode ahead of the drive, seeking a source of water for the night's camp, and looking for Indian sign as he rode. But the herd safely reached the area Story had chosen and was bedded down for the night.

"Nighthawking as usual," said Story, "and no dozing in the saddle. I don't know what those coyotes are up to, but when it comes, I aim for us to be ready."

But the night passed without disturbance, and the outfit again took the trail. Before scouting ahead, Story paused for a word with Shanghai. The old rancher pointed to the smoke on the northern horizon, and Story nodded.

"The varmints purely know how to work on a man's nerves," Shanghai said. "If we got to fight, then let's fight an' be done with it."

"Exactly how I feel," said Story, "and I think that's exactly what they have in mind. They want us so spooked we couldn't hit a buffalo at ten yards. Then they'll come after us."

It was Tom Allen's day to ride drag. Lorna and Curly drifted out of earshot, so the two could talk, if they wished.

"You reckon them two are makin' plans for when we get to Virginia City?" Curly asked.

"I don't know," said Lorna, "but I won't be surprised. You should have been at drag when we were crossing that river, when the drag steers spooked and a horn raked Jasmine's horse. When that horse tore off down the back trail dragging Jasmine from a stirrup like a bundle of rags, I just knew she was dead. Tom Allen was like a madman, beating his way through those steers with a doubled lariat, trying to reach her."

"Well at least he's got some kind of claim on her," Curly said. "Bud's been pestering the hell out of me ever since he saw me with my shirt open and my Levi's down."

"Until then he didn't know you were a girl," said Lorna.

"That's when he started tryin' to reform me, make me say things and do things the way he thought a girl should."

"I can't see that you've changed that much," Lorna said wryly.

"I ain't," said Curly. "He finally said he'd ruther I swear at him than not talk to him at all."

"Have you been swearing at him?"

"Not since he stopped hounding me 'cause I wasn't acting like a girl," Curly said.

"Maybe you should just leave it like that till we reach Virginia City," said Lorna. "Both of you may see things different by then."

The several days after leaving the canyon had been a nightmare. There had been substantial snowfall, and it had drifted deep. When the snow began to melt in the face of a warming trend, there was mud. The wagons, even Sandy Bill's, mired down repeatedly. The third day after the storm, an anemic sun appeared, and only then did the mud begin to lose its grip on their wagon wheels.

"We might as well of stayed in that canyon till the sun come out," said Arch Rainey. "We'd of saved ourselves the misery of spendin' two days of haulin' them wagons out of the mud."

Story had to admit it was gospel. They and the teamsters had wasted two days, doing the hardest work imaginable, and they hadn't gone anywhere. Five days out of the canyon, they were still within spitting distance of it, and when they had the herd bedded down, Shanghai presented Story with another problem and another delay.

"In the last little while," Shanghai said, "we had three hosses throw shoes, an' there'll be more, pronto, if we don't stop an' take care of 'em."

"Damn it," said Story, "the horses were shod at Leavenworth."

"Only them that needed it at the time," Shanghai said. "We didn't shoe none of them we took from that bunch of renegades. They was all right at the time, but they ain't all right now, an' them that *was* shod at Leavenworth ain't gonna make it on t'Virginia City. We put ever'body t' the task an' work like hell, an' mebbe we kin finish in a day."

"Then we'll take tomorrow and do it," said Story.

So they had lost another day, and the lot of them had worked from first light until almost dark, taking some satisfaction in the fact that all the horses needing shoes had been shod. Besides, the muddy trail had dried for a day.

"God," said Hitch Gould, "that's got to be the hardest work I've done since leavin' Texas."

"I've knowed you awhile," said Arch Rainey. "What did you do in Texas that was all that hard?"

"Anything I can't do from a saddle is hard work," Hitch said, "and I had to shoe horses in Texas too."

October 14, 1866. The Bozeman Trail north.

Nights were cold, but the skies remained clear. Story believed that within two weeks, if there were no more delays, they would cross into Montana Territory. It would be friendly Crow country, and the Sioux threat would be left behind. But Nelson Story was no optimist where the Sioux were concerned, and not for a minute did he believe that Red Cloud and Crazy Horse would allow them to pass without a fight. Again Story took the trail ahead of the herd, preparing to scout the country ahead, his eyes searching the horizon for "talking smoke." There had been none yesterday, and there was none today. The absence of it bothered Story more than its presence. It had become a habit with him to pause when approaching the crest of a ridge, taking a hard look at the country beyond before riding on. He had ridden no more than three or four miles ahead of the herd, when he reined up short of riding over a ridge.

Walking his horse forward until he could see, he caught his breath, for there was a column of Indians riding across the valley below. Quickly, he estimated the number at a hundred, for there was no time to count them. They seemed in no hurry, certain of their destination. Story turned his horse and kicked it into a fast gallop. The showdown they had been expecting was at hand.

Sandy Bill saw Story coming, riding hard, and the old cook reined up.

"Indians," Story shouted. "Hold up where you are."

Gus Odell and Virg Wooler, horse wranglers for the day, had heard Story when he warned Sandy Bill, and began heading the horses. Story rode on, waving his hat when he was within sight of Shanghai Wolfington, at point.

"Indians," Story shouted. "Head the herd and bunch them." Story rode on, warning the flank and swing riders, and finally the drag. From there he rode to the farthest of the four freight wagons.

"Indians," he shouted. "Circle the wagons as near the herd as you can, and unlimber your rifles."

They barely had time to follow Story's orders. By the time the last wagon lumbered near the herd, the Sioux came thundering in, yipping like demented coyotes. But the range was still too great for their arrows, and Story's riders cut loose with the long-range Remingtons. A dozen Sioux were shot from their horses in the first volley, and seven more were hit with the second. The stunned Sioux rode madly away, not having loosed a single arrow.

"Hieeeeyah," screeched Quanah Taylor. "Run, you varmints, run!"

"Keep your rifles ready," Story warned. "They may be back."

The Indian method was to sweep in, making swift attacks while within arrow range, and then retreat. Their attacks were repeated, as they whittled down their enemy, confident they could escape before muzzle loaders could fire a second time. So perfectly did they know the range and limitations of the soldiers' Springfields, they couldn't believe what had just happened to them.

"Here they come again," shouted Story.

The Sioux leading the attack wore buffalo horns. Story suspected he was the medicine man and that he'd managed to work the rest of them into enough of a frenzy for another attack. Now he galloped well ahead of his comrades, determined to show them how strong his medicine was. Story shot him off his horse, and as the rest of the Remingtons began to thunder, nine more Sioux were cut down before they could turn their ponies and gallop away. This time they did not regroup, for their loss had been too great.

"That's the end of it," Story shouted.

The riders gathered around, astonished that they had slaughtered almost half of the attackers without suffering so much as a scratch.

"By God," said John Catlin, "I believe we've sent a message that even Red Cloud can understand."

"Don't count on it," Story said, "but I think we've proven something to ourselves. Let's move on, so they can return for their dead. We won't deny them that."

The dead lay in the path the drive would have taken, and the smell of blood and death would have stampeded the herd. Story and Shanghai headed the leaders to the west until they were well past the scene of death, and then circled back until they were again traveling north.

"Keep them moving, Shanghai," said Story. "I'll ride ahead and find us a place to bed down for the night, and I'll look for Indian sign as I go."

But Story saw nothing to alarm him, and for the rest of that day and all of the next, there was no more "talking smoke." It resumed, however, on the third day.

"They ain't done with us," said teamster Levi Puckett.

"We may of put a crimp in Red Cloud's tail, but we ain't convinced Crazy Horse yet."

"He be convinced when he git a dose of Remington medicine," Oscar said.

"We'll continue using outriders," said Story, "and after I've scouted ahead, I'll ride well in advance of the drive. The only way they can hurt us is if we're strung out for a mile. We must have time to bunch the herd and bring in the wagons. Cal, I want you and Quickenpaugh with the freight wagons, always watching our back trail. When it comes to firepower, we have an edge, but I don't expect that to stop them. They can outnumber us maybe a hundred to one, if they choose, so expect five, maybe ten times as many of them when they strike again."

The weather continued to hold, with mild days and cold nights, and with each passing day Story marked off their progress. The riders took to eagerly searching the horizon at dawn, seeking the "talking smoke."

"We can't count on anything, based on that," Story said.

"Maybe not," said Tom Allen, "but last time, two days after the smoke stopped, they came after us. Since we can't make anything else of it, that's something."

The drive moved steadily on, and each morning, ahead of them and behind, the smoke was there. Finally, in the closing days of October, the "talking smoke" again ceased.

"Maybe you're right, Tom," Story said. "Win, lose, or draw, I think we're about to meet Crazy Horse, chief of the Oglala Sioux."

Story began choosing campsites with an eye for defense. At the end of the second day after the "talking smoke" ceased, Story was scouting ahead, seeking water. Ahead was a sheer, towering butte that rose high above the plains. At the base of it, on the east, water gurgled from a crevice in the rock. Story rode from one side of the *picacho* to the other, satisfying himself that there was no means of scaling the steep flanks. He then rode back and met the herd, leading them to the spring, with its runoff.

"That's as good a natural defense as I've ever seen," said Bill Petty, viewing the massive butte.

"I can only agree," John Catlin said. "With these Remingtons, we could put our backs to that and hold off every Sioux in the territory."

"We may have to," said Story. "Every time they've hit us in the open, it's been a busted flush. From now on, we'll choose every camp with an eye for defense. A surprise attack could come at dawn, and that means we'll likely still be in camp."

The attack came on the morning of the third day after the "talking smoke" had ceased. The Sioux came in such numbers that, even with Remingtons in their hands and a sheer stone wall at their backs, Story's riders were awed. The outriders circling the herd were the first to see them coming, and Oscar Fentress was the first to reach camp.

"De Sioux be comin'," he shouted, "an' Lawd God, dey be a million of 'em."

All the wagons were already drawn in close to the butte in anticipation of just such an attack, and it was only a matter of moving the herd near enough that the Sioux couldn't stampede them before coming within range of the Remingtons. The teamsters and many of the riders lay behind wagon wheels or steadied their rifles across a wagon box. Lorna, Curly, and Jasmine lay behind their saddles, using them to rest the Remingtons. The Sioux seemed bound for a head-on clash, but before they were within range of the rifles, they split their forces. Half their number rode north of the butte, while the rest circled to the south.

"They aim to ride in from both flanks," Story said. "Those of you who are handiest to the left, concentrate your fire in that direction. If you are nearest the bunch attacking from the right, go after them. We can't come out of this with whole hides if we're all shooting at the same fifty Sioux. There are many more of them this time, and with the greater number, they figure some of them will get close enough to hurt us."

The rest of the outfit followed Story's lead, and when he judged the galloping horsemen were close enough, he fired. Twenty-nine rifles roared, and suddenly there were twenty-five riderless ponies. A second volley dropped twenty more riders, and the rest galloped frantically out of range.

"God," said Gus Odell, "there must of been a thousand."

"Close," Story said, "and they're regrouping. They're not done with us."

"Maybe more than they think," said Bud McDaniels. "They ain't even got close enough for their arrows."

"Here they come again," said Smokey Ellison.

"Let 'em come," shouted Sandy Bill from beneath his wagon. "We got the guns an' we got the outfit."

Again the Sioux galloped as close as they dared, and again they were cut down by merciless fire from the long-range Remingtons. Three more times the attackers swept through, and each time the hail of lead took a devastating toll. Out of range, the remaining Sioux paused, as though uncertain. Then they simply rode away. Their loss had been too great.

22

Following the fight with the Sioux near the butte, Story had again taken the trail north. Riding ahead, he looked for Indian sign, but found none. The weather remained cold, especially at night, but the icy clutches of winter spared the high plains. Story located water, and although defense wasn't as good as that near the butte, it would have to do. The riders were jubilant following their early morning victory. Even Sandy Bill seemed to walk straighter. Nelson Story was no less elated, for his judgment had been vindicated, and except for Coon Tails, he hadn't lost a man.

"I'm starting to think that someday we're going to reach Virginia City," Lorna said. "How much farther, Mr. Story?"

"About four hundred miles," said Story. "Wouldn't you say so, Waddy?"

"No more'n that," said the teamster as he hunkered down with his supper.

"Six more weeks," Story said, "if we can average ten miles a day. We'll continue nighthawking as we've been doing, the rest of the way to Virginia City. We'll soon be in Crow country. They're friendly, but good horses can sometimes pose greater temptation than they can overcome."

The rain that had plagued them in the early months of the drive hadn't created any problems on the high plains. The Tongue River was low in places, and they forded it without difficulty. Three days later they crossed the Big Horn River, and since it was late afternoon, Story decided to bed down the herd there. Sandy Bill barely had supper started when nine Indians rode in, making the peace sign. One of them rode forward and spoke.

"Crow," he said. "Amigos. Me Buffalo Tail. Want eat."

Story nodded. He pointed to the Indian, then to the ground. He had been invited to dismount. He did so, followed by his companions. Sandy Bill eyed the bunch without any enthusiasm. He had seen Indians devour an entire deer at one setting. When supper was ready, the Crows didn't even look at the beans, but they devoured every biscuit in sight, and nearly all the fried steak. Story's riders glared malevolently at the feasting Indians, and Sandy Bill cursed them as he set about frying more steak.

The first watch was saddling up when one of the Crows wandered over to Russ Shadley's horse. He reached for the walnut stock of Shadley's Remington, lifting the weapon from the saddle boot. Seeing the action, Shadley drew his Colt and smashed it against the back of the Indian's head. The Crow slumped to the ground, and Shadley was about to kick him when Cal Snider intervened. He caught Shadley by the collar of his coat, and fisting his right hand, he slammed it into Shadley's jaw. Shadley went down, but he wasn't out. He had dropped the Colt, and now he scrambled for it, but Cal kicked it away.

The fallen Crow's companions no longer looked friendly. Two of them, including Buffalo Tail, had drawn knives. Obviously, all that had held them at bay had been Cal restraining Shadley. Nelson Story helped the fallen Crow to his feet and then led the Indian to Sandy Bill's wagon. From it Story took one of the Winchesters and a tin of ammunition. These he gave to the Crow, who quickly forgot his pain, as his grim visage broke into a grin. His companions gathered around to admire the weapon, but he refused to let them handle it. Story was relieved when the nine of them mounted and rode away. He found Shadley mounted, ready to begin the first watch.

"Shadley," said Story, "I'm going to pay you ten months' wages, which is more than you deserve. Then I want you to ride out, and keep riding."

"It's gittin' dark," Shadley said sullenly. "Wher' am I s'posed to go?"

"You can ride on to Virginia City, back to Texas, or go to hell," said Story. "I don't care. Just ride, and keep riding."

"Sorry I had to be the one to slug him," Cal said. "He's had a mad-on all the way from Texas."

"If anybody's sorry, it's me," said Story. "He was overdue for that."

November 28, 1866. The Yellowstone.

Story and his outfit crossed the Yellowstone just ahead of another winter storm. There was more freezing rain, and with the wind whipping it out of the northwest, it was a fight just keeping the longhorns moving. This time there was no canyon and they were forced to take shelter in a stand of pinion pine. The wagons were semicircled, with canvas sheets thonged between them. That, and the heavy boughs of the pinion pines, offered some shelter. With their lariats looped around saddle horns, the riders snaked in logs, limbs, anything that would burn. There was no source of water except that which the wind flung at them, and Sandy Bill relied on the water barrel to make coffee. The storm had struck two hours before dark, but with the overcast sky and the driving rain, the riders had already circled the herd.

"Longhandles aren't very warm when they're wet," Lorna said.

Curly laughed. "You was worryin' about gettin' wet crossing the Yellowstone. We get across the river almost without wettin' our boots, and here we are soaked to the hide, with it lookin' like it might rain forever."

"There's good news," said Jasmine. "Mr. Story says we're only about fifty miles out of Virginia City."

"Good place to get snowed in for the winter," said Bud, who had ridden up behind them.

But the rain continued, and miserable as they were, nobody complained much. Wet and cold was one thing, snowbound was another. Dawn broke, and while the rain had slacked, sleet clattered off the wagon canvas and stung their faces as it rode a chill wind out of the northwest.

"It's going to be hell driving the herd into the wind, with ice slapping them in their faces," Story said, "but we can't stay here. God only knows why the snow's held off as long as it has, and it won't much longer. Double your lariats and keep them moving. If we travel only three or four miles today, we'll be that much closer to Virginia City. I'll be riding ahead, looking for a better shelter for tonight."

Slowly, doggedly, they pushed on, heading the long-horns who continually broke ranks seeking to get their backs to the storm. Just when it seemed their circumstances could get no worse, they did. The freezing rain started again, and the hides of the longhorns and the rumps of the horses became coated with ice. The long-horns bawled their misery and frustration, and intensified their efforts to get these hated elements at their backs. Story, riding ahead of the herd, knew they must have shelter, and soon. He had hoped, with only the wind and the sleet, they could control the herd. But the wind had risen, and the sleet was now mixed with freezing rain. Story's horse shook its head, and ice shattered like fine glass. Somewhere ahead, even with the shriek of the wind, Story could hear rushing water.

He topped a ridge and found himself looking down into a valley that seemed to widen near the northern end. While the stream was not of the magnitude of the Yellowstone, it was a fast-flowing river, and by the time he reached it, the air already felt warmer. The west wall of the valley grew steeper, and eventually it became a blind canyon. Water cascaded off a rock shelf sixty feet above Story's head, forming a large pool, and then went racing down the valley. Most of the trees lining the river and those on the farthest slope were coniferous. There were pinion pines, some ponderosa, with some quaking aspen. It would provide a haven for the cattle and horses, while the uppermost end of the canyon would shelter the riders and their cook fires.

Story rode back the way he had come, and when he reached the crest of the ridge, it seemed the storm had grown in its fury. While the struggling herd was no more than three or four miles on the back trail, it seemed much farther, for the freezing rain had changed to snow. Already the ground was covered and there were few recognizable landmarks. Story's back was to the storm and he could hear nothing but the shriek of the wind. Convinced he'd lost his way, he reined up, and then heard the distant bawling of the cattle. Reaching the herd, he found the rebellious longhorns virtually out of control. Snow-encrusted cowboys rode after bunch quitters, only to have another bunch break away before the first bunch could be headed. A dozen steers broke loose and headed for the back trail, Story hard on their heels. Finally he got ahead of them, drew his Colt, and fired in the snowy air over their heads. The bunch galloped on as though they hadn't heard. Story holstered the Colt, doubled his lariat, and rode headlong into the fleeing longhorns. Swinging the lariat like a club, he slashed the brutes across their tender muzzles. This furious madman who inflicted pain was more fearsome than the storm, and the longhorns suddenly decided they wanted to rejoin the rest of the herd.

Slowly the riders regained control of the herd. Smokey Ellison and Arch Rainey, wranglers for the day, slowed the horse remuda. With the horses ahead of them, the longhorns more willingly faced the storm, and the drive went on. Finally they were over the ridge and the serenity of the valley below seemed like paradise. The horse remuda broke and ran, the longhorns following. Story guided the wagons across the river and to the upper end of the canyon.

"Line them up along the canyon wall, under the overhang," Story told them. "Unharness your teams and take them to the river with the longhorns. The rest of us are going to drag in limbs, logs, and anything that will burn."

The storm raged for the rest of the day, all night, and most of the next day. When it had subsided, Story saddled up and rode down the canyon until the west wall leveled down enough to accommodate the wagons. Riding up the rise, there was little accumulation, but that quickly changed. Once over the ridge, it was hard going, for the snow had drifted deep. Story rode back the way he had come, his hands numb with cold, even with gloves. This was Story's country, and his riders waited expectantly, trusting his judgment.

"We're going to be here awhile," he told them. "The drifts are deep, and God knows how long it'll be with us."

The rest of the day and the night that followed was bitter cold. The riders had three fires going, and it took all the wood they could gather. Clouds moved in during the night, and by dawn the sky was an ominous gray.

"Damn it," said Tom Allen, "more snow."

"Maybe not," Story said.

His optimism was justified. By nightfall the wind had lost its bite, and during the night it began to rain.

"Cold rain," said Manuel Cardenas, "but it is not freezing. It will melt the snow."

"I ain't gittin' too excited," Levi Puckett said. "We'll be swappin' three feet of snow for three feet of mud."

And that's about the way it turned out. When the rain quit, the land was a virtual quagmire. There were bogs where oxen from one wagon had to be unhitched to assist another team whose wagon had sunk down to the axle. It became a three-day nightmare that ended only when they reached the destination Story had in mind. Gallatin Valley was a few miles east of Virginia City. It was a land rimmed by blue, snow-patched ridges, and their first sight of it was a time none of them would ever forget.

"God Almighty," said Shanghai Wolfington, "I feel like Moses lookin' at the Promised Land."

Story laughed. "With one difference. You're going in."

They rode into the picturesque valley where grand processions of snow-topped mountains marched south to the continental divide, and loosed their horses, long-horns, and oxen along the Madison River.

"I can't wait t'git t' the land office an' grab me one of these valleys," said Shanghai. "Now that we brung a herd from Texas, they'll be more."

"Not until there's peace with the Sioux," Story said. "We'll give the herd time to settle down and graze for a few days. Then we'll have four herds to separate. Yours, Bill Petty's, Tom Allen's, and mine. We lost some, but at last tally we had gained almost a hundred calves. We'll each take some of the loss, and divide the calves in a way that's fair to everybody."

"You know these plains," said Shanghai. "Do we start buildin' cabins now, er wait fer spring?"

"Suit yourself," Story said. "This is shaping up like a mild winter. Soon as I've secured my land, I aim to start building some kind of shelter. I aim to hire twelve riders, and I'll gut-shoot anybody that tries to take Sandy Bill away from me."

John Catlin and Steve Grover wasted no time in riding on to Virginia City, for they hoped to find work in the mines. With the drive finished, the outfit would be breaking up. Story arranged to meet privately with Bud McDaniels, Bill Petty, and Tom Allen.

"We're at the end of the trail," Story said, "and I don't want to leave any of our outfit to drift. Sandy Bill's staying with me, and I've hired Hitch, Arch, Mac, Manuel, Quickenpaugh, Quanah, Gus, Virg, Dutch, and Jules. Cal will become my segundo, so there'll be a home for Lorna. Bill, you and Tom have cows of your own, and you'll be building spreads. I reckon we've been amigos long enough for me to get personal. Unless I'm barking up the wrong tree, Bill, I expect you'll be putting a roof over Alicia Blackburn's head."

"You figure right," said Petty. "I know it's proper to wait a year, her bein' a widow, but this is the frontier."

"That's how I see it," Story said. "Now Tom, since I bought their herd, Jasmine and Bud aren't poor. They won't lack for a roof over their heads, but I don't want anybody feeling slighted. What concerns me is Curly Wells, and Bud, that brings me to you. Curly's too young to drift from pillar to post, even if she *had* been a man. Is there any hope that you and Curly will make a go of it?"

"I ain't sure," said Bud. "It's up to Curly. I'm willing, but I won't hog-tie her against her will. Now that we're here, I aim to talk to Jasmine about us getting a spread of our own. Then when the Sioux settle down, we can go back to Texas for a herd of our own. Curly could stay with us until she decides what she wants to do."

"Well, hell," Tom said, "I've *got* cows, and if I can wrassle Jasmine into double harness, that would make Bud a third pardner. We could start with my cows, and like Bud suggested, go back to Texas for another herd. I reckon if Bud could sweet-talk Curly all the way to Texas and back, he could win her over."

"You've been nuzzlin' Jasmine all the way from Texas," said Bud, "and I don't see no ring through her nose."

Story laughed. "I should have stayed out of this. When you've reached some conclusions, tell me. From now on, I promise to mind my own business."

December 9, 1866. Virginia City, Montana Territory.

Three days after reaching the Gallatin, Story, Shanghai, Bill Petty, and Tom Allen rode into Virginia City. Story had been away for a year, and he had no idea what to expect as they rode up the mountain trail. What might his reception be? He couldn't help wondering if there were others of Ken Tanner's stripe who had escaped the noose at Alder Gulch, and if they might recognize him and come gunning for him.

"I'm glad you kept Quickenpaugh," Bill Petty said, "but I can't figure what you aim to do with him, unless you're goin' back down the Bozeman and fight the Sioux again."

"Quickenpaugh has a weakness," said Story, "and I took advantage of it. He likes horses, and so do I. The next thing I aim to do is establish a horse ranch, and who do you reckon will be gentling the horses?"

Story was astounded at the change in Virginia City. There was now a newspaper, two more hotels, an opera house, eateries, saloons beyond number, and a Masonic hall. The newspaper boasted there were ten thousand people in Virginia City, and more on the way. There was a sawmill and lumber yard, too.

"We'll go to the land office first," said Story. "Then I aim to sell some longhorn cows."

Story had left his outfit busy felling cedars for a cabin and bunkhouse. Cal Snider, the new segundo, swung an ax with the rest of them. When Sandy Bill got supper ready, Story and his companions still hadn't returned from town. Although not part of Story's new outfit, Alicia Blackburn, Curly Wells, Oscar Fentress, Smokey Ellison, Jasmine and Bud McDaniels, had been invited by Story to remain as long as they wished. After supper, Curly and Bud took a walk down the river without any explanation.

"Lorna," said Cal, "why don't you open that package Emma gave you before we left Fort Worth? She asked you to wait until we reached Montana, and we're here."

The parcel hadn't left Lorna's saddlebag. Part of its wrapping had included oilskin, so it had survived rain, sleet, snow, and river crossings. Carefully, Lorna opened the package to reveal a white satin dress. She held it up in front of her, and it swept the floor. There was exquisite lace at the throat and sleeves.

"I've never owned anything so beautiful," Lorna said.

"There's a letter that was in the parcel," said Cal. As he read it, Lorna read along with him.

Dear Lorna:
    This is your wedding dress, my dear. I cannot be there, but I will be with you in spirit. When you wear it, be happy, and don't forget your friend.
                                        Emma

23

A week after reaching the Gallatin Valley, Story, accompanied by Hitch, Arch, and Mac, drove two hundred head of longhorns into Virginia City. Story sold the animals for a hundred dollars a head, and the town rejoiced. There would be beef for Christmas. The arrival of the Texas cattle created a stir, and the editor of the newspaper cornered Story, insisting on an interview. There were those who remembered Story being captain of the vigilance committee that had hanged Sheriff Henry Plummer and his gang, and despite Story's embarrassment, he was forced to elaborate on that. But there was more to come. With Red Cloud and Crazy Horse riding rampant on the Bozeman Trail, Virginia City was virtually isolated. The town wanted news of the trail, what it was like to meet the dread Sioux in battle, and in their midst was a man who could satisfy them on both counts. Before Story managed to escape, he had been roped into appearing at a public forum the Saturday before Christmas, where he would tell of his experiences on the Bozeman.

"By God," Arch yipped, "you're famous."

"Famous be damned," said Story. "I reckon I'll have to start ridin' to Butte."

Story was in for considerable hoorawing from the outfit, but it ceased to bother him when he realized his riders actually were proud of him. One week before Christmas, Cal got up after supper and made an announcement.

"Christmas Eve," he said, "Lorna and me's gonna buckle on that double harness."

"I feel kind of responsible for this," said Story when the whooping and hollering had died down. "There's a grand ballroom at the Palace Hotel. I'm going to pay for that ballroom for the night, and for you and Lorna, a room in the hotel after the ceremony."

Nobody slept that night, some due to merriment and hoorawing, others because the proximity of such an event forced them to consider their own circumstances. Jasmine McDaniels and Tom Allen often spent their evening hours together, even on the trail, but Cal's announcement had somehow changed things, and they both knew it.

"We knew they were going to do that," Tom said, "but it's still hard to believe."

"I know," said Jasmine. "Lorna's five years younger than me. God, I feel so old."

"You *are* old," Tom said, "and so am I. I was twenty-five in July."

"I envy Lorna and Curly. Especially Curly. I'm so damn old, no man would want me."

"I'm a man," said Tom, "or I was last time I looked, and I want you."

"Why?" She frowned and he realized she was serious. He tried again.

"I want to strip you naked and have my way with you." He leered at her.

"Why, besides that?" She ducked her head, blushing furiously despite herself.

"That's it," said Tom. She hid her embarrassment behind mock anger.

"Damn you, Tom Allen. It's the money, isn't it?"

"Half the money belongs to Bud. I'd want you if you were broke."

"Then damn it, take me, before I change my mind."

"Christmas Eve," Tom said, "with Cal and Lorna."

She came to him, smiling through her tears, and he held her close.

In Virginia City there was much excitement, as a committee made plans for Story's appearance. But there was one man, hard-eyed with a tied-down Colt, who anticipated the event for more sinister reasons. Strong on his mind was that winter day when his friends had died at the end of a rope, and the man on the vigilante end of that rope had been Nelson Story. . . .

After Tom and Jasmine announced their intention, the shaky truce between Bud and Curly threatened to collapse.

"I don't care a damn *what* everybody else does," Curly said. "Am I some kind of dancing bear that's got to shuffle its feet to somebody else's tune?"

"Let me put it another way," said Bud, "and this has nothin' to do with you and me. Jasmine and Tom aim to start a spread, and I'll be pardners with them. When the Sioux trouble is over, we'll be goin' back to Texas for another herd. Damn it, you've got to be somewhere, and I want you with us."

"I can *be* somewhere without bein' with you. Anyhow, I don't want your charity."

"No charity," Bud said, struggling to control his temper. "I'm talking riding, roping, and branding. You're a better-than-average cowboy, even if you're never worth a damn as a woman."

He'd said it with a bitterness he hadn't intended, but it wasn't lost on her. With a cry more of anguish than of anger, she hit him, not with the flat of her hand, but with her fist. He was staggered, his nose bleeding, and he caught her wrist as she was about to slug him again.

She swung at him with her other fist and he caught her wrist just shy of his already bloody nose. With both arms imprisoned, she aimed a boot at Bud's crotch, but he was expecting that. He let go her right hand, caught the offensive foot, and sat her down without hurting anything but her dignity. He then got astraddle of her legs so she couldn't kick and then caught the freed hand before she could fist it and hit him again. She retaliated in the only way she could, cussing him and his family back three generations.

"By God," Bud panted, "I can hold out as long as you can. We're goin' to talk normal to one another like a man and woman ought, if I have to keep you here till dark. I'll turn you loose when you promise to stop swearing and fighting. You've showed me you can be a lady when you want to be. Is that askin' too much?"

"No," she said softly. All the anger had gone out of her eyes when they finally met his, and tears slid down her pale cheeks.

It was enough for Bud. He got up, helped Curly to her feet and led her to a windblown pine. He sat down, pulling her down beside him.

"I haven't cried since I was six," she said. "When Mama left me. When Daddy died I couldn't cry. I stood beside his grave and I . . . I just felt all dead inside."

Bud held her close while she wept long and hard. When there were no more tears, she looked into his eyes and his heart leaped at the promise in hers.

"I do want to go to Texas with you, Tom, and Jasmine," she said, "but I'm not ready for the preacher yet. When we get back, if you still want me . . ."

"I'll want you," he said, "and I'll wait. Just so you're with me."

Leaving the trail drive, Russ Shadley had ridden on to Virginia City. He had taken a room in a boarding house occupied by miners. He had no interest in them or in the dingy mines where they labored. While he had no intention of returning to Texas, he found Montana Territory desolate and even less desirable. He had money, but boomtown prices were taking their toll, and he decided to move on to California. But first he had a score to settle. He was on the outer fringes of the crowd the day Story and some of his riders had driven in the longhorns, but there had been no sign of Cal Snider. In one of the saloons, however, there was talk of Story having rented the grand ballroom at the Palace Hotel. Snider was getting hitched to the woman he'd brought from Texas, and in Shadley's sadistic mind, it seemed an appropriate time for his act of retribution. He went to the hotel, found the ballroom unoccupied, and wandered through it. The room was encircled by a balcony that was an extension of the second floor. It had possibilities, and Russ Shadley grinned to himself. . . .

When Bud and Curly revealed their plans to Story, the big man laughed. "This is grand." He wrung Bud's hand, and to Curly's surprise, he grabbed her and kissed her.

"One big ranch," said Tom Allen, grinning. "With Jasmine and Curly to do the ridin', ropin', and brandin', I reckon Bud and me can get in plenty of time hunting and fishing."

"Don't make any hard and fast plans in that direction," Jasmine said. "If the next drive from Texas is anything like this one, I reckon Curly and me will have enjoyed all the cowboying we can stand. If you lazy varmints want cowboys, you'll have to hire them, not marry them."

December 22, 1866. Virginia City.

Tom, Jasmine, Bud, and Curly moved to the hotel, Tom and Bud sharing a room, Jasmine and Curly sharing another. Bill Petty had taken a room for himself and one for Alicia. Story had tried to talk them into becoming part of the big event on Christmas eve, but they seemed satisfied to wait until another time. A podium had been set up before the courthouse, and it was from there that Story would speak. Without giving them a reason, Story had arranged for Bud, Arch, Hitch, and Cal to wander among the crowd, discouraging anybody who seemed inclined to pull a gun. But the crowd was not unruly, and for December, the day was unusually mild. The sun put in a brief appearance, and that's all that saved Nelson Story. He had just reached the podium, the sun to his back, when there was a wink of light from atop the two-story Masonic building. Story dropped, rolled, and came up before the courthouse door, Colt in his hand. Two slugs slammed into the wooden podium, screaming off the stone steps. Story was off and running toward the Masonic building, his riders right behind him.

"The bastard's on the roof," Cal shouted. "Come on, Arch."

Cal and Arch found the front door standing open, and once inside, took the stairs two at a time. Hitch and Bud followed Story as he circled the building. The roof was flat, with a false front, tapering off toward the back.

"He ain't had time to get down," said Hitch, "unless he jumped off the back. We could see the door. Cal and Arch may have him cornered."

"The two of you move around back," Story said. "There's a back door."

Cal and Arch crept cautiously up the narrow stairs to the second floor, and but for tables and chairs, it seemed deserted. A ladder ran up the back wall, and at the very top of it was an open skylight.

"The varmint's still up there," said Cal. "I'll climb up and take a look."

Story crept along the side of the building, considering

possibilities. At the very back, extending well above the second floor, was a pinion pine. The branch moved just a little, and there was no wind.

"Drop the gun and come on down," Story said. "You're covered." Story dropped to one knee as he spoke, and when the bushwhacker fired, the lead went well over Story's head. Story fired three times. Once at the puff of smoke, once to the left of it, and again to the right. A Colt hit the ground first, and then with a thrashing among the branches, the body of the dead man followed. Within minutes most of those who had come to hear Story speak had gathered around. Arch and Cal had come down from the roof and were working their way through the throng. Rolling the dead man over, Story didn't recognize him, but others did.

"Why, that's Brace Jackman," somebody said.

"I don't know him," Story said, "or why he'd be gunning for me."

"There was talk," said the man who had identified Jackman, "that he was part of Plummer's gang. I reckon the sheriff will shake your hand, 'cause he didn't have proof enough to do nothin'."

Story spent some time with Sheriff Jules Hardy, and the sheriff soon confirmed what Story had heard.

"Everything pointed to him bein' one of the Plummer gang," said Hardy, "but I couldn't prove it. There's more of 'em, but they've hightailed it out of the territory. Somebody else will have to hang or shoot the varmints."

Story had taken advantage of the new sawmill and lumber yard, ordering enough two-by-sixes for the new cabins and the proposed bunkhouse to have decent floors. The first cabin on Story's spread was finished two days before Christmas.

"That one belongs to the segundo," Story said. "It'll be a place for Cal and Lorna to come home to."

"Now we can start on the bunkhouse," said Quanah Taylor.

"You'd better," Story said. "I've never seen Montana weather so mild this late in the year. You'd best take advantage of it."

Despite the attempt on Story's life the day before, preparations were begun on Sunday for the cowboy wedding on Christmas Eve. It was rare that anything taking place on the frontier could be considered ordinary, but nobody could remember there ever having been two knot-tyings on the same day, by the same preacher. Story had donated three whole steers for a Christmas barbecue. The weather turned bitter cold during the night of the twenty-third, and snow-capped mountains to the west left little doubt that the long-delayed winter was indeed on the way. Huge tents were thrown up, guy ropes pulled taut and stakes driven deep, and the barbecue went on. The big event would take place in the Palace Hotel's grand ballroom at eight o'clock that night, and long before the prescribed time, the hotel was filled to overflowing.

To Shadley's dismay, tables and chairs were placed along the balcony overlooking the ballroom, and every table was jammed with drinking, laughing people. Shadley drifted back to the ballroom on the main floor, losing himself in the crowd. A not-quite-in-tune piano had been borrowed from one of the saloons, and a not-quite-sober saloon musician to play it. Jasmine and Lorna had been in their rooms on the second floor, and shortly before eight o'clock the two of them descended the stairs. Lorna wore her white satin while Jasmine wore pink. Somehow they had managed to find slippers that matched their dresses. For a heartbeat there was total silence. When the men got over the shock, their shouting and whistling drowned out the howling of the wind.

"Quiet," Story shouted when the uproar showed no

signs of ending. He finally pounded on a table with the butt of his Colt until there was silence. "Save it for after the ceremony," he said. "These ladies have no fathers to give them away, and I've been asked to do the honors, so let's get on with it."

Story turned to find a duo of cowboy grooms struck dumb with awe.

"God Almighty, Jasmine," said Tom, "is that *you?*"

The women thought that was the funniest thing they'd ever heard, and burst into a fit of giggles. Their mirth proved contagious, and when most of the crowd joined in, Story again had to pound the table for silence. Story nodded to the preacher, and before there was another diversion, the ceremony was under way.

When it was over, Story kissed the brides and did a better job of it than either of the lucky cowboys. The piano tinkled on, the man punishing it seemingly unaware the event was over. Everybody wanted to shake hands with the grooms and kiss the brides. Even Quickenpaugh was there, having bought a hat for the occasion. He looked at the couples, and when he spoke, it was directly to the men.

"Get squaw," he said. "Kill buffalo, squaw scrape hide."

"You heathen varmint," Jasmine said. "I get my hands on you, and I'll scrape your hide."

Those who had heard the exchange told others, and the Indian was soon surrounded by laughing, shouting men. Either they had forgotten he was Indian or they didn't care, and drinks were thrust at him from all sides.

"Givin' whiskey to an Indian," said Tom Allen. "If Colonel Carrington was here, he'd have the whole town under military arrest."

The handshaking, drinking, and back-slapping went on until Cal grew weary of it. He found Story and excused himself and Lorna.

"I feel like I been throwed and stomped," Cal said. "We're goin' up to that room you reserved for us."

Story laughed. "I don't blame you. I reckon this bunch will have to be run out of here at daylight."

Cal and Lorna started up the stairs, and Russ Shadley slipped down the hall toward the back door. It would suit his purpose eventually, but now he was interested in the stairs that led to the second floor. Reaching the landing, he eased the door open as Cal and Lorna paused before the door of their room. Shadley cocked his Colt and stepped into the hall. Lorna saw him first.

"Cal," she cried.

Cal dropped the key and went for his Colt, but Shadley had the drop. The first slug ripped splinters from the door frame, and the second slammed Cal against the door. He slid to the floor, and Lorna took the Colt from his limp fingers. Hoisting the long dress to her knees, she ran toward the door through which Shadley had vanished. Already she could hear the thump of boots on the front stairs. Cal would have the attention he needed, but Shadley was getting away.

But Russ Shadley's luck had run out. The back door at the end of the first floor hall was locked. He had his shoulder to the door when Lorna's first shot crashed into the wood just inches from his head. He hadn't expected this, and he blasted a shot at the girl. He missed, but Lorna didn't. She shot Shadley just over his belt buckle, and he dropped the Colt. His back was to the door, but his knees buckled and he fell facedown. When Story and the riders found Lorna, she was sitting near the bottom of the stairs, still gripping Cal's Colt with both hands.

Lorna seemed in shock. Story took the Colt from her, while Jasmine and Curly helped her up the stairs. When they neared the door of the room where Cal had been shot, it all seemed to come back to her.

"Cal," she cried. "Cal!" She ran, tripped on the long dress and fell.

When they got Lorna into the room, the doctor was working over Cal. He had been stripped to the waist and his boots removed. Quanah Taylor, Arch Rainey, and Bud McDaniels were there. The doctor had forced the rest of them to remain in the hall.

"How is he, Doc?" Story asked.

"I had to dig the slug out," said the doctor, "but it wasn't difficult. I've never seen the like of this. He's been shot before, and this one hit him almost exactly where the first one did. He'll recover, as long as we can keep down the infection and he doesn't do anything foolish."

Three days later, Nelson Story knocked on the door of Cal's room. He found Lorna sitting beside the bed and Cal awake for the first time since he'd been shot.

"Well," Story said, "how's married life?"

"Nothing's changed," said Lorna. "Everytime he gets in bed, he's been shot, and I end up in a chair, waiting for him to heal."

Story laughed. "He does seem a mite accident prone. When I reserved this room, I didn't know he'd be here two weeks."

"I ain't stayin' two weeks," Cal said weakly.

"The doc says different," said Story. "Seems like we've been through all this before. Snow's almost neck deep, and there's nothing you could do if you were up. The rest of the outfit's holed up in your cabin, and with you and Lorna thrown in, it'd be a mite crowded."

"I reckon." Cal grinned. "Maybe I'll just stay here for a while."

Story left, allowing the rest of the riders to visit Cal, and they did. For together they had been through the fire, accomplishing what the Union army said couldn't be done. They were more than an outfit, more than just

friends. They were a family, and they had the feeling
they had become a part of history, for the odds against
them had been a hundred to one. They had whipped
Red Cloud, Crazy Horse, and the bloody Bozeman.
They believed Nelson Story was destined to ride into
the pages of western history, to leave his mark on Montana Territory, and they would side him all the way. Just
as they had sided him for a treacherous twenty-six hundred miles, on the Virginia City Trail. . . .

EPILOGUE

Nelson Story married the former Ellen Trent, of Neoshe, Kansas, and five of their seven children reached adulthood. One son, Nelson Story, Jr., became Montana's lieutenant governor. In addition to Story's cattle empire, he brought two hundred brood mares from California and established a horse ranch. Story supplied beef to the Crow Agency, Fort Ellis, Fort C.F. Smith, and to regional army posts. Before the railroads came, Story had thousands of oxen in freighting and industrial service. Story had wholesale houses in St. Louis that ran freight steamers up the Missouri, delivering cargo to Story wagons that freighted from ports in Dakota and Montana. Story had keel boats on the Big Horn and Yellowstone rivers, as well. He invested in mines, industry, and lands. Story was instrumental in opening the first bank in Montana. It later became the Gallatin Valley Bank of Bozeman, with Story as president. In 1919 the Story Flour Mills merged with other plants to further develop the state's milling industry. Story eventually retired, selling his ranching empire, financing skyscrapers in California. He owned two family homes, one in Bozeman and one in Los Angeles. Nelson Story was an empire builder, but in western history, one deed is honored by elective membership in the National Cowboy Hall of Fame and Great Western Heritage Center at Oklahoma City, and that is Story's cattle drive from Texas to Montana Territory in 1866. Story died in 1926, at the age of eighty-eight, in Los Angeles, California.

Colonel Henry B. Carrington, commanding officer at

Fort Phil Kearny, is best remembered for his participation in events leading up to the infamous Fetterman massacre of December 21, 1866, in which seventy-eight soldiers and two civilians died.

John Wesley Hardin was shot to death in El Paso, Texas, on August 19, 1895. He was shot in the back of the head by Constable John Selman. At the time of his death, Hardin had more than thirty notches on his gun, and was considered one of the deadliest gunmen ever to come out of the state of Texas.

FOLLOW THE HERD IN *THE DODGE CITY TRAIL*—ANOTHER *TRAIL DRIVE* TITLE FROM RALPH COMPTON. AN EXCERPT FOLLOWS:

The bawling, cantankerous herd plodded on, defying all efforts to prod them into a faster gait. It became a futile race with time, and Dan's eye was on the ever lowering sun. Since the wagons and the horses had gone on ahead, Dan rode to the point position. The longhorns had their heads down, their tongues lolling, but they still needed something or someone to follow. The oppressive heat seemed to rise out of the very earth, surrounding them, and not a breath of air stirred.

The critical time would come after sundown, when a tantalizing wind from the northwest could bring a hint of water. In but a few seconds their cause could be lost, their efforts in vain, as the massive herd thundered across the plains, out of control. Repeatedly, Dan turned in his saddle, watching the lead steers. The faster gait, which he had fought to establish at the start of the day, had dwindled until the herd seemed moving even more slowly than before. But there was nothing more the riders could do. The brutes bawled in dismal cacophony as they stumbled along a trail that seemed endless.

The westering sun seemed to rest on the distant horizon for a few minutes, and then began to slip away in a burst of crimson glory. Dan removed his hat, sleeving the sweat from his eyes. He judged they had maybe an hour before a treacherous wind might betray them. With that thought in mind, he distanced himself from the herd, riding far enough ahead that he might escape a thundering, thirst-crazed avalanche if he had to. The sun was long gone and purple twilight approaching when Dan received the first hint of impending disaster.

So weary was he that at first he didn't notice, but the thirsty longhorns did. Their frenzied bellows seemed to come simultaneously from twenty thousand parched throats. There was a gentle breeze from the northwest, cooling to Dan's sweaty, blistered face. There was a thunder of hooves as the thirsty longhorns responded, and Dan rode for his life. When the herd fanned out, they would come at him in a deadly swath a mile wide. He rode west until he was sure he was out of the path of the stampede. He waited until the danger was past, and then rode back, catching up to the drag riders. Dejected, they sat their saddles amid the settling dust, watching the last of the herd vanish into the twilight.

"A hard day for nothing," Odessa Chambers sighed, "and God knows how many days rounding them up."

"One thing in our favor," said Dan, "they won't run beyond the water."

"No, but they might scatter the length of it," Adeline said wearily.

"That's something we'll have to contend with in the morning," said Dan. "It'll be dark before we reach the river. Let's ride."

Dan estimated the distance at five miles. Eventually they smelled smoke, evidence that they were nearing the river and their camp. Silas had a fire going, and somewhere beyond it was the sound of cattle splashing around in the river.

"We got here with the wagons in time to fill all our pots and kegs with clear water," Silas said. "Them thirsty varmints is likely to muddy it up for the rest of the night."

"Let's hope they stand right there in it till daylight," said Monte Walsh. "Last time the bastards stampeded, it took us a week to round 'em up. Now we got twice as many."

Dan rode across the river to find the horse herd and see to the safety of the young wranglers. To his relief, he found them and their charges a quarter of a mile north of the river.

"They was all watered and out of the way when the longhorns hit the water," Denny said proudly.

"The four of you handled it just right," said Dan. "It's something to keep in mind. If there's a water problem somewhere along the trail, we may be faced with this again. The longhorns have settled down, so we can drive the horses a little closer to the river. By then supper should be ready."

Supper was mostly a silent affair. Nobody even wanted to think about tomorrow, and the task of rounding up the scattered herd.

"Watches tonight as usual," Dan said, "but you can forget about the herd. Just stay close to camp, keep an eye on the wagons, and join the wranglers in seeing that nobody bothers the horses."

THE DODGE CITY TRAIL BY RALPH COMPTON—ANOTHER EXCITING ADDITION TO THE *TRAIL DRIVE* SERIES!

THE TRAIL DRIVE SERIES
by Ralph Compton
From St. Martin's Paperbacks

The only riches Texas had left after the Civil War were five million maverick longhorns and the brains, brawn and boldness to drive them north to where the money was. Now, Ralph Compton brings this violent and magnificent time to life in an extraordinary epic series based on the history-blazing trail drives.

THE GOODNIGHT TRAIL (BOOK 1)

THE WESTERN TRAIL (BOOK 2)

THE CHISOLM TRAIL (BOOK 3)

THE BANDERA TRAIL (BOOK 4)

THE CALIFORNIA TRAIL (BOOK 5)

THE SHAWNEE TRAIL (BOOK 6)

THE VIRGINIA CITY TRAIL (BOOK 7)

THE DODGE CITY TRAIL (BOOK 8)

THE OREGON TRAIL (BOOK 9)

THE SANTA FE TRAIL (BOOK 10)

THE OLD SPANISH TRAIL (BOOK 11)

THE GREEN RIVER TRAIL (BOOK 12)

THE DEADWOOD TRAIL (BOOK 13)

AVAILABLE WHEREVER BOOKS ARE SOLD
FROM ST. MARTIN'S PAPERBACKS

CRIES FROM THE EARTH

A PLAINSMEN NOVEL

TERRY C. JOHNSTON

By MID-1877, trouble in the Northwest is brewing like a foul broth. Ill will is growing between white settlers and the Non-Treaty bands of the Nez Perce. The American government is forcing the Indians from their homelands onto the reservation. Many go quietly, thinking more about their families than of the pride of their warriors. But for a few hold-outs, there's no room for compromise. Their history, their heritage, and their ancestors are buried beneath that land. Although severely outnumbered and outgunned, a few brave warriors will heed the call of cries from the earth . . .

"Rich and fascinating . . . There is a genuine flavor of the period and of the men who made it what it was."
—*Washington Post Book World*

"The author's attention to detail and authenticity, coupled with his ability to spin a darned good yarn, makes it easy to see why Johnston is today's best-selling frontier novelist. He's one of a handful that truly knows the territory." —*Chicago Tribune*

AVAILABLE WHEREVER BOOKS ARE SOLD
FROM ST. MARTIN'S PAPERBACKS

CRIES 5/91